C

M

Mend 1/02
Ls/ SP

FUTURE INDEFINITE

Round Three of The Great Game

DAVE DUNCAN

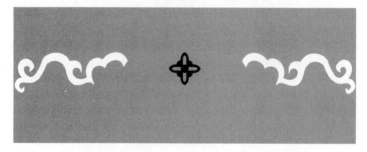

FUTURE INDEFINITE
Round Three of The Great Game

AVON BOOKS ◆ NEW YORK

Excerpt from *Mahatma Ghandi: Essays on His Life and Works* edited
by S. Radhakrishan used by permission of HarperCollins Publishers Ltd.

Excerpt from "Reflections on Ghandi" in *Shooting an Elephant and
Other Essays* by George Orwell, copyright 1950 by Sonia
Brownell Orwell and renewed 1978 by Sonia Pitt-Rivers,
reprinted by permission of Harcourt Brace & Company; copyright the estate of
Sonia Brownell Orwell and Martin Secker and Warburg Ltd,
reprinted by permission of A.M. Heath & Company Limited.

AVON BOOKS
A division of
The Hearst Corporation
1350 Avenue of the Americas
New York, New York 10019

Copyright © 1997 by Dave Duncan
Interior design by Kellan Peck
Visit our website at **http://AvonBooks.com**
Visit Dave Duncan's website at **http://www.cadvision.com/daveduncan**
ISBN: 0-380-97586-6

Library of Congress Cataloging in Publication Data:

Duncan, Dave, 1933–
Future indefinite / Dave Duncan.
p.   cm. — (The great game ; round 3)
I. Title.   II. Series: Duncan, Dave, 1933-   Great game ; round 3.
PR9199.3.D847F88   1997   96-48715
813'.54—dc21   CIP

First Avon Books Printing: August 1997

AVON TRADEMARK REG. U.S. PAT. OFF. AND IN OTHER COUNTRIES, MARCA REGISTRADA,
HECHO EN U.S.A.

Printed in the U.S.A.

FIRST EDITION

QPM   10   9   8   7   6   5   4   3   2   1

In dedicating books I have too long overlooked someone who deserves a dedication more than almost anyone—my agent, Richard Curtis. He not only makes my job more profitable, he also makes it much more fun. One day his Collected Correspondence will be the humorous bestseller of the twenty-first century. So, thanks, Richard! This one is for you. (Have you sold the Swahili rights yet?)

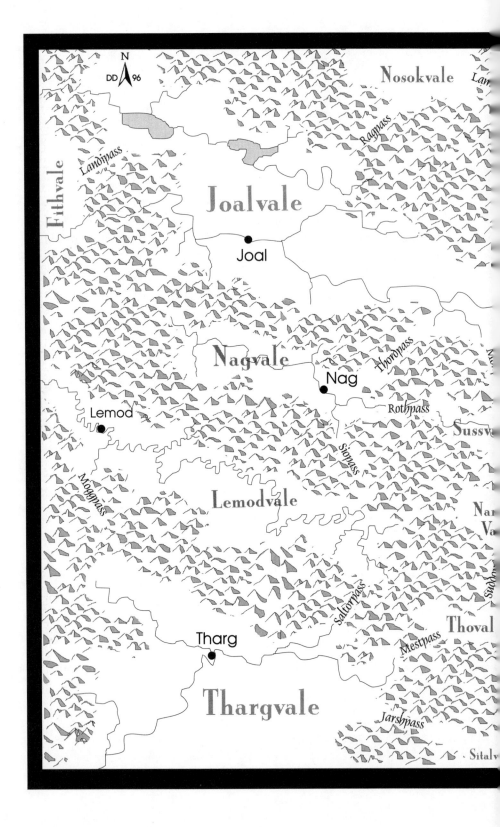

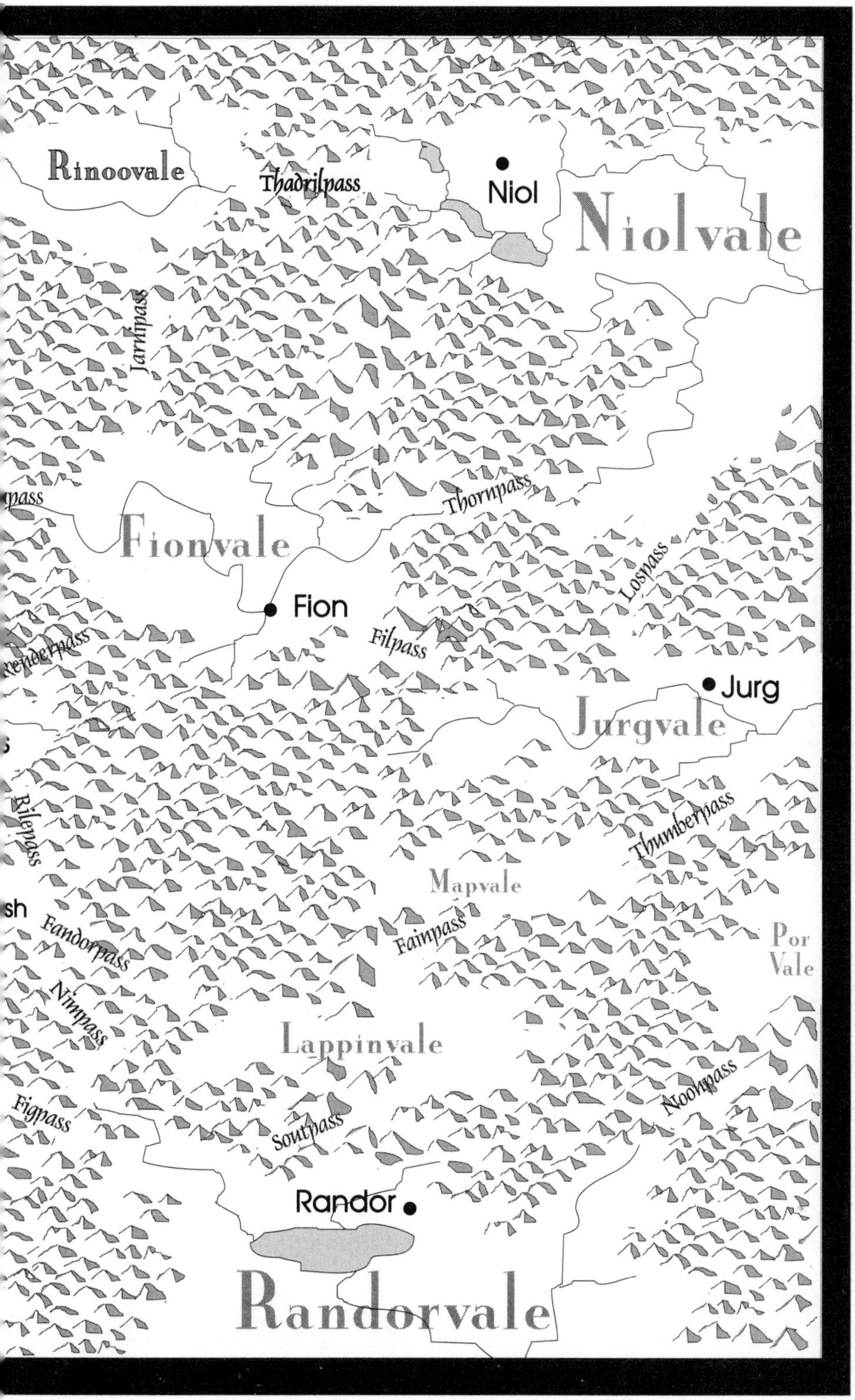

Rinoovale

Thadrilpass

Niol

Niolvale

Jarripass

Thornpass

Fionvale

Lospass

Fion

Filpass

Jurg

Jurgvale

Rilepass

Thumberpass

Mapvale

Por
Vale

Fandorpass

Fainpass

sh

Nimpass

Lappinvale

Noonpass

Figpass

Soutpass

Randor

Randorvale

Men say I am a saint losing himself in politics. The fact is that I am a politician trying my hardest to become a saint.

MAHATMA GHANDI

Saints should always be judged guilty until they are proved innocent.

GEORGE ORWELL

In wrath the Liberator shall descend into Thargland. The gods shall flee before him; they shall bow their heads before him, they will spread their hands before his feet.

FILOBY TESTAMENT, 1001

Contents

The Players

The **PENTATHEON,** the five paramount "gods" of the Vales:
    Visek the Parent
    Eltiana the Lady
    Karzon the Man
    Astina the Maiden
    Tion the Youth.
They acquire mana from the native population by terror or deception, and while away the centuries playing the **Great Game** with human pawns.

    Their many minions are known as avatars,* especially the **Chamber,** who are the worst of them, led by:

    Zath, the "god" of death. Although officially an avatar of Karzon, he has become dominant by empowering murderous devotees known as **reapers** to offer him human sacrifice, a most potent source of mana.

The **SERVICE,** a group of altruistic strangers who are attempting to overthrow this malignant tyranny by promoting a new faith, the Church of the Undivided.

The **FILOBY TESTAMENT,** a book of prophecy that predicts the coming of the Liberator who will bring death to Death, but identifies him only as the son of **Cameron Exeter,** a member of the Service in the late nineteenth century.

---

*Neither they nor the Five are really gods, merely humans who have crossed over to Nextdoor from Earth or some other world. Being **strangers,** they automatically have **charisma,** the ability to absorb **mana** from the admiration or worship of natives.

HEAD OFFICE, an organization of strangers on Earth who frequently cooperate with the Service on Nextdoor and who sheltered Cameron Exeter when he fled back to Earth to escape Zath's efforts to break the chain of prophecy by murdering him.

The **BLIGHTERS,** another group of strangers on Earth, who will sometimes attend to the Chamber's dirty work there, and who in 1912 hunted down Exeter and his wife at Nyagatha in Kenya and slew them.

EDWARD EXETER, the only son of Cameron and Rona Exeter, and thus the **Liberator** foretold.

The Game So Far

In August 1914, just as the Blighters succeeded in provoking World War I, they also came close to killing Edward. Rescued by Head Office and Julius Creighton of the Service, he found his way to Nextdoor, fulfilling the prophecy that said he would come into the world in Sussland during the seven hundredth Festival of Tion and be aided by someone named **Eleal,** who turned out to be a juvenile member of a troupe of actors. When Edward made contact with the Service, he refused to undertake his prophesied mission, determined to return to Earth and fight for King and Country. He also rejected Tion's efforts to bribe him with an offer to cure Eleal's deformed leg.

Further attacks by Zath's agents caused him to lose touch with the Service. Lacking knowledge of the keys and portals, he was stranded on Nextdoor. In **Nagvale,** he was befriended by the young men of **Sonalby** and accepted into their age group. War broke out between **Joalia** and **Thargia,** two of the three great powers of the Vales (the third being **Niolia**). Because Nagland was a Joalian colony, the junior warriors were conscripted to participate in an invasion of **Lemodvale,** a Thargian ally. Through charisma and innate ability, Edward advanced to supreme command and rescued the Joalian-Nagian army from disaster. He escaped from Zath with the assistance of Karzon.

After further wanderings, Edward located **T'lin Dragontrader,** a native Service agent, and eventually **Jumbo Watson,** one of the senior members, who led him to the station at **Olympus.** He still insisted on returning to Earth, but the Service was seriously divided on the merits of the Liberator prophecy and procrastinated. Eventually Jumbo offered his personal assistance and instructed Edward in the workings of a portal—which dropped him into the middle of a Belgian battlefield. Arrested as a suspected German spy, he was rescued by his cousin **Alice Prescott,** former school friend **Julian Smedley,** and Head Office agent **Miss Pimm.** In order to warn the Service that Jumbo was a traitor, Edward returned to Nextdoor with Julian, meaning to stay only a few days. He discovered that Olympus had been sacked by Zath's agents and the girl he loved was among the dead. Roused to fury at last, Edward swore revenge and walked out of Olympus.

FUTURE INDEFINITE

Round Three of The Great Game

Behold! Exalted, I have come. I have escaped from the nether world. The roads of the earth and of the sky are open before me.

THE BOOK OF THE DEAD, 78

1

Prat'han Potter was growing tired of waiting to die. He had been standing in chains in the courtroom since dawn, and pretending to be brave for so long had turned out to be much more wearing than he had expected. Seventeen of his age brothers had already been tried, convicted, and taken out to be whipped. But he had been the ringleader and this was his third offense, so he had been assured he would be found guilty and put to death. He was starting to think it would be a welcome release, the sooner the better, and if the Joalian crotchworms had not gagged him, he would be telling them to get on with it. He hoped his martyrdom would be the spark to light the revolution that Nagvale so badly needed.

"Granted that death is the only possible sentence in this case," the advocate for the defense said in a bored voice, "impalement is an exceptionally painful, lingering form of execution, and I would ask the court to stipulate more merciful means for this defendant, if My Lord Judges will permit me a brief word on the subject."

"Briefly, then," the president conceded with poor grace. All three judges were Joalians, as were all the other court officials. Most of them were sweltering in formal robes and floppy hats, for the courtroom was as hot as a kiln. Indeed, Prat'han's only consolation was that he was clad in nothing but his usual leather apron. And chains, of course, lots of chains.

The courthouse was the largest and most splendid building in Sonalby, recently erected by the Joalian overlords as a symbol of the enlightenment they brought to their colonies. It contained at least four rooms, all with shiny plank walls and windows of stained glass. This room was the largest, but even with only one defendant remaining, it still contained far too many people for its size—the judges up on their bench, two advocates, four clerks, half a dozen sword-bearing guards. Although the door in the tiny area railed off as a public gallery stood open in a vain attempt to let in some air, it admitted nothing but a view of the village huts of wattle and thatch. The street was deserted. There was not even a mongrel cur left in Sonalby today to hear the victims howl at the whipping post or watch Prat'han die. The inhabitants had vanished before dawn, to show what they thought of Joalian justice. It was not much of a rebellion, but it was the best the poor sheep could manage.

"My Lords are gracious," said the advocate. He had not spoken ten words to his supposed client, and all they had in common was that they were both bored.

"First, I respectfully point out that the only crime the defendant committed was to paint his face. My Lords will forgive me if I concede that I might be tempted to do the same if I had such a face."

The judges smiled thinly. There was absolutely nothing wrong with Prat'han's face except that he was not allowed to paint it the way his forefathers had done for a thousand years. Women told him he was handsome even when his face paint had been smudged to a blur. He tried again to lick the roof of his mouth and was again balked by the foul-tasting wooden bit. His jaw ached from being held open so long.

"Objection!" said the prosecutor, half rising from his seat. "The paint is itself not the issue. The issue is that the governor has prohibited a specified list of barbaric tribal customs such as ritual self-mutilation. Face painting is one of the forbidden procedures."

The left-hand judge smothered a yawn. "And the law specifies impalement. Have you anything else to say?"

"Yes, My Lords," the advocate for the defense said hastily. "Briefly, the accused, Prat'han Potter, had a distinguished military career in the recent war against Thargia. He was troopleader for Sonalby during the campaign in Lemodvale and the subsequent glorious and historic invasion of Thargvale, fighting alongside our noble Joalian warriors. When the victorious joint army returned to Nagland three years ago and was forced to suppress the usurper Tarion, the accused strangled the usurper with his own hands during the assault on the palace. He acquitted himself throughout with great distinction, receiving a commendation for personal bravery from our own noble Kalmak Chairman."

The judges exchanged annoyed glances. They were all political appointees, and Kalmak was currently top dog in the Clique and hence effective ruler of both Joalia itself and its colonies.

Prat'han made loud protesting noises around his gag and rattled his chains. If the court decided to refer the appeal for mercy all the way to Joal, then he might have to wait two or three fortnights for an answer, and he could not see that strangulation would be enough of an improvement to justify the delay.

"Silence that man!" said the left-hand judge.

A guard punched Prat'han in the kidneys. Taken by surprise, he screamed and fell to his knees in a rattle of chains, choking for breath, fighting nausea. The courtroom floor swam before his eyes. Long before he was ready to be brave again, he was hauled to his feet to hear the sentence. He could barely straighten up properly or control his breathing.

". . . previous convictions," the judge president droned, "have used up any goodwill earned in the war. You have been found guilty of treason against the Nagian People's Democratic Republic. The sentence of the court is—"

"Wait a moment!" said a new voice.

It was not a loud voice, but all heads turned. The speaker was a tall youth standing in the hitherto deserted public enclosure. Lean as sinew, tanned to walnut, black haired, empty-handed, naked except for sandals and a leather loincloth—just a typical Nagian peasant in from minding the herds? But Prat'han recognized him instantly and forgot the sickening throb of pain.

"You have a very short memory, T'logan," said the newcomer. "So have you, Dogurk. I remember when you were T'logan Scribe and Dogurk Scholar. Have you forgotten so soon, My Lord Justices?"

He swung a long leg over the railing, revealing a glimpse of very pale thigh under the leather. As he brought the other leg over, one of the guards lurched forward, drawing his sword. D'ward just looked at him, and he stopped as if he had hit a wall.

D'ward resumed his approach to the bench. Two of the judges had lost color, even in that steaming sweat house. Where had he come from? All this time and never a word—yet he walks in at this very instant . . .

"Three years ago, My Lords, you were under my command, remember? Not quite four years ago, you were about to die outside Lemod, trapped by a guerrilla army and the onset of winter. The only thing that saved you—and all the rest of your great Joalian army—was that the Nagians took the city in the nick of time and found you safe haven. That is correct, isn't it?"

He was in the center of the courtroom now. He folded his arms and scowled up at the bench. Judges T'logan and Dogurk nodded in horrified silence.

D'ward, D'ward! Where had he come from? He had vanished in Thargvale three years ago, and no one had heard anything of him since. He had not changed at all. Prat'han knew how his own once-taut belly had begun to thicken and how the hair had crept back from his temples, but D'ward was still that same wiry youth he had been then—a boy with a black-stubble beard.

The third judge began, "What is the meaning of this—"

"Shut up!" said D'ward. "I *respectfully* remind the court that Prat'han Potter was the third man up the rope in that assault. He saved your lives, you miserable slugs! And you, T'logan—I remember him jumping into the freezing torrent and lifting you out bodily when we were making our escape from Lemod in the spring. I saw it with my own eyes! He saved you again."

The judge president made incoherent choking noises.

"And now?" D'ward added enough scorn to turn the oven into an icehouse. "And now Joal has enslaved the entire population of Nagvale. Oh, I know! I know you think you're raising them from barbarism to civilization, but they don't see it that way, and the complete suppression of a culture seems like enslavement to me. Civilization, you call it? Because Prat'han Potter is a proud man as well as a brave one and chooses to decorate his face with what he regards as sacred symbols of his manhood, you plan to put him to death in the foulest way you can think of?"

An agony of silence filled the courtroom.

Then Judge T'logan spoke the forbidden name: "The Liberator! What are you doing here?" He glanced uneasily around the courtroom, as if expecting to see reapers assembling.

D'ward Roofer, D'ward Troopleader, D'ward Hordeleader, D'ward Battlemaster . . . D'ward *Liberator*! He had never accepted that title before, but this time he did not refuse it.

"Just passing through. But if you harm my age brother Prat'han, then I may decide to stay here and organize the Nagian Freedom Fighters. And if I do choose that option, My Lord Justices, I will throw every last Joalian out of the vale inside two fortnights. I will trample you as I humbled the might of Thargia. *I am the Liberator foretold!* Do you doubt my word?"

The three judges shook their heads in unison, although they probably did not know they were doing so.

"So, My Lords, you will now issue the prisoner a severe reprimand and release him."

Judge T'logan spluttered and drew himself up. "That is not—"

"Now!"

The judge subsided again. He glanced at his associates. Dogurk nodded. Trillib nodded, more reluctantly.

"Release the prisoner!"

Two minutes later, Prat'han staggered out into the blinding sunlight, leaning on the Liberator's shoulder.

Five minutes later, the two of them arrived at his shop and he could drink his fill of tepid water, cleanse his mouth, slump onto his work stool and gape at D'ward. The stabbing pain in his back had faded to a dull ache.

No one had seen them, of course. No one had screamed out D'ward's name, or even Prat'han's own, for he would be something of a hero himself now, being so unexpectedly alive. The people would not return until after dark, and the rest of the senior warriors must be off tending one another's stripes.

Under its thick reed-thatched roof, the shed was cooler than the sun-drenched street outside, but not by much. The heavy smell of clay that always hung in the air had faded in the last fortnight, while the potter languished in the village jail. Sunlight blazed in through the open door, glowing on the warm pinks of the wares that cluttered the floor—dozens of jars, bowls, jugs, plates, all waiting for buyers. Flies droned around or walked on the wicker walls. Prat'han was both surprised and delighted to see his spear and shield still leaning against the wall. He would feel castrated without those old friends, although it was illegal to take them outdoors now, and rumors persisted that the Joalians would soon confiscate every weapon in the vale.

D'ward inverted a ewer and sat on it. He sighed deeply and wiped his forehead, then grinned at Prat'han as calmly as if he were one of the regulars who dropped in to chat every day. There was no need to ask how he had worked that miracle in the courtroom. He was D'ward Liberator. The shockingly blue eyes and unforgettable white-toothed smile could spur a man to do anything.

"The years have been good to you, old friend?"

"You . . . you haven't changed!"

D'ward's smile narrowed a little, but it was still a smile. "Not on the outside, I suppose. You're not much different yourself, you big rascal! Married now?"

Prat'han nodded, while his gaze wandered over D'ward. His beard was trimmed close in Joalian style. His ribs . . .

D'ward looked down where he was looking. "Oh. I seem to have lost my merit marks, don't I? Well, you know they were there once. I can't help it if I'm good at healing, can I?"

The potter pulled himself together. "I owe you my life again, Liberator, and . . . Oh! I must not call you that, must I?"

"Yes, you can!" Blue eyes twinkled. "My time has come! As of today, you may call me the Liberator. From now on, I bear the title proudly and will teach the world to respect it. I am happy to start by liberating you. It was pure chance; I came by four days ago and heard what was bubbling."

He stared thoughtfully at Prat'han, who felt a thrill twist his gut. Why had the Liberator come? Was there blood on the wind again? He said, "You have been away too long! We are your family."

"Always! But I have many sad things to do in the world. I came to see my old comrades in arms and discovered that most of them were in jail. I had hoped that the old Sonalby Warband might be willing to help me in a dangerous venture, but . . ."

There *was* blood on the wind! Prat'han crossed the shack in three long strides to snatch up his shield and spear. "Lead, Liberator! I will follow."

D'ward rotated on the ewer to face him. "I'm afraid not. Not you. And none of the others either. You see, brother, now I march against the gods themselves. I can't lead followers who sport the symbols of the Five—green hammer, blue stars, the skull of—"

"Faugh! Face marks do not matter. If you want me like this, then you get me like this."

"Oh?" D'ward seemed to be having trouble keeping his lips in line. "But do I want a helper so fickle? Ten minutes ago you were prepared to die horribly for the right to paint your face. Now it doesn't matter?"

Of course it didn't! But Prat'han was not accustomed to thinking *why*, and he had to rummage frantically in unfrequented corners of his mind before he could say, "You offer me a choice. Joalians tell me. Quite different."

D'ward laughed. "I see! But the next problem is that you and the brothers seem to have a revolution of your own under way. What I'm planning has nothing whatsoever to do with throwing the Joalians out of Nagvale."

Prat'han shrugged to hide his chagrin. "I only fight Joalians from boredom. Whatever your cause, I will support it. Your gods are mine."

"It will involve long travel and grave danger."

"Good!"

"But you said you were married. As I recall, married warriors are reserved for defense."

Why had Prat'han been such a fool as to admit to Uuluu? "I am only very slightly married—a matter of a couple of fortnights." Or thereabouts. "No children! My wife can go back to her father unchanged."

D'ward raised his eyebrows in disbelief. "That she may go back I will believe, but unchanged? This I doubt, you big male animal, you!"

"Not much changed." Feeling as if he had been counting every hour in three long years for this moment, Prat'han fell to his knees. "Liberator, I would kneel to no other man. I would not plead with any other, either, but I swear that if you leave me behind, then I shall die of shame and despair. Take me, Liberator! I am yours to command, as I always was. I will follow you wherever you lead."

"Don't you even want to know what I'm planning?"

"You are going to bring death to Death, as is foretold in the *Filoby Testament*?"

"Well, yes. If I can."

"I wish to help. And all the others will, too! Gopaenum Butcher, Tielan Trader, Doggan . . ."

D'ward grimaced. "I let them all get flogged today. I dared not intercede for them, Prat'han, because I wasn't sure I had enough . . . had enough power to rescue you. It was a damned close thing, there, you know! A couple of times I really thought you and I would be gracing adjoining fence posts. How long until they'll be well enough to travel?"

"They are well now! I've had those beatings. Nagians shrug them off. We have thick skins."

"You have thick heads, certainly." D'ward ran his fingers through his hair— curly, bushy, shiny black. He pulled a face. "What is your wife going to say? I warn you, this will be bloody. Many who go with me will not return. Perhaps none of us will."

Prat'han rose. He put his heels together and laid his spear against his shoulder, as D'ward himself had taught him, long ago. Staring fixedly at the far wall, he said, "Lead and I follow."

D'ward rose also. They were of a height, the two of them, both tall men, although Prat'han was thicker.

"I can't dissuade you, can I? Never thought I would, actually." He took Prat'han's shoulder in the grip that brother gave to brother in the group. "You have been a shaper of clay, Prat'han Potter. Follow me, and I will make you a shaper of men."

II

And he is the guardian of the world, he is the king of the world, he is lord of the universe—and he is myself, thus let it be known, yea, thus let it be known!

KAUSHITAKI-UPANISHAD, III ADHYAVA, 8

Ripples raised by that encounter in Sonalby were to spread throughout the Vales in the fortnights that followed and give rise to major waves. Before the green moon had eclipsed twice, they disturbed the normal calm of a certain small side valley between Narshvale, Randorvale, and Thovale, whose only claim to distinction was that the little settlement near its north end was home to the largest assembly of strangers on Nextdoor. They called it Olympus.

The Pinkney Residence was not as grand as the palaces of the monarchs or high priests of the vales, but it was spacious and luxurious by local standards, having recently been rebuilt from the ground up. In design it more closely resembled the sort of bungalow favored by white men in certain tropical regions of Earth than anything a native of the Vales would have conceived. Within the oversized and overfurnished drawing room, lit by a multitude of candles in silver candlesticks, a man with a fair baritone voice was singing "Jerusalem" accompanied by a lady playing a harp, because the Service's efforts to instruct their local craftsmen in the construction of a grand piano had so far failed to meet with success. The audience consisted of eight ladies in evening gowns and six gentlemen in white tie and tails.

" 'I shall not 'cease,' " the singer asserted, " 'from mental fight, Nor shall my sword sleep in my hand. . . . ' "

Two more men had slipped out to the veranda to smoke cigars and contemplate the peace of the evening. The warmth of the day lingered amid scents of late-season flowers and lush shrubbery, although the sky was long dark. Amid an escort of stars, red Eltiana and blue Astina peered over jagged peaks already dusted with the first snows of fall.

"It is a rum do." The taller man was spare, distinguished by an unusually long nose. He had grace and confidence and—on appropriate occasions—a wry, deprecating grin. Like most strangers, he did not discuss his age or past. Although he appeared to be in his middle twenties, he was rumored to have participated in a cavalry charge at the battle of Waterloo, more than a hundred years ago. "Never expected him to start that way."

"Never expected him to start at all," his companion complained. "Thought we'd heard the last of him. Thought Zath had got him, or he'd gone native."

"Oh, no. I always expected Mr. Exeter to surface again. I just didn't expect him to cock a snoot at the Chamber quite so blatantly or quite so soon." The taller man drew on the cigar so it glowed red in the gloom. Then he murmured, "Very rum! I wonder how he went about it."

"I wonder how he's managing to stay alive at all." The other man was shorter and plump, although he appeared to be no older. He parted his hair in the middle and tended to close his eyes when he smiled.

"That's what I meant. Zath should have bowled him out in the first over. Think we ought to stop him, do you?"

"Stop who?" demanded another voice. "What are you two plotting out here? Arranging a little something behind the Committee's backs?" Ursula Newton came striding out and peered suspiciously at the two men, one after the other. She was below average height, but her evening gown revealed very muscular arms and unusually broad shoulders for a woman. She was loud and had never been compared to shrinking violets.

"Certainly not!" said the shorter man.

"Jumbo?"

"Of course we were," said the man with the long nose, unabashed. "Pinky was just about to ask me to name the most efficient assassin on our staff at the moment, weren't you, Pinky?"

His companion muttered, "I say!" disapprovingly. "Nothing like that."

"The fact is," Jumbo explained, "that young Edward Exeter has surfaced up in Joalvale, preaching to the unwashed, openly proclaiming himself to be the Liberator foretold."

"Great Scot!" Ursula frowned. "You're sure?"

"Quite sure," Pinky said fussily. "Agent Seventy-seven. He's a very sound chap, knows Exeter quite well. Very well, actually."

"And how long has this been going on?"

"He'd been at it about three days when Seventy-seven saw him. Seventy-seven scampered back here right away to let us know. Very sound thinking. I commended him on his initiative. It did take him four days to get here, though, so the situation may have undergone modification."

"Exeter may be dead, you mean. But if we've heard, then the Chamber's heard, sure as little apples."

"Oh, quite, quite."

The patter of applause having died away, the baritone had unleashed his next song.

> " 'And this is the law I will maintain,
> Until my dying day, sir. . . . ' "

The men smoked in silence, and Ursula leaned on the rail between them, scowling at the night.

"Could be serious," she said.

> " 'That whatsoever king shall reign . . . ' "

"Absolutely," Pinky agreed.

" 'I will be the vicar of Bray, sir. . . . ' "

"You're going to send someone to bring him in?"

"That was what we were debating when you arrived," Jumbo remarked, sounding amused.

"It's a matter for the Committee," Ursula said, "but of course you haven't told Foghorn yet, have you? Want to get it all settled beforehand, don't you? You two and your cronies."

"Not settled," Pinky protested. "Dear me, no. Not settled. Didn't want to spoil a delightful evening by bringing up business. But I knew Jumbo would be interested. Thought he might have a few ideas. And you, too, my dear. You agree we ought to send someone to have a word with Exeter?"

"Just to have a word with him?"

"The emissary's terms of reference would have to be very carefully drawn," Pinky said cautiously. "A certain amount of discretion might be permitted."

Jumbo coughed as if he had swallowed more smoke than he intended. "Spoken like a true gentleman—Cesare Borgia, say, or Machiavelli. Well, he certainly won't let me near him. Not after what happened the last time."

"If he has any brains at all," Ursula said, "he won't let any of us near him. Except Smedley, perhaps. Old school chum? Yes, he'd listen to Julian."

Pinky closed his eyes and smiled beneficently. "Captain Smedley is an excellent young man. But he is rather new here. Do you think he could comprehend all the ramifications of the situation? I am sure he would deliver a message, but would he plead our case with conviction?" He peered at her inquiringly.

"He certainly won't do the dirty work you've got in mind. But remember he has no mana. I think you need to send two emissaries to Exeter—his friend Smedley and someone else, someone who can help the captain out if there is need for a little muscle."

"Ah! Brilliant! I expect we should have seen that solution in time, Jumbo, what? Two emissaries, of course! And who should the other one be? What do you think?"

Jumbo sighed. "I don't like this. Not one bit. Rosencrantz and Guildenstern. We need someone with damned good judgment."

"And very few scruples?" Ursula inquired scathingly.

"Now, now," Pinky said soothingly. "Don't go jumping to conclusions. I am quite hopeful that Mr. Exeter will see reason."

"It's a matter for the Committee. Let them decide. Now come on back inside, both of you, and stop this inner-circle intriguing." She spun on her heel and strode off into the drawing room, a surprisingly abrupt departure.

Two cigar ends glowed simultaneously. Two smoke clouds wafted into the night air.

"Obvious!" said Pinky. "We'd have thought of her on our own, wouldn't we? Eventually?"

Jumbo sighed again. "Truly it is written that the female of the species is more deadly than the male."

"Oh, quite," said Pinky, smiling with his eyes closed. "Quite."

3

SEVEN STONES IN RANDORVALE HAD ONLY FOUR STONES—ONE VERTICAL, two leaning, and one fallen. The missing three were either buried in undergrowth or had been carted away in past ages. The remaining four were set in a grassy glade walled around by enormous trees like terrestrial cedars that crowned the level summit of the knoll. It was a spooky place, dim and pungent with leafy odors, stuffy as a Turkish bath on this breathless autumn afternoon. Staying well back from the crowd, hidden behind shrubbery, Julian Smedley could feel his skin tingling from the virtuality.

Using the fallen stone as a pulpit, Kinulusim Spicemerchant was thundering the gospel of the Undivided at a flock of forty or so people sitting cross-legged on the grass. Men and women, even some children, they were a fair sampling of the local peasantry from Losby and other nearby hamlets. Forty was a good turnout at Seven Stones. Julian had already identified a few familiar faces, the faithful. Others were here for the first time, investigating this strange new religion their friends now professed. Soon it would be his turn to try to convert them.

Meanwhile he was changing into his work clothes. Standard Randorian dress was a single voluminous swath of flimsy cotton, apparently designed to keep off insects, as Randorvale was well supplied with bugs, but its main attraction for Julian was that it had no tricky buttons or hooks. Feeling like a human Christmas present, he unwrapped yards and yards of gauze, enough bunting to decorate a battleship. When the silkworm finally emerged from its cocoon, Purlopat'r solemnly held up his priest's robe for him to step into—hood, long sleeves, girdle. He thought of it as his Friar Tuck costume. It was a drab gray, because the Pentatheon had already appropriated all the better colors.

Purlopat'r Woodcutter was a nephew of the spice merchant, somewhat more than life-size. He had the face of a boy of twelve, but from the neck down he was about seven feet of solid muscle, which gave him a certain air of authority, and he wore a gold circle in the lobe of his left ear, the sign of a convert to the Church of the Undivided, so Kinulusim must regard him as an adult. Purlopat'r was serving no real purpose at Julian's side. He had probably volunteered to wait on the saintly guest so that he need not suffer through another of his uncle's interminable sermons.

Kinulusim was a convincing lay preacher, one of the best the church had. His faith was strong; he proclaimed it in rolling, sonorous torrents of words, waving his fists in the air as he denounced the evil demons of the established sects of the Vales. If he became any more heated, his beard would burst into flames. The old boy was always a tough act to follow. Julian was neither a natural orator nor truly proficient in the Randorian dialect, and he lacked Kinulusim's faith. He also considered the Church of the Undivided to be a load of guff.

"Holiness?" Purlopat'r spoke in a high-pitched whisper unsuited to his size. He was one of those people who can rarely remain silent for two breaths at a time. "Did my uncle tell you about the troopers he saw?"

"Yes, brother." Julian smiled up at the worried young face. He wanted to run over his sermon notes again, but apostles were expected to demonstrate both patience and faith. Troopers were worrisome news.

"Do you suppose King Gudjapate has been misled by the demon Eltiana?"

"Undoubtedly. The demons will mislead anyone who listens to them."

Purlopat'r nodded, rolling his eyes. "If the troopers come against us here today, the Undivided will defend us, Holiness?"

Julian sighed and adjusted the tie on his gown, mostly to give himself time to think. The young woodcutter had just thrown him the worst paradox in monotheism: Why does an all-powerful god tolerate evil in the world? That was not something to be answered off the cuff, even if Julian had had a cuff handy.

"I do not know the answer to that, brother. We must do our duty and have faith that the One will prevail in the end, even if sometimes our limited vision does not reveal all the details to us."

"Oh, yes, Your Holiness. Amen!"

Julian thumped the kid's shoulder, curious to know if it was as solid as it looked. It was. "We are both humble servants of the Undivided, brother. We are in this together."

And in this case, laddie, you can be confident that your apostle will not vanish in a flash of magic and leave you in the lurch, as slimy Pedro Garcia did down in Thovale. This apostle hasn't got any mana.

He took a quick look through the greenery to see how Kinulusim was doing. The audience seemed suitably impressed.

Julian liked Randorians, who were mostly simple peasants, working the land in the ways of their ancestors. Their dialect was more tuneful than those of vales closer to Tharg, whose harsh, guttural tongue seemed to have infected all their neighbors. They were taller than most Valians and laughed a lot when they were not engaged in solemn activities like worship, and they had wonderful folk music.

Having been allowed to choose between Randorvale, Thovale, Narshvale, and Lappinvale for his missionary work, Julian had selected Randorvale and proceeded to specialize in its dialect. He was happy with his choice, perhaps because most of the natives had faces a tone darker than his. Preaching to them, he could almost convince himself that he was back Home, in some remote colony of the Empire, enlightening the heathen, bearing the White Man's Burden. With people the same pale pink he was, he would lose that illusion. Then he might wonder about historical accidents, the possibility that some flip of a divine coin might have gone otherwise and resulted in Narshians and Randorians saving souls in England—a discomfiting thought.

Like most of the Service, he had little faith in souls anyway. He did not promote the Church of the Undivided for theological reasons, but because it was the only possible way to undermine the tyranny of the Pentatheon. Only when the Five had been overthrown would the Vales ever progress to true civilization. It was the worldly lot of the natives he sought to promote, just as the European powers bettered the economies of their colonies. Here in Randorvale, Julian Smedley would preach with a clear conscience, doing what he did for the good of the natives, the *lesser breeds without the law.*

Already he could feel mana flowing. As the spice merchant worked up to his thunderous peroration, his listeners' veneration for the Undivided god was becoming infectious, magnified by the virtuality of the node like organ music reverberating in a church.

Purlopat'r had been silent for thirty or forty seconds. The strain must have become unbearable, for again his whisper came from somewhere above Julian's head. "Was it not most wonderful what miracle the most holy Saint Djumbo performed in Flaxby two fortnights ago?"

Julian craned his neck. "I don't think I heard about that. Flaxby, in Lappinvale? What happened?"

The boy's eyes widened. "It was a mighty miracle, Holiness! The laws in Lappinland now proclaim that all the faithful are to be rounded up and punished most barbarously."

"Yes, I know. That, too, is the work of the demons. But what about Saint Djumbo?"

"A magistrate sought to arrest him, Holiness! He had two soldiers with him, and he accosted the holy apostle as he was leaving a prayer meeting like this one. But Saint Djumbo called upon him to repent and instructed him, and lo! the magistrate and his companions fell upon their knees and heard the word of the True Gospel. Then all present departed in peace, singing the praises of the Undivided!"

The devil they did! "Saint Djumbo has true modesty, brother. He has never reported this to us, and I thank you for bringing it to my attention."

Purlopat'r beamed. He was no more pleased than Julian was, although Julian interpreted the story differently. Obviously Jumbo had used his stranger's charisma—and perhaps a shot of mana as well, because even for Jumbo, those three together would have been a tough egg to crack. He had not abandoned his flock, a bloody sight better performance than Pedro's craven desertion! But to hear of persecution in Lappinland was bad news. The Pentatheon's pogrom against the Undivided heresy had begun in Thargland half a year ago, then spread to Tholand and Narshland. Today Kinulusim had reported troopers in the vicinity. Had the poison now reached Randorvale, too?

Ah, the old windbag had run out of steam at last. He wiped his hairy face with a corner of his wrappings and drew breath.

"We are most blessed today, brothers and sisters! Come among us to honor us is one who can speak to you with true authority. I am but a humble merchant, no better than any of you, perhaps worse than some. Most of you have known me all your lives. How can this man have wisdom of holy things? you ask, and you are right to ask. But now I give you one of the blessed apostles themselves, one chosen by him whose name may never be uttered, chosen to lead the rest of us into righteousness and save us from damnation. He is already one of the saved. He can speak to you with authority. He can teach you holy matters with the voice of perfect truth. Brothers and sisters, hearken unto the words of the most holy Saint Kaptaan." He raised his hands overhead to form the circle. Then he stepped down from the pulpit rock.

Julian straightened his shoulders, confirmed that his long sleeves hung straight, and walked out from behind his tree. As he came into the worshippers' view, he felt the rush of mana like a tingle of electricity, a surge of exaltation. He sprang up on the stone and smiled benevolently at all the earnest faces.

This was always the moment when he wondered what his father would say if he could see him now—bearded, dolled up in a long robe like an illustration from a children's Bible, a Moses from Hyde Park Corner. Actually, he had a fair idea what his father would say. Sergeant-Major Gillespie of His Majesty's Royal Artillery would be even more explicit. What of himself? What did he say? Did he really want to spend the next few centuries like a horoscope huckster, touting nostrums and panaceas like a monkey up a stick?

No time for doubts; he was here to do good. He raised his arms briefly to make the circle. The congregation bowed their heads for that blessing, so the chances of his maimed hand being noticed were slight. He had already settled on sermon six, but before he got into that, he would have to correct Kinulusim's minor theological error.

Standard opening first: "Brothers and sisters in the true faith! To be here with you all today gives me wondrous pleasure and a great sense of humility. The first time I visited Seven Stones, there were only three of you. . . ." He droned his way through that, and yet his stump was already aching by the time he had done.

Then to Kinulusim's slip. He slowed down, wrestling his thoughts into sing-song Randorian. "Our virtuous brother Kinulusim spoke well, revealing many great truths to you. Carry them with you in your hearts when you leave this place. He is a worthy servant of the Undivided. In his humility, he may have given you the impression that I am in some way more worthy than he is. Do not let his modesty deceive you into believing so. I am one of the apostles, yes, but this does not make me any better than Kinulusim—or any of you—in the eyes of God. The Undivided chose me to bear his word to the world, but not because of any great virtue of mine. I am a sinner, too. I am only a man as Kinulusim is." And so on.

Having spread that little fiction, he began the sermon. He had rehearsed it many times and the dialect came readily. Number six was his favorite, straight plagiarism of the Sermon on the Mount. The Service's synthetic theology always made him feel hypocritical, but the ethics were fine. He had believed in these ethics all his life.

Blessed are the poor. . . . Blessed are the meek. . . . It worked. Of course it worked! Fascinated bright eyes stared at him out of brown faces.

Soon the mana was pouring in. His stump burned as if it were dangling in molten lead. He could feel the fingers of his right hand, which had rotted away in the Belgian mud, back in 1917. At least the pain reminded him to keep his arms at his sides. He need not draw his audience's attention to the fact that he wore gloves, and hopefully few of them would notice or guess why. There was nothing in doctrine to say that apostles must be perfect human specimens, although in practice their steady diet of mana kept them ageless and healthy. He would not create theological paradoxes if he displayed his mutilation. He would if he cured it.

Many of these worshippers had seen him before, and he hoped most of them would see him again in future. A visible miracle of regeneration would not fit the Service's definition of sainthood. If such a miracle became known, Julian Smedley would be promoted in the eyes of the people into a supersaint or even acquire godhood, and the Service was very much on guard against that. It had lost too many missionaries to the opposition already, most recently the mealy-mouthed Doris Fletcher, who was now the divine Oris, avatar of Eltiana and patron goddess of the newfangled art of printing.

He was hitting his stride. "Murdering chickens in a temple will not save you from the wrath of the Undivided, brothers and sisters! He does not judge you by what you sacrifice to the demons but rather by every moment of your daily lives. Virtue and kindness are the offerings he demands of you. . . ."

It was hackneyed stuff to a man raised as a Christian, but to many of his listeners it must be startlingly new and unexpected. They had been brought up to respect the rich and powerful, not to pity them. The Pentatheon did not teach compassion or humility. The Five demanded only obedience, for that brought them mana.

"Not great temples!" Julian thundered. He liked this bit. "Pouring your alms into stones and gilt does not honor the Undivided! Rather use that money to feed a starving child or ease the lot of a cripple. This is the road you must take to find your place among the stars. . . ."

That was pure bunkum, but for centuries the Pentatheon had bribed their victims with a promise that the obedient would dwell evermore amid the constellations. To remain competitive, the One True God must offer nothing less, and it had seemed safer to adopt the local faith than invent a new afterlife. Potential converts might hesitate to accept an unfamiliar heaven.

The words drifted away through the steamy glade; sweat streamed down Julian's face. Then a flicker of movement caught his eye. And another. In the patchy shade at the outskirts of the wood, sunlight glinted on metal. All around the grove, soldiers were moving in, pushing their way through the shrubbery. They held naked swords in their hands.

Oh damnation!

His audience was waiting, puzzled by his sudden silence. He had lost his place. Where in Hades had he got to? He smiled comfortingly at his frightened flock and jumped a few mental pages to be certain he did not repeat himself. Meanwhile his mind was racing.

So was his pulse. He had not felt terror like this since the day a Boche shell had buried him alive.

He was not Jumbo Watson, who could preach a magistrate and two soldiers to their knees, and there must be thirty armed men out there, maybe more. He was not Pedro Garcia, who had magicked himself out of danger in similar circumstances. Julian Smedley could not save himself with mana, even if he wanted to. Every scrap of mana that came his way went into healing his hand—that was not a conscious decision, it just happened. When he had come to Nextdoor a year and a half ago, his arm had ended at the wrist. Now he had a palm. On his last circuit, it had begun to sprout five stubs. He assumed that one more tour would give him recognizable beginnings of fingers and thumb.

Wrong! This tour was going to kill him. He was likely to die on the wrong end of a bloody sword unless he could do something dramatic.

Right. The first thing was to keep control of the meeting. So far the congregation had been too intent on his words to notice the intruders. If they leaped up in panic and tried to flee, they would undoubtedly be hacked down in a bloodbath.

He stopped preaching. He raised his arms in the sign of the circle.

"Brothers! Sisters! We are greatly honored. We have visitors. See the noble company of His Majesty's brave soldiers come to join our worship. Nay!" he shouted over the sudden screams. "Do not be afraid!"

In one simultaneous surge, the worshippers were on their feet. Damn!

"*Stay where you are!* Welcome these worthy men; admit them to our fellowship in the name of the True God! Enter, friends!"

The captain, distinguished by a scarlet plume on his helmet, was emerging from the undergrowth almost at Julian's side. A grizzled boar of a man, in leather and steel, he was showing his teeth in a gloat of triumph at having cornered his prey so easily. "Desist in the king's name!" he bellowed, raising his sword.

Julian bellowed right back at him. "God save the king!" He turned to his cowering, paralyzed flock again. "God save the king!" he repeated.

Wily old Kinulusim echoed him at once: "God save the king!"

"Long live His Majesty!"

This time the response was stronger. "Long live His Majesty!" The congregation had huddled in around Purlopat'r and his uncle, with the young giant towering head and shoulders over everyone else. All those frightened eyes stared at Julian in mute appeal.

"Let us pray, brothers and sisters. Let us pray that good King Gudjapate be granted long life and wisdom to reign over his people. Let us pray that he be granted health and prosperity and true counsel, that his beloved queen . . . that the noble young prince . . ." And so on and so on.

The captain was nonplussed, unwilling to interrupt these patriotic sentiments. His band had come to a halt, all in full view now, a ring of dangerous young men waiting for the word to begin the roughhousing.

Julian roared on. He prayed that the king might continue to be a beloved father to Randorland. He prayed that the king be saved from the wickedness of evil demons. The faithful would know that he referred to Eltiana, the Lady, patron goddess of the vale, but he was careful not to mention her by name nor any of the other local deities either, not even the Undivided. He gave the captain no excuse to interrupt. Gathering words from the wind, he gradually edged his prayer into a sermon again, and this time he used number three.

Julian disliked sermon three more than any other of the current year's issue. He had spent little time studying it, because he had not truly believed that he would ever use it. Just to read the words made him feel more than usually hypocritical, although he had known that three would be a good crowd rouser, pure hellfire: The Five promise you an afterlife of bliss among the stars—they lie! The Pentatheon and all their avatars are not gods at all, they are foul demons, who will be destroyed by the One True God at the Day of Judgment, and all who worship them and serve them here will be similarly wiped out. Solid stuff. Solid balderdash! Who could know what happened after death? Certainly not Prof Rawlinson or the other scribblers of the Service who had written the True Gospel. At least they had not designed a god so malicious that he would torment sinners forever. An eternity of black and solitary boredom was the Valian concept of hell, and the Service had been content to stay with that.

Julian tossed in a little brimstone for good measure.

What he could not remember, he improvised, ranting and roaring. With one small, unoccupied corner of his mind, he registered that it was working. He was holding his own. Sheep and wolves alike, his listeners were rooted to the spot, intent on the torrent of words. Three cheers for charisma!

But it was not enough. He could not go on forever. As soon as he stopped, the captain and his men would snap out of their trance and remember their duty.

He was starting to repeat himself.

His stump had stopped hurting. He was soaked in nervous sweat, but he was also soaked in mana, loads of it—this was a node, after all, and a powerful one. He could feel mana like crackling static in the air, and he must be spewing it right back at the worshippers so fast that his mutilation had no chance to steal it on the way.

There was the answer! For the first time since he crossed over to Nextdoor, he was capable of working a little magic. If he were Pedro Garcia he might use the trapdoor, but he was a true-blue Englishman, who would never desert the ship.

"You ask for proof?" he demanded, although no one had spoken a word. "You want evidence of the powers of the Undivided? Then behold and I shall show you." He thrust out his arm. "You—Purlopat'r Woodcutter! You have known me for a year now, have you not?"

The big youth nodded, eyes wide as soup bowls.

"Then tell your brothers and sisters why I wear a glove!"

"You have only one hand, Holy One," Purlopat'r cried out squeakily.

"Wrong! I did have one hand. My right one was cut off at the wrist, wasn't it? See now what is there!" He ripped off the glove. "My hand is restored to me. My fingers are coming back. Next time I visit you, brothers and sisters, I shall have a hand here as good as the other. This is how the One Who Cannot Be Named rewards those who serve him."

The Service would disapprove thoroughly. The Service would accuse Julian Smedley of promoting superstition, raising false hopes, seeking self-aggrandizement. Under the circumstances, he could not care less what the Service might think. He just wanted to keep on breathing.

"A holy miracle!" yelled old Kinulusim, falling to his knees.

"A miracle!" chorused the faithful, copying him. Young Purlopat'r actually prostrated himself full-length, like a falling cedar. Only the soldiers remained standing.

The captain stood openmouthed and irresolute. Julian swung around to flaunt his maimed—his partially unmaimed—hand at him. He gathered up all that crackling sense of mana and mentally hurled it at the man in desperation. *Kneel, damn you! Kneel!* It was doubtless a very tiny ray of mana by the standards of the Five or their avatars, but it was enough to overpower one crusty, intractable old veteran. *Repent! Repent!*

Slowly, reluctantly, the captain sank down on his knees, and all around the glade, his followers followed his example.

Jesus!

"Let us pray!" Julian barked. "Let us give thanks for the evidence of mercy and goodness—"

He gasped as flames of agony enveloped his hand. Then he caught his breath and plunged ahead. The mana was boiling in now, not just from the already overawed believers, but from another thirty converts also. He had worked a miracle. He was a holy man. The captain was weeping and half his men had thrown away their swords.

4

AMORGUSH HAD GONE TO SLEEP ON DOSH COACHMAN'S ARM, BUT HE managed to slide it free without waking her. She rolled over on her side, breathing loudly. He slid out of the bed and wriggled his toes in the thick rug.

Sunlight streamed in through the windows, gleaming on silk sheets, marble walls, and furniture polished to a glassy luster. Just one of those gold-framed paintings would keep him in luxury for the rest of his days, or possibly get him hanged. Outside, acres of manicured garden swept down to the shores of Joal-water. A small fortune in jewelry lay scattered on the dressing table, making his fingers itch.

He must resist the temptation if he wanted to continue living on old Amor-gush. He stooped for the clothes he had dropped on the floor an hour ago. They were fine clothes. Give the old bag her due—she was generous. That was about the only good thing to be said of Amorgush, though. She claimed to be forty, and the gods should strike her dead for perjury. She was reputed to be the richest woman in Joalvale. She was certainly one of the stupidest, although not quite stupid enough to believe the words of adoration he whispered to her every day about this time. She knew he was only a hired man.

He slipped into his pink linen breeches and kid shoes, fastened his wide leather belt lovingly. That did not come from Amorgush. It was probably of Randorian make, although he had stolen it in Mapvale a couple of years ago. A twist would bring the ornate buckle free, bearing a thin strip of steel, flexible yet razor sharp on both edges, a beautiful thing. He loved it. Poor little Dosh always felt naked without at least one weapon concealed somewhere on his person.

He donned his silk tunic—a delicate lilac shade, exquisitely embroidered with many-colored wildflowers—and admired himself in the mirror for a moment, then looked more carefully, checking for love bites. He found none. What he did notice, with annoyance, was the gleam of scalp through his curls. Blond men always went bald young, and he was no longer as youthful as he liked to think he was. There were faint lines starting on his forehead. He turned away angrily from his reflection.

The old hag was still asleep, snoring now. That relieved him of the obligation of a sticky, hypocritical farewell embrace. Amorgush was a good living, but he felt he earned every crust of it, and he headed for the door with the conviction that he had just done a noble day's work. After such a session, his nominal duties in the stable always seemed positively recreational.

The corridor was deserted. He strode along it, admiring the pillared grandeur, intent on a quick bath to get the stench of her perfume off him. All things considered, though, his position in the Bandrops household was the most en-joyable sinecure he had found in his highly varied career. For one thing, Joal was the finest city in the Vales, with every facility a man could dream of. He was paid enough to indulge his versatile taste in vices. Best of all, he need not fear the wrath of a jealous husband, because Bandrops knew exactly what his coachman did during siesta hour.

It had been Bandrops who had first brought Dosh into the house. Bandrops Advocate was an up-and-coming politician—which in Joal meant a man with the instincts of a killer spider—who was widely expected to bribe his way into the Clique when the next vacancy occurred. He had married Amorgush for her money, as his personal tastes ran more to the likes of Dosh than to matrimony. For a while poor Dosh had been required to satisfy both of them regularly, which had been hard work, but now the master had found himself a tender juvenile page, and his calls upon his coachman's evenings were much rarer.

As Dosh reached the head of the staircase, who should be trotting up it but that very same Pin't Pageboy, looking hot and flushed and positively adorable. He stopped, and the two of them appraised each other warily. Dosh had a faint worry that Pin't was after his job with the mistress. Pin't was distrustful of Dosh's own advances, although he had so far managed to resist them admirably.

"Feeling the heat?" Dosh inquired. "It's a remarkably warm fall."

"You don't look very cool yourself," the brat retorted. He had a dark curl trailed artfully over his forehead—Dosh wished he knew how the kid organized that so consistently. "I was looking for you."

"Wonderful! I'm just heading for the bathhouse. Come along."

Pin't curled a lip in refusal. "The master wants you."

Dosh regretfully dismissed the thought of cool water. At this time of day, Bandrops would be wanting a coachman, not a catamite—probably. He shrugged. "Then I'd better go to him. But keep my offer in mind."

"I can't think why I should."

Dosh trotted down. "Experience, my boy!" He reached out in passing, aiming an affectionate pat, which Pin't foresaw and dodged. "I could teach you some very useful tricks."

"I doubt it," Pin't retorted.

He was certainly wrong.

Dosh knocked and was bade enter. The master's office was a sumptuous, sun-bright room overlooking a manicured garden. The rugs alone represented more wealth than most men earned in their lifetimes. Amorgush left all the financial decisions to her clever husband.

Bandrops's perpetual stoop seemed only to emphasize his bulk. He sported the thickest, blackest eyebrows Dosh had ever seen, under a shiny bald pate, although every other part of him sprouted dense black hair. He had a mellifluous, orator's voice, a raging ambition, and sadistic tastes in recreation. He was wearing a loose silk tunic of sky blue and leaning his fists on his ornate desk.

He greeted his coachman with a disagreeable scowl. "I am sorry to drag you from your work."

"I am entirely at your command, sir, of course," Dosh remarked airily as he crossed the sumptuously colored Narshian rug. He was much more interested in the other man standing near the window.

The other man was younger, leaner, even harder, with a cold intensity in his face to warn the discerning observer of potential trouble. He, too, wore the standard Joalian tunic and breeches. In contrast to Bandrops's, his forearms were almost hairless, well muscled, and also much paler than his hands. As were his shins. His cheeks above his close-trimmed beard were darker than his ears and forehead.

"This is the boy, Kraanard," Bandrops declaimed. "Dosh, this is Kraanard Jurist. He has need of your services."

"As my master bids me, sir." Dosh bowed to the stranger, wondering what sort of services were implied. He wondered, too, why an obvious soldier, a man who normally wore greaves, vambraces, and helmet, would be masquerading as a jurist.

Kraanard regarded him with unconcealed contempt. "Have you a moa, boy?"

If Dosh wished to be impertinent, he could now ask where a lackey like him could ever acquire the wealth to own a moa, but that was not what was meant. Moas resisted new riders with murderous zeal; it took months to attune a moa to a man. Dosh was skilled at many things other than seduction. He could harness the household stock to the master's coach and drive it. Officially, that was all that was expected of him.

When Bandrops had hired him, though, he had set out to imprint one of the household moas—mostly because he thought the brute would make suitable severance pay if he had to leave without notice. Bandrops knew he had been trying, because he had commented on the numerous bruises and tooth marks poor Dosh had acquired in the process. What he did not know, apparently, was that Dosh had persevered. There seemed no reason not to tell the truth in this instance, for the other servants knew.

"There is one I can usually manage, sir."

The other men exchanged pleased glances.

"You will come with me," Kraanard announced. "We shall be gone only a few days."

Dosh had survived so long in his perilous career only because he possessed an acute sense of danger. Now tocsins clamored in his mind. There was something extremely fishy here. He contrived an expression of youthful anxiety, which had always been one of his most effective.

"I doubt I can handle Swift for that long, sir. I am only an amateur on a moa."

Bandrops reddened, but it was the soldier who answered.

"The matter is extremely important. Even if you suffer some scrapes, you will be well rewarded."

"I am sure to be thrown a few times, sir. Then Swift will escape."

Kraanard's eyes narrowed. "We shall have others with us. We shall round it up for you. They never go far."

Now the details were starting to take shape—a troop of lancers!

"If you need a moa rider, sir, surely there must be hundreds of native-born young Joalians far more expert than I am."

Again the two men exchanged glances. Then Kraanard strode across until he was right in front of Dosh and could stare down at him with cold gray eyes and unmistakable menace. He was considerably taller.

"But I understand that you are familiar with a man named D'ward."

If he wanted to shock, he succeeded. Dosh felt as if he had been dropped into ice water and for once his self-control failed him. *"The Liberator?"*

Kraanard was pleased by the reaction. "Some call him that. He is here in Joalvale, somewhere over by Jilvenby."

D'ward! It had been more than three years. They had been traveling with a band of Tinkerfolk, Dosh's own people. Dosh had tired of the grinding poverty and run out on them. But before that . . .

"No!"

A dangerous silence . . . Kraanard said, "What does that mean?"

Dosh himself did not know what that meant. He did not know what he was thinking. D'ward!

"It means he wants money," Bandrops growled in the background. "He's a greedy, grasping scoundrel with the heart of a whore, but he'd sell his own mother for a few silver stars."

Mother certainly, but not D'ward!

Why not D'ward? Dosh did not know. He needed time to think.

Kraanard smiled. He closed a fist in Dosh's hair and bent his head back. "How does thirty stars sound, boy? All you have to do is identify him for us. We'll handle the rough stuff. You won't be hurt."

Dosh uttered the plaintive cry he used to indicate pain or fear, but at the moment he was feeling neither. He was filled with an inexplicable fury. Thirty stars? That was too much. What sort of gullible fool did they think he was? Far too much! Thirty stars was more money than he'd ever owned in his life.

"What's the Liberator to you, boy?" Kraanard demanded. His breath stank of fish.

Good question! "Sir, you're hurting me!" Dosh wailed, but his mind was churning. What, indeed, was the Liberator to him? Betraying friends had always been one of his specialties, so why should he feel so different about D'ward? Was it because D'ward, although he had known exactly what Dosh was, had always treated him as an equal, another human being? He was almost the only person who ever had. Dosh slid the knife out from his belt.

The trooper did not notice the movement. Snarling, he twisted Dosh's hair harder. "Answer me!"

Dosh gave him his answer. Flexible blades were tricky for stabbing, but he drove it expertly between Kraanard's ribs. He had a very intimate knowledge of anatomy—he knew the way to a man's heart. The knife came free easily as the body dropped. Bandrops gaped, then dived around the desk, heading for the door and opening his mouth to shout, but he should have done the shouting first. Dosh leaped, took him from behind, and cut his throat.

He had wiped the blade clean on Bandrops's tunic before the blood stopped pumping out of its owner. Meanwhile, he was thinking hard. Killing had never bothered him—nor excited him either. His heart was beating quite normally—but he had certainly behaved in a very uncharacteristic fashion. Why refuse an offer of thirty stars, however remote the chances of collecting?

More to the point at the moment, how had the authorities known that Bandrops Advocate's coachman could identify the Liberator? He could think of no reasonable explanation in mortal terms, which meant the gods must be meddling again. Dosh revered no god. He despised most of them—especially Tion, the Youth.

Which god was mixed up in this? Many men and women affected special loyalty to a specific god, swearing allegiance to a mystery. Tion had the Tion Fellowship and probably several other cults also; Thargian warriors would belong to the Blood and Hammer, loyal to Karzon. Dosh knelt beside Kraanard and peered carefully under the neck of his tunic, looking for a chain. Not finding one, he undid the laces, but then he was forced to conclude that the late, un-lamented Kraanard had not been wearing an amulet. He stripped the tunic off the corpse and began to inspect it—a nice, well-muscled body. He noted with approval how tiny the wound was and how little it had bled, like a deadly snakebite, he thought proudly.

He did not find what he was looking for until he removed Kraanard's breeches. High on the inside of the man's right thigh he discovered a small red birthmark in the shape of an Ø. Dosh would bet his ears that the man had not been born with that birthmark.

Well! He had expected a five-pointed star, symbol of the Maiden. Astina was presiding deity of Joalia, her resplendent temple standing not a mile away. In her avatar of Olfaan, she was patron goddess of soldiers. If a Joalian trooper was sworn to any deity, it should be Astina, but Ø was the symbol of Eltiana, the Lady. The label was so inconspicuous that the cult must be a very secret one. The Lady was goddess of such things as passion, motherhood, and agriculture. None of her aspects was especially threatening, so far as he could recall; a few of them demanded ritual prostitution from their worshippers, but Dosh had no quarrel with that.

He patted the dead man's cheek. "You rascal! You're a spy—or even an assassin, perhaps? I misjudged you!" But the evidence was clear—the Lady was after D'ward and could be assumed not to have his best interests at heart.

He rose and surveyed the carnage. Moments ago those two had been rich and powerful, and he a lowly flunky. Now they were dead while he was still alive. Such is life. Situations change, though—having slain a prominent citizen and a soldier, poor Dosh would soon be as dead as they were if he lingered long in Joalvale. All he would have left to look forward to would be a prolonged and very public death.

Besides, whatever D'ward was doing in Joalvale, the lunatic ought to be warned of Eltiana's concern. It would be an hour or two before anyone thought to interrupt the master at his business. That was long enough for him to get well out of town. Amused by a sudden inspiration, he took the time to undress Bandrops's corpse also—that should confuse the issue a little.

Investigating the secret compartment in the desk, Dosh found a bulky purse he estimated must hold fifty or sixty stars. Unfortunately the jewelry he had seen there on earlier inspections was absent. He considered the possibility of running back upstairs to collect Amorgush's, but concluded reluctantly that the old cow might be awake by now. Hanging the bag on his belt, he headed for the door. Jilvenby lay to the northeast, near Joalwall. A fast moa ought to make that in a day, and despite his earlier disclaimers, he was now extremely skilled at handling Swift.

He was skilled at many things.

5

THE SUN HUNG LOW OVER THE SNOWY PEAKS OF RANDORWALL AS JULIAN
Smedley headed back to Losby through a green jigsaw of paddy fields and or-
chards, divided by winding hedges of bloodfruit bushes. Here and there between
the trees, he could see small groups of the faithful making their way homeward.
Randorvale was very lush, vaguely reminiscent of the south of France if one did
not look too closely at the vegetation or question what mountains those were.

His stump ached fiercely—the finger stubs were already visibly longer than
they had been this morning—but all in all he felt as if his feet were barely
touching the ground. His dander was still up, a fizz of mana. The old spice
merchant trudged along at his right in triumphant silence, while on his left, young
Purlopat'r ambled with gigantic strides that would not have shamed a moa,
prattling shrilly about the glorious miracle the One had vouchsafed his believers.

It had been quite a good show, actually. Before setting out from Olympus
three days ago, Julian had equipped himself with two dozen gold earrings for
converts he might bring into the fold during his two-fortnight circuit. He had
thought he was being grossly optimistic, but he had used up eighteen of them
already. Eighteen in one day was certainly a Service record—he had heard of
Pinky Pinkney managing twelve. Seventeen of the troopers, including Captain
Groud'rart himself, had also clamored to join the church on the spot, but the
rules required them to take a course of instruction first. Some of them would
change their minds, of course, but some would not. To have believers within
the royal army could be a tremendous advantage for the Undivided, perhaps
leading to infiltration of the Randorian government itself. When Julian Smedley
returned to Olympus and submitted the usual report, it was going to be a very
unusual report. The new boy had scored a stunning success. It was too bad that
he had done so by flaunting his personal miracle cure, and there would be
whispers about that. Shag 'em! The alternative had been martyrdom, and the
Service did not demand that of its agents. He had not used the trapdoor like
Pedro Garcia. He had turned certain disaster to pure triumph. He had even
outscored Jumbo Watson.

There was Kinulusim's cottage now, on the outskirts of Losby, flanked by his
storage shed and the paddock. There were two rabbits in the paddock.

"Someone has come," Purlopat'r squeaked.

The someone would be from Olympus, almost certainly, and Julian's first
thought was that now he had an audience to brag to. His second was that of

27

course a fellow didn't brag, and his third was perverse annoyance that whoever it was would get the story in spades from Purlopat'r and Kinulusim. Dammit! He wanted to slip his miracle into his written report without comment, not make a great shemozzle out of it.

Their approach had been observed. The man heading out to meet them was short and stocky, wearing brown breeches and tunic—Joalian garments that were well suited to riding but which at once made Julian acutely conscious of his own absurd Randorian draperies. In a moment he identified the newcomer and his mana fizz flared close to anger.

Alistair Mainwaring was a plumpish, brown-haired man of indeterminate age. His English bore a faint Highland brogue that showed up even when he spoke Joalian and quite strongly in Randorian. He was one of the most effective missionaries the Service possessed, known around Olympus as Doc and to the natives as Saint Doc, although his degree was in anthropology, not medicine. He was also head of the Randorian section, thus Julian's boss, and a sanctimonious twit. Had he come all this way just to check on his most-junior assistant's progress?

They met, and Julian raised his gloves overhead to make the circle—thereby demonstrating that he had no fears of unfriendly onlookers and had the district under control. The other three copied him instantly. Kinulusim and Purlopat'r would be much impressed to have two holy apostles honoring Losby at the same time. The old spice merchant would also be frantic with curiosity to know why.

Disturbingly, Doc looked about fifty. Strangers' apparent ages were defined by their current mood, and the fatigue of the journey alone should not be so evident. He was also grimy and windswept, so he must have just arrived. He spoke curtly. "Blessings upon you, brothers, and greetings, Saint Kaptaan."

"Your Holiness is most welcome at my humble abode." Kinulusim rubbed his hands eagerly. "May we hope to be honored with your company for an extended period?" He would expect to prolong the greetings with flowery phrases for at least ten minutes, but Doc was clearly in no mood to soft-soap the natives.

"Possibly—that will indeed be a pleasure—but it is likely that Saint Kaptaan will have to leave very soon. I need a quick word with him."

Failing to hide his affront at this summary dismissal, Kinulusim assured the honored apostle that of course he understood and would at once see about preparations for refreshments, and so on. He stumped angrily off along the road, accompanied by the titanic woodcutter, who peered back in juvenile curiosity at the guests.

Alistair sank down on the grass with a weary sigh. "How did it go, old man?" He looked as if he expected a string of excuses.

Still tipsy on mana, Julian felt absolutely no need to sit and was quite certain he had nothing to excuse. "Not bad."

"I hear there have been peelers seen in the area—no trouble, I hope?"

"Nothing we couldn't handle."

Doc dismissed the matter with a shrug. "I've got some queer news. Your chum Exeter is reported to be on the loose up in Joalvale, marching up and down telling everyone he's the Liberator of the *Filoby Testament.*"

Julian was too astonished to say anything but, "I beg your pardon?" Exeter? Come out of hiding? Parading around in public? Godfathers! He was going to be frightfully dead frightfully quickly if Zath heard of it. Somebody would have to do something. Oh, it couldn't be! He interrupted Doc's explanations. "There's been a mistake! That would be suicide! I mean, he would never—"

"Sorry, old son. No bally doubt about it."

"It can't be!"

"It is. Seventy-seven says so, and he knows him as well as any. It's definitely Exeter and he's definitely calling himself the Liberator, quite openly."

Julian felt sick. "Zath will fry him."

"The tough one, old chum, is why Zath hasn't fried him already."

"What does that mean?"

Alistair raised a sardonic eyebrow. "Our information is that Exeter started a week ago or longer. It's old news, of course, but if he's still alive, then he must have made himself reaper-proof, mustn't he?"

"I fail to follow you." Julian would gain nothing by losing his temper. Nor could he defend Exeter's behavior when he did not even know what it was.

"You've been here long enough to know the rules. If Exeter can protect himself against Zath's killers, then he must have picked up some jolly powerful mana. I mean, little things like the trapdoor are fine if native bullyboys come after you, but you'd need a sight more heft to take on Zath. How can he have done that?" Doc's upper lip was very close to a sneer.

Julian caught his temper just before it escaped. So that was what was in the wind, was it? The Service had never done a damned thing for Edward Exeter, although his father had been one of the founders. It had kidnapped him, ignored him, hindered him, and tried to kill him. Now, apparently, he was going to be maligned as a turncoat. That would be a good excuse to give him even less help in future.

"Mana? Human sacrifice or ritual prostitution. Like the Chamber does. He took the medal in sixth form for human sacrifice."

A long ride on a rabbit was not the best sauce for humor, and Doc's eyes glinted angrily.

Julian pressed on. "I haven't heard a word from him, if that's what you're wondering. I don't know what he's up to any more than you do." Almost two years ago, right after the massacre at Olympus, Exeter had walked out of the station and disappeared. Perhaps he had gone insane. That felt like a very disloyal thought. "So why come to me?" Was he going to be tarred with the traitor brush, too?

Doc shrugged. "Committee wants you back at Olympus. For consultation. I'll take over your tour here." He did not add that he would do a much better job of it, but his manner certainly implied that.

Dammit! The Committee was probably chasing its tail, trying to decide what to do. Because Julian had been at school with Exeter they would assume that he knew him better than anyone else did, but that had been a long time ago. Rivers of blood had flowed since those days. Still, orders were orders, and he couldn't deny any call that involved Exeter, however unlikely the story sounded at the moment.

"Then I'd better scoot."

Doc blinked. "Tonight, you mean?"

"It's a fine night. Should be lots of moonlight. Why not?"

"It's your arse." Doc hauled himself painfully to his feet. "I'm going to stagger down to the village bathhouse and thaw mine out."

"Then I'll see you when the nabobs have done with me," Julian said cheerfully. With luck he could disappear over the horizon before anyone told Alistair about the eighteen converts. That was a pleasing thought.

ϟϲ~ 6 ~ϛϛ

It WAS CLOSE TO MIDNIGHT, AND CHERRY BLOSSOM HOUSE WAS HAVING A poor night. Half the tables were empty, the roar of conversation was so muted that Potstit Lutist's playing was audible at the far end of the big dark room.

The true artist, so Grandfather Trong had always said, regarded a poor audience as a challenge to excel. Thus Eleal Singer was working the crowd, making her way from group to group, smiling, laughing, chatting up the clientele. The paying customers were all men, of course, a galaxy of hairy, flushed faces under the hanging lamps—young men, old men, just men. The women beside them or draped over them were staff. The air stank of cheap wine and stale cooking, lamp smoke and unwashed bodies.

The tables were very close together, by design, but that let her lean on chair backs or men's shoulders as she moved, concealing her limp. She wore a black leather bra and a short leather skirt, both studded with brass. It was not the sort of outfit a normal girl would wear outside a nightmare, but an actor dressed as the part demanded, and this was the only costume that could justify the heavy boots she needed. Her hair hung lush and raven dark around her shoulders. Apart from her short leg, her body was the best in the house, which explained the deadly stares from the harlots at the tables. And they couldn't sing.

Eleal could. She was going to sing in a few minutes.

She knew most of the regulars by sight, but they were not what she was looking for. She flirted and taunted them a little, relishing the wistful lechery in their eyes, but she was not for them. They knew she was not one of the whores. Suddenly she had a chance to prove it. A calloused hand slid up her thigh. She swung around on her good leg and struck as hard as she could. Fingers almost fell off his chair, and the slap was clearly audible over Potstit's lute playing. So was her roar, professionally projected to reach the farthest reaches of Cherry Blossom House.

"If that's what you want, there are those here who sell it. I do not!"

Fingers's companions yelled with laughter and pulled him down on his chair as he tried to rise. If he got out of hand, Tigurb'l Tavernkeeper would send in his notorious bouncers.

Under the cluster of lamps hanging over the little stage, Potstit ended his solo and reached for the bottle beside his stool. There was no applause. Tigurb'l appeared beside him—a gray, lizardy man like something dreamed up after drinking too much perfumed wine. He rubbed his long thin hands together and flicked a pale tongue over his lips.

"My lords!"

His customary salutation was met with the usual hoots of derision. He proceeded to give a long buildup, introducing Yelsiol Dancer—the *great,* the *sensuous,* the *seductive* Yelsiol Dancer, and the audience responded with drunken whoops. Yelsiol was a great, sensuous, seductive barrel of grease with the wits of a cockroach. Her legs looked fat as full-grown hogs, but they must be solid muscle to stand the pace. Tonight was a real stinker if Yelsiol had to come out again so soon.

Potstit struck a chord and began the beat. Eleal Singer started heading for the front. She was on next, and she still had not found one single friend. Most nights there would be half a dozen of her admirers scattered through the audience, those who came here especially and only because of Eleal Singer, and on a good night . . . Wrong! There was one, sitting alone at a table next the wall. She changed direction. What *was* his name again? It was only four or five nights since he had been here. A perfect memory is the absolute first requirement of an artist, Trong had always said, but she couldn't remember.

"Darling!" She slid gracefully onto the next chair and pecked his cheek. "Darling, how *wonderful* to see you again!"

He was fiftyish, flabby, and vaguely frail, as if his health was poor. His mustache was silvered and his face lined, but he would have stood out in Cherry Blossom House just from the quality of his attire. He was obviously a very successful businessman, which explained how he could afford to patronize the arts so expansively.

He smiled and squeezed her hand and they exchanged pleasantries. In the background, Yelsiol dropped a veil and the audience cheered and yelled for her to get on with it. Fat rolled and pulsed.

Potstit flubbed a few notes and recovered. Potstit had played at court when he was younger, long before Eleal was born. When on form, he was still good, but he was rarely on form. His pay and the rare tips he received, he converted at once to wine. His fingering was very shaky early in the evening, became reliable or even inspired around midnight, and went into eclipse before dawn. Tonight the tempos seemed to be deteriorating faster than usual. Time to go.

Ah! She had it—Gulminian Clothier.

"*Darling* Gulminian, I really *must* rush! I'm on next. But *it's* been *ages*! Don't you *dare* run off without a word. *Do* come and see me *right* after my number, won't you? I shall be *heartbroken* if you don't."

Gulminian promised. Greatly relieved, Eleal heaved herself up with a friendly hand on his shoulder and resumed her journey toward the front. She would be so humiliated if not a single admirer came to congratulate her after she sang! It had never happened yet. It would certainly give Tigurb'l Tavernkeeper ideas if it did.

She reached for another chair back and lurched to the next table, turning on her smile. Again, only one man . . .

"Eleal?"

Oh, by all the gods! For a moment she turned away, as if to flee. Then she forced herself to meet his eyes, while her innards curled up in knots.

It was Piol Poet. How he had aged! A thousand years old—tiny and shriveled. His face was as white as his hair and as thin. He hunched over a beaker clasped in both spidery hands, with no bottle in sight. Normally he would not rent his chair for long at that price, but the house was so poor tonight that he was welcome decoration. He stared up at her with a strange appeal.

She forced the smile again. "Piol!" She squeezed down on a seat beside him, too shaky to stand. "It's been a long time! How are you?"

"I'm well." He wheezed. He did not sound well. He did not look well. "And you?"

"Oh—I'm very well!"

The audience screamed enthusiasm and hammered on the tables as more of Yelsiol came into view. Potstit lost the beat and then found it again.

"What are you doing these days?" Eleal said hurriedly. "Who's performing your plays now?" She wondered if he was eating regularly.

He blinked a few times. "No one at the moment. I have several being considered. I hope to hear shortly on two or three of them. You may be confident that my name will appear at the Tion Festival again next year."

"That's wonderful!" Wonderful hogwash. Piol's plays needed Trong to direct them, and Trong was no more.

The old man fumbled inside his robe. "And I had a book published. Here—I brought you a copy."

She took it, thanking him, congratulating him, remembering how Piol had always despised printed books. Like its author, this one was notably thin. "I shall enjoy this. Will any of them make songs?"

"Possibly. Feel free to use any of them that take your fancy." His wizened lips smiled uncertainly. "And you?"

"Oh . . . It takes forever to get one's name known. But I have had quite a few auditions in the last fortnight." More hog, more wash. She dismissed Cherry Blossom House with an airy wave. "This is just to keep my hand in, you understand. I get so bored otherwise." Unless old Piol had lost every last wit in his head, he knew that the only money in music was in dramatic roles and a crippled singer had no real future.

"I remember you singing in the king's house," he quavered.

"But only as a member of the troupe. I plan to win my way back there on my own merits." That would certainly be the day water ran uphill. "Er . . . Have you heard any news of the others recently?"

He sighed and shook his head, a skull balanced on crumpled parchment. "You know that Golfren went back to farming? Sharecropping, of course. And Uthiam gave him a son at last? Klip joined the Lappinian army."

None of that was new. To think of Uthiam, that beautiful, wonderful actor, working in fields, probably as fat as Yelsiol now, nursing babies! Gartol had died. Eleal had even heard a rumor that young Klip had been killed in a minor mutiny, but she would not pass on such tidings. She wondered how much bad news Piol was keeping from her.

"Those were the good old days!" she said brightly.

It had been the Trong Troupe, but it had not been her grandfather who held it together. None of them had really appreciated that fact until Ambria had been carried off by a sudden fever and the troupe collapsed like a puffball. Trong had died of a broken heart. The troupe had been Eleal's family, the only life she knew. They had never had money, even in the good times, but they had had fellowship and good cheer.

"At your age, the good days are still to come, dear Eleal."

She laughed. "I certainly hope so." It wasn't the good days, it was the bad nights. . . .

Yelsiol was working up to a frenzy now, thumping around the stage, raising clouds of dust and yells of encouragement. Only two wisps to go. Eleal must get up there and wow the fans. No time for finesse.

"Are you eating regularly? Where do you live now? You need money, Piol?"

He shook his head violently, pulling back his lips in a grimace. "No, no! I'm very comfortable."

"Look, this isn't much of a scene, but it pays well. Are you sure—"

He continued to shake his head, pointing at the chapbook she held. "I have a room above the print shop . . . help set type, proofread sometimes."

A deafening howl . . . Yelsiol was down to the last wisp. Eleal pushed back her chair.

"That's my cue, old timer! It's wonderful to see you again, Piol." It was, too, however unwilling she was to be seen in a place like the Cherry Blossom House. She wondered how Piol had found her, and how many of the other survivors of the troupe knew. "I want to have a long talk with you, I really do."

He smiled eagerly. "I look forward to hearing you sing again, Eleal. Come back here after you're done?" For a man who had been a literary genius in his day, Piol had always been blessed with an astonishing streak of naiveté.

"Er, not tonight, I'm afraid. I—I promised my boyfriend. Sorry. One afternoon, maybe?"

Whatever he tried to say was lost in the roar as all of Yelsiol came into view. A couple of her admirers rose and hurried forward through the storm of applause—hoping to visit the star's dressing room and congratulate her, of course, as admirers did. As Gulminian Clothier and hopefully some others would come to visit Eleal. Tigurb'l Tavernkeeper's terms would be reasonable tonight.

Eleal patted Piol's bony, blotched hand and stood up. "Come back one afternoon!" she shouted. She began to hobble away, heading for the stage.

He twisted and reached out to her. "Eleal!"

She looked around. She should be up there by now.

"Eleal," Piol quavered. "I forgot to tell you. Have you heard the news about the Liberator?"

She staggered as if he had struck her with a rail. *"Who?"*

Piol blinked rapidly and beamed. "There's rumors in town that the Liberator's appeared in Joalvale. I wondered if you'd heard."

"D'ward?"

"I assume it must be D'ward."

She stood frozen, barely aware that Tigurb'l was already onstage, introducing her. D'ward! After all these years! The floor rocked under her boots. D'ward! That *slime?*

Piol had not noticed her reaction. "It's very strange! I can't imagine how he would dare to flaunt that name when he knows about the *Filoby Testament.* I mean, Zath is certain to hear. So maybe it isn't D'ward at all, just an imposter, although even an imposter would be very stupid to call himself the Liberator. But just in case it really is D'ward, I thought you might like to know, because I remember how fond you were of—"

"Fond! Fond of D'ward you mean, you old fool?"

Piol's face fell. "What's wrong? I thought you'd like . . . What's wrong?"

He was so stupid that she wanted to grab his stringy neck and shake him. She tried to scream and her throat produced only a whisper. "Nothing's wrong, Piol. Nothing's wrong at all! I'd love to meet D'ward again!"

And I will tear his lungs out and make him eat them and then there will be even less wrong than there is now. It's all his fault that I work here as a harlot in a brothel.

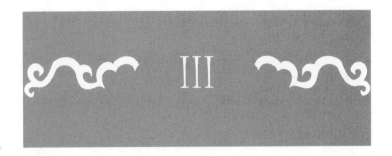

III

Rise up and get ye forth from among my people.

THE PENTATEUCH: EXODUS XII 31

ALL MORNING, DOSH COACHMAN HAD BEEN ENJOYING A LEISURELY RIDE across Joalvale. He arrived at Jilvenby around noon. The moa could have made the journey faster, but he had not pushed her, for he was not worried about pursuit. Yesterday's little episode would not have been discovered for hours, and who then could have known that the murderer had headed east? Kraanard had been a soldier, certainly, but even if he have been acting in an official capacity, his superiors would need time to organize a pursuit. His brethren in the Eltiana cult would be equally eager to peg out the culprit's hide, but they might not hear the news for days, so Dosh had every reason to believe he was free and clear. His life to date had been a hard one. He deserved some good fortune, and now he had earned it with quick wits and the foresight to imprint a moa.

Jilvenby was an unprepossessing hamlet, much what he had expected—a cluster of adobe hovels and waving palm trees set in the middle of farmland. Its inhabitants could be assumed to be honest, hardworking, impoverished, and dull as mud. The only good thing that might be said about the place was that it had a spectacular backdrop of jagged mountains already topped with the first snows of winter, but the same could be said of almost anywhere in the Vales.

The problem would be to locate D'ward. That would not be difficult in a place so small, except that he must be living under a false name—obviously that was why Kraanard had needed a witness to identify him. A man who had the god of death as his sworn foe could not survive for long otherwise. He might have been hiding out in this pigpen for years, earning his bread with honest sweat—horrible thought! Rural yokels did not take kindly to strangers, but that difficulty cut both ways. If D'ward had won some sort of acceptance from the locals, they would be even more suspicious of another foreigner asking questions about him. Silver would usually loosen tongues.

The village stood on the far side of a small river. As Swift waded across the ford, Dosh noted a peasant eating his lunch in the shade of some parasol trees. The evidence lying around this stalwart yeoman indicated he had been repairing a rail fence. Common prudence suggested that Dosh interrogate him before venturing into Jilvenby itself.

He rode over and bade Swift crouch. He slid gratefully from the saddle and hobbled her by tying the reins around one of her hocks. Taking his lunch from the saddlebag, he strolled over to the native, affecting the aloof bearing of a man rich enough to own a moa.

"Care for some company this fine day, my good man?"

The good man in question was a grizzled, overweight specimen wearing a loincloth and a surly expression. He was hairy and none too clean. Taking another bite from a hunk of bread, he continued to chew in relative silence.

Prepared to be patient with the bumpkin, Dosh chose a patch of shady moss on his upwind side and settled down with relief. A moa was a comfortable ride, but he was not accustomed to long journeys and had sprouted blisters. He unwrapped his bundle, selected a slice of sausage, and began to eat, admiring the fall sunshine much more now that he was not exposed to it. This part of Joalwall looked higher than he had expected, leaping from the narrow green foothills in shards of dark rock and sparkling snow. The frondy trees swayed in lazy dance. Swift hobbled around, crunching grass in its big teeth.

"You're too late," the yokel announced. "He's gone."

Now it was Dosh's turn to ruminate. "Who's gone?" he asked eventually.

"The Liberator."

Well! More chewing. "Who's he?"

"The one prophesied. Been here three, four days. Him an' his rabble. Locusts!" The workman spat.

This information would require more digesting than the sausage. Dosh rejected his previous theories on D'ward's activities. He discovered he had nothing to replace them.

"Never heard of him. What rabble? What're they up to?"

"They're up to trampling my field to mush, knocking down my fences, camping, littering, singing hymns half the night, preaching a lot of heresy." The peasant was becoming disturbed, working himself up to righteous wrath. "Must've been a hundred of them by the end, more trooping in every day." He skewered Dosh with an accusing glare.

"Not me! I never heard of any Liberator. Where'd they go to, so's I can avoid them?"

"Said they were heading over Ragpass."

"To Nosokvale? Oh, that's all right then. I couldn't take my moa over Ragpass, anyway, could I?"

"Why not?"

"Thought it was too high for them."

"No." The inspection continued. "Where're you heading, then?"

That was a valid question that must not be given a valid answer.

If D'ward had publicly declared himself the Liberator and was leading some sort of religious uprising, then all of Dosh's previous assumptions were trash. The Joalian government would move far more swiftly and drastically to crush a potential rebellion than it would to flush out a solitary fugitive in hiding. If the late trooper Kraanard had been acting officially in a case of suspected insurrection, then his death might be taken as evidence that the conspiracy had reached into the capital already. The authorities would view the affair much more seriously than Dosh had expected.

In other words, pursuit might be a lot closer than he had been counting on. He had better start laying a false trail.

"Me? I'm heading down Sussvale way."

"Can't take your moa over Monpass," the oaf said triumphantly. "Nor over Shampass neither!"

"I have a friend near there, who'll look after her for me while I'm gone."

The yokel scratched himself busily, not commenting, more obviously suspicious than before.

If D'ward was not in hiding and already had a hundred followers, then he was in much less need of Dosh's information about the Eltiana cultist, and the emblem on Kraanard's leg might be totally irrelevant anyway, because his military superiors were far more likely to be worried about an uprising than the Lady would be. But now poor Dosh was trapped in eastern Joalvale, with only one pass out that he could take with his moa. It seemed he was going to follow the Liberator to Nosokvale whether he wanted to or not.

He began to eat more quickly. "And what exactly are these crackpots preaching?"

"I don't know," retorted the peasant. "And I don't shitty care. The Maiden's good enough for me, praise her name."

"Amen!" Dosh said piously. He wondered how far it was to Ragpass and how much start D'ward had. He wasn't about to ask anyone in Jilvenby.

ᏉᏒ 8 ᏕᏉ

IN JOALIAN, THE PRINCIPAL DIALECT OF THE VALES, THE ANIMAL THAT MEMbers of the Service termed a "rabbit" was a *rabith*. English dictionaries traced "rabbit" back to old Flemish and dismissed earlier etymology as unknown, but undoubtedly the word came from some native of Nextdoor who had crossed over to Earth centuries ago and applied the Joalian name to the comparable animals he found there. Nextdorian rabbits were considerably larger, of course.

They also had tusks. From tusks to bunny tail they were longer than horses, but only about half the height, so that their riders must sit with feet raised in a posture that became very uncomfortable after a few hours. Although they had amazing endurance and an incredible turn of speed, they could not maintain a steady pace. They would flash over the ground for fifteen or twenty minutes, then slow down until another sharp kick sent them off again at their original breathtaking rush. Every hour or so, they needed a break to eat. They were steered—and only constant attention would keep them on a straight course—

by gentle tugs on their long ears. Julian thought of them as hay-powered motorcycles. They were certainly no smarter.

For a man with only one hand, a rabbit was a much harder ride than a horse would have been. Braking required tugs on both ears simultaneously, so the only way Julian could stop was to steer straight at a high wall. Even then, Bounder would sometimes try to jump the obstacle, with unpredictable results. A rabbit must be tethered before its rider dismounted or it would run away, and Julian had difficulty doing that. Experience had taught him that it was easier to keep on going until he arrived at his destination, and thus he was very glad to arrive back at Olympus at dusk, after almost twenty-four hours on the road.

He was always happy to return to the station, though. The air alone was worth the price, as Jumbo said. Cosy and wooded, the little glen nestled between the peaks the Service called Mount Cook, Nanga Parbat, the Matterhorn, and Kilimanjaro—native Valians rarely gave names to mountains; there were just too many of them to bother with. Julian's pleasure now was marred only by the knowledge that the person he most wanted to see would not be here, because she had set out the day before he had, on a mission to the Lemodians.

He had given much thought to the Exeter problem and had concluded that the man up in Joalvale must be an imposter. Zath would probably welcome a few fake Liberators showing up to discredit the legend; he might well have set up this false Liberator himself, as some sort of trap for the Service or for Exeter.

The one time Julian had heard Exeter discuss the prophecy, he had been adamant that he would never try to fulfill it. He could not bring death to Death, he had said, because the only way to do so would be to become a more powerful pseudogod himself, and the only way to acquire such mana would be to stoop to the rotten tactics the Chamber used. Out of the question, Q.E.D.

But of course, if this reported Liberator was the real McCoy, then Exeter must have found another answer, and in that case Julian had a worthy friend engaged in a worthy cause. He would have to go and help, whether the Service was willing to support him or not.

Or had the man just snapped under the strain? For almost five years Exeter had known that the Chamber was after his blood; he had been harried from world to world and watched his friends die in his stead. Julian Smedley had seen enough of the effects of war to know that even a regular brick like Edward Exeter must have a breaking point. He had seen it happen to dozens of men almost as good.

Same answer—rally round and help!

Bounder loped wearily along the banks of the Cam, past the Carrots' village. Copper-haired children gawked at the *tyika*. A few adults bowed or made the circle sign. Soon after that, Julian came in sight of the station itself, a cluster of villas grouped around the node. The first time he had seen it, a year and a half ago, it had just been sacked by Zath's henchmen, but it was all rebuilt now. There was even a new cricket pitch, and a few chaps were still out there, practicing in the fading light. The latest addition was a polo field. The first thing he would do when he'd finished growing his hand back was take up rabbit polo.

He rode straight to the paddocks, where he steered Bounder into a corner and then turned him over to the Carrot grooms. He set off on foot for his own bungalow, staggering with fatigue but knowing he could not have come so far so fast on a horse, or even a relay of horses. He had a recurring dream where he somehow took a rabbit Home and rode it in the Derby, leaving the rest of the field at the post. Alas, the dream must remain a dream, for only people could cross between worlds.

He had not even reached the gate when he saw a man he knew in the next paddock, leaning on a fence and chatting with a couple of stable hands.

Julian bellowed, "Dragontrader!"

T'lin looked up, said a word to his companions, and clambered over the gate. He came trotting in Julian's direction, not moving quite as fast as Julian would have liked.

Political Branch's Agent Seventy-seven was a huge man with a monstrous ginger beard. His origins were obscure, although his habit of wearing a turban suggested that he hailed from Niolland or one of its neighboring vales. His fur jerkin had once been dyed blue, his voluminous bags were a faded green, his boots had started out as scarlet, and he would have some yellow and white about him somewhere. Those were the sacred colors of the Pentatheon, but the tiny gold circle of the Undivided glinted in his left earlobe.

He arrived, stopped, and made the sign of the circle. Julian ignored it, for the Service did not bother with religious mumbo jumbo within Olympus.

"I understand you met *Tyika* Kisster in Joalvale?"

T'lin stood well over six feet tall and could look down on Julian easily, even at his present respectful distance. His expression gave away nothing. "That is correct, Saint Kaptaan."

"Did you speak with him?"

"I did, Your Holiness."

"Just call me '*tyika*' here, Seventy-seven, if you please. Did he say what he was doing?"

T'lin's emerald eyes regarded him coolly under hedges of russet eyebrows. "I asked him. He just said, 'Preaching,' Holiness. I already knew that, because I had watched him. I heard little of what he was preaching, although I believe it was the True Gospel."

"Did he say anything else?"

The green eyes twinkled. "He asked how you fared, Holiness, and if your hand had healed."

Damn! Julian was momentarily thrown off balance. His hand slid behind his back without any orders from him. "You have no doubt that it was the real *Tyika* Kisster?"

"None, Your Holiness. He reminisced extensively about the days when he traveled with me, pretending to be one of my men. No one else could have known the stories."

Damn again! And damn Exeter for foreseeing this very conversation! "Thank you. That will be all."

"Holiness." T'lin hinted at a bow and stalked away. *Tyika*, of course, meant "master." Red beard or not, Dragontrader was not a Carrot.

Julian resumed his walk home.

As he trudged up the bungalow steps, Dommi Houseboy appeared on the veranda to greet him, bowing respectfully. The groom handed him Julian's bag and hurried off. Like almost all the natives of the valley, Dommi had flaming copper hair, although as a domestic he was required to keep it cut short. He was losing the all-over freckles of youth, but he was just as eager to please as he had been when Julian first hired him. As always, his white livery was faultless.

"Evening, Dommi. How's Ayetha?"

"Oh, she is indeed most well, *tyika*, thank you. And you are very welcome back."

"And glad to be so," Julian admitted, heading straight for the bathroom. "I need to shed about twenty pounds of dust."

"I have a warm tub waiting, *tyika*."

He did. The big copper basin was steaming. How on Nextdoor had he ever managed that? He could have had only a rough idea of when Julian would turn up and likely was not supposed to know even that much. He must have arranged for someone in the village to signal to him somehow. Couldn't keep secrets in Olympus—damn Carrots knew everything.

Accepting help to undress, three hands being faster than one, Julian caught a glimpse of his bristly beard in the mirror. Shave? Usually when he came home to Olympus, a smooth chin stood right at the top of the order of battle. Doc had taken over his tour . . . but there was still the Exeter problem. Think about it. He sank blissfully into the water. Dommi bustled around, laying out clothes and towels.

Now for the news, which Dommi must be eagerly waiting to impart.

"The Peppers back yet?"

"No, indeed, *tyika*. They are now four days overdue."

That was odd. Normally members of the Service went Home on leave every couple of years, but the Great War had interfered. Now that it was over, everyone was very eager to catch up. The Peppers had won first slot and were making themselves extremely unpopular by being late returning. It would be at least eighteen months before Julian's number came up.

"There is many excitements around, *tyika*. You are not the only *tyika* to be summoned back. *Tyika* Corey, and *Tyika* Rollinson, and *Entyika* Newton, and *Votyikank* Garcia, and *Entyikank* Olafson and McKay." Dommi's head disappeared into the linen cupboard for a moment. "But *Entyikank* Corey and Rutherford have not been summoned for, nor *Tyikank* Newton and McKay."

It sounded like the Committee was in one of its paper-throwing frenzies, but it would not be good form to say so to Dommi.

Julian rolled an eye to inspect the garments awaiting him. "Dinner?"

"You are invited to *Votyikank* Pinkney, *tyika*."

Julian groaned. He needed sleep! "What time is it?"

"It is approaching six. I checked our clock with the sundial this morning, *tyika.*" Olympian clocks were individualists and rarely agreed with one another about anything.

"Then I will have a nap and arrive late." Reaching wearily for the soap, Julian recalled his adventure of the previous day. "Blast!" The Randorian intervention would have to be reported. Political Branch would be interested, and the other missionaries must be warned. "Take down a letter for me, will you?"

Dommi beamed. "Of course, *tyika!*" He loved to demonstrate his literacy, although his spelling was legendary. In seconds he was sitting cross-legged beside the tub, with pen, paper, and ink.

"To *Tyika* Miller. Dear Dusty. Some Randorian soldiers intruded on the meeting at Seven Stones yesterday. Fortunately they proved amenable to reason and did no harm. Doc knows, of course, but we must expect trouble in future. Yours."

Dommi carefully blew on the paper to dry the ink, then held it up for Julian's inspection. Had he really said "enterooded"? or "iminiable to reesson"? or "I have the oner to be uor most humbille and ubidiant sirv'ntt"?

"That's fine. Thanks. Remind me to sign it." He realized that Dommi had not produced the razor. "How about a shave now?"

"If the *tyika* feels it is advisory."

Julian contemplated that remark sleepily. "Or perhaps I'd better keep the beard."

"It might be for the best, *tyika.*"

So Julian was not going to be staying long in Olympus and the Carrots knew it. They had ears like hawks!

"I'll need a snack before I turn in. I'm famished."

"At once, *tyika.* Would tea and bubbler sandwiches be sufficiencies?"

"You know I love bubbler sandwiches." Julian roused himself to attend to his ablutions.

Dommi headed for the door, then paused. "*Tyika?* If it is not too much presumptuousness . . ."

"What say?"

"When you go to meet the *Tyika* Exeter . . . may I come also?"

Julian was so startled he rubbed soap in his eyes and swore. The Liberator problem was none of Dommi's business! He could not recall Dommi ever leaving the valley before, and Ayetha was close to term. But he had been Exeter's houseboy once, and Exeter had always had a gift for inspiring loyalty—when he had been house prefect at Fallow, the juniors had worshipped him. If the *Filoby Testament* had not kept him out of the war, he would have made a great officer. None of which concerned Dommi.

"I haven't been told I am going anywhere to meet anyone."

Dommi murmured, "Of course, *tyika!* I beg the *tyika's* pardon," and padded away.

Julian began contemplating a long evening. The dinner at the Pinkneys' might be more important than any formal Committee session, for the real decisions would be made there, over port and cigars. And of course Dommi had been careful to tell him that his mistress was back, but her husband was not.

9

A CRUEL WIND WAILED ALONG THE STREET, INCITING DEAD LEAVES TO RUN races, whipping up the rank smell of horses from the stones. It tugged at Eleal's cloak and tried to snatch her precious load from her arms. It threw dust in her eyes. In this corner of the town the evening's activities would not normally begin for hours yet, but twilight was coming early under the storm clouds and she must complete her business and be well away before it did. Bending into the gale, she trudged with her uneven gait—*clip-clop, clip-clop-clip*. The wind repeatedly tried to push her off balance or rip the cloth wrapping from the burden she carried.

Jurg was a fine town, her favorite town in all the Vales, but all towns had seamy corners and River Street was seamier than the backside of a patchwork quilt, a fetid alley that made the area near Cherry Blossom House seem dull as a virgin's diary. She had only ever ventured here before once, and then in broad daylight. The Cherry Blossom whores came regularly, but always around noon, and even then Tigurb'l Tavernkeeper sent bouncers along to protect them. Eleal could have asked a couple of those thicks to escort her this evening, but they would have been more dangerous than the ill-reputed denizens of River Street. They would have demanded to know what she carried wrapped in that rag and then promptly relieved her of it. The brighter ones would also have cut her throat so she couldn't tattle back to Tigurb'l.

It had cost more than five Joalian stars. If she let it slip, it wouldn't be worth a copper pig. If she fell and went down on top of it, she might not be, either. The sucker was as tall as a two-year-old child—and *heavy*. The push of the wind was uneven. The cobbles were uneven. Her legs were uneven. *Clip-clop . . . clip-clop . . . clip . . .*

There were few other people around. The town mice had fled the coming dark and the cats had not yet emerged. The one or two men who came hurrying past all looked at her as if they could not believe their eyes—this was no place for a woman alone. She should have borrowed some less pretentious garments, too. Her cloak alone had cost almost half a star, burgundy-colored Narshian llama wool with white goose-fur trim.

But here was her destination. Amid all the shabby tenements, run-down stores, and mysterious anonymous doorways stood a grand pillared entrance, far older than all of them. The original proprietor was still in business, for the portico bore a massive metal hammer, the symbol of Karzon. Usually the holy buildings in a city were clustered close together. Isolated temples like this one were so rare that Eleal knew of no others—it was as if the god who lived here had been spurned by the other gods of the city, as if they would not associate with him. This was the home of Ken'th, avatar of the Man in Jurg.

She dared not pause to catch her breath, although her heart was racing like a cheetah. One more effort to think this project through and her courage would fade like mist. Blinking the wind tears from her eyes, she hurried up the steps, clutching her precious bundle. *Clip-clop, clip-clop . . .* The old tiled steps showed signs of wear. That amused her, because no one ever admitted to worshipping at the temple of Ken'th. Mother Ylla, that horrible hag, had told her once that only boys and old men did—she had overlooked harlots.

The door stood open. It was a small door for so large a portico, and the interior beyond seemed dark. Again, Eleal felt her nerve waver. Her insides had tied themselves into hard knots; her arms shook so violently that she feared she was about to drop the figurine. That would ruin all her plans! But gods should be approached with humility and reverence, not this burning anger, this vitriolic craving to *get even.* Who ever brought a plea for justice to the Man? Justice was the prerogative of the Maiden, especially her aspect of Irepit, who had once sent one of her nuns to save Eleal from a reaper and must therefore be well disposed toward her. Unfortunately, Astina's aspect in Jurg was Agroal, goddess of virginity, not at all the right goddess to handle a problem like this—nor one that Eleal Singer would dare to petition, whereas she had a special call on Ken'th. *Get even!* I will be revenged on D'ward! She clenched her teeth and lurched forward into the temple. *Clip! Clop! Clip!*

The circular chamber was small for the home of an important god, but that was because Ken'th attracted solitary worshippers, not great congregations. To her intense relief, it was presently inhabited only by a restless wind, which rustled leaves it had brought in as offerings and stirred the draperies covering the walls. High, narrow windows above them shed little light on the gloomy hall. In the center, two oil lamps burned on the low dais, their flames jumping nervously— they could not be half as nervous as she was! Above them stood the figure of the god.

Unlike the Youth, the Man was normally portrayed clothed, but of course this was Ken'th. Lit mainly from below by the lamps, the carving was impossibly priapic. She had been only a child on her previous visit, yet even then she had been confident that the anatomical details were based on wishful thinking. Now she knew that from experience, but she could also tell that the sculptor had been much more skilled than whoever had painted the pornographic murals in the upper rooms of Cherry Blossom House. The musculature was superb. The set of Ken'th's hands on his hips and the tip of his head demonstrated male arrogance beautifully—man the irresistible. The face bore an expression at once sensuous, demanding, and callous. She thought of her mother, wondering if she had come here of her own free will, or if the god had sought her out somewhere else.

Eleal limped closer. She should kneel, she supposed, and yet she felt strangely reluctant to do so. Her heart was fighting to escape, a terrified bird in a bony cage.

A curtain swished open, revealing a dark little room behind. She jumped, almost dropping the figurine. A man strode out silently on bare feet—a priest, of course, although he did not look like a priest. Male servants of other deities wore long robes, and most shaved their scalps and faces. Being Ken'th's and on duty, this one had only a green wrap tied around his loins. His hair hung to his shoulders, his beard merged with the fur mat on his chest. He was tall and well-built, an exemplar of young manhood, but the temple of virility would have many more applicants to choose from than most did.

He came around the plinth and stopped near one of the lamps, regarding her with approval. "You are welcome to this holy place, beloved."

Eleal clutched the figurine tighter—much tighter and she would break it. "Thank you, father," she said, and was annoyed to hear the quaver in her voice.

He nodded slightly, eying her burden curiously. "I see you bring a substantial offering. How may I aid you? What mercy do you seek from mighty Ken'th?"

"I wish to speak with the god himself."

"An elderly husband, perhaps? An embarrassing delay in conceiving?" He would be willing to remedy the matter, with the god's help and a suitable fee. He might even waive the fee in her case.

"No, father."

He smiled, unable to conceal his eagerness. "Then too much success in conceiving? You wish the god to withdraw his blessing? This, too, may be arranged, beloved."

That was why the harlots came. It would be all much the same to him, for although that ritual included some complicated preliminaries to appease the god and ensure the required result, all Ken'th's rituals included coitus. All that involved women, anyway. What happened with the boys and old men, she did not know and did not want to.

"Not that, either. I wish to speak with the god."

A flicker of impatience. "Present your offering, make your prayers, and then I shall aid you in the rites."

"No. I—I wish to meet him in person."

The man blinked. Then he grinned broadly. "You are ambitious, daughter! Whatever your need, I am authorized to represent the god in the performance of his sacrament."

Eleal had never met a man who did not think that of himself, and she could recognize the too-familiar eagerness in the priest's manner. He advanced a step. She backed away. He noticed her limp and frowned.

Unable to think of anything more to say, Eleal pulled the cover from the figurine, a female dancer poised on one toe, about to take flight from its plinth, carved Niolian crystal flashing in the lamplight. Its beauty was heart-stopping. She had spent all afternoon haggling with the dealer, and even then he had emptied her purse to her last twelfthpiece. Surely such an offering would earn the god's attention?

The priest sucked in his breath. "You bring a rich gift, lady!" he admitted. "It is fitting." He tore his eyes away from the carving to study her again, noting the quality of her robe. She could almost hear him concluding that a woman who wore such a garment to visit River Street must be out of her mind.

He reached out. "Let me take it for you."

"No!" She moved it away.

"Then lay it on the dais, carefully."

"No! I wish to give it to the god in person. *I want Ken'th in the flesh!*"

"You are verging close to blasphemy, daughter!"

His tone annoyed her. He was little older than she was.

"Tell the god that—"

"Give me that carving before you drop it." He reached out again.

Again she lurched back. Seeing she could not evade him any longer, she turned and hurled the figurine at the feet of the idol. The crash echoed from the stone walls; a hail of diamonds danced across the floor. The priest cried out in horror.

"There!" Eleal shouted. "I have given my offering to the god! Now let him hear my prayer!"

The priest backed away, watching carefully where he put his feet. "You are crazy, woman!" His voice was unsteady. "You commit sacrilege and blasphemy! Begone, lest Holy Ken'th smite you in his wrath!"

"I want Ken'th!" she yelled. "I have words for his ears alone!"

"Go! You are out of your wits, I say. Beware that he does not curse you, so that no man will ever consummate his holy sacrament with you."

"He is my father!"

The young priest curled his lip in disgust. "One of those, are you? Be thankful to mighty Ken'th for giving you life and do not trouble him further." Coming around, staying clear of the shining fragments, he grabbed her arm so hard that she cried out.

"I have a special service to offer him!"

"Begone, madwoman!" He began pulling her to the door.

She struggled and clawed at him. He took hold of her other wrist and manhandled her easily, practically carrying her.

It was not working out as she had planned. She had thrown away everything she had ever earned and would have nothing to show for it. She was going to be balked of her revenge. "I want to tell him of the Liberator!"

"I am sure you do. And you doubtless have a few prophecies he should hear also. Pray to him in the privacy of your bedroom, and he will hear." They had reached the door. "Out with you!—and do not linger in these streets, for the god's presence here makes men bold. It is no place for a woman alone."

With that cold warning, the priest threw her out. The door slammed behind her as she sprawled down on the rug.

10

Rug? Not a woven rug but a thick alpaca fleece. She raised her head to look into a cheerful log fire, crackling and sputtering in a stone fireplace. She could have sworn that the priest had thrown her outside on the steps. His words had said so. To her left, a leather couch . . . another couch on her right. She was indoors in a large and comfortable chamber.

She moaned in fear and pushed herself up on her arms. She had sung in the king's house when she was a child and she gave private recitals now, so she knew how the rich lived. She had seen nothing to better this: floors of polished wood overlain with soft fleeces, walls bearing shelves of books, racks of bows and spears, mounted trophy heads. The furniture was solid, upholstered in browns and russets, subdued and harmonious. Scents of beeswax, leather, and wood smoke hung in the air. Bewildered, she rose to her knees. This was very much a man's room, a rich man's den, cozy and friendly and appealing.

She peered around for a door but saw only full-length drapes of umber velvet, which might equally well conceal windows. None was close enough to explain how she came to be where she was. This was certainly not that fusty little cubicle she had glimpsed in the chapel. On the shelf above the fireplace stood two gold candlesticks, a golden vase of autumn flowers—and a carved crystal figurine of a dancer poised to fly. She scrambled to her feet to stare at it. It stood a little higher than eye level, and with candlelight dancing over the shiny facets, she could easily imagine that it was already flying. There could never be two identical and yet she had smashed . . .

"Thank you. It's very beautiful." The voice came from somewhere behind her.

There had been no one there a moment ago. She knew who must have spoken, who must have re-created the dancer. Her prayer had been granted. She spun around and simultaneously sank to her knees, touching her face to the rug, not daring to look upon the god without permission. Her heart thundered in her throat.

The Man was an ambiguous deity. Creator and destroyer, he must be both feared and adored. As D'mit'ri he was the builder of cities; as Krak'th he shook them down. As Padlopan he was sickness; as Garward, Strength. He was husbandry and battle. As Zath he was Death, as Ken'th he quickened the womb to bear new life. As Karzon he was all of them.

Piol Poet had written the Man into his plays many times, but never as Ken'th,

48

although there were many fine legends of the Lover. Most were variations of the tragic tale of Ismathon, the mortal who pined away and eventually slew herself rather than live without his love. The Trong Troupe would never have performed any play with Ken'th in it.

"It is an exceptionally fine piece," the god said, his voice coming closer. "It cost you dearly, so whatever it is that troubles you must be a serious matter." Then he chuckled. "Are you comfortable down there?"

She had not expected a god to *chuckle*. "Er . . . yes, Lord." She raised her head a fraction and saw two bare feet. A strong hand reached down and raised her. She kept her face lowered until a finger lifted her chin and she met his smile.

Back in her theater days, she had seen Karzon in his various aspects depicted by many actors—Dolm, Trong himself, Golfren, men with other troupes. He was always portrayed with a beard, often in armor, and whenever possible by a large man. Ken'th did not look as she expected at all. He was younger, for one thing, and not especially big, although his arms and shoulders were solid enough. He had curly hair and a Niolian-style mustache. He wore a sleeveless shirt and knee-length breeches—in green, of course. At least the color was right. But there was no sense of divine majesty about him. Nor did she sense any stunning, overwhelming sexuality. He was just a chunky, cheerful young man, handsome in a rugged sort of way, faintly scented with musk and lavender. He was smiling reassuringly. His eyes . . . perhaps the eyes . . .

"Why not begin by telling me your name?"

She struggled to find her wits. "Eleal Singer, Lord."

"Welcome to my house." He unfastened her cloak, glanced at it approvingly, and tossed it over a couch. He took a step back to look her over. "Mm! You are not only a startlingly beautiful woman, Eleal Singer, but you have exquisite taste in clothes!"

She gasped out her thanks. She had money to indulge her whims now, and this gown was her newest and best, just bought for winter. She had not worn it before—fine white wool, decorated only with big rhinestone buttons down the front and brocade on the collar. She always chose clothes with long skirts to hide her boot; she suspected that the long sleeves and high collar were a reaction to the skimpy things she wore to perform. It was snug around the bodice, though, with a high, tight waist supporting her breasts, and from there it fell full and loose. To have her clothes praised by a god was a heady sensation. She avoided his eye, feeling herself blush.

He led her to a russet leather couch, seating her next to the fire and settling down beside her. She clasped her hands on her knees and stared at them as if she were a fourteen-year-old with her first man.

"And you claim to be my daughter? Who was your mother?"

"Itheria Impresario." When there was no reaction, she continued. "She disappeared for a fortnight, here in Jurg. I know very little about her. She bore me and then she just died, and I was reared by my grandfather, Trong Impresario, and his wife—his second wife, Ambria. She said my mother hadn't been a bad woman, she had . . ." Been seduced by the god, but she couldn't say that. "Pined away for love?"

Ken'th sighed faintly. "That does happen, I'm afraid. I don't recall the name. It could have been me. I'm not usually quite that fickle—only a fortnight? But it is possible, I suppose." He slid an arm around her, making her heart flip. "You are certainly beautiful enough to be the child of a god. You sing for a living?"

"Yes, Lord."

"Where?"

"Oh, all over the place. I have performed in many of the Vales and at many places here in Jurg." That was all true. The Trong Troupe had traveled. Tigurb'l often arranged for her to perform in private houses.

"Fascinating!" the god said softly. "And you mentioned the Liberator! Are you the Eleal named in the *Filoby Testament*?"

"Yes, Lord."

"Father?"

"Yes . . . Father." She glanced sideways.

He raised dark eyebrows and waited. He was smiling, but his amusement held none of the mockery the priest's had. He was taking her concern seriously.

Talk . . . "I did what was prophesied. When the Liberator came, I tended him, washed him. He fell very sick, and I nursed him. I did everything I was supposed to, Father!"

Ken'th frowned. "You know, I find I dislike that title? I have no experience at being a father, Eleal. That's not my job. For that you need Visek."

"Of course, Lord!"

"I am god of virility," he said apologetically. "I do have duties. If I tried to keep track of all the bastards I have fathered in the last few hundred years, I would have no time for anything else. You do understand?"

"Yes, of course, Lord!"

"Call me Ken'th."

She hesitated, appalled.

"Go on!" he said, teasing. "You wanted me in the flesh. You have me in the flesh, so call me Ken'th!"

"Yes, Ken'th."

"That's better."

For a moment he just smiled at her. She smiled back with mounting confidence. He was handsome, now she saw him close—handsome and attractive. His face did not at all resemble the face on the statue. Not arrogant, not callous, but kind and trustworthy and sympathetic.

"How old are you?"

"Seventeen . . . Ken'th."

"So when the Liberator came you were only a child. He was not a baby, of course, although the text implied he would be. How old was he?"

"Eighteen, he told me."

"Lovers?"

"Oh *no*! Of course not!"

The god's arm tightened around her. "And what did you want to tell me about him?"

This was where matters might become just a trifle delicate. Her heart began to speed up again. "He's reported to be up in Joalvale."

"That's the story that's going around, yes."

She drew a few long breaths, as she did just before starting to sing an especially difficult song. "I thought . . . perhaps . . . I wondered if you might want to get in touch with him. If you do, I could identify him for you . . . if you wish. . . ." Of course it was Zath who would be interested in catching the Liberator, but Zath was Karzon and Karzon was Ken'th, although she couldn't in any way relate this chunky, likable young man to the dread god of death.

"An interesting offer!" the god said thoughtfully. "What is wrong with your leg?"

Normally she was furious if anyone mentioned her impairment, but this was her father, so his interest was excusable. "One's shorter than the other." She raised her leg so he could see the thick sole on her boot. "I fell out a window when I was a baby."

"It does not hinder your ability to perform?"

"Not— Well, yes, of course it does! My ambition has always been to be an actor, but I can't clump around a stage like this! I would not be allowed to enter the Tion Festival!" There, she had told him!

And Ken'th murmured sympathetically. He understood! "Let's hear you sing. Sing for me—nothing elaborate, something simple. Something unusual." He took his arm away and reached over the back of the couch to produce a lute. He strummed expertly; it was in perfect tune. "What'll it be?"

She had not expected this! To sing for a *god*! She racked her brains. " 'Woeful Maiden'?"

He smiled and played a verse, although it was an obscure song, one that not many people would know. He was much better than Potstit had ever been. "Higher? Lower?"

"No, no, that's just right!" Daringly, she added, "You play divinely!"

He laughed. "Well, of course!" He began the introduction.

She sang the first verse, but then he stopped and put the lute away.

"Just what I expected. Your voice is reedy, your timing eccentric. You put terrific feeling into the words and get by on drama, but you wouldn't be admitted to the Tion Festival in a thousand years."

"Lord! I mean Father . . ."

He swept her into his arms and squeezed her tightly. He kissed the tip of her nose playfully. "You must be very hot in that dress?"

"I'm your daughter!"

His eyes gleamed in a look she knew well. "And I'm a god! Gods do not have to obey petty little rules!"

Then he kissed her lips.

It was not an especially long kiss. It did not have to be. When he had done she leaned back and gaped at him. She was limp. No man had ever kissed her like that.

He chuckled with satisfaction. "Now, Eleal Singer, let's have the truth. Not just what you want to believe is the truth, but the real truth. Where do you sing?"

She clenched her teeth. And her fists. But the god was waiting, regarding her with big brown eyes. "Well, several places. I mean . . . sometimes . . . well, Cherry Blossom House."

"So you are a whore!"

"Certainly not!"

He raised his eyebrows. "My, you are a determined little prickleback, aren't you? We'll try some more, then."

He was firm; he did not hurt her, but her struggles were useless against his strength. His lips pressed on hers, his hand stroked her breast—the dress was down around her waist, although she did not know how that had happened. Tingles rippled through her, from her scalp to her toes. She was melting and struck by lightning, both at the same time. Excitement surged through her in fiery waves. No man had ever taken over her body like this, nothing like this had ever happened to her before, she was floating away in clouds of pink fog— but then he stopped.

"Oh, Ken'th, Ken'th . . . Darling . . ." She reached down to remove the dress completely.

He took her hands between his and clasped them. "The real truth now!"

She heard her own voice from far away. "Yes, darling. Yes, I'm a whore. After I sing, Tigurb'l sends men back to my dressing room. I bring in three times what anyone else does, he says. Sometimes he sends me to perform in private houses . . . just for men, of course. I don't want to do these things, but there's no other work for a crippled singer. I was so hungry! Kiss me again, please."

He uttered that surprising chuckle again. "You don't shock me, Eleal. Did you think I would disapprove? You are doing what women should do—aiding men in the performance of my sacrament. And the Liberator?"

One of her hands broke free and began to unbutton his shirt. "I don't care much about him," her voice said. "He was supposed to go to Tion's temple. This was in Sussvale, where the Youth is patron. The priests commanded that D'ward—that's the Liberator's name, D'ward—that D'ward come to the temple, and Kirthien Archpriest said I had done well and Holy Tion would heal my leg, but the Liberator just ran away. He disappeared! So my leg didn't get cured . . ." The memory of that awful injustice flickered faintly through the pink fog. *Coward! Ingrate!* "He ran away! He betrayed me. I want. . . . You're my father. When I learned that, when we came back to Jurg, I came and prayed to you, here in the temple. Until a priest found me and said I was a dirty little girl and threw me out!"

"I didn't hear you," Ken'th said grumpily. "I may have been away. Or busy."

"Well, this morning I decided you might hear me if I mentioned the Liberator. And if I brought a big offering." She hoped she could stop talking now and he would kiss her again. She had his shirt open and could run her fingers through the manly thatch on his chest.

"You want revenge on the Liberator. . . . No, mostly you hope to bribe me to heal your leg."

"No, no, no! I just want to help you, because you're my— I want to help you!" She tugged one-handed at the big gold buckle of his belt.

Ken'th was frowning, though. "I could cure you, of course, but I'm god of lust, not god of healing. That's one of Tion's attributes. I suppose I could claim that repairing a harlot was within my field, because he certainly plays around in my garden when he's in the mood. Damn you, you little shrew-cat, you've put me in a confounded mess!"

Eleal choked. "M-mess?"

"Mess. If Zath ever finds out I had a lead like you and didn't follow it up . . . Never mind. You can't understand."

Why did he speak of Zath as if he were someone completely different, not just another aspect? She had thrown away her savings, angered a god, probably angered Tigurb'l Tavernkeeper, too, because she was going to be late—and she still had to get out of River Street without being raped. But at the moment none of those things mattered. "Kiss me again. Please!"

"No. I need you with some wits about you. Here's what you're going to do, Eleal Singer. You're going to go and find this D'ward Liberator, you hear? You're to go up to him and put a hand—"

Black panic cut through the pink fog like a sword blade.

"No, no!" She writhed and struggled. "You're not to turn me into a reaper!" A reaper like Dolm Actor, with all those horrible rituals he had known—to slay people with a touch, to walk through locked doors, even to summon Zath himself . . .

"By the Five, you do have resistance, don't you? Tough as marble!"

"Not a reaper! I won't, I won't!"

"I couldn't make you a reaper. That's Zath's speciality. But I have a trick or two of my own. Don't I?" Ken'th smiled and removed her hand from his belt. He spread her arms wide and leaned on her, bringing his lips to hers again.

The world danced for her. She soared into heavens of delight. She melted. But it was all too short, only seconds. When he pulled back from her, she could see his big brown eyes appraising her calmly. She was gasping for breath, soaked all over, quivering violently. More, more!

"Now, Eleal Singer. I shall give you money and have the priests escort you safely back to the whorehouse. Tomorrow you will go and find the Liberator. Get very close to him, touching him. In his bed would be best, but a hand on his arm will do. Then you will sing that song you sang for me. You must never sing it again until you are touching D'ward, you understand? And when you come back, I shall heal your leg for you. I'll find you a nice rich husband—rich, anyway, the two together are rare."

He released her hands, which immediately reached for her bundled dress, to push it off her completely.

He chuckled. "No! Put it on again. Do as I say, and I'll give you what you want when you come back. Truly, I look forward to it! But now you will leave here at once and you will not remember this conversation. When the priests deliver you to your door, you will forget ever coming here. But tomorrow you will do as I have told you."

ᔕᓄ   11   ᔭᓇ

DOSH KNEW MOST OF THE OFFICIAL PASSES IN THE VALES AND A FEW UN-official ones also—the secret "back doors" patronized by smugglers and Tinkerfolk, who were frequently the same people. Although he had not crossed Ragpass in years and had only vague memories of it, he remembered it as soon as he saw it. The Nosokvale end, he now recalled, was quite gentle, but the Joalvale side angled up a sheer cliff. In many places the trail had been notched into the buff-colored rock like a half tunnel, and those artificial parts were too narrow to let two men pass. The natural ledges were mostly wider but often canted unpleasantly toward the scenery. The only good thing to be said about the ascent was that it zigged and zagged so much that anyone who blew off could have some hope of flattening a fellow traveler or two as he bounced his way down.

Convinced now that his continued survival depended on leaving Joalvale with haste and as few witnesses as possible, Dosh had not paused to talk with any more natives. His Tinkerfolk childhood had given him skill in tracking, but any fool could have read the footprints in the dust, and they would have been erased by the wind if the Liberator and his gang were more than a few hours ahead of him. When he drew near the base of the cliff, he could see small groups of people like mites, trailing upward, far above him. In the warm glow of a setting sun, he proceeded to ride his moa up the nightmare.

The first third or so went comparatively easily. All he need do was urge his mount on and resist a temptation to close his eyes. Being suspended seven feet above the path was much worse than having one's own feet on it, and he had to curl into a knot at the overhangs, but at least he need not exert himself. Joalflat began to expand below him like a painting. He caught up with some of the stragglers and passed them. They were mostly old folk or families with children—not the normal run of travelers at all—so he assumed that they were the tag end of D'ward's army. He did not stop to speak with them, merely shouting at them to stand aside and let him pass.

The moa repeatedly battered his knees and ankles against the rock. As he drew higher, the wind flapped at his clothes and ruffled his curls.

The rule of thumb in moary was that moas would go no higher than the tree line. Swift must have read the rule book, because she suddenly concluded that the total absence of trees hereabout meant that she was excused from further effort. She stopped dead and tried to bite him.

Dosh kicked hard, winning another few minutes' progress. Then Swift stopped again. Wishing he had thought to wear spurs, he pulled out his dagger and gave the brute a jab in the shoulder. The result was a hair-raising tantrum of leaping and bucking, followed by a serious effort to run back down to Joalvale. Pebbles flew over the edge and rattled away into space. Dosh wrestled the beast around and jabbed again. Swift took off like a Nagian warrior's spear. Warned by his yells, other travelers cleared the way, and he went by them in a blur.

It could not last, of course. Eventually they reached an impasse. Swift absolutely refused to budge any farther. Concluding that more jabbing would merely exacerbate her already vicious temper, Dosh dismounted.

Moas could be led, in which case they tended to bite. Their teeth were blunt and rarely drew blood but could certainly hurt. Moas might also be driven, in which case they would kick with their sharp hooves. Dosh elected to drive, untying the reins and using the thong as a tether. As he had hoped, Swift was too winded and too unsure of the footing to do much serious kicking. They proceeded up the hill at a reasonable pace.

The sun was drawing unpleasantly close to the horizon. Joalflat stretched out to infinity, vanishing into haze to the west. Moa or not, Dosh was determined to reach the top of this accursed ascent before dark.

He passed a few more of the Liberator's rabble, which was a fair description of them. A majority seemed to be women, and none of them looked prosperous. Obviously no one with a good living would throw it up to follow the Liberator, although why anyone at all should want to follow the Liberator just because he was the Liberator escaped Dosh completely. D'ward had been a superlative leader when he was battlemaster of the combined Joalian and Nagian armies, but these derelicts were no army. And who was the enemy? *Zath?* That seemed like a war to avoid at all costs. Dosh wished wholeheartedly that he had washed his hands of the Liberator and headed west to Fithvale.

As the sun swelled to a scarlet cushion on the skyline, he reached the top of the ascent. Suddenly there was no more cliff above him, only trees and two great peaks flanking the pass. A gale was howling through the gap. As far as he could recall, though, from here the road wound gently downward all the way to Nosokflat.

"There, you brute!" he told the moa. "Trees! You're back on duty."

She kicked at him and he dodged.

He paused to catch his breath and look back, letting his sweat cool. Half of Joalvale was visible, its shadowed landscape a tapestry of green and gold fields, woodlands, blue waters. The rivers were silver ribbons, the roads red threads. If the light were better, he would probably see Joal itself.

He saw dust. Something was raising a smudge of dust on the road he had come. It might just be a caravan of wagons, but his instinct for self-preservation told him not to bet on that. Far more likely it was a troop of Joalian cavalry. They probably would not attempt the ascent in the dark—he hoped. They might not be after him or the Liberator.

Pig puke! His lifelong motto had always been to assume the worst, and it had never failed him yet. He should have heeded it sooner.

The sky was cloudless. Trumb had risen, almost full, and could be counted on to bathe the world in bright green light until dawn. Dosh turned to give battle with the moa. "You," he said grimly, "are going to run as you have never run before."

Swift expertly kicked him on the shin, hurling him to the dirt, and then landed another kick on his ribs as he rolled away. Fortunately it broke no bones and he did not let go of the tether.

Who owned a pass was a question that had started many a war, but the ultimate answer depended on the relative strengths of the parties involved. When the neighboring states were Joalia and Nosokia, there was no argument. The Nosokian rulers were Joalian puppets and would not talk crossly to Joalian troopers if they pursued a fugitive into Nosok itself and hacked him to bits on the main street. When the fugitive spoke no Nosokian and knew of no back doors out of Nosokvale, his only option was to head east as fast as possible. If he could reach Rinoovale, he would be into Niolia's sphere of interest, safely out of Joaldom.

All four moons graced the night. Although Kirb'l, Ysh, and Eltiana combined could not match the green glare of Trumb, they did help lighten the shadows, and Dosh rode swiftly along the valley. Mainly the track clung to the banks of a chattery stream, avoiding the head-smashing branches of the forest. He passed more of the Liberator's followers. If the Jilvenby peasant's numbers had been anywhere near correct, there could not be many more of them ahead.

After a mile or two, Dosh rounded a bend into a section of the valley that was more open. Its walls rose steeply from a flat floor, carpeted by shrubs but few trees. He saw the flicker of fires ahead, a cluster of fallen stars among the bushes. There were many more of them than he would have expected.

There was nothing to stop him riding right on by. He could be in Nosokland by morning, whether or not it killed his moa. That was what he should do. On the other hand, he must have at least an hour's start on the Joalians, even if they risked the ascent in moonlight. He had come this way to warn D'ward, so he might as well do so.

His sentimentality would be the death of him.

He even decided as he turned Swift off the trail that, if he were to be completely honest—not something he encouraged in himself—he would admit that he would dearly love to spend a friendly evening with D'ward beside a campfire, chatting of old times and finding out just what all this Liberator racket was about.

He headed for the fires and the sound of crying babies. He noted people moving around in the shrubbery and guessed that they were gathering berries. How many berries would it take to fill a hundred empty stomachs?

A man appeared as if from nowhere, right in his path. He wore only a leather kilt—chilly covering in the mountains at night—and he carried a spear and a round shield. He said, "Halt!"

Dosh halted. The spear was a serious matter.

"State your business!" The sentry had a familiar accent, and suddenly his face was familiar also.

"Doggan! Doggan Herder! It's me—Dosh!"

"Five gods! I mean, *Bless me!* It's the faggot himself! What you doing here, slime?"

"I could ask the same of you." Dosh considered dismounting, but he was more worried now by Swift's teeth than Doggan's spear. He wondered how many more of D'ward's old Warband might be around and concluded that there would probably be quite a few of them. Nagian age groups were fanatically loyal and did everything in bunches. "Where's your face paint, warrior?"

"Face paint is out!" Doggan said firmly. He was a short, broad man, more notable for muscle than brains. He seemed unaware that what he had just said was rank heresy to a Nagian. "I asked you what you wanted."

"I came to see D'ward."

Doggan thought about it. Then he gestured with the spear. "Follow me. And if you let that brute bite me, then it's cutlets."

"Lead on." Dosh began rethinking strategy. A troop of Nagian warriors would be a fair match for the Joalians. If D'ward was willing to protect him, he might be out of danger.

A few minutes brought them to a campfire. Having hobbled Swift, he limped wearily forward into the light, his leg throbbing like hammers where the moa had kicked it. Half a dozen shivery-looking Nagians squatted around the flames, apparently listening intently to D'ward, who was sitting on a rock, expounding. He broke off what he was saying, his teeth flashing in a smile.

"Well, see who's here! Our old messenger! Welcome, Dosh!" He was dressed in a dark, long-sleeved priest's gown. He wore a close-cropped beard and hints of black curls showed under his cowl, but he would look more like a priest if he shaved both his face and his head. That would be a pity.

"Thanks." Dosh moved closer to the fire and the others quickly made room for him, lots of room, as if he carried some contagious disease. He crouched down to warm himself, registering that these men were all from the old Sonalby troop—Prat'han Potter, Burthash Wheelwright, Gopaenum Butcher, and the rest. Every one of them would cut himself into small cubes if D'ward asked.

Silence alerted him; he looked up and saw that D'ward was waiting for him to speak.

"I heard you were at Jilvenby. A trooper in Joal told me. Thought I'd come and warn you."

Even in the flickering firelight, D'ward's eyes showed blue, twinkling with amusement. "That was very friendly of you, Dosh. The Joalians were no threat to me—but it was a kind thought."

He had not changed at all. If he wanted people to think of him as a leader, he ought to let his beard grow longer. No, that might be true of other men, but it wasn't true of him. He seemed too young, yet he was completely calm, absolute master of the group and of himself. Dosh felt the old magic at work again. This was a man who commanded respect and loyalty without ever asking for it. He talked with gods. He was foretold by prophecy. He elicited trust—and also confidences.

"He wasn't quite what he seemed," Dosh said. "He bore the mark of the Lady."

Big Prat'han grunted, but what he meant remained unclear.

D'ward pursed his lips. "The only male Eltiana cult I know of is the Guardians of the Mother. They're said to wear her symbol in a very intimate place."

"That's it."

The smile faded. The stare seemed to sharpen. "And how did you discover that, Dosh?"

A couple of the men muttered inaudibly.

"No," D'ward said. "If he was sworn to Eltiana, then he wouldn't be doing that. Well?"

"I killed him."

D'ward sighed. "Why?"

"He wanted me to betray you." Dosh looked around the group hopefully. If he expected approval, then he was disappointed. These lunks had never approved of him. They had let him continue breathing only because D'ward had told them to. He cared nothing for their opinions, but he would like to think D'ward appreciated what he had done. He had felt that way about very few men in his life . . . no others at all that he could think of just at the moment.

D'ward said, "I suppose it explains why you ride by night. How did you ever get a moa?"

"Stole her, of course."

"You haven't changed a bit, have you?"

"No, I just got better at it."

D'ward scratched at his beard, seeming more exasperated than anything else. "I appreciate the news about Eltiana. The Guardians are her doers of dirty work—not as bad as reapers, but they can be dangerous. I just wish you hadn't gained the information the way you did. Will you spend the night with us or are you in a hurry to admire new scenery? 'Fraid we can't offer much in the way of hospitality."

All the eyes turned toward the intruder, waiting for his reply. The Nagians were hoping he would leave very soon and thus clean up the neighborhood. He could not tell what D'ward wanted.

Wearily, he held out his hands to the fire again. The air was cooling off, leaving the night cold and dark. And lonely. "There's a troop of Joalian cavalry—" His tongue was not usually so eager to run away with him, and he reined it in.

Gopaenum threw more brush on the fire. Smoke and sparks billowed up to the stars.

"Not after us," D'ward said. "I doubt they're even coming to make sure we've left, because our safe-conduct runs for three more days yet. Are they on their way up the pass now or waiting for daylight?"

"Don't know." Dosh rose stiffly, wincing at the pain in his leg. "Well, I've told you my news. I'd best be going." He thought of the long, lonely ride to Nosokvale.

"We welcome recruits," D'ward said quietly. "You're welcome to join us."

Prat'han growled.

D'ward said, "Hush!" and Prat'han flinched as if he'd been slashed with a whip.

Dosh went down on one knee by the fire as a sort of compromise between going and staying. "Join what? What are you up to?"

"Tell him, big brother."

The muscular potter scowled at Dosh. "The Liberator is fulfilling the prophecies. We are the Free, and we are on our way to Thargvale, where he will bring death to Death, as is foretold."

That was utter insanity, but Dosh knew better than to argue with Prat'han. His head was as empty as his pots.

"What conditions?"

"Ah!" D'ward thought for a moment. "You're a murderer, a thief, a liar, a sexual pervert of every description, and a traitor. Does that about sum you up?"

Burthash guffawed. D'ward looked at him sharply.

He shriveled guiltily, muttering, "Sorry, Liberator."

"I think you've covered all my good points," Dosh said. "I also drink to excess and smoke poppy when I can afford it."

"We can't accept a man who does any of those things."

"Then why are you wasting my time?" Dosh began to rise.

"Because you could promise to stop doing them."

Dosh wondered if he'd heard correctly, and the others looked equally bewildered. With anyone but the Liberator, he would have assumed that he was being mocked, but D'ward's eyes held no ridicule, only challenge.

"I don't care what a man was, Dosh, only what he is now."

"You mean you'd take my word for it? Mine? You think I could possibly keep such a promise, even if I wanted to?"

"Yes I do. You once told me you were the toughest bastard in the army, and I said I believed you. I'd believe you now. If you'll tell me now that you'll give up all those vices, then you'll keep your word."

The fire began to crackle more loudly, its smoke drifting away in the wind. Out in the dark valley were low voices, children, and someone singing what sounded like a hymn. Who were the Free? Just the Sonalby troop or all that ragtag collection of humanity? Join them? Him?

"Gods!" This was the greatest insanity yet.

"Only one god here. Your decision." Suddenly D'ward laughed. "I've never seen you look scared before, Dosh!"

He *was* scared. His hands were shaking. "I couldn't!"

"I think you could."

That was what he'd wanted D'ward to say, but he still didn't believe it.

The Liberator was watching him very closely. "We knew you as Dosh Envoy. If the troopers ask for you by whatever name you're using now we can say we don't know you." He grinned faintly. "Besides, you'll be a new man altogether, won't you?"

New man? This was the sort of decision that needed a lot of thinking over. Dosh wouldn't be a loner anymore. He would be one of this harebrained Liberator cult, heading for certain death in Thargvale or sooner. He had been one of the gang, once. Briefly.

"Why haven't the reapers caught you already?"

D'ward shrugged.

"Reapers?" Gopaenum laughed raucously. "You want to meet some reapers? We've got a dozen or so around somewhere. Soon as they get near the Liberator, they aren't reapers anymore."

"Huh?"

"Never mind that," D'ward said. "You're avoiding the issue."

Dosh looked uncertainly around the firelit faces. He couldn't actually *see* the scorn and contempt, but he knew it was there. They were hiding it out of respect for D'ward, that was all. He heaved himself to his feet, feeling as if he weighed more than all of them put together.

"I wish you luck. You're all crazy. Go and bring death to Death if you can. Me, I want to keep life in the living."

He turned away. He had taken only a couple of steps when he heard D'ward call out, "See you in Nosokland."

He walked on, paying no heed.

℘℘ 12 ℘℘

T HE FIRST *TYIKA* HOUSES AT OLYMPUS HAD BEEN LAID OUT ON THE PERIMeter of the node. When that loop was full, an outer circle had followed, forming the other side of a street, and after the Chamber had sacked the station, it had all been rebuilt to the same plan. Being "Boots," the junior officer in the regiment, Julian lived even farther out, in a new suburb just beginning. A man's residence defined his status very clearly, but it wasn't all swank, for the innermost locations provided a distinct occult advantage. When followers of the Undivided anywhere in the Vales prayed to the apostles, a little mana would flow to those located on a node. It would not compare to the power the gods received from the worshippers in their temples but, year in and year out, it must mount up.

As the sky flamed blood red behind the peaks, he headed inward, feeling the first tingling of virtuality as he paced up the Pinkneys' garden path to their front door. Through the open windows, he heard the polite laughter of the *tyikank* enjoying themselves. Three minutes later, he was clutching a glass of the sickly fluid that passed for sherry in Olympus and pretending breathless interest as his hostess described the new rock garden her Carrots were building for her.

Escaping from Hannah Pinkney's horticultural saga as soon as he decently could, he began to circulate from group to group. He was required to discuss polo and cricket—the Carrots had taken it up and were becoming too bally good at it, old man—and of course the weather. Not a word was said about the Liberator.

"Fascinating news from Fithvale," Prof Rawlinson declaimed. "Seems that Imphast has ordered her clergy out of red and into blue!"

Delores Garcia said, "Really!" Then she added vaguely, "Who's Imphast?"

"Goddess of, um, female puberty. Obviously she's changed allegiance from Eltiana to Astina! A major move in the Great Game!"

"Gracious!"

Prof began to explain, at great length. Julian knew nothing of Imphast and cared less. He moved on, analyzing who was there and who was not. Some people were only window dressing, not relevant to the Exeter problem—people like Hannah, for instance. Ineffectual people, gossipy, garrulous people. Some undoubtedly were relevant: Prof Rawlinson, Jumbo Watson, and a couple of the others Dommi had mentioned as having been recalled. In the background he could hear Foghorn Rutherford, this year's chairman.

About three of the women might be significant: Delores, who had a body to drive men out of their wits and was reputed to be the only faithful wife in Olympus; Ursula Newton, with the shoulders of a wrestler and the unerring competence of a sergeant-major; Olga Olafson, who was unmarried, voluptuous, and a nymphomaniac. Scandal whispered that she even pursued Carrots.

He detoured away from Foghorn, who was leering at Cathy Chase, who in turn was portraying bored indifference, although they were current lovers. Extramarital affairs were the main source of entertainment in Olympus, but it was understood that they must be kept strictly confidential in case the Carrots gossiped. That deception was the second most popular game. Admittedly, there were few other games to play in a land so backward, but Julian considered it absurd early-Victorian hypocrisy. Of course, many of these people *were* early Victorian. In practice, everyone knew exactly who was sleeping with whom. If they didn't, they could always ask their Carrots.

The Service were a very rum lot, and somehow that was even more obvious than usual tonight, but it took him a while to work out what was different. There was nothing conspicuously wrong with the dinner party—a dozen men, a dozen women, two Carrots serving drinks and probably twenty or more laboring away behind the scenes. Conversation swung from triviality to banality and back again.

Under the glitter of the chandeliers, the men wore tails, the ladies long gowns.

This sort of dinner party happened almost every night of the year, for there was no restricted social season in Olympus. No one would ever mistake it for a formal dinner in Town. The discerning London hostess would look askance at the outdated fashions. She would eye the furniture with curiosity and inquire politely where in the Colonies this or that had come from, although she might well praise the Narshian rugs or the Niolian brasses, which were as good as anything from Benares.

On the other hand, the gathering was a reasonable facsimile of a social occasion in an outpost of Empire almost anywhere on Earth—dinner with His Majesty's district commissioner. The Service did not serve the Empire on Which the Sun Never Sets, but it had the same altruistic motives as those who did. Like them, Olympians were dedicated to uplifting the benighted savage. They were just exiled a little farther away, that was all, or no distance at all, if one preferred that view of the paradox. The node here was a portal. Walk out on the grass, perform the key ritual, and you could be Home instantly. Unless you had made arrangements to be met by Head Office, you would be naked and penniless, of course, and you would certainly be mortal again. No fear! It was a lot better to better the lot of the natives here in the Vales.

Then he realized what was wrong: A party that should be as lively as gaudy at Oxford was as flat as a geriatric Mafeking reunion. Strangers never revealed their age, and to discuss it was strictly off-limits, always, but he was the baby of the group. None of the rest of them would ever see twenty-two again. Olga had probably weathered several centuries. Jumbo and Pinky and Ursula Newton had been co-founders of the Service, along with Cameron Exeter and Monica Rogers, fifty years ago. Nonetheless, at a do like this strangers ought to be sparkling like a gang of adolescents. Tonight they seemed middle-aged. They displayed no wrinkles or silver hair, and their bodies were still trim, but their mood gave them away.

Joalvale was not the problem. The Church of the Undivided had no significant presence there and nothing to lose if Exeter provoked the civil authorities into repression—in fact a few martydoms were good for business, although it would be poor form to say so. No, the Chamber was the danger, and always had been. The Service feared the prophecies of the *Filoby Testament* almost as much as Zath himself did, for any attempt to fulfill them must provoke an all-out war that Olympus could not hope to win. Then the men and women of the Service would be faced with a choice between death and flight back to Earth and mortality. Their cosy fiefdom here would be wiped out.

They had the wind up!

He discovered Marcel Piran and Euphemia McKay in a secluded nook behind some potted shrubbery and invited himself into the conversation. Euphemia was a right-down stunner with green eyes and hair so authentically Irish red that it made the Carrots' seem drab by comparison. Culture and intellect were not her strong points, but she had a devilish wit and a keen sense of mimicry—she was, in fact, a bundle of fun. Unfortunately she also had the worst clothes sense in two worlds. Tonight she was squeezed into a satiny gown of royal blue, which should have flattered her coloring and figure but made her seem frumpy and hippy. She looked much better without any clothes on at all.

In a few moments, Marcel tactfully eased away to speak to Hannah.

"And how is my delicious Wendy?" Julian assumed a lecherous growl, while pretending to study the shrubbery.

Euphemia peered around the room indifferently. "Randy as an alley cat. How about my Captain Hook? Ready for boarding? Got your cutlass well sharpened?"

"Primed, loaded, and cocked. Why don't we nip behind the sofa and have a quick one?"

"I'd rather wait for a slow one later."

"Just one? It's not like you to settle for just one, Wendy."

"Well, think what you tempt me with! How's a girl expected to refuse that?"

This verbal foreplay was interrupted by the arrival of Olga and the evening's host, Pinky Pinkney. Conversation veered to a discussion of the latest news from Home, which was over a fortnight old.

"It is most unfair of the Peppers to keep the Goldsmiths waiting like this!" Pinky proclaimed. "Deborah is desperate to see London again."

"You haven't heard what's delayed them?" Euphemia asked.

"Of course not. The Montgomerys are due back in a couple of days—perhaps they'll know what's keeping them."

"No word from Head Office?"

"I'm afraid Head Office has been badly disorganized by the war. They're not what they used to be."

She sighed, and her dress struggled to contain the movement. "William and me aren't due to go for years!"

Pinky made sympathetic noises. He was as slick as an oiled eel and parted his hair in the middle. "Are you quite sure of that, my dear? I think there were some changes made to the schedule while you were gone."

"Really?" Euphemia asked with surprising interest.

"Dolores will know. Let's go and ask her, shall we?"

Without a word of apology, the bounder led her off across the room. Julian sipped some of the nasty sherry.

"Don't glare, darling," said a throaty murmur. "People will think you're jealous."

He jumped. Olga was a heart-stopping Nordic blonde, a female Viking— something Wagner might have invented if he had dared. Tonight she wore a scarlet gown in a way that implied one deep breath would cause it to explode.

"Jealous? Of Pinky and Euphemia? There's nothing between them."

Olga fluttered golden lashes. "The way Pinky was looking at her, darling, there won't be anything at all between them in a few hours."

Julian drained his glass in one great Philistine gulp. Olga unnerved him on several levels. First, he had no idea whatsoever of her background—her English was too perfect to be her genuine mother tongue; she might not even be from Earth at all. Second, she was probably the oldest person in the Service, because she was a convert. Before changing sides, she had been a minor goddess, an avatar of Eltiana.

And third, she was blatantly promiscuous. No other woman on the station would dare to look at a man the way she was looking at him right now. She was probably not serious, because she had hung Julian's scalp on her belt years ago, a few days after he arrived. He hoped she wasn't serious, but at least a fellow need not watch one's tongue with Olga. She was unshockable and never took offense. And at the moment she was trying to put the boot in.

"I think you are attributing unseemly motives to a perfectly innocent conversation. Mrs. McKay and Mr. Pinkney are—"

"Are rutting, dear. He is, anyway. He's as loud as a wapiti."

"What the deuce is a wapiti? And even if he is, why should Euphemia—"

Olga rolled her sea-blue eyes dramatically. "Julian, darling, I thought I cured your innocence years ago. Don't tell me all my work was wasted! Weren't you born in India? You should know that imperial exiles are the same everywhere."

"Nextdoor is hardly a blooming colony," he protested. "The Empire doesn't reach quite this far—not yet, anyway."

She smiled sardonically. "They like to pretend it's a colony, though. Olympus is deliberately modeled on a British government station somewhere in the bush, isn't it? Don't deny it; you know it's true. Lording over the natives, dressing for dinner . . . I remember Foghorn trying to get us to put up a flagpole so we could fly the Union Jack. Cameron threatened to strangle him with it if he tried."

Julian blinked. He had not known that Olga had been around Olympus so long, for Cameron Exeter had gone Home thirty years ago. "What has that to do—"

"You're not worried, darling?" she purred.

"Not about Pinky," he said staunchly, fairly sure he was not even blushing, which was a jolly sight different from how he would have reacted to Olga's claws two years ago. Pinky would get nowhere tonight—or any other night either—because Euphemia considered him a bore and a toad in the grass. It would not be Pinky skin to skin with Euphemia tonight, it would be Captain Smedley (Royal Artillery, ret.), and the sooner the better.

He made his escape from Olga as soon as he could without seeming to be running away. No one had mentioned the reason for his recall yet or told him whether he was scheduled to appear before the Committee itself. If he were, it would be an irrelevant formality, because decisions in Olympus were made by the inner circle, Pinky and his cronies. That was another characteristic of the Service—nobody trusted anybody; too many had gone over to the opposition. There had been traitors, one of whom had very nearly scuppered Edward Exeter by sending him Home into the middle of a battle in Flanders. Mana was addictive, and the Pentatheon could offer better sources of mana. Even a very minor god with his own temple collected far more of it than a preacher holding secret prayer meetings in the bush.

★   ★   ★

Euphemia and Pinky reappeared, but Julian's efforts to resume his wooing were persistently defeated by Pinky, who clung to her like a treacle shampoo until his wife announced that it was time to go in to dinner.

Julian was alarmed to discover that he was paired with Olga, who proceeded to flirt shamelessly with him. Fortunately they were seated across from Jumbo and Iris, who were good company. Euphemia, he was annoyed to notice, had been placed next to Pinky.

Dinner went off as usual, with inconsequential small talk. It was all frightfully civilized—damask tablecloth, silver plate, hovering servants—and a welcome relief from the peasant hospitality he should have been enduring in Randorvale right now. The only time anything approaching business was discussed was when someone brought up the story of Jumbo's miracle at Flaxby, deflecting a magistrate and two soldiers. Julian had learned of it from Purlopat'r, but apparently the news had leaked out just after he left.

It was impossible to dislike Jumbo. He was tall and lean and had gained his nickname from the length of his nose. He had a notably wry sense of humor and a becoming modesty.

"It was nothing much," he protested. "I didn't set out to work any miracles. I was so scared at the sight of those jolly swords that I started babbling my head off. Before I knew it, the chaps were on their knees, begging for mercy—wanting me to shut up, I expect. If I did spend some mana, then I got a whole lot more back in return. Jolly fun, actually. You should have seen the magistrate's face. . . ." He made a good story out of it, everyone laughed.

Julian did not mention his adventure in Randorvale. The conversation veered to the unusually warm weather.

If it was impossible to dislike Jumbo, it was still possible to distrust him. He had been the one who sent Exeter to what should have been certain death in the battle of Third Ypres. He claimed that he had been deceived by Jean St. John, but Jean had either died or done a bunk when Zath's reapers caused the sack of Olympus, so there was no way to confirm the tale. Jumbo had been friends with both Exeters, father and son, during their respective times in Olympus. He was an adamant opponent of the Liberator prophecy.

Julian struggled not to yawn as he kept up his end of the conversation. The people around the table were all worried; they were all scared. It showed.

The meal was over, decanters waited on the sideboard. The hostess glanced around the table to make sure everyone had finished. Hannah Pinkney was a lightweight, far more interested in her proposed rock garden than in the Service's mission to save the heathens or her husband's slimy advances to Euphemia. Tonight she was dressed in lace and chiffon, all pink and fluffy, well suited to her personality.

"Well!" she said brightly. "Shall we leave the men to their cigars, ladies?"

The expected shuffle of movement as men rose to lift back their companions' chairs . . . Olga removed her hand from Julian's thigh.

"I should like a cigar tonight," said a loud voice.

Hannah tracked it down to Ursula Newton and stared at her in consternation. Julian struggled against an urge to burst out laughing.

Ursula had not been drinking unduly. She was merely irate and consequently dangerous. Although not unattractive, she was too broad for her height, built like a Victorian mahogany dresser—muscle, not fat—lacking feminine grace. But she could preach damnation with the best of them or raise hell with a tennis racket, being aggressively good at anything she cared to try and inclined to bark at those who were not. Tonight she wore a lilac gown that displayed her powerful arms and shoulders and clashed with her dark coloring. Where Euphemia lacked taste, Ursula didn't give a damn.

"You're not serious, are you, dear?" Hannah bleated. "I mean, I'm sure we can find a cigar for you if—"

Ursula ignored her, scowling at Pinky. "No, I'm not serious about the cigar. I am serious about the Committee. I am very tired of discovering that every matter brought before it has already been settled. You men are planning to cross-examine Captain Smedley tonight and tomorrow you will tell the rest of us what to rubber-stamp."

Pinky smiled graciously, but when Pinky smiled nothing showed of his eyes, only their heavy lids. "Aren't you being a little unfair, my dear? You must agree that we men are free to discuss whatever we wish, as are you ladies. Surely you are not suggesting we should banish Captain Smedley from the table, mm? Wouldn't that be unkind? Of course it would. If you have complaints about the way the Committee is being run, then you should address them to the chairman. Formally, I mean. In writing."

Foghorn Rutherford was this year's chairman. That did not matter. Despite the Service's professed determination to remain a democratic association of equals, Pinky Pinkney was the one who pulled the strings, this year and every year.

Foghorn was loud, large, windy, and uncouth, a rubicund human bagpipe, likable in an uncomplicated sort of way, typecast from birth to be captain of a county rugby club. Now he harrumphed a steam-hooter noise. "I assure you that the Committee will have ample opportunity—"

"I don't believe you!" Ursula snapped. "You are going to deal with Captain Smedley exactly the way you did with the man who brought in the news."

Rutherford guffawed like a mule. "Ursula, old girl, if you imply that Pinky invited that rascally dragon trader to dinner, then he will demand pistols at dawn on the croquet lawn."

Hannah tried to start a laugh, but no one picked it up.

Ursula returned her fearsome glare to Pinky. "If you will give me your word that no one here will as much as mention Edward Exeter for the rest of the night, then I shall happily withdraw. If not, I stay. So does Olga."

Like the rest of the men, Julian had resumed his seat. Olga had resumed her fondling. Olga would certainly be involved in the ad hoc group dealing with the Liberator crisis—he should have realized that. She would have been coopted at once, for she knew better than any how the Pentatheon thought.

Pinky surrendered, smiling sleepily. "Stay by all means. Yes, I expect we shall talk shop. Why not, mm? Don't we always? Any of you who want to stay, may stay. If shoptalk bores you, you may depart in peace and migrate to the drawing room. Is that fair enough? Very fair, I'd say." He nodded to the waiting Carrots to bring out the port.

Everyone elected to stay, of course, and the men all refused cigars, which annoyed Julian, who needed a smoke. Nextdoor's equivalent of tobacco tasted like burning pine needles, but it did pack a wallop of nicotine. The port came around, Ursula pouring herself a glass and passing it on with the correct hand; most of the women just passing it. Small talk fluttered like awkward moths until the Carrots had departed. Then Pinky nodded to Foghorn who boomed obediently, "I expect Doc told you, Captain? Edward Exeter is on the loose up in Joalland, proclaiming himself the prophesied Liberator chappie."

With T'lin Dragontrader so sure of himself, there was no use trying to cast doubt on the identity of the culprit. "Yes, sir."

"What's he up to, hm?"

"I have no idea. I haven't heard from him since he left here." Julian could feel that statement being weighed all around the table. They didn't trust him, which was fair enough, because he did not trust them.

"You know him better than any of us, Captain." The speaker was Pedro Garcia, who had done a bunk in Thovale and left his flock to pay the piper.

"We were school chums, yes, but I've hardly seen him since—once, very briefly, two years ago. You lot know him better than I do, actually."

Guff! Exeter in 1917 had been exactly the same person as the house prefect who had left Fallow in 1914. He was one of those people who never change. He had been as self-reliant at eighteen as he would be at eighty—or eight hundred, if he stayed on Nextdoor that long. He would sail his own course, guided by his own sense of what was honorable, letting nothing sway him. He had been upright, unassuming, admirable—all those proper things—and thoroughly square on top of it. He would be till the day he died.

Garcia shrugged, greasy as a Dago fish fryer. "He went native."

Julian's fist clenched. "Did he? I thought he went off back Home, to enlist and do his bit in the war. That was the plan." Olga squeezed his thigh, but whether that was intended as a warning or encouragement, he did not know. Or care.

"Indeed, Captain? In his farewell address he told the Carrots he was going off to fulfill the prophecy."

"What if he did? That prophecy has blighted his whole life. It killed his parents. It branded him a murderer in England. It kept him from enlisting. It cut down his friends like corn." It had even killed the girl he loved, although Ysian had been a native and to mention her would do no good. "He walked out of Olympus to save the rest of us. If he'd stayed here, Zath would have struck at the Service again."

Directly across the table from Julian, Jumbo said, "Hear, hear! You're not being fair, Pedro old man. Exeter survived his first two years on Nextdoor without any help from us. It's hardly cricket to call that 'going native'! I'd call it 'surviving under adverse conditions.' Adopting local color, if you prefer. When he finally did get here to Olympus, he was a perfectly civilized young gentleman again."

Julian smiled gratefully at him and reached for his port. He hoped the discussion was now over and he could trot off to bed. Euphemia's bed.

Rutherford broke the awkward pause with a throat-clearing like a carillon of church bells. "We were wondering, Captain . . . Do you know a young lady named Alice?"

Julian took a sip of port. They were ganging up on him. "Sounds like a limerick. Did she live in a palace?"

"We can all think of a good rhyme for the last line," Jumbo said, "but I don't think that was what the chairman was getting at."

"Alice Prescott, Exeter's cousin? Yes, sir, I've met her. Why?"

"Just wondering!" Foghorn boomed. The port was turning his red face redder. "If we asked for her help to make Exeter see reason, do you suppose she would cooperate, what?"

Not in a thousand years. Alice had far more respect for her cousin than that. At least, Julian thought she probably had. Alice was on another world anyway.

"I really could not say, sir." That sounded uncooperative. "I only met her once or twice."

"We just wondered. Well, that ought to conclude the shoptalk, so—"

"No." Apparently Jumbo had other ideas. Jumbo was quick; he had a sight more gray matter than Foghorn, perhaps even more than Pinky. "Let's review the problem. I have never made a secret of my dislike for the prophecy. Exeter's father agreed with me all the way."

Heads nodded, but the eyes were on Julian. He said nothing, waited for the haymaker.

"First," Jumbo said, "it's crazy to take on Zath. He's not officially one of the Pentatheon, but he's undoubtedly stronger than any of them. The Five are scared stiff of him."

"Human sacrifice!" Olga said. Her hand was exploring busily. She must have decided that Julian's scalp had grown back in again. "None of the others stoop to that."

Jumbo nodded. "And it won't only be Zath. The Pentatheon may not like Zath, but they won't approve of an upstart stranger preaching reform, so Exeter can't hope for much help from the Five. Second, the civil authorities will not take kindly to hundreds of people galloping off after a new prophet. We're already meeting resistance, and we're nowhere near to being the sort of threat that the Liberator would be."

"Powers that be always want to go on being powers, you know," Pinky remarked sagely.

Pinky himself was a prize example, so Julian couldn't argue with that. They were picking on him because he had been Exeter's friend. A chap must stand by his friends. "Civil authorities can be diverted, sir. You proved that yourself in Loxby."

"Not if the Pentatheon throws its weight behind them!" Jumbo shook his head wearily, looking twenty years older than usual. "The next stage is likely to be plague and thunderbolts, you know. We don't have anything like enough mana to protect the church against direct assaults."

"The argument cuts both ways. Exeter as Liberator may draw the Chamber off. They won't worry about us while he's on the rampage."

Jumbo was unconvinced. "They're more likely to lump both heresies together and declare a general pogrom. Exeter's a threat to all of us and everything we're trying to do. We're still terribly vulnerable. A hundred years from now, things may be different."

Heads nodded solemnly all around the table. Bloody bunch of chickens!

Olga spoke up demurely. "Historically, if any one of the Five began to grow too powerful, the other four have always combined against him or her. They didn't spot what Zath was up to until it was too late."

She unfastened a button in Julian's fly. He removed her hand and refastened it. She'd had her chance at what was in there two years ago.

Farther along the table, Prof Rawlinson took up the argument. "There is another point. Didn't T'lin Dragontrader say that Exeter is preaching the Undivided?" Rawlinson was colorless, owlish, and clever in an impractical sort of way. He had the pedantic manner of a divinity student, but in the past he had been one of the pro-Liberator group. The Service had always been divided over the Liberator; now it seemed to be united. No one was on Exeter's side except Julian Smedley.

"He could hardly do otherwise, I fancy," said Pinky smoothly. "He did do some missionary work for us, remember? Mostly in Thovale, was it not? Yes, mostly Thovale. He will need a gospel to preach. The *Testament* by itself would not be enough. Couldn't work just from that. He'd need something more, mm? So it's quite natural that he would adopt our theology. Ready-made for his purpose, I'd say."

"You mean he is stealing our church?" Hannah cried. She subsided into blushing silence under her husband's frown.

"So if Exeter tries and fails," Jumbo said, watching Julian, "he may bring us down with him."

"Worse!" Prof chirruped. "Suppose, against all odds, he succeeds? If he does fulfill the prophecy, then he'll be stronger than Zath. What will he become? What could he do with such power?"

No one seemed very worried about that improbable hypothesis, but Jumbo said, "That's what bothered his father. Cameron didn't want his son to become another pseudogod."

Obviously everyone was against Exeter, whether he won or lost: Zath, the Pentatheon and their lesser gods, the various rulers of the Vales, the Service—they were all opposed.

Julian decided it must be his turn.

"You are asking my opinion?"

"Go ahead," said Pinky. "You have the floor. The port is with you, Duffy."

"I don't believe it. I know Edward Exeter, and he was as much against the prophecy as anyone. There's been some mistake."

"Seventy-seven's a sound chap."

"But a native, sir. Would you expect Exeter to confide all his plans to T'lin Dragontrader?"

"That's an interesting point, Captain. Very interesting." Pinky filled his glass. "But the fact remains that Exeter is calling himself the Liberator. In public. Do we have a consensus that he should be stopped? Is that the sense of the meeting?" He glanced around with a smile, his eyes seeming to be shut. "Unless anyone has changed his mind, of course?"

What did *stopped* mean? Julian risked another glass of port as the decanter went by him. "Sir, Zath has been trying to break the chain of prophecy for thirty years. It's too late to work on any of the other stuff in the *Testament*. The only way to stop it now would be to kill Exeter himself."

Hannah and a couple of the other women gasped.

Foghorn boomed out, "Balderdash!" without meeting Julian's eye.

Only Jumbo was looking at Julian, staring challengingly across the table at him. "Perhaps Exeter himself is trying to break it by committing suicide."

"Not the Edward Exeter I knew."

"That's how it looks," Foghorn said firmly. "Damned fool stunt! We owe it to him for his own sake to bring him to his senses."

Here it came. It was Jumbo who put the question. "Are you with us on that, Captain?"

Julian held up a hand, the one without fingers. He sensed the surge of anger and embarrassment. "I agree with everything you've said about the dangers of the prophecy, yes. I support what the Service stands for absolutely—and so does Edward Exeter, as far as I know. I also feel that Zath is the embodiment of all that's evil in the Pentatheon and we have a duty to overthrow him as soon as possible. I hope *you* are all with *me* on that! It would be the greatest service we could perform for the people of the Vales." Was the Service really interested in the natives' welfare or only in its own survival? "He's not unlike the Kaiser, really. We've been fighting a hellish war to stop him, back in Europe. Victory did not come cheap."

He glanced around the table. He wasn't increasing his popularity terrifically. "The war cost millions of lives, but it was worth it. Destroying Zath may be worth some sacrifice too, so I cannot dismiss whatever Exeter is doing without knowing more about his thinking. He may have seen something that the rest of us have missed. I think you owe him a hearing before you condemn him out of hand."

Pinky drooped his eyelids again. "Quite right. Very sound. We ought to find out how the land lies. Would you be willing to go and talk to him, Captain, mm? Drop in on him, feel him out?"

"I'd be glad to. Always wanted to see Joalvale. I'll leave first thing in the morning."

Pinky nodded graciously. "Very obliging of you, Captain. It would put our minds at rest. But that's quite a long jaunt. You will pardon my mentioning this, but you don't have the experience some of the rest of us have. Two heads are always better than one, what? Not that we don't trust you, of course."

They trusted Julian as far as they could throw Kilimanjaro. He decided to make it easy for them. "I'd be very happy to have company, sir. You all know I can't use mana. It won't stick to me—or it sticks too well, rather."

His preferred companion would be Euphemia, of course, and everyone could guess that, but he must not say so. The watchdog they chose would be Jumbo. He had been Exeter's closest friend, his father's friend, and a founder of the Service; he was adamantly opposed to the prophecy. He was a jolly dog, though, and a journey with him would be fun.

Foghorn Rutherford recalled that he was chairman of the Committee and fired a broadside of decibels. "That's damned white of you, Captain! The sooner you can go and talk some sense into our young friend the better. We may send someone Home to seek out Miss Prescott and enlist her help, too, but that will take time."

That was pure bosh, designed to lower Julian's guard. The Service had already condemned Exeter. How far were they prepared to go to stop him? Jumbo was looking a bit shifty—were they setting Julian up as a Judas goat? Dammit, a chap ought not to go calling on a chum with an assassin in tow.

But obviously the business of the evening had been concluded. Tomorrow Julian Smedley would head north to find Exeter. The only remaining problem was to escape from Olga and find his way to Euphemia's bedroom to do his lover's duty.

℘ℛℭ 13 ℛℭ℘

"I SHALL BE LEAVING IN THE MORNING," JULIAN SAID, PULLING ON HIS PA-jama jacket. "Pack a bag for me, will you?"

Dommi closed the wardrobe door and turned with a smile. "It is already taken care of, *tyika*. I have laid out winter garments in tribute to the advanced season and in presumption that you will be dragon traveling and may therefore cut short across country."

"Good show. Um, Dommi . . ." It had occurred to Julian on his way home that, whatever dark deeds Jumbo Watson might have in mind, there was one person in Olympus who could be trusted to support Edward Exeter through Hull, Hell, and Halifax. Not that a native could do much in practice against a stranger, but a friendly face was worth a third arm on a black day. "I'll be heading up north, going to find *Tyika* Exeter. I'm not sure there'll be a spare dragon, but if there is, then you're welcome to come. If you still want to, that is."

Dommi beamed. "I shall be most and assuredly honored, *tyika*."

Why would the man leave his wife at such a time? Carrots were not expected to have such unexpected foibles, but it would not be right to ask. "I'm sure you'll be a great help. I think that's all, thank you. Night, Dommi."

"Good night, *tyika*. Do you wish me to open the window wider?"

"Yes. It's a little stuffy in here."

Dommi pulled the sash up another foot and departed, closing the door in silence.

Julian snatched up his dressing gown and headed for the window.

It was a black dressing gown.

Love was a rum business, and even rummier in Olympus than anywhere else. "Till death do us part" became meaningless frippery when life expectancy stretched out to three or four digits. All evening he and his sweetheart had smiled politely across the room at each other, exchanged meaningless small talk, behaved just like all the other guests. Thus was the game played, and everyone played it. But every dressing gown on the station was black.

He clambered over the sill. There was no reason why he should not just walk out his own front door, except that certain things should be done in traditional ways.

The night was a symphony, cool without being chilly, lit by the red and blue moons and a million stars and scented with the innumerable night-flowering blossoms of the Vales. The mountains looked as if they had been arranged by an expert stage designer, and the squirrel-like nightingales caroling in the bottle-gourd trees were almost as tuneful as the birds of the same name back Home. He hurried along the road, keeping to shadows as much as he could, seeing no one. It was embarrassing to meet a friend on such occasions, although by convention neither party would take notice of the other. The total absence of lights in the station did not mean that all the inhabitants were sleeping the sleep of the innocent.

His quest led him inward again, and soon the ancient thrill of lover hurrying to meet beloved was augmented by the familiar skin-tingling awareness of virtuality. As he passed Olga's house, a bat-owl soared overhead, circled a few times to decide if he was prey, then decided he wasn't and floated away behind the trees. Reaching the McKay residence, he picked his way around the side path until he came to a garden bench, which just happened to be under a window.

Which just happened to be closed.

Well, bother the woman! What was she thinking of? She knew he was coming. They'd been doing the drink-to-thee-only routine all evening, making sheep's eyes and sending just-wait signals. William was still away exhorting the unbelievers—not that William cared two hoots who tumbled his wife. He slept with Iris Barnes these days . . . these nights.

Julian stepped up on the bench and rapped fingernails on the glass. He waited. Nightingales serenaded. He was tingly and twitchy already.

He knocked harder, with knuckles.

Light flared as the heavy drapes were moved, then vanished again. Now a pale figure knelt on the other side of the pane. It lifted the sash about an inch.

"Go away," it whispered through the gap.

"No. What's the matter?"

"Nothin'. Everythin'. Please! Not tonight." The lilting Irish voice thrilled him as always. He had told her it was the sound of rain on peat, although then he'd had to explain that he'd meant it as a compliment.

She was crying!

"Darling Euphemia, tell me what's wrong. No, let me in first."

"Just go . . . please!"

"I will not go." A nightmarish vision of Pinky in pink pajamas . . . "Not unless you have another man in there."

"No! But please, Julian? Not tonight. We can talk when you come back from Joalvale."

"Why? No! There's something wrong? Look, if you don't let me in here, I'll go 'round and beat on the front door until I waken every Carrot in the house." That ought to do it, for every woman in Olympus lived in dread of what the Carrots might be saying about her, even though she knew that every other woman was doing exactly the same thing and the Carrots really did not care anyway. The only thing that was *not* done was doing it with Carrots. "You're upset. I want to help. I love you, darling!"

Euphemia made unromantic sniffing noises.

"I'm not going to rape you!" Julian protested, mentally reserving seduction as a definite option. "We can just talk, if that's all you want." If that was all he could achieve. She'd never been unwilling before, not once that he could recall. She would enthusiastically try anything he suggested, which had been almost anything he'd ever heard of or could imagine. . . .

She rose and the light flared again as she departed, but she had left the window open. He slid a hand and a half under the sash and lifted. A moment later he pushed through the drapes and blinked in the glow of the candles on the dresser. She was standing in the middle of the room with her back to him, wearing a diaphanous pink nightgown, half transparent and completely the wrong color for her, but her gorgeous hair hung almost to her waist, a Titian waterfall that excited him as much as the glimmer of milky skin through filmy fabric.

He put a hand on one shoulder and a stump on the other and tried to turn her. She resisted and moved away. He restrained himself.

"What have I done?" Had any man since Adam not asked that question at some time in his life?

"Nothing, nothing at all. Just not tonight, darlin'. When you come back from Joalvale."

"Right-oh!" he said thickly, although everything was obviously wrong-oh. "You sit there, and I'll sit over here, and you tell me what's the matter." He went over to the chair. He wished he knew more about women.

She sank down on the edge of the bed, hunching herself small, arms tight around her breasts and face down. Candlelight on that hair was enough to detonate him all by itself, but there was also the deep cleavage, the bulge of nipples like pale strawberries, the russet shadow at her groin. His heart was running the Grand National, jumps and all. He adjusted his dressing gown to hide the incriminating bulge.

"Now Wendy can tell Captain Hook what's wrong."

For a long time she just sat there, heaving with dry sobs, not speaking. He had very little experience with women. Olga had bedded him a few days after he had arrived in Olympus—just once. That once had satisfied Olga's curiosity. It had been a devastating experience for a crippled, shell-shocked, war-damaged virgin of twenty-one. He had not begun responding to the hints again for several months, and even then he had not dared risk a commitment until that magical day when he had gone for a walk up the hill and had run into Euphemia purely by chance. One thing had led very quickly to the next thing, and they had ended up lying in some badly crushed wildflowers clad only in a healthy perspiration. Since then there had been no one else. She was everything he had ever hoped a woman would be.

She was not, by any stretch of the imagination, a lady. Her father had sold fish in Donegal. The other women tended to snub her. Bill McKay had gone Home on leave and returned with this common, working-class slip of a girl and . . . Lord knew how long ago that had been. One did not ask. Back Home, Julian would not even have considered her. His monstrous regiment of aunts in Cheltenham would succumb to mass hysteria if he ever brought home a woman like Euphemia McKay. The thought of her at the opera or even helping out the ladies at the church garden fête just did not pass muster. But this was Olympus, not Cheltenham, and she was his mistress. His, not Pinky's!

"I've been greedy," she whispered.

"What say?"

"I've been greedy." She glanced up briefly, eyes red-rimmed, then dropped her gaze to the floor again. "I shouldn't be keeping you all to myself like this." *Sniff, sniff!*

"You are not communicating, darling."

"Why don't you understand? I've had my turn. They all want you! You're young, really young, not just stranger-young. You're handsome and a wonderful person and really no older than you look and so innocent, and Olga's told them all about—about what a man you are, and you're a hero, a real hero! So you ought to share yourself around and—"

Julian spoke a word he had not used since he left the Western Front. Then he stood up and began to pace back and forth across the room. He wanted to sit down beside her, but if he ever got his hands—hand—on her in his present mood, he wasn't sure what might happen. Well, he knew what might happen, but not how.

"This is absolute——" He used another expression ladies were not supposed to know, although Euphemia would. "Am I a bloody stud horse? They think they can pass me around like a good book? Don't I have any say in who I sleep with? Whom, I mean. Hell's bells, woman, I want you, not anyone else. And screw Olga and all the rest of—" He choked and then laughed nervously. "I mean, no, I won't. Screw them, that is." Let them suffer. Flattering to think they might be thinking that way, even if he didn't believe it. Did they really? Strewth!

No answer except more snuffling.

"What's Pinky been telling you?"

She made a sound that was half sob and half gasp, but she did not look up.

"Well?"

"You're going off to Joalland tomorrow."

"So? I'll be back. I'll take you with me gladly if you'll come." It would cause a scandal, but he wouldn't care if she didn't.

"With Ursula Newton."

Julian stopped pacing. "I thought I was going with Jumbo." But no one had said so. He'd just assumed.

Euphemia shook her head, making the curtain of hair sway. He could not see her face at all. "Ursula."

"Darling, that was not my choice! And if you think there's anything between me—" He shuddered, and there was no faking required. Never Ursula! That female blacksmith? She hit a tennis ball harder than any man on the station. Mannish women repelled him. "I'd sooner crawl into bed with Foghorn."

"You think it'll matter what you are thinking?" she demanded, suddenly loud. "She's been around longer than any of us!"

"Yes, but . . . What do you mean?"

"I mean no one's ever known Ursula to work any miracles, have they now?" Euphemia's brogue grew thicker when she was excited, and she was excited now, even if she was still wringing her hands and talking to the Narshian rugs. "She must have more mana saved up than any livin' soul on the station, and if she wants you—and she does, I know it—then she'll have you and you won't have any say in the matter."

Godfathers! That would be rape.

There were even nastier implications. "Why are they sending Ursula?"

After a moment, Euphemia whispered, "To stop Mr. Exeter."

Julian shuddered again, even harder. He was being sent along to get Ursula Newton in under Exeter's guard so that she could nobble him with mana? Judas goat! He sat down on the bed beside Euphemia and put an arm around her to comfort her. He really wanted her to hold him and comfort him, but she squirmed away, not understanding.

There was a very nasty taste in his mouth. He had to solve the Euphemia problem before he could even think about the Exeter problem. He cleared his throat harshly. "What else did Pinky say to you tonight?"

Silence.

"What did you say to Pinky, then?"

Another silence, then she said softly, "Go away, love. Stop asking questions. I don't want to be hurting you."

"You can't hurt me more than you're hurting me now."

She sniffed and wiped her eyes with the back of her hand. "Yes I can."

"Try. I want the truth, Euphemia, the whole truth."

Sniff! She rubbed her nose. "They're going to send someone Home to see Alice Prescott, ask her help. Just a very quick trip, there and back."

He waited, not understanding. Again he tried to put an arm around her, but she pushed it away. He noticed that his dressing gown no longer bulged.

"William and me won't be going for months yet. There's someone I . . . someone I haven't heard from since the Great War started. Not a word. I asked the Peppers, but they may not remember . . . and they had so many requests. I only need a few minutes on the phone, just one call. . . ."

"That filthy devil is blackmailing you? I'll rip out—"

"No, no!" She squirmed around and clapped a hand over his mouth. "All he said was that they were going to choose someone to make a quick trip Home. Then he said he always sleeps with his window open. That was all."

That was enough. Julian could hear Pinky saying it, in his sly way.

"That sleazy, slithering bugger! I'll—"

"No! You mustn't, or he won't let me go! There's lots of people want the chance, but he said he thought he could arrange it—"

He pulled her hand away. "Jolly right he can! He can arrange anything for a price, can't he?"

"Oh, it isn't the end of the world, Julian. I've done it before."

"What? With Pinky? No!"

"Yes!" she shouted.

"You said you never cared for him."

Her laugh was bitter as lemons. "Oh, you young idiot! I've cared for almost all of them at one time or another. Haven't you guessed that yet? You think you got me as a virgin?"

One never asked. "It doesn't matter." It did, though. He wished she hadn't said it. How many? Who? They all did it, all the time. He was the baby. "Who is it that you're so thumping keen to get news about?"

"A—a relative."

"What relative?" He jerked on her wrist. *"Answer me!"*

"All right with you, then!" she shouted. "I'll tell you and you'll wish you'd never asked. It's Tim—Timothy Wood, my son!"

"Son?"

He always thought of her as being younger than himself. His rational mind knew that was nonsense; but his emotions went by appearance and behavior. She had never seemed any more than eighteen to him, and often less, but staring at him now, green eyes awash with tears, inflamed with weeping, red blotches of anger burning on her cheekbones, she was much more than eighteen, much much more.

"He's older than you, Julian Smedley."

"Your son is? Not William's son?"

She shook her head, eyes searching his face. "Big, strapping broth of a lad, he is. Has red hair. Like his mother."

He guessed from her eyes. *Don't say it!* he thought, *please don't say it.*

But she did. "And like his father."

She did it with Carrots.

Julian's world collapsed.

It wasn't just that Carrots were natives. At least they were white. They were rustics, primitives, uneducated. . . . But Mrs. McKay was working class herself, wasn't she? No, the snake in the grass was that Carrots were mortal, and romance between mortal and immortal was simply not on. Inexcusable. Exeter had discovered that.

"You see why you should go now, Julian? You go and have a brave holiday in Joalvale with dear Ursula, and I'll go and be nice to darling Pinky."

Still he hesitated. She pushed him roughly. "Be gone with you. I tried to save you, and you so innocent, but now you know I was breeding Carrot bastards before you were even born, my lad. So be off with you."

He stared. How old was she? How many dozens or hundreds of men had gone where he had gone? Some trick of the candlelight made her a nightmare hag.

"If that's what you really want." A gentleman could hardly stay around a lady's bedroom when he wasn't welcome. He stalked over to the window, climbed out, and went home, feeling about a thousand years old himself.

14

THE FAIR CITY OF JURG WAS JUST AWAKENING FOR BUSINESS AS ELEAL Singer came limping along Market Street, weaving between the carts, being jostled by fresh-scrubbed apprentices hurrying to their labors and maidservants out buying fresh bread for their masters' tables. A few late-rising roosters still crowed in the yards and alleys.

She labored under the weight of a pack that held all her worldly goods: spare clothes, three books, two spare pairs of boots, and a few keepsakes. She was also suffering from some very painful bruises, although her face was unmarked, fortunately. To compensate, she was buoyed up by a strange exhilaration, a sense of destiny, a conviction that her life was about to turn an important corner. The sunlight seemed strangely bright, the day itself sweetly scented. Cynical inner voices told her that she was merely suffering from lack of sleep, for dawn more usually marked the end of her working day than her time for rising. That was all behind her now, though. She was a new woman.

A new life beckoned. She had resigned, retired, absconded. Last night she had gone for a stroll and returned late for her gig, something she had never done before. Tigurb'l Tavernkeeper had been unreasonably annoyed. He had not struck her himself, but he had an infinite number of ways to punish, and he had chosen to send some very nasty customers to her dressing room. After the second one, she had packed up her valuables and departed by way of the window.

Here was the place she sought. A garishly painted sign in the shape of a book hung from a bracket above the leaded windows: BALVON PRINTER, MAKER OF EDIFYING TOMES, TEXTS, & TRACTS. The wide door stood open, so she marched right in.

She had never been in a print shop before. It was surprisingly large, with seven or eight people already hard at work. The heavy brass contraption in the center must be the press itself. The air bore an aromatic tang of mingled dust and ink. She glanced around, trying to figure out what everyone was doing so busily at tables and benches around the walls. Two men seemed to be setting type, fishing letters out of rows of boxes. One boy was spreading ink, another carrying away freshly done sheets to dry, another cutting the dried sheets into pages. An old man was pushing a broom around. Three men seemed to be sewing, and one with a mallet was pounding leather on a bench. Fascinating! All this fuss to produce silly little books?

A heavyset man swept forward to greet her. His arrogant demeanor and domineering eyebrows suggested that he might be Balvon Printer himself. She braced herself to meet his inspection. She had shed all her paint and perfume. She was a respectable woman again and need not let this artisan bully her. What if she did carry her own luggage? Her cloak was a great deal grander than his ink-stained apron, even if he did have a jewel in his turban.

His bow was peremptory, but it was a bow. "How may we be of service to my lady?"

Not bad! She savored the respect. Then she wondered if that was suspicion glinting in his eyes—or recognition, perhaps? Could he be a patron of Cherry Blossom House? Might he have recognized her? Might he even have been one of her admirers? She could not recall his face.

She would not consider such a possibility. She must be the daughter of a wealthy landowner, a patron of the arts. She assumed a suitably ladylike manner. "Good morning, my man. I am sorry to disturb you at your labors. I merely wished to speak for a moment with . . ."

The old man holding the broom was staring at her in rank dismay.

Before she could prevent it, a very unladylike blast of laughter erupted from the patron of the arts. "Piol!" She composed herself. "I wish to have a quick word with an old friend." Seeing a glower of disapproval compressing fat old Balvon's heavy features, she raised her chin again and hid her amusement.

"I shall not keep him long from his duties, master. Surely your janitor's time is not so valuable that I need buy a library to earn the privilege of a moment with him?" That seemed like a good exit line, so she turned and swept out into the street.

Piol followed her out, trailing his broom, and blinked at her ruefully in the sunshine.

"Good morning, Piol!" She could not keep her mirth from her voice.

He looked even frailer in daylight than he had under the lamps two nights ago. His straggly white hair was awry, his skin yellow as old parchment, his wrinkles were deeper than Susswater Canyon. His robe was a shabby, dusty thing, and he was barefoot.

"Good morning, Eleal."

"Now we share each other's dreadmost secret, don't we?"

He nodded, smiling without much conviction. "I'm afraid we do." He made a few desultory strokes with his broom, as if he had come to clean the doorstep.

"Oh, Piol!" Where had that terrible lump in her throat come from?

He glanced around, perhaps afraid his employer might be standing at his back, glaring at him. "What is it, Eleal? Be quick, please."

For a moment she could hardly remember what it was she wanted. Piol Poet, who had won the playwright's rose at the Tion Festival an unprecedented twelve times! Piol Poet sweeping floors!

"I want you to come with me."

"What? Where? It is not much of a job, Eleal, but even old men must eat. I don't need much, but I do need a dry, warm place to sleep."

"You shall have it!" she said hurriedly. "Piol, I have decided to go for the big time! Joal beckons! I shall seek to further my art in the artistic capital of the Vales!"

He smiled uncertainly. "Well . . . well, that is wonderful news, my dear! I am sure you will prosper there. Joalians appreciate talent."

"But I need company on my journey. You!"

His toothless jaw dropped, and he stared at her as if he had taken leave of his wits or thought she had lost hers.

"I am on my way to Joalvale, Piol. It was your mention of the Liberator that gave me the idea. It will be fun to see D'ward again, so we shall contrive to meet him there. But I need a companion, and you are the only one I can trust. Besides, I feel my career requires a manager. Come with me!"

"The Liberator?" He shook his head in disbelief, then made an effort to straighten his bent shoulders. "But that isn't necessary! The Liberator is coming here. All you need do is wait in Jurgvale. He will come. No need to go to Joalvale. In fact, he probably isn't even there anymore."

She felt an inexplicable stab of dismay. "Not there? But you said he was in Joalvale!"

"He was. He will certainly have moved on by now. And what use can I be? I am old. I am not very well, Eleal. . . ."

"Nothing a good meal or two won't fix! If D'ward isn't in Joalvale, then where is he? And how do you know?"

"From the prophecies, of course. He is on his way here, I am sure of it."

That would not do at all! "Then we shall go and meet him in Fionvale."

Piol's eyes narrowed. "I doubt he will be coming that way. He will be coming around by Niolvale, I'm sure. Are you especially eager to leave Jurg, Eleal?"

She laughed and glanced around nervously. The bouncers were not usually operational so early in the day, but Tigurb'l must be very, very mad. She had no time to waste. "You're still as sharp as ever, you old rascal! Yes, I do believe a change of scenery would be beneficial and absence thereof detrimental. Let us head for Niolvale, then. There will be opportunities for an artist there, too. I shall require a good manager—I see now that that was where I made my mistake. How do you know D'ward will come that way?"

Piol blinked his rheumy eyes. "Verse six sixty-three: 'In Niol's shadow, by the silver waters, multitudes shall flock to hear him, and the sharp swords shall drink, spilling blood into the sands. Young men leave their bones where the Liberator has passed.' "

Oh! "Well, we're neither of us young men, are we? Please, Piol! I am carrying quite a lot of money. I do need someone with me, and who else can I trust?"

"Not me! Eleal, what are you planning? Who has put you up to this?"

She had expected him to leap at her offer, but he seemed ready to flee back into his cage.

"No one except you! I'll explain all that when we're on the road." Some of it, anyway. "I need you, Piol. Surely you'd rather come adventuring with me than stay here sweeping dirt? It'll be like old times, Piol! A little like old times, at least. The trader caravans leaving at noon from . . ."

Piol was shaking his head. "I can't leave, Eleal," he whispered.

"Can't? Why not?"

He glanced behind him again, having to turn his whole body in the manner of the aged. Then he looked back to her, his face crumpled with shame. "It costs money to print a book. I still owe rather a lot of it, I'm afraid."

She reached for the money bag under her cloak. "How much?"

"I can't take your gold!" He recoiled from her.

"Piol! Whatever do you mean? Are you implying there is something shameful about my money? I earned this with my singing."

Still he hesitated, shaking his bony head.

"How much do you need? I have lots of money! On a long journey I need a man to accompany me. Go back in there and shove that broom down old Balvon's throat, then gather up your things and come with me! Meet me over there in that bread shop. We'll have some fresh hot rolls and plan our journey. Please, Piol?"

The bakery was hot and rather dark. It was thronged with servants and housewives impatient to acquire their daily bread, but it did have a few rickety tables and chairs. Eleal sat in a corner and fidgeted. She ordered rolls and some of the weak, sweet beer that Jurgians drank in the morning, although she was neither hungry nor thirsty. She had spent the night at a very fine inn, a hostel patronized by gentry, and had eaten well this morning.

Tigurb'l did not own her, but he behaved as if he did. Furthermore, in a few frantic minutes just before leaving her dressing room, she had achieved a remarkable amount of destruction—it was quite amazing what could be achieved in complete silence with a sharp knife. The thugs would be trying to find her to take her back. Definitely a change of scenery was called for.

And it would be fun to see D'ward again. Perhaps he had a very good explanation for running out on her in Suss. She should not judge until she had heard his excuses.

She stifled yawns. What little sleep she had achieved had been broken by strange dreams of an admirer she could not place, a chunky, ruggedly handsome young man with a mustache. It was odd that she could not remember his name or anything more about him except his face and his very hairy chest.

Piol appeared at last, staggering under the weight of a bulky bag. His robe was a threadbare rag, well patched and faded until its original color could not be guessed at. He had wrapped up his head in a whitish turban, which was a Niolian custom, but not uncommon in Jurgland. He tucked in to the buttery rolls with his scanty teeth and ample enthusiasm as if he had not eaten for two fortnights.

He showed much less enthusiasm for her project. "By all means try your luck in Joal, my dear. I shall be happy to help in any way I can. I probably still have friends in the artistic community there, and as you say, it is the greatest of them all. But D'ward . . . I was wrong to mention him to you. Now I think you should avoid opening old wounds."

Whatever could be worrying the old coot?

"Oh, bygones are bygones. It will be fun to see him again."

"You didn't seem to think so when I told you about him."

"Nonsense! I was merely surprised. Tell me why you think he is coming here."

"He must," he mumbled with his mouth full, "go to Thargland, right? That's what the *Testament* says. You can work it all out from the places named."

"Tell me."

He glanced down at his bag. "I have a copy . . . but I think I can remember. You have to fit them together in the right order. . . . Verse one thousand and one: 'In wrath the Liberator shall descend into Thargland. The gods shall flee before him; they shall bow their heads before him, they will spread their hands before his feet.' Tharg is where Zath has his temple, the temple of Karzon, so that's where D'ward must seek him out."

"But if he's in Joalvale, then the quickest way for him to go is through Nagvale and Lemodvale."

"He isn't going the quickest way!" Obviously Piol had been giving much thought to the prophecies. However old and sick he might be, his brain was still working. "Verse two twenty: 'In Nosokslope they shall come to D'ward in their hundreds, even the Betrayer.' "

She forced herself to meet his stare. "Who's the Betrayer?"

"I don't know." He was wondering about it, though.

She shrugged uneasily. "Then let's not go to Nosokvale. What's next?"

"Then the one about Niol—the sharp swords and the young men leaving their bones."

She did not think that could apply to her. She certainly had no sharp swords to hand. "Niol won't get him any closer to Thargland."

"Then Verse fifty-six: 'The Liberator shall hail the Free in Jurgland.' There's a lot more about him promising to bring death to Death and being acclaimed by the multitude. But that one must come next. There's a verse about the king of Randoria and one about hunger in Thovale."

Eleal took a large bite of bread and chewed busily to keep her face occupied. "Prophecies aren't inevitable, though, are they?"

Piol sighed and took a gulp of his beer. "No. If you can break one link in the chain, all the rest must fail. If I were Karzon, I would be trying to kill D'ward before he killed me." He watched carefully for her reaction.

She laughed gaily. "You don't look much like a god to me!"

"You know what gods look like, Eleal?"

"Well of course—I mean, no. Only in general. Why mention Karzon? It doesn't say D'ward will kill Karzon! Only Death, and Zath is just one of the Man's aspects. Of course I don't know what gods look like, except on stage."

"Where did you get so much money, Eleal?"

"I earned it, of course." At least, she thought she had. In her hasty flight, she had emptied all the little caches where she kept her savings hidden. When she went to count it this morning, she had discovered that her money belt contained about four times as much as she expected. It was odd but certainly nothing to complain about. She could live for a year on it.

"So if you're right, then I don't need to go all the way to Joalvale. We can just go over Lospass to Niolvale. If he isn't there yet, then we'll go on to Rinoovale."

"I thought you were going to Joalvale and the Liberator was incidental?"

"Well . . . It would be nice to see him again."

The old man nodded in resignation, making the flaps of his neck wave like flags. "If you insist. Have you enough money to buy a sloth and cart?"

"What do I need a cart for? Or a sloth?"

He smiled for the first time since he had arrived. "If you have money, Eleal, then you always have trouble. If you can't find a better defender than me, then you have serious trouble! You need to discourage the young and greedy. Let's buy a sloth and cart and load it up with sewerberries."

"Yuck!"

This time he actually chuckled, just like his old self. "Exactly! Nobody's going to dig through a load of sewerberries looking for gold. Nobody will come within yards of us! It's a profitable cargo, too—we may make money, which is better than paying for a ride in a caravan and for guards whom we couldn't trust anyway."

Suddenly she felt much better. She leaned over and squeezed his hand. "Brilliant! That's the Piol I used to know! You write the play and we'll star in it together. Two tragic figures? You shall be the noble old campaigner, called forth once more to bear arms in a worthy cause! And I shall be your granddaughter, perhaps? A forsaken maiden going in search of the man who betrayed her but whom deep in her heart she still . . ."

Then fell one of those deathly silences, as if someone had forgotten his lines. A shadow had settled on Piol Poet's face.

"I will write that role gladly, Eleal, if you will play it."

ᎶᏨ 15 ᏁᏩᏋ

OVERHEAD THE SKY SHONE PURE WEDGEWOOD BLUE, ALTHOUGH THE SUN had not yet cleared the peaks. Morning was a symphony of pearly light and cold as a bugger. Rimy grass crunched underfoot as Julian trudged along, shivering inside his furs and fleece-lined boots. He was in no mood or state for an argument, but he could see one coming whether he wanted it or not.

His eyes were gritty. He had slept very little, tossing the night away thinking about Euphemia prostituting herself to bloody Pinkney just for a chance to make one phone call. It made him feel so bloody inadequate, a man who couldn't defend his woman! It wasn't the ritual that was the problem—she must know at least one of the keys as well as bloody Pinky did—it was the timing. The Olympus portal connected to St. Galls in Wiltshire and a cemetery in Edinburgh and other places as well. You had to know what hour of day or night it was at Home now and when Head Office would have helpers standing by, or you could find yourself in very hot water indeed. The Committee kept all that information under its hat.

Well, it was over. Pinky had had his fun by now. And here came more trouble. Dommi was at his heels, bent almost double under a bag as big as himself. Pind'l and Ostian, Dommi's juvenile assistants, brought up the rear with the rest of the baggage. The air was sharp as swords, and yet they wore only flimsy cotton livery. Dommi was bareheaded, although the rest of him was swathed in a ragtag assembly of moth-eaten furs.

The dragon paddock lay upstream from the station, far enough off to muffle the brutes' incessant burpings. Four dragons were being loaded by a group that included two men in black turbans—simple arithmetic foretold trouble. Turbans came from Nioldom, black was the color of Zath, to be displayed with caution. The only men who ever wore black turbans were T'lin Dragontrader and his hands; it was a sort of uniform with them, dating back before T'lin's conversion to the Undivided.

Julian was in the soup because Dommi expected *Tyika* Kaptaan to keep his promise. A man's word was his bond, and all that. Dommi's furs must have come from the Carrot village, so the whole valley would know that he was bound for Joalvale with *Tyika* Kaptaan. He had roused Julian before first light, having already laid out the *tyika*'s warmest garments, heated a tubful of water, packed the bags, summoned bearers, and prepared a hot breakfast. But two and two made four, on any world, and there were only four dragons in the pen. Olympus owned three of its own, but it was not unusual for all of them to be absent from the valley, as now. Most of those half-clad redheads bustling around would be grooms or polishers or whatever the correct name was for men who shoveled dragon shite, but the dragons themselves all belonged to Agent Seventy-seven, alias T'lin Dragontrader. And both the black-turbaned men were armed, dammit! Julian hadn't even thought of that problem.

Dragontrader himself he could override; Ursula was another matter alto-blooming-gether, especially at this time of day, after two nights without sleep. Blast Edward Exeter and his blasted prophecies! Still, a man's word was his bloody bond.

"Dommi?" he croaked.

Dommi took two fast steps to draw alongside, craning his neck to peer up at him from under the pack. *"Tyika?"*

"You know how to handle a sword."

A worried frown disturbed Dommi's honest freckles. "Is regretful, *tyika,* that I have never had experience with weapons, excepting the short bow for bird-hunting and—"

"Don't argue. You know how to handle a sword."

"As the *tyika* wishes."

Dragons were hay-eating nightmares, a cross between a rhinoceros and the Loch Ness monster, but gentle, helpful creatures in spite of it, the only species capable of crossing from vale to vale without using the standard passes. Exeter had once referred to the dragon as the Rolls-Royce of Nextdoor, and Julian was looking forward to his first real chance to ride one. With his entourage at his heels, he strode into the center of group. Amid a crowd of freckled, lightly clad Carrots, Ursula was well bundled up in white fur with only her face visible. She looked as friendly as a rabid bulldog, and T'lin's expression was equally hostile. They disapproved of Dommi's costume.

"Morning all!" Julian chirruped. He jumped as the two youngsters' packs hit the ground beside him, shaking the valley. Dommi lowered his more circum-spectly. "You're looking very charming this morning, Mrs. Newton, an Eskimo's dream. Everything all ready to go there, Dragontrader?"

T'lin raised his massive arms to make the sign of the Undivided. "We are honored to serve, Holiness."

"Rather! Well, sharp's the word! Let's get this stuff loaded, shall we? Then we can be on our way, what?"

"Captain," Ursula growled, "what does this mean?" She spoke in English, aiming a loaded finger at Dommi.

"What? Dommi, you mean? Oh, need a valet. Can't handle buttons and all that, you know." Julian waved his right hand, making the fingers of his glove flap.

Her glower darkened perceptibly. "I am sure Dragontrader won't mind helping you dress, Captain." Was she implying that she would help him *undress*? *From ghoulies and ghosties and long-leggèd beasties . . .*

"Humbug! Dommi's an excellent cook, and I'm sure he can help out with the livestock too. Can't you, Dommi?"

With great eagerness, Dommi said, "Indeed, *tyika,* I had experience many years as a stripling here in the paddock, helping tending with the dragons."

"There! That's settled." Julian turned away.

"No!" Ursula barked. "This is not a Sunday school picnic, Captain Smedley. We have only four mounts. Goober Dragonherder is a skilled swordsman. So is Seventy-seven, of course, but an additional guard will be invaluable. We won't take any houseboys."

The surrounding Carrots raised their pink eyebrows at her tone, although few of them would understand the words.

"Dommi can handle a sword. Can't you, Dommi?"

Dommi favored Ursula with a gaze of earnest innocence. "Most assuredly, *Entyika* Newton, I was juvenile fencing champion of the village running three years in my youth, and my father sent me out to Randorvale to study with the noted blade-master—"

She uttered a snort that startled even the dragons. "Tell it to the marines, boy! We're going to Joalvale. You're going back to the kitchen. Now, Dragontr—"

"Joalvale, *entyika?*" Dommi exclaimed. "But *Tyika* Kaptaan told me that Niolland would be your most primordial destination, because of the notorious prophecies."

Tyika Kaptaan had said no such thing and wondered if he looked as surprised as Ursula did. Dommi glanced from one to the other, apparently worried that he might have revealed a confidence.

"Prophecies?" she demanded. "What prophecies?"

Totally at sea, Julian sighed. "Oh, go ahead, Dommi. You tell her."

Dommi beamed with innocent youthful pleasure at this honor and began to gabble. "*Tyika* Kaptaan explained to me, *entyika,* how the words of the *Filoby Testament* can be construed to elucidate the route that Liberator must follow to reach his intended dread purpose in Thargvale, *entyika,* which is where he must going be if the slaying of Zath is his object, which we are all knowing it is, yes? Likewise, *Tyika* Kaptaan was instructing me how there are eight references only to the Liberator and twelve to D'ward, whom we know to be the same with *Tyika* Kisster and also himself the Liberator, overlooking a few ambiguous abstrusenesses that may also refer but not specify by name, yes? And of the twenty, fifteen either specify a place or imply one, *Tyika* Kaptaan says."

Julian wondered if perhaps he had not awakened at all and was dreaming this. In that case, why was Ursula gaping like a dead fish?

"Incontrovertible it is," Dommi continued, flushed with excitement until his freckles hardly showed, "that numerous of these place-naming verses may be ordered so as to predict *Tyika* Kisster's chosen path, and while it is not certain that he has already left Joalland, where he was observed in motion a half fortnight ago, *Tyika* Kaptaan pointed out that his chances of interception to the Liberator would be magnified by regressing this indicated itinerary backward, and consequently it will be advantageous to make progression directly to Niolvale—or perhaps Jurgvale, even-—and retracing his tracks before he makes them."

Ursula looked aghast at Julian. "Damn my eyes! You mean he isn't just *letting* the prophecies happen, he's going to fulfill them *deliberately* to prove he's the bloody Liberator?"

"Well, surely that's obvious, old girl?" It was obvious to Julian now that his bottle washer had pointed it out. Resourceful chap, Dommi, the perfect gentleman's gentleman. Of course Exeter would make it his business to fulfill all the prophecies—half a Liberator would be no bally good to anyone. And of course he would have to do it in some sort of geographical order, and why the blazes had the Carrots worked that out before the *votyikank* did?

Ursula's eyes burned dark with suspicion. "Why didn't you mention this last night?"

Julian shrugged. "I assumed you could all see it as well as I could, old girl." Nothing untrue there.

"Niolvale or Joalvale, wherever we're going, we still only have four dragons."

Not trusting his Joalian, Julian switched to Randorian, which he knew T'lin understood, and flourished his crispest military tone. "We'll head for Niolland. Dommi, get our kit loaded." Immediately a wave of gleeful Carrots swept through, bearing away all Julian's baggage—and Dommi's also, of course—to pack it in the dragons' panniers. "I'm sure someone will turn up with another mount in a day or two, Dragontrader, and your man can follow us then." Before anyone could argue further, he added, "Oh, and do get him to lend Dommi his sword, will you? No use taking along a first-class fencer without arming him."

ᘒᘒ 16 ᘈᘈ

İT WAS NOT DOSH'S FAULT—HE COULD HAVE GONE ON FOR HOURS AND almost certainly escaped from Nosokvale, free and clear. The festering moa failed him in the night. Just where Ragpass widened out and merged with the foothills of Nosokslope, the brute began staggering, stumbling, and falling over things. Reluctantly, he rode off the trail and took refuge in a wood. There he unsaddled and hobbled her, then stretched out under a bush and slept.

By the time he awoke, it was well into morning. He ate his last scraps of food before doing battle with Swift, who was still lame and did not want to go adventuring again. When he returned to the trail, he saw at a glance that a company of moas had passed recently. If they weren't the Joalian troopers, he was a virgin. He considered turning back and decided against it. He had no supplies, he was hungry, and he felt strongly disinclined to run into D'ward and his ragtag rabble again. More to the point, if the cavalry leader knew his business, he would have foreseen the possibility of the fugitive doubling back and left a squad behind to guard the pass.

So Dosh went on, riding down to Ragby, which was a sorry little excuse for a village. Nosokvale was a shoddy land altogether. It must have been fertile and prosperous once, for there were more ruins around than houses, but it was too close to Joalvale for its own health. The Clique and their friends had exploited it, evicting the inhabitants and setting up huge ranching estates. Amorgush owned great tracts of land in Nosokvale.

Knowing no back doors out, poor Dosh had no option but to head east to Lampass with all the speed he could force out of Swift, who no longer deserved her name. He was not so stupid as actually to go into Ragby itself, for the troopers would certainly have mentioned blood money in the village, but the nagging hunger in his belly forced him to stop at an isolated hovel and buy a meal. Either the old couple there betrayed him or he was just observed on the trail; Nosokflat was a tablecloth of grass with very little cover, and by noon Dosh knew he was being watched. He saw isolated riders tracking him in the distance—herders, probably, servants of the absentee landlords. No one was closing in on him, but he must assume that they had sent word ahead to the Joalians. He wondered if there was more than mortal justice hunting him now, if Kraanard's murder had brought the wrath of the Lady upon him.

When pursuit became chase, he would have no chance at all. Most of the troopers' moas must be as exhausted as his, but some of them would still be in working order. Reluctantly, he turned around and headed back. In an ironic echo of the previous day and at about the same time in the evening, he entered Ragpass from the opposite end, confident that he must have the same hunters on his trail again by now.

As the track wound up through the Nosokslope foothills, he began to see people, scores of people in small groups, all heading in the same direction he was. They could not be planning to cross Ragpass tonight, for already the grasping shadows of Nosokwall were reaching out over the landscape. Most were clearly local peasantry, the same sort of rabble that had been following D'ward from Joalland—looking even more impoverished and downtrodden. Others were astride llamas or rabbits or rode in carriages. Apparently, word of the Liberator's arrival had preceded him, and the gentry were also assembling to view the wonder.

Regrettably, he saw not one solitary moa to make his own less conspicuous. He went with the crowd, which merged with the tail end of the self-proclaimed Free coming down from Joalvale and then flowed off into a side canyon. There, obviously, D'ward had set up camp again, and so had his followers. Fires twinkled in the dusk. Dosh met tantalizing odors of cooking, noting that they were mostly associated with parked wagons or coaches and hobbled animals. Those must belong to Nosokians who had brought provisions, although some enterprising groups were selling meals from carts. What were those without money eating? Probably nothing. There were no berry bushes here—precious little of anything except grass and a few emaciated trees. He could hear children crying, but when did children not? Soon he drew near a steep hillside closing off the little valley. From the ruined walls of some ancient building at its base came the sound of many people singing. If they were singing for their supper, they would have to sing much louder than that.

His situation had improved very little. True, there must be three or four hundred pilgrims here to hide among. He could buy himself a meal from one of those entrepreneurs and pick out some respectable citizens to blandish with his polished charm. If that would not uncover a few temporary brothers or cousins to vouch for him, then his money should, provided the price on his head was not too high. The main thing would be avoid the notice of the Liberator and his—

"Dosh!"

Too late. The three men running toward him bore spears and circular Nagian shields. The big one in front was easily recognizable as Prat'han Potter, and behind him came Gopaenum Butcher and Tielan Trader—all from Sonalby, all veterans of the Thargian campaign.

Dosh barked at Swift to crouch, and she seemed to collapse under him. He slid down from the saddle, not worrying about hobbling or tethering, for the brute was too spent even to try to bite him. Feeling just as weary himself, he leaned against her flank and waited for the warriors, wearing an unfamiliar sense of failure like a shroud. He had been in tight corners often enough in his life, but rarely had he lacked confidence in his ability to wriggle out again. Now he was too tired to run and could not hope to hide. These men had always despised him; now they could turn him in as soon as the troopers appeared. Here he was, with more money than he'd ever had in his life, trapped by idiots too stupid to be bribed.

Prat'han arrived first, with the other two close on his heels. They grounded their spears.

"Greetings!" the big man said.

Dosh looked for the mockery he expected. Surprisingly, he did not find it. "Greetings to you," he responded warily.

Tielan chuckled. "The Liberator said you would turn up! Been a long time, Dosh!" The trader was a small, wiry man. He had always had a flippant, juvenile air about him and he had not lost it. Yet even he did not seem to be gloating. He stepped forward and grasped Dosh's shoulder in the Nagian greeting. Prat'han and Gopaenum quickly did the same, as if caught out in a breach of manners. Dosh responded doubtfully.

Well, well! All old friends together now?

"You look as if you've had a hard day." Prat'han peered at the moa and frowned. "You've ridden that poor brute into the ground!"

"It was it or me."

"The troopers came by not long after you left us last night," Gopaenum said. "I'm surprised they missed you. And pleased too, of course!" he added without much conviction. In the last few years he had gained weight and moved most of his hair from his scalp to his chest.

"You told them where I'd gone, though?"

The three exchanged glances.

Prat'han shrugged. "You'd refused the Liberator's offer."

Dosh waited for more, but they waited too.

"And what happens when they turn up tonight? Will you tell them I'm here?"

Gopaenum and Tielan looked expectantly at Prat'han. The big man was their leader, after D'ward. He sidestepped the question.

"We were hoping you'd changed your mind, Dosh."

"You're lying. D'ward may be hoping that, but you aren't, none of you. Join you? Why should I trust you?"

"Because we're prepared to trust you, of course."

"You are or D'ward is?"

Prat'han put his weight on his spear as if he expected to be there for a while. "Whatever D'ward wants is enough for us. He said we were to look out for you and make you welcome if you want to join the Free."

Dosh snorted in disbelief. "I just have to promise to be a good boy in future and you'll accept me as your long-lost brother? You?"

The big man bared his teeth. "I'll try. I really will try. You were our friend once."

His memory was very selective. Friend? Never. After the sack of Lemod, they'd stopped spitting at Dosh Catamite but that was about all.

"You mean you'd defend me from the troopers? You'd lie to them? You'd *fight* for me?" Dosh laughed.

The other two scowled at him. At least Prat'han was trying, although the effort was making his forehead shiny. "We'd do that for a friend, of course—for a brother, I mean. D'ward says you weren't a Thargian spy at—"

"Ha! But I was a spy. Did he mention that?"

"Yes. But he told us to remember how you proved yourself at Lemod, how you went out with him that night, how you went over the wall right after him. He said if you do want to join the Free, you'll prove it."

Startled and then suspicious, Dosh said, "Prove it how?"

"He didn't tell us that."

Tielan said, "He said it's up to Prat'han. You gotta convince Big Pots here. Go ahead and convince. I'm sure it will be an interesting performance."

Gopaenum chuckled. "I'm looking forward to it, too. Actions speak louder than words, the Liberator says."

The bastards were really enjoying this. Dosh peered around, hoping to see some alternative. He didn't. The valley was almost dark now, so that the scattered fires shone brighter. The singing had stopped. The crowd at the ruins had fallen silent, listening to someone speaking—D'ward, probably, but the snatches the wind brought were too faint to make out. The only other sounds were thuddings of axes as the last trees turned into firewood. The moa was useless; if he took off on his own feet, he'd be run down easily. The Nagians knew he was here and would tell the troopers. It was join them or die. He was shaking now from cold and exhaustion, but these boneheads would think it was from fear. Maybe they were right. He'd have to join the Free, at least until morning.

Join them how?

"You're going to bring death to Death?"

"To try," Prat'han said. "We're not fools, Dosh. We know this is dangerous. Some of us may die. All of us may die. We think it's worth the risk, that's all—no more reapers."

"If it scares you, you don't have to, of course," Tielan added.

There was one thing he could do, but his whole self shied away from the prospect like a fiery death. "Suppose I agree now and change my mind tomorrow?"

Prat'han chewed his lip unhappily for a moment. He was having to *think*, and he usually managed not to get involved with that. "Suppose you'll be free to go. Anyone's free to go. One or two of us turned back; missed their wives, they said."

Gopaenum shivered noisily. "You going to stand there all night? Come on—convince!"

Dosh thought it over again and reluctantly came to the same conclusion as before. He sighed. "You still a butcher?"

"I was until a coupl'a fortnights ago. Why?"

"Lot of hungry people out there tonight. I don't need this moa if I'm going to join you, do I? Take it, kill it, share it out. The saddle can go to make shoes for some of the kids."

Gopaenum and Tielan looked inquiringly at Prat'han.

"Doesn't prove much, Dosh. It makes you conspicuous and it's half dead already."

"I haven't finished!" Dosh snapped, although he'd had hopes. "And it's still worth a hundred stars! Here, I've got some cash, too." He pulled out his money bag, wishing he'd had the foresight to divide his riches between two bags.

Tielan snarled, "We don't want your filthy gold!"

And him a trader!

"Not for you, shitface. For those hungry people. Come and watch."

Hardly able to believe he was letting himself be suckered like this, he stumbled off into the gloom, heading for the nearest campfire, Prat'han and Tielan stalking along at his heels. Gopaenum stayed with the moa, and it cried out briefly in the background as Dosh handed the first coin to an astonished child. More children flocked around; he gave them silver. He strode over to the next fire and the next, choosing those that were not cooking food. He dropped coins to mothers with babies, laid others beside sleeping children. He found himself laughing rather shrilly at the expressions on the adults' faces. Then the bag was empty. He turned to the two Nagians.

"Well? Have I convinced you now?"

Tielan beamed and opened his mouth.

"Why stop now?" Prat'han demanded, frowning. "That's a pricey-looking outfit. What's in the pockets?"

"Nothing, you stupid ox!"

"Well, you can't cross a river halfway, D'ward says. Finish the job, Dosh. Do it all."

Cursing under his breath, Dosh stripped. He gave away his tunic, his boots, his precious knife belt. He exchanged his fine linen breeches for a grubby loin-cloth off an astonished beggar. Then, penniless and barefoot, he turned on Prat'han. "Well? You want my skin, too? Because that's all I've got left. You want to pull out my toenails, you, you . . ." He wanted to scream.

With a bellow of joy, Prat'han enveloped him in a bear hug so tight his ribs creaked. "Well done, Dosh! Well, well done! D'ward said you'd prove yourself and none of us believed him!"

Then it was Tielan's turn. He not only hugged Dosh, he kissed his cheek. "Welcome, brother! Come and meet the others, Brother Dosh."

They led him back to where Gopaenum was passing out hunks of still-warm meat to an excited throng. More of the Warband emerged from the darkness. Told what he had done, they embraced him and bade him welcome to the Free. They all smiled as if they meant it, although he couldn't see their faces clearly. It was easy enough for them. They hadn't had to throw away a fornicating fortune to join a madhouse.

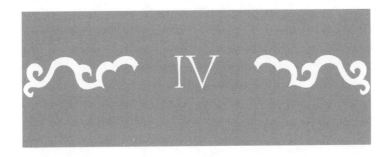

IV

Now this, O monks, is the noble truth of the cessation of pain: the cessation, without a reminder, of that craving; abandonment, forsaking, release, non-attachment.

BUDDHA

ʃʀʀ 17 ᴚʆʀʓ

IT WAS FEBRUARY. IT WAS ALMOST DARK. IT WAS RAINING. TO SAY RAIN was falling would be inaccurate—it moved in gray sheets parallel to the ground, sweeping horizontally across the sodden flatland of Norfolk so that it could needle into Alice's face, insinuate its cold presence under the edges of her sou'wester to soak her hair, creep down the tops of her Wellingtons, trickle icily into the neck and sleeves of her raincoat. The wind tugged and wrestled at the coat, which was much too large for her and probably Tudor, or at least Georgian. She had found it in hanging on a nail in the cottage, overlooked or unwanted by those who had taken all the other contents. No wonder the English had conquered half the world—a race toughened by such weather could overcome anything.

Her hands and face ached with the cold. She had been a fool to come out for a walk and an even bigger fool to head downwind. Now she had the gale in her face all the way back and the going was much harder. She had wanted some fresh air, but not quite this much, thank you. She was still so weak that it had blown her over twice already, sliding her feet from under her in the mire, so she was almost as muddy as the track itself. She would have no one to blame but herself if she caught a chill; the doctor had warned her not to get overtired, but he had not thought of hypothermia. Wistful dreams of hot, steaming tea in large quantities drove her onward.

But not far now. She turned into the little driveway to her door. The hugely overgrown hedges on either side gave her shelter from the wind.

She ought to fill up the coal scuttle before she went in, while she had her coat on. Had she ever truly appreciated the gas fire in her flat in London, or the roof there that did not leak? Even the screaming boredom of the office had taken on a certain nostalgic glow now. Frailty, thy name is Alice! She had made her decision and would live with it. Tonight she would finish painting the ceiling if it killed her. She had started four days ago and she could still see more mildew than paint.

As she left the shelter of the hedges, the wind grabbed at her, flapping her coat, making her stagger. She almost walked into the car before she saw it. She stopped in astonishment, wiping rain from her eyes.

It was a very large motorcar, parked right at her door. Large and black. Just for a moment, it reminded her of D'Arcy's old Vauxhall. A wild, crazy fantasy . . . *It was all a horrible mistake, darling. I've been in a German prison camp. . . .*

No, that was madness. Even if it were true, she had seen the Vauxhall wrecked by bombs in Greenwich eighteen months ago during those few chaotic days when Edward had returned from fairyland. And the other, corresponding, daydream, of Terry turning up saying, *No, love, I wasn't drowned* . . . that was even more impossible. If Terry were to come back from the dead, he would not do so in a car.

But who did she know who had an automobile and access to petrol? No one. The war had not been over long enough for such luxuries to have reappeared. And almost nobody would have known where to find her anyway. She had not yet written all the letters she meant to write, ought to write, must get around to writing.

A neighbor coming to call? Leaving cards? She would not expect the locals to drop around and leave cards—that seemed a ludicrous idea in a rural wilderness like this. She had been expecting someone to drop in before now, just to check out the newcomer. She had not been expecting a car to come by itself, and this one was certainly unoccupied.

She fingered the big key in her pocket. She was quite certain she had locked the door, although that would probably seem an unfriendly act to the locals. There were no other houses within a mile of her and she had no telephone. Until now, that situation had not bothered her. She really should not let it trouble her now. . . .

But where was the driver? In the outhouse? In the shed at the back? It made no sense to take shelter in either of those, for the car itself would be more comfortable. If her visitor had evil intentions, it made even less sense to lie in wait for her somewhere with the car standing in full view. She moved slowly to the door. The cottage's two tiny, secretive windows both faced the front, and few people would be able to clamber in through them anyway. Neither was broken or showed conspicuous signs of tampering. The long grass under them had not been trampled.

Very gently she depressed the latch; the door was still locked. More relieved than she cared to admit, she twisted the key in the keyhole and heard the antique lock clatter. The wind hurled her into the cottage in a cloud of rain. She heaved the door back and slammed it. She shot the bolt.

Panting and shivering, she stood for a moment, hearing the patter of mud and water on the newspapers covering the floor at her feet, grateful to be in out of the storm, unable to see anything except the twinkle of firelight. Bring in more coal? Coal could wait. If her unknown visitor had merely gone to visit the privy, she would hear him return to the car.

She hauled off her hat. The reek of turpentine in the room was sickening. Gradually her eyes adjested to the light and she saw the sink and counter in the corner, the stepladder, the tins of paint, the paraffin lamp, the sofa and chair draped in dust covers as if veiled for a funeral. All the rest of the furniture had been crammed away into the bedroom. The woman on the sofa was drinking tea.

Yelping with shock, Alice jumped back and cannoned into the door.

The visitor frowned and lowered her cup into the saucer she held in her other hand. "Good afternoon, Miss Prescott. I'm sorry if I startled you." She sat tall and erect in a sensible brown tweed coat with a fur collar. A cumbersome handbag lay beside her on the sofa. Her bright-glinting eyes and angular features were oddly birdlike.

For a moment Alice had no breath to speak but every muscle in her body tried to move independently in all directions. Then she croaked, "You're younger!"

The visitor raised carefully penciled eyebrows to suggest that the remark was in questionable taste. "Younger than what? Magna Carta?"

"Than when I last met you, of course. Are you still Miss Pimm?"

She was completely dry, from her neat hat to her practical, square-toed shoes, although the path outside was awash in mud. There was no sign of moisture on her fur collar.

"That name will do, I suppose, Miss Prescott."

Suddenly shock gave way to anger. "And mine is Pearson." Alice struggled with the buttons on her coat.

The witch glanced briefly at the ringless fingers and considered that information for a moment. "You are living alone, though, Mrs. Pearson. I take it that condolences are in order?"

An explanation would be much more in order. Not the locked door. That was easy enough to understand, for Miss Pimm had once removed Alice herself from a bicycle and placed her in the backseat of an automobile while the two vehicles were approaching each other at a hundred miles an hour. Why, though, had she invaded Alice's hard-won solitude in the depths of darkest Norfolk? Could she not recognize a hermitage when she saw one?

Then understanding and excitement: "Edward? You have news of Edward?"

"He is alive and well, as of a couple of weeks ago. And he is the reason for my intrusion, of course. He always is, isn't he?" Miss Pimm shook her head in mild exasperation. "I must have an impacted mother instinct where that boy is concerned."

"He has returned?"

"No. He is still on Nextdoor. He never came Home, as he promised. I should have informed you promptly if I had had word of him. This is the first definite news I have heard."

And the first Alice had heard of either of them in years. She hung her hat and muddy coat on the nail by the door. "You had had *in*definite news?"

"I received a report that he had announced his intention of fulfilling the prophecy and had then left Olympus. The details were so vague and so unlikely that I chose not to trouble you with them."

Alice chafed her cold and aching hands, then pulled her feet out of the Wellingtons. "And what is more definite this time?"

"I shall get to that in due course. I made some tea." Obviously. And the teapot in its cozy was perched on the ladder, one step up from the milk jug, the sugar bowl, and a second cup and saucer. All those things had come out of the jumble in the bedroom. Miss Pimm was a very efficient busybody, for Alice had not been gone more than twenty minutes.

"It was very kind of you to come so far to let me know," she said sweetly, heading for the tea. She had no need to ask how the old hussy had tracked her down.

"You have been ill."

"Is it so obvious?"

"Not to most people, no."

"I had a touch of the Spanish flu."

"You were in good company. You must find this place very lonely after London?"

"By choice." Anger made her hands shake as she poured the tea. In the month she had been here, no one had come to call except tradesmen: milkman, butcher, grocer, and the postman twice. Not a single neighbor. She had wanted solitude and found a ton of it. Until now. Now her privacy had been raped. She sat down on the lumpy, shrouded chair and sipped at the tea while trying to face down Miss Pimm's penetrating scrutiny. "How is Head Office?"

Miss Pimm pouted. "Licking our wounds."

"But you won, didn't you?"

"The result might best be described as a draw. We won in the West. We definitely lost Russia and we are seriously concerned about the Peace Conference. The struggle against evil continues; the Blighters have regrouped. They outwitted us with the Spanish flu."

"*That* was their doing too?"

"Indeed it was—influenza is not normally so deadly. It was an attempt to keep the Americans out of the war. It began in America, you know, and turned up in all forty-eight states within a week. It has already killed more people than the war did. It may not be over yet. Does that sound like ordinary flu to you?"

A tale so outrageous ought to defy belief but did not when spoken by Miss Pimm.

"Pestilence! The fourth horseman?"

"Quite. In the end, it backfired. It was the flu that crippled the German Army and ended the war." A thin, gloating smile came and went quickly.

"That is not true!"

"That is what General Ludendorff says." Miss Pimm dismissed the German High Command with a shrug. "But we did come out better in the war than we initially feared, yes."

The light from the window was failing. The fire threw the visitor's shadow on the wall, larger than life and ominously like the shape of a bird of prey. "Why Norfolk?" she demanded.

"I inherited this place. It has been in the Pearson family for generations." Irrelevant! Alice took another sip of tea, feeling its warmth running hot down inside her.

Miss Pimm eyed the ceiling acerbically. "Obviously none of them believed in paint. So why did you throw up your London job and bury yourself here in the swamps?"

That was absolutely none of her business, but one did not say such things to Miss Pimm.

"I'm not sure. The war was over. I needed a new start? Turn a new leaf? Or just postflu depression. Now, what news of Edward?"

Miss Pimm nodded briskly, as if agreeing that the time for small talk was now over and the meeting could get down to business. "He has apparently decided that he is Jesus Christ."

"I consider that remark to be in poor taste."

"Moses, then. Or Peter the Hermit. He is trying to fulfil the *Filoby* prophecy." Miss Pimm might have shed thirty years, but she had not shed her stranger's authority.

"He swore he never would."

"Apparently he has changed his mind."

"His privilege," Alice said carefully.

"Not if his whim endangers others, it isn't. We have a visitor from the Service, a Mrs. Euphemia McKay. She says that your cousin is now openly proclaiming himself the Liberator of the prophecy. He is going up and down the landscape preaching a religious revolution."

"*Edward* is?"

"Apparently."

"Well, I expect he has his reasons." Alice's memories of her cousin and foster brother were mostly memories of a boy, but she had seen a very strong-willed young man in 1917. He would not do anything lightly.

Miss Pimm sighed. "I am sure he does have reasons, and I must confess that my presence here today is largely prompted by sheer curiosity. I should love to hear what those reasons are. His father was most adamant that the Liberator gambit would be a grievous error, and from what I know of the matter, I tend to agree. That is irrelevant. Mrs. McKay was sent over because the Service are seriously worried. What Edward is doing could have catastrophic consequences for them."

"In what way?" Alice asked. And why should that concern her? Why, even, should it concern Edward? The Service had done nothing for him except shanghai him to Nextdoor and then frustrate his efforts to return Home. It had also tried to kill him—or one of its members had. She could not see that he had any obligations to the Service. She certainly did not.

"I believe they are mainly concerned that he will fail," Miss Pimm said thoughtfully, "and that their work to date will thereby be discredited. That is a charitable view. I could present less favorable hypotheses."

Alice decided not to pursue that train of thought. She did not like the direction this conversation was taking. "I am glad to hear that he is alive. It was kind of you to bring the news in person. Thank you." *Good-bye.*

Again, Miss Pimm's smile was fleeting but sinister. "Mrs. McKay crossed over to this world specifically to appeal to you for help."

"Me? How? Write a letter . . . No, that's not possible, is it? My help to aid Edward or try and stop him?"

"The latter."

"Why should I? I fail to see that whatever he is up to is any concern of mine."

"Or of mine. I am becoming a trifle peeved that the Service keeps appealing to us for help. We did not seek to involve them in our struggles with the Blighters."

That remark seemed irrelevant, so Alice ignored it. "He is of age. I have every confidence in his judgment."

"So do I. That is why I am curious." The admission was appealing, suddenly making Miss Pimm seem almost human . . . normal.

For a moment, neither spoke. It was Alice who looked away first, of course. She discovered that her cup was empty, but the effort of going for another was beyond her.

"The suggestion is absurd. For me to intrude on him, to presume to advise him, when he knows the situation—indeed the whole world—so much better than I do . . . it would be an intolerable presumption. I refuse. Please indicate to Mrs. McKay . . . Where is this Mrs. McKay?" Alice glanced uneasily at the door to her bedroom.

"I left her prostrate on a bed in the Bull in Norwich. She is suffering from lack of sleep, because Valian days do not coincide with ours at the moment. She also wanted to make a telephone call. You wish me to convey your regrets to the Service, then?"

Alice wondered if it was possible to shock this formidable lady. "You may tell them to go and get stuffed."

The basilisk expression did not change. "The sentiments, if not the precise phraseology, are exactly what I predicted."

Again, a silence, and this time longer. Miss Pimm appeared to be waiting for something, but Alice could not imagine what. She was certainly not going to go and wag her finger at Edward on behalf of strangers. Even if she knew all the facts, which she certainly did not, and even if she thoroughly disapproved of his actions, which she might, she would not presume to meddle. So what was there left to discuss?

"Have you anything planned for this evening?" Miss Pimm inquired softly.

Try to finish painting the ceiling and the cupboards, by the light of the paraffin lamp. Then open a tin of sardines or something for supper. Whatever it was, it would taste of turpentine. And then go to bed with a candle and *Wuthering Heights*. She could not even play the gramophone, because it was packed in under the bed behind her books and pictures and general paraphernalia. Come to think of, it the kitchen table and the rug were on top of the bed.

"Not much," Alice admitted.

"Then you shall come and have dinner with us at the Bull. I can bring you back afterward, if you wish."

Why should she not wish?

"The last time we met, you didn't drive."

"'Didn't' and 'couldn't' are not the same," Miss Pimm said firmly. She rose and headed for the teapot. "Go and change."

Alice opened her mouth and then closed it, knowing that arguing with a *stranger* was not likely to be productive. Besides, the thought of a decent meal in civilized surroundings had a definite appeal. She hauled herself out of the chair and walked across to put her cup and saucer in the sink.

"Don't," Miss Pimm added, "put on anything you would mind losing. Just in case you change your mind."

Alice swung around, fright and anger boiling up together. "Are you planning to abduct me? Is that what you're hinting? Because——"

"Of course not. If I planned a kidnapping, Mrs. Pearson, I should not have wasted all this time in conversation."

18

"MRS. MCKAY, MRS. PEARSON," MISS PIMM SAID.

Alice was cautious at first, unsure of the correct protocol. "I trust you had a comfortable journey?" seemed a peculiarly banal question to pose to a traveler from another world—but the mysterious Euphemia turned out to be extraordinarily ordinary, almost disappointing. Her dress was dowdy, her accent working-class Irish, and her manner decidedly unladylike. If she had been smitten by fatigue earlier, she had now recovered, for she sparkled with prankish humor, openly teasing Miss Pimm and making racy little remarks about the handsome soldiers she had seen hanging around the Bull. At a guess, she was in her very early twenties, but she had the confidence of a much older woman.

"The news was good?" Miss Pimm inquired archly.

"Oh, it was grand!" Mrs. McKay said. "They say he's doing just splendid. Telephones are marvelous, aren't they?"

The three ladies proceeded to the dining room. It was gloomy and low ceilinged, but it was warm and did not reek of turpentine. At this early hour they had the place to themselves and were granted a table next to the fire and tended by an antiquated and very deaf waiter. As soon as they sat down, Miss Pimm withdrew from the conversation, behaving as if she had cast an invisibility spell on herself. Mrs. McKay, in contrast, began chattering breezily about the rigors of occult travel, how wonderful it was to be Home in England, even if only for a brief stay, the disgraceful weather, the changes she had seen already, and the misfortunes of a couple named Pepper, who had won the lottery for the first postwar leave and had both been stricken with flu a few days after they arrived.

Olympus would not have sent an unprepossessing ambassador, and Alice soon realized that her first impressions had not done Euphemia justice. She was personable and witty in a sharp, juvenile way. If she would just get a fashionable haircut, if she weren't wearing too much powder, an ill-fitting dress of dowdy brown, and a rouge that clashed horribly with her coloring, then she would be quite a beauty. Men would probably regard her as a stunner already, for her hair was a cascade of fiery auburn and she had an impressive figure. To be fair, her makeup and clothing must be other peoples' castoffs, for she could have brought nothing with her from Nextdoor. Who was Alice to criticize when her own hair was full of paint?

The food was vastly better than wartime London had offered, although the only vegetables available in February were turnips and soggy potatoes. Alice gorged herself on roast pork, washing it down with an excellent white wine. Her indulgence in the wine might possibly be an aftereffect of Miss Pimm's driving—just because the old witch could see around corners did not mean that she had to keep proving the point—but by the time Alice realized that alcohol might be unwise under the circumstances, it was too late to care. Much to her surprise, she discovered she was enjoying herself more than she had in months.

Eventually, of course, Mrs. McKay got down to business. She confirmed what Miss Pimm had said about Edward—he had returned to Nextdoor in 1917, then walked out of the station and disappeared. Since then there had been no word of him at all. Now, according to reliable reports, he was openly preaching to the natives in some place called Joalvale, professing to be the foretold Liberator.

"He is taking a terrible risk," she proclaimed earnestly, although it sounded more like *turrible roosk.* "I just don't know why Zath and his gang did not kill him immediately. It may very well be too late already."

Too late to do what?

The green eyes widened—she really ought to try mascara on those sandy lashes. "You do know of the prophecies, Mrs. Pearson?"

"Roughly. Please call me Alice."

"And you must call me Euphemia!" Euphemia took a sip of wine, then leaned forward with a conspiratorially intent expression. Here came the grifter's patter. "You understand that what he's doing could have serious repercussions on the poor natives?"

Whose vocabulary was that? Not hers.

Alice said, "I know that Edward insisted he would not do what you say he is now doing. If he has changed his mind, then he must have good reasons for doing so. Did he take anyone with him when he left Olympus?" He had spoken of a girl Ysian, who had become somebody's cook. . . .

"Oh, no. Well, at least I don't think so." Either Mrs. McKay had never considered that possibility or she had not been briefed on it. "There was a lot of muddle just then, of course. . . ."

The query had thrown her off balance and Alice followed up her advantage. "Muddle? What can muddle a coven of sorcerers?"

"A what?" Looking startled, Euphemia took another drink of wine, then began to speak in her normal manner again, as if abandoning a prepared script. "We're not that! The Chamber attacked Olympus while Edward was away, and he was the first one back after it happened. Just terrible! The houses were all burned. We've only just got the place shipshape and Bristol fashion again. And there were deaths! Not all of us managed to escape in time. Several people were never accounted for. We think one of them was a spy who ran away with the killers, but I suppose it's possible that one of the others went off with Edward. . . . Why are you asking?"

Alice chewed for a moment while she tried to think of a tactful way of inquiring about Edward's possible romance. She couldn't find one. "It must have been quite a shock for him to cross over and find himself in that. And a worse shock for Captain Smedley." She had forgotten to ask for news of Julian.

"Oh, yes! They organized the Carrots to bury all the dead."

"*All* the dead? It was that bad?"

"Dozens! Only four of them were strangers, though."

"And natives don't count, of course?"

"They count with me!"

Oh lordy! "I beg your pardon. That was unforgivable. They would count with me, too, and I know they would with Edward. We were both raised in Africa, you know. . . ." As Alice struggled to extricate herself from her embarrassment, she noted that Mrs. McKay was blushing bright enough to make the rouge on her cheeks seem pale, but she was sure that she must be as pink herself. How could she have said such an appalling thing? *Alice, you have been drinking too much!*

Mercifully, the waiter arrived then and interrupted the conversation. When he hobbled away, leaving offerings of trifle, generously laced with sherry, Alice tried a fresh start.

"Doesn't one of the prophecies say that the dead will rouse him? The Liberator, I mean. Two years ago, I thought that referred to the dead he saw in Flanders, but perhaps the seeress meant the dead in Olympus?"

Mrs. McKay shrugged vaguely. "Oh, I don't pretend to be understanding the prophecies."

Dead plural, the massacred Carrots? Or *dead* singular, the girl Ysian? To ask that of this twittery woman would be a waste of time, but obviously something had roused Edward.

Two other parties entered the dining room and were seated. Euphemia seemed to have forgotten or postponed her mission, which Alice had begun to suspect mattered much less to her than the unexplained good news she had received earlier. She was tossing down wine wholesale, as if celebrating something more than a flying visit to England—not that Alice herself was far behind. Drinking had been frowned on during the war, but now it was all right again.

"It is wonderful to be Home again, even if it's so brief-like. The war must have been terrible?"

Yes, Alice found herself agreeing, it had been very bad. Millions had died. At the end, the flu had come and killed millions more. Even here in England, it had been bad—food shortages, bombs, the daily casualty lists, women working in factories, social upheaval.

"But it is getting better?" Euphemia demanded. "The men are coming back? Things are getting back to normal?"

"Things will never get back to normal, if you mean what was normal before the war." Somehow—was it the wine talking or reaction to the loneliness of the cottage?—Alice found herself describing the past bombings, the continuing shortages, and now the strikes, the frustrations, the eternal squabbling that filled the newspapers with gloom and made one wonder what good four years of slaughter and sacrifice had accomplished.

Euphemia made sympathetic noises, her green eyes wide. "And the war touched you personally?"

"Too personally."

"I was told to find a Miss Prescott. Of course, if you would rather not talk about it . . ."

"There is hardly anything to talk about," Alice said bitterly. "I was married for less than a week. I had lost a very dear friend in Flanders. He was killed in action the very day that Edward returned to Nextdoor. I married Terry on the rebound, one of those crazy wartime affairs. You probably won't understand. He was young and brave and terrified. They had this awful urgency, you see, this sense that every day might be their last. They were all so tough and so frightfully fragile at the same time." The wine drove her onward. "It sounds terrible to say, but it may have been for the— I don't mean that. It was tragic and I mourn him, of course. What I mean is just I can see now that our marriage was foolish, one of those impetuous wartime romances that might have turned out to be a mistake—"

She clenched her teeth as one might rein in a runaway horse. She had been starved for company so long that her mouth was going to make an ass of her if she gave it half a chance. So much had happened since that bewildering day when Miss Pimm had saved her life and Edward's with a display of magic. First D'Arcy, then Terry . . . It was D'Arcy she thought of most, still. Terry had been a transitory madness. The only thing they had had in common was a complete lack of family. A smile, an aura of vulnerability, a lightning romance, a wedding, five frenzied nights of love, a frantic farewell, a telegram . . . and a cottage.

"I inherited the cottage. It was all he had to leave, his grandfather's home. His ship went down six days after our wedding. A U-boat. I get a small pension. . . ." She felt guilty every time she spent a penny of it.

She stared down at her empty plate and bit her lip until the pain brought tears to her eyes. Then she took another drink. Her plate was removed. Cheese and biscuits and coffee arrived. The dining room buzzed with conversation, an unfamiliar sound.

After the silence, Euphemia said, "I am terribly, terribly sorry. Our troubles must all seem very trivial to you."

"No. Not at all. Tell me about Olympus itself. Edward was confoundedly vague about it, and he had so many other things to tell us."

"Olympus? It's a monkey house!"

Bewildered, Alice said, "In what way?"

Euphemia seemed to have second thoughts. "Oh, you know—outpost-of-Empire stuff. Exiles in the bush going wild-crazy from boredom. There's no other stations to visit, no big, fancy Port Said or Singapore within reach. The climate's so darlin' that we don't need to rush off to the hills in the hot season. The men can't go big-game hunting, because the only weapons around are bows and arrows. There are no letters from Home."

"And the *Times* is never delivered?"

"Never. Olympus is worse than a lighthouse. We inmates may not admit it, but at times we all became bored to madness. That's why the Service allows women to be missionaries, dear. Try leaving the little women at home all the time, and they get the crackers. We're bored, we gossip, we squabble. We—" Euphemia hesitated, then said bitterly, "Monkeys in a monkey house." She drained her wineglass.

"Oh!"

"The rules don't apply there, you see. We don't grow old. The fires don't cool. We don't settle into comfortable, down-at-heels middle age."

Alice was annoyed to discover that this frankness discomfited her. She liked to think of herself as modern. "Edward definitely did not mention that."

"Ha! No, he was different. Of course he wasn't there very long, but he was definitely the only man who ever refused Olga Olafson."

Nettled, Alice said, "I'm not surprised. His morals were always the most rigid thing about him."

Euphemia found that remark hilarious, and Alice laughed with her.

"To chastity!" Euphemia said, raising her glass, which had mysteriously re-filled itself.

Alice clinked it with her own. "In moderation!" They drank. "And how has Captain Smedley fared in Olympus?"

"Oh! Um. Jolly well. Just went off to see if he could help Mr. Exeter. Very popular . . ." Euphemia's already flushed complexion became noticeably pinker. "His hand is growing back, you know."

"No! Really?" Magic in a vague, general sense was hard enough to swallow, although Alice had seen enough of it now to believe in it. To associate a miracle with someone as ordinary and practical as Julian Smedley was somehow more difficult.

"Of course," Miss Pimm said quietly. The other women both jumped, as if they had forgotten she was there. "Did you ever doubt that it would, Mrs. Pearson?"

"Yes."

"You should have more faith! A stranger can always heal himself—or herself." She skewered Alice with an extremely disconcerting stare. Had she grown taller since the evening began or was that just an illusion?

"What—what do you mean?"

"I mean that what you need is a nice tropical vacation."

"Me?"

"You. Soldiers are not the only people who suffer from battle fatigue. The whole world is suffering from battle fatigue. You have experienced two bereavements in eighteen months. You lost your uncle not long before that, and you thought your cousin also. I suspect your encounter with the Spanish flu was more serious than you admit. Your decision to seclude yourself here in Norfolk was probably very sound, but the vacation I have suggested would be a better alternative."

Battle fatigue? Shell shock? Alice had never thought of applying those sinister terms to herself. They seemed like a very glib excuse. What she had experienced was nothing to compare with the hell the men in the trenches had endured. " 'Nervous breakdown,' we used to call it."

"The name does not matter," Miss Pimm said firmly. "'Emotional exhaustion,' would suffice, and you are probably badly run-down physically, also. So why not a holiday—all expenses paid? A few weeks in exotic surroundings? Perhaps not quite as relaxing as a Mediterranean cruise, but probably more enjoyable at this time of year. It is late autumn in the Vales, but the weather will be clement."

"Much better than this," Euphemia agreed hopefully.

Alice struggled to adjust to the concept of holidaying on another world. Her mind slithered helplessly, like a puppy on an icy pond.

"Very beneficial for the convalescent," Miss Pimm remarked. "Of course, if you do decide to go on and see Edward, the journey may be strenuous. The Vales are a more primitive land than England, so it would be foolish to deny that there may be risks, but no more than you would incur on a safari in Kenya or yachting on the Broads, for that matter. At this time of year you would have to travel on dragonback. A chance to meet your only living relative?"

"But I refuse to—"

"I do not believe the Service's invitation has any strings attached to it. You can make it quite clear that you do not commit yourself to supporting any particular viewpoint in the dispute. Is that not correct, Mrs. Mackay?"

Euphemia started to shake her head and then nodded uncertainly.

"Jolly good!" Miss Pimm said as if the matter was settled. "And if you do agree to go and see your cousin, you can explain your motives to him. I am sure he will accept them and be very glad to see you again."

The dining room rocked in waves of unreality and disbelief. To hear Edward talk of crossing over to other worlds had been bad enough. For Alice to consider actually doing so herself was a unicorn of another color.

She glanced suspiciously at Euphemia, who seemed to be having trouble keeping up with the conversation. "What guarantee do I have that I shall be allowed to return?"

Miss Pimm pursed her lips. "I can give you mine. The Service personnel are all eager for Home leave, now that the war is over. For that they require our cooperation. If you do not return in a month or so—or whatever time you stipulate beforehand—then I can arrange for serious consequences. Take hostages, in effect. We can set up a code message for you to send me if you wish to remain longer."

Gibber! Alice thought of the cottage: dark, damp, dingy, and drear. No one would care whether she finished the painting now or months from now—or never. No job. No friends who would notice her absence unless it was prolonged. Why could she not jump at this incredible offer?

Miss Pimm frowned. "I honestly do not believe that the Service will make trouble for you. They are basically decent people, perhaps a little out of their depth at the moment."

Euphemia said, "Ha!" and emptied her wineglass.

Alice drained her coffee cup. Outside was rain, loneliness, mud, and skeletal, leafless trees. To see a warm, tropical land again! How long since she had enjoyed a real holiday? She could not recall one, not ever. A week now and again visiting great-aunts at Bournemouth. Stolen weekends with D'Arcy before the war. The fire hissed and smoked.

"The milkman," she muttered. "The butcher . . ."

"Your bills are all paid up? We can go past the cottage on our way. You will leave a note on the door, requesting no deliveries until further notice."

"An invitation to burglars?"

"I can make the cottage secure against intruders. Now, is it settled?"

Alice looked doubtfully at Euphemia. "As long as I am not committing myself. I trust Edward. I won't betray him."

℘℘ 19 ℘℘

OMBAY FALA, INKUTHIN . . .

They had not long left the cottage for the second time, passing through Norwich again and heading southwest toward Cambridge, when Alice's sense of collapsing reality made her wonder if her mind had come unhinged completely. Or was the wine wearing off? She huddled in the back of the car with Euphemia McKay, while Miss Pimm drove like a maniac through the night. Rain streamed on the windscreen, mocking the wipers' efforts to clear it; the fancy electric headlights showed nothing ahead but silvery torrents.

Indu maka, sasa du.

Teeth chattering, slapping her hands on her knees to beat time, Euphemia was attempting to teach Alice the words of the key, the age-old chant that would open the portal at St. Gall's and lead them through to another world. Alice could recall a similar drive, a year and a half ago, when it had been Miss Pimm instructing Edward and Julian in the same gibberish. Words from before the dawn of history, a complex, troubling rhythm. But that had been a sun-baked summer afternoon and the driver had been the solid, sane Mr. Stringer. He did not overtake on blind hills in pitch darkness or cut corners on the wrong side of the road.

"*Hosagil!*" Euphemia cried triumphantly. "That's the first verse. You want to try it now?"

No, Alice did not want to try it. Alice wanted to go home to her lonely hermitage and jump into bed and pull the blankets over her head. She wanted this insanity to stop. Now! Instantly. The wine had scrambled her brains or she would never have agreed to this madness. Vacation on another world? They had no luggage, either of them. They weren't going anywhere. They couldn't be. It was all just a gigantic hoax; it must be. Now the wine was wearing off, she could see that.

"Let me try it one line at a time first, please."

"Right-oh!" Euphemia chirped. "*Ombay fala, inkuthin.*"

"*Ombay fala, inkuthin.*"

In Cambridge they were going to pick up Bill and Betsy Pepper, the couple who had come Home from Nextdoor on leave and then succumbed to the flu that still lurked around England. Euphemia had explained at great length how the poor Peppers' failure to return on time had made them very unpopular back at Olympus.

Bugger the poor Peppers! Why, oh why, had Alice ever consented to this?

> "*Aiba aiba nopa du, Aiba reeba mona kin.*
> *Hosagil!*"

"Now the second verse—"

"Just a minute. Shouldn't I learn this beat you're doing, too?"

"Oh, you'll pick that up. Miss Pimm will drum for us. Won't you, Miss Pimm?"

The car tilted into a corner and slewed sideways before accelerating again into the rushing, silver-streaked darkness. Alice's half-formed scream failed as she realized she was still alive.

"Do you *have* to go so fast?"

"Yes, I do!" Miss Pimm said loudly. "We have a long way to go. We must complete our mission, and I must be gone, before the locals wake up and notice odd things going on."

Odd things? Neolithic shamanism in this day and age? In a *church?*

"The vicar will be celebrating matins," Miss Pimm added, as if that excused everything.

"St. Gall's is still in use," Euphemia said cheerfully. "The center of the node is right in front of the altar, but there are some standing stones in the churchyard. It's been a holy place for thousands of—"

"I know. I've been there."

"Oh, yes. You said."

Alice had witnessed Edward and Julian go into that church. To the best of her knowledge, they had never come out. It was in the Cotswolds, somewhere. That was right across England: Cambridge, then probably through Northampton, and Oxford. Wiltshire? It was going to take hours.

"Let me get this straight. We dance and chant, and then the magic comes and we find ourselves on Nextdoor? Just like that?"

"Just like that. One second you're in St. Gall's, and the next you're on the node at Olympus. On a lawn with a hedge round it."

In Colney Hatch with a straitjacket on, more likely.

"There will be four of us," Euphemia continued blithely. "It's much easier with a group. Coming over I was all alone and it was frightfully hard. It took me at least twenty minutes before I could catch the mood. I was absolutely fagged out, all that dancing. . . . Now the second verse—"

"Just a minute! If Miss Pimm's doing the drumming, what's to stop her passing over with the rest of us?"

"It's happened," Miss Pimm bellowed from the front. "The wrong person going through, I mean." She swerved to avoid a suicidal lone cyclist fighting his way against the wind and rain with no light on his bicycle. "But I shall stay well back from the center of the node, and I shan't be singing or dancing."

Pagan orgies in a respectable rural Anglican church?

"Besides," Euphemia added, and the tremor of amusement in her voice should have been a warning of what was coming, "Miss Pimm will have her clothes on."

"What? You mean we have to . . . in this weather?"

"Oh, yes. So let's learn our chant, shall we, so that everything goes off smoothly and quickly and we don't have to hang around too long."

"No clothes at all?"

"Not a stitch. But it will be almost dark. Don't worry about Bill. He's done this lots of times and seen everything there is to see. First verse again. . . ."

20

THE NIGHT WENT ON FOREVER, TO THE LIMITS OF UNREALITY AND FATIGUE and then beyond, into total madness. As morning neared, Alice found herself cavorting around with three other lunatics before the altar of a respectable little country church, an ancient, down-at-the-heels conventional place of worship like a thousand others scattered over the face of England. The first rays of dawn showed the tints of stained glass in the eastern windows, the glimmer of a sputtering acetylene lantern cast wild shadows over oak and flagstone and memorial tablets.

And this was only the dress rehearsal! She mumbled the gibberish as well as she could, she copied the others' movements as the four of them leaped and gestured and gyrated, dancing around in a circle between the pulpit and the front row of pews. Miss Pimm sat farther back, thumping intricate rhythms on a drum. No one else seemed to recognize the insanity of what they were doing. None of them even seemed to see that it was rank sacrilege.

Alice never thought of herself as religious. What her true parents had believed, she could not remember. Uncle Cam and Aunt Rona had been upright, moral people, but not members of any formal sect. They had taught her that deeds mattered more than words, that love and duty counted more than ritual or any specific creed. Like Edward, she had been repelled by the overt fire-and-brimstone dogmas preached at them by their Uncle Roland. She had entered a church only once in many years, and that had been only because Terry had wanted a Christian marriage. She had mourned him without clerical assistance.

Nevertheless, St. Gall's was a church, a place of worship sanctified by the devotions of humble, honest people over many centuries. To profane it with this mumbo jumbo was not merely disrespectful, it was horribly wrong. The sense of wrongness grew steadily stronger until she felt she could endure it no more. She was just about to stop dancing and say so, when Miss Pimm ended her tattoo.

"That will do. We'll try it now."

Alice said, "But . . ." and then her courage failed her. She stifled her protest and followed the others back to the vestry, picking her way along the dark nave by the light of the lamp Euphemia was carrying. She waited at the door with the other women while Bill Pepper went inside. She averted her eyes when he emerged without his clothes. She kept telling herself that she had had enough, that she was not going to play this stupid game any longer, and yet she entered with Euphemia and Betsy—who still had a racking cough and certainly ought not to be exposing herself to the icy cold in this unheated church on a rainy February night. Cursing herself for a dupe, a gullible maniac, Alice undressed with them and hurried back to the altar when they did, shivering at the touch of dank air on her skin and the cold stones underfoot. If it been wrong before, how much worse it must be now!

"Ready?" Miss Pimm boomed, and began the beat without waiting for a reply.

"*Ombay fala, inkuthin . . .*"

Jump, twist, wave arms.

"*Indu maka, sasa du . . .*"

Mr. Pepper was a tall, hollow-chested man, but he had an astonishingly loud bass voice. Supposing some early riser happened to be passing the church and saw the light of the lantern flickering through the stained-glass windows or heard the drumming and all this gibberish? Next thing anyone knew, the police would be at the door. The gutter press would shriek about satanic orgies. Bare limbs and torsos writhed like pale ghosts in the darkness. It was wrong! It was sacrilege. It was obscene.

With no warning, the gloom split, as if the fabric of reality had ripped. A brilliant jagged rent opened overhead, too bright to look upon. It spread instantly, down beside the pulpit, across the floor, dividing the world in two halves. The ground vanished below Alice's feet and she fell through into hot daylight, rolled on grass. A wrench of anguish twisted through her. She screamed and heard others screaming also. Brightness blinded her. Pain, despair . . . Then someone enveloped her in a blanket and hugged her tight, lying beside her, clasping her.

"It will be all right, *entyika,*" said a gruff female voice in her ear. "I will hold you and it will pass in a minute."

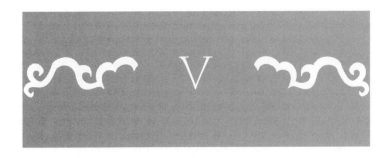

V

Where are the fiends? Where are the worshippers of the fiends? Where is the place
whereon the fiends rush together? What is the
place whereon the troops of the fiends come
rushing along?

THE ZEND-AVESTA: VENDÎDÂD, FARGARD VII, 8

21

DOSH HAD NOT VISITED RINOOVALE SINCE HIS CHILDHOOD. BRACED against the wind on a vantage where Lampass road emerged in Rinooslope, he stared down at the flats with disgust, seeing it as even bleaker than he remembered—a small, drab basin wedged in the teeth of gigantic peaks. Cowering under those terrible white fangs, the land was more gray than green, smallholdings and pastures struggling to survive between the mounds of slag that would eventually engulf them all, tiny isolated hovels spread like pepper grains, plumes of dust drifting from the active mines. He thought he could recall trees, but there were no trees now. The only touches of color were specks of lurid reds or purples on the slimy, poisonous ponds in abandoned workings. At the hazy limit of vision, he thought he could make out a village. That must be the only real settlement in the vale, the self-proclaimed city of Rinoo, where the Niolian military governor ruled.

Of more immediate interest, sunlight was flashing off a troop of bronze-mailed soldiers about half a mile ahead at the base of the long descent. They were lined up across the trail, so the Liberator's entrance was going to be disputed. This would be interesting. Would D'ward loose the Warband on them or talk his way through or turn back? Having no weapons other than his fingernails, Dosh did not intend to get involved, but it would be interesting to watch.

He turned away, blinking back tears and wishing he had more clothes than one threadbare rag. Twice in his life he had gone adventuring with D'ward Liberator, and twice he had ended up poor as beggars' lice. Some people never learn.

To his left, the Warband had come to a halt on the top of a little knoll and formed up around the leader. That seemed to be the warriors' main task—to keep the crowds away from D'ward when he wanted some peace. The rest of the time, he was buried in eager pilgrims, mobbed by them. Dosh had not spoken with him since he had joined the Free. He had just hung back and watched, trying to understand this madness. He sat on the edge of the crowd when D'ward preached, which he did two or three times a day. He was a wonderful speaker, of course. In the old days, Dosh had watched him inspire an army often enough, and he was even better now.

He spoke Joalian like a native, but if anyone addressed a question to him in Niolian, he would reply in that tongue. He was very slick at answering trick questions. He told stories. He uttered homilies, enjoining faith, humility, honesty, chastity, and other absurdities. He disapproved of fun things like lechery, avarice, and gluttony. He quoted the *Filoby* prophesies that he would bring death to Zath, so that there would be no more reapers collecting souls by night. Much of what he said was pure blasphemy, denying the gods, the Pentatheon and all their lesser avatars. He insisted that they were merely mortals with magical powers, sorcerers. That should have provoked his listeners to riot and stone him to death, but so far they hadn't. A surprising number of them seemed to believe him and believe in him.

Dosh couldn't. He knew something of the gods; he did not like all of them and he hated the Youth especially, but he knew enough to fear them. He would love to believe D'ward's claptrap heresy, but he could not. It would be even more wonderful to be able to swallow the Liberator's idealistic moral drivel, but he knew too much of the world, and it just wasn't like that. The world was made up of wolves and sheep, and wolves could not eat grass, no matter who preached to them. He wasn't about to tell D'ward that, though.

And he certainly would not say so to Prat'han or the other henchmen. Dosh's only contact with the Sonalby Warband had been when he dropped in at their campfires to eat. They fed him willingly, kidded him a little, and in general were friendly enough. They had concealed him from the troopers. They even seemed prepared to trust him, but he was not at all sure he trusted them. Their fanatical faith in the Liberator proved that they were all crazy, and a prudent man did not consort with armed lunatics.

From habit, Dosh had kept himself to himself. He had been a loner all his life, a man of unnumbered lovers and no friends. Now Prat'han Potter was heading his way, striding purposefully over the grass, tall and dangerous with his spear and shield. Evidently he had been sent to summon Dosh. Dosh waited for trouble to arrive in its own good time.

Behind them, the ass end of the procession was still trickling down the trail from the pass—the runts, the women with babies, the old men on canes, the cripples and invalids. The Free had increased in Nosokvale; there must be half a thousand people following the Liberator now. Most of them had no food and no money. Many of them were wearing no more than Dosh was. They were going to pour into barren little Rinoovale like a plague of locusts if the soldiers let them. If the soldiers turned them back, they would starve or freeze in the hills. Winter was coming.

"Greetings, Brother Dosh!" Prat'han boomed. It was still surprising to see a Nagian warrior without face paint.

"Greetings to you, Troopleader."

"I am no troopleader. The Liberator is our leader. I am but one of the Free, like you." The big man grounded his shield and surveyed the vale. "You been here before?"

"Long ago."

"What place is that?" The spear pointed.

"Rinoo."

"That's the city?" Prat'han snorted. "That? Who owns the temple there?"

"There isn't one that I know of. Just a few shrines. There's a temple a few miles east of Rinoo, though, to Gunuu. He's god of courage, an avatar of the Youth."

"No gods!" Prat'han snapped menacingly. "Enchanters. Imposters, all of them!"

"If you say so."

"D'ward says so! That's good enough for me, and for you now."

One of Dosh's personal rules was not to argue with armed young men more than three feet tall, and Prat'han was twice that. "Sure. The main, er, enchanter's foundation in Rinoovale is the convent of Irepit."

Prat'han sneered. "And what does she claim to be?"

"Goddess of repentance. You've heard of the Daughters of Irepit?"

"No. And I do not wish to. The Liberator wants you."

Obviously Dosh had no choice. They began to walk back up the knoll.

"What's the matter with this land?" his companion demanded. "It looks like a well-used feedlot."

"It is overblessed with mineral wealth. Dig anywhere and you turn up nuggets of gold and other metals, even jewels."

"A waste of good grazing."

"Niolians don't think so. They strip it down to the water table, so nothing ever grows again. Why don't you ask D'ward these questions? He's been here more recently than I have."

The warrior glanced down at Dosh suspiciously. "How do you know?"

"Well, I assume he has."

Prat'han thought about that and frowned. "Don't *assume* about the Liberator." End of conversation.

To anyone with less muscle and more brain than an ox, it was obvious that D'ward knew exactly where he was going, in precise detail. He chose the damnedest places to make camp, but he set off every morning straight to the next. Some days he would walk his ragged congregation to exhaustion and others he would hardly go any distance at all. If Dosh were a gambling man—and he must assume that now he wasn't, at least not at the moment—he would bet everything he owned—which was currently nothing, of course—that D'ward had walked out his entire route from Joalvale to Tharg in advance, using the *Filoby Testament* as a guidebook.

When Dosh had first met him, he had known almost none of the prophecies. He must know them all by now. He must know the one that said, *In Nosokslope they shall come to D'ward in their hundreds, even the Betrayer.* Dosh himself had joined the Free in Nosokslope.

He reached the outskirts of the crowd behind Prat'han and began to pick his way through. Whenever D'ward stopped moving, a halo of followers would gather on the grass around him, sitting patiently, their numbers steadily growing as the stragglers arrived and settled at the edges. The Warband stood guard in the center, clustered around D'ward, who was sitting on a rock, talking as always. His gray robe flapped and billowed in the wind, he had his cowl up, and yet he seemed oddly hunched, as if he felt the chill more than the men around him, who were all nearly naked.

Seeing Dosh slipping in between the shields, he jumped up with a smile. He grabbed Dosh's shoulder in a Nagian greeting.

"Welcome! How are you feeling?"

"Cold and hungry and poor."

D'ward grinned, as if truly pleased to see him. "But not hunted? You've been lying low! But we're not in Joaldom anymore. If you want to slide over the horizon, now's your chance."

Dosh glanced at the frowning faces of the Warband all around him. Even the smallest of them was at least a hand taller than he was. "With no clothes and no money? You think I'm crazy?"

"I think you're just fine. Tielan? Give him the bag."

As if he had been expecting the order, Tielan Trader stepped forward, pulling a strap over his head. He handed Dosh a leather satchel—small, well worn, and so unexpectedly heavy that Dosh almost dropped it. He looked up at the Liberator in bewilderment.

"From now on," D'ward said, "you hold our purse."

"What do you mean? This is money?"

D'ward nodded, seeming amused. "That's the war chest of the Free. It's everything we've got. You can look after it for us."

"How do you know I won't vanish with it?"

"I don't, but I'm willing to gamble." His blue eyes sparkled brighter than the sky. "Most of it was yours originally, you know. We pass the hat after the sermons, and just about every coin you gave away came back eventually."

Why did he have to say so? Oh, temptation!

"And what do I do with it?" The warrior animals were scowling at him because he was talking back to their precious Liberator.

D'ward shrugged. "Keep it safe."

"Set a thief to catch a thief?"

"Of course. Everyone has his own talents, Dosh. You can count, which some people can't. You still got those great legs you had once?"

Dosh had done no real running since those far-off days when he had been D'ward's messenger; his feet were soft and already blistered, but he wasn't going to say so in front of the louts. "Sure."

D'ward smiled as if he saw through that lie. "Then when we get down to Rinooflat, I want you to run on ahead to Rinoo. Tonight we'll camp at the burial ground at Thothby—"

"Burial ground? Why camp in a burial ground?"

The answer was a flicker of authority from those sky-blue eyes. Dosh's spine chilled all the way down. "Sorry," he muttered.

"All right." The Liberator scanned the vagabond army sitting patiently around the knoll. "How many are there now, do you suppose?"

"Five or six hundred. At least."

"Well, it's your job to feed them tonight. Buy livestock, buy grain, buy firewood—arrange for it all to be delivered to Thothby. There's no village left, but they'll know where it was. All right?"

Dosh nodded. He could run to Rinoo, certainly. Then perhaps just keep on running? He would decide when he got there. "You still have to get us down to Rinooflat safely."

"Ah!" D'ward said, and pushed back his cowl so he could scratch his head. "I was just explaining when you got here. There isn't going to be any trouble. I had a safe-conduct for Joalvale and Nosokvale. I've got another for Rinoovale. Once we get to Niolvale, things may get sticky." He glanced around at the listening warriors. "That's when you sharpen your spears."

" 'bout time!" said Gopaenum and the others laughed nervily. Did they know verse 663, the one about young men's bones?

"Safe-conduct from whom?" Dosh demanded.

D'ward hesitated and then replied to the group, not just to Dosh. "The authorities. Not all the enchanters are totally bad. Remember that always—nobody is totally bad! Nobody is totally good, either, of course. Some of the enchanters are on our side. A few of them are helping us." He looked around the Warband to locate Prat'han, who was the senior, even if he would not admit it. "Remember, no bloodshed!" His eyes glinted mischievously. "But perhaps we can start to stir up a little trouble now."

Prat'han chuckled throatily. "What sort of trouble, Liberator?"

D'ward scratched his bushy black locks again. "Only the Thargians keep slaves, right? Do any of you know who those miners are down there?"

Silence. These Sonalby rustics knew of nothing outside Nagvale.

"Convicts," Dosh said.

D'ward turned a sky-blue smile on him. "And what does it take to become a convict in Niolland?"

"Forgetting to bow when the queen's name is mentioned? Life sentence in the mines! Having a pretty wife that some official fancies? Ten years for that, I expect."

"Probably. With time off for good behavior on her part? Understand, lads? Rinooland is nothing but a Niolian penal colony. Now, if a multitude of pilgrims like this just happened to swarm right through one or two of those pits on their way by, then I don't think the jailers would be able to do very much about it, do you? And there might not be any miners left when we'd gone by, right?"

The oafs all guffawed and thumped their spears against their shields.

D'ward grinned at them. "But, please, no bloodshed! Stun them if you must. No more than that. Recruit them if you can. They'll be in deep trouble with their superiors after we've gone, so they may be open to reason. . . . I think we've had a long enough break. Let's move on. I'd better stay in front this time."

At that he strode forward and the Warband opened to let him through. The massed pilgrims began scrambling to their feet, some of them running forward to accost the Liberator and ask him questions. D'ward waved them away, the warriors blocked them, and soon most of them had been left behind. Very conscious of the weight of the money bag on his shoulder, Dosh found himself hurrying along at D'ward's side, while the armed band escorted them both. That might not be a good place to be when they reached the checkpoint at the bottom of the hill, but it would do for now.

He asked the question. "What do you really want of me?"

The Liberator looked down at him for a moment in silence, his stare strangely frightening.

"Bagman?" Dosh demanded. "Runner, like before? I'm not a kid any longer, D'ward."

"More than those, Dosh. I think you have a really important part to play in this." Suddenly D'ward smiled, and it was as if the heavens had opened. "Just be a friend, if you want. You're under no compulsion to stay, but I do hope you will."

Dosh looked away to break the spell. Time had not blunted his feelings toward the Liberator. D'ward could still melt the flesh off his bones with that smile. *Idiot! He didn't want you even before you started going bald.*

"What happens when you get to Niolvale itself?" Dosh was surprised to realize how little he doubted that the Free *would* get to Niolvale, despite that army ahead blocking their path.

For a moment D'ward stalked on down the track, staring straight ahead and not replying. His bony features seemed oddly shadowed. He still had his cowl back, and the sun glinted on his black hair like starlight. "That's when we start playing the Great Game with real money."

"Verse six sixty-three says that in Niolvale the bones of young—"

"I know that, Dosh. I just hope it won't be too many young men. The trouble will start in Niolvale, though. There must be visitors on their way to see me by now. The kings and politicians are starting to take notice. More than all that, Niolland is Visek's turf. Visek can nip me in the bud if he wants."

Visek the Parent, Father and Mother of Gods, greatest in the Pentatheon, patron deity of Niolvale, god of destiny, god of prophecy . . . The Liberator was not going to bring death to Death if Holy Visek did not want him to.

"So you'll go and pray to Visek?"

"I may go and have a chat with Visek. Not quite the same."

"But you do cooperate with the gods when you want to?"

"They're not gods, Dosh. Just enchanters, sorcerers, magicians."

"Tion? Or Prylis? He cured my scars!"

"That doesn't make him a god. He's at least a thousand years old, I agree, but he's human. They all are. They can die, as Zath will die when I kill him. They will all die one day. They were born of woman, every one of them—wet and bloody and screaming, just like us. One day they will die, whimpering and frightened, just like us."

"They are gods!"

D'ward shook his head sadly. "No, they're not. They want you to think they're gods, because that gives them power. When you believe they are gods, you expect them to judge you. Accept that they're mortals and you can judge them. Some things they say are true always. Some aren't true, ever. And some were true once and now aren't true anymore. Watch out for those. Those are the tricky ones."

It took Dosh some time to think through the words and discover that they didn't mean anything much. "Forget Visek. What about Elvanife?"

"Who? Oh, the queen?"

"Yes, the queen of Niolia! She's just a kid. Too young, and female."

D'ward shot a puzzled glance down at him. "Why does that matter, Dosh?" Sometimes he seemed incredibly naive.

"It matters because she's not safe on her throne! The nobles are conspiring against her. Haven't you heard? She's been throwing her weight around, showing how tough she is, stamping out dissent. You're going to present her with a peasant revolt! She'll have no choice but to jump on you."

D'ward shrugged. "She'll do what the priests tell her, I hope, and the priests will tell her what Visek tells them to tell her."

Maybe, but then Dosh realized that they were almost at the base of the hill and there was someone else stalking along on D'ward's other side. He hadn't seen where she had come from. She was tall, shrouded in a long blue nun's habit, her face concealed by a voluminous blue hat whose flaps tied under her chin. At her side dangled a long, shiny naked sword, so she must be a nun from the convent he had mentioned to Prat'han, one of the Daughters of Irepit. They had a very sinister reputation. D'ward must know she was there, yet he was ignoring her.

They had almost reached the roadblock. Dosh tried to ease back, only to discover there were spears and shields close behind him. He was trapped out in front, where he had vowed not to be at this point. The Warband was at his heels, but there were only twenty of them, whereas the force facing him was at least a hundred shiny bastards, all glittering with bronze, their shields blocking the way like a wall. Each man was set with one foot forward, javelin poised to throw. Their leader waited a couple of paces in front of them, sword drawn.

Niolia was not engaged in any war at the moment, so far as Dosh had heard, and only when engaged in active hostilities would a ruler muster the peasants. This must be a sizable portion of Elvanife's permanent army, the Royal Niolian Guard.

"Halt in the name of the queen!"

D'ward halted. Everyone halted. Dosh pressed his knees together to steady them and glanced around to plan his escape. There was no cover anywhere. Good legs or not, if he took off over that stony plain, he was going to have an ash shaft sticking out of his back in seconds. The pilgrims, he noted, were well behind the Warband now, waiting to see what would happen. If it came to bloodshed, they weren't going to throw any stones to help their precious prophet.

D'ward drew a deep breath and then out-bellowed the captain. "Stand aside! I am the Liberator."

"Turn around and liberate elsewhere! You and your followers are forbidden entry to Nioldom, on pain of death."

"It is prophesied that I shall go to Tharg and bring death to Death."

"Go another way, then. I shall count to three. *One!*"

In the terrible silence, Dosh could feel the sweat running down his ribs. D'ward seemed to have run out of bright ideas. The way the wind played with his curls was very appealing, but it wasn't going to be enough to get him past the Niolian military.

"Two!"

Dosh prepared to throw himself flat.

The nun laughed. "Well? Do you want my help after all?"

D'ward sighed. "Yes please, ma'am."

She took a step forward. She had her sword in her hand and she raised it, pointing it straight at the captain. Dosh didn't think he could have held such a weight steady, but the point was not wavering. In a voice as strong as the men's she cried, "Repent!"

It was if the soldier had not noticed her until then. He started violently and dropped his sword. It fell on the stones with a clang. His lips moved, but no sound emerged. Behind him, the bristling ranks of javelins wavered, their blades glittering like shards of ice in the sunlight.

"Repent!" she cried again. "You dare oppose the Liberator who is prophesied? Rather you should join his ranks and march in his service. Repent, I say! Throw down your arms or die on them. Stand aside!"

The captain spun around and screamed orders. The Royal Niolian Guard dissolved in panic. In seconds the road was clear, while on either hand men were tearing off their armor and hurling it down on the weapons that now littered the ground.

"Thank you, ma'am," D'ward said quietly.

She glanced at him. Dosh had a brief view of a face both surprisingly youthful and yet ageless, beautiful but stern—sad, lovely, unforgettable. "I keep my word. Go with my blessing, Liberator."

He nodded, then raised his arms in benediction, hiding the nun from Dosh's view. He called out to the soldiers over the clatter of metal and the moans of fear.

"Brothers! We are the Free, for we go to bring death to Death. Your repentance has been accepted; you are forgiven. Those who wish to join our pilgrimage are welcome. Leave your weapons, arise, and follow me."

He began to move and at once pebbles rattled under the Warband's horny feet behind him. Dosh was butted forward by a shield, so that he had no choice but to follow. Smiling, D'ward marched along the road, his arms outstretched to the Niolian military that knelt on both verges. A few were still armored, many had stripped almost naked, almost all of them were sobbing with terror, hands reaching out to the Liberator and beseeching his blessing. The blue nun was nowhere to be seen. A horde of excited pilgrims came yelling and jabbering along behind.

Thus did the Liberator enter into Rinoovale and Nioldom.

〜 22 〜

LOSPASS, BETWEEN JURGVALE AND NIOLVALE, WAS NEITHER VERY STEEP nor very high, one of the easiest passes in the Vales. Sloths, on the other hand, were well named. If they moved faster than mushrooms, it was not by much. Eleal Singer and Piol Poet had been on their journey for several days, and only now were they truly into Niolvale. The air was muggy, scented with a vegetable odor that seemed alien to her. In her childhood, the troupe had rarely visited Niolland. Most years they had returned home to Jurgvale from Jiolvale by way of Fionvale.

Piol had been clever to suggest the sloth and cart. As they rattled out through the city gate of Jurg, Eleal had seen a couple of the Cherry Blossom House bouncers inspecting passersby, but they had not looked twice at her or her malodorous conveyance. She was used to the stench of the sewerberries now, although they had nauseated her for the first couple of days. They certainly deterred everyone else. Other people went by the wagon like birds in flight, no brigand had accosted them to poke through their cargo in search of gold. Niolians used sewerberries to make the patina on their famous black bronzes, Piol said, and only Jurgvale could grow them. No matter. No matter, either, that the travelers were both so saturated with the foul stench that no inn would admit them. They had been blessed with fair weather; they had slept under the stars or under the cart, and they had eaten as well as could be expected when Eleal herself was doing the cooking.

Now they were in Niolland, the sun shone, the road stretched out level before them, winding between little lakes, fording streams. Niolvale had more water than any other vale, Piol said. Men wearing only turbans were harvesting rice from paddy fields. The villages were blobs of white walls and red tiled roofs against the green and silver landscape. It was very idyllic.

But not too helpful.

Eleal awoke from a wonderful daydream of . . . of what? She wasn't sure. Her nights were full of dreams of D'ward, but a strangely changed D'ward—thick and chunky, instead of tall and lean, and wearing a floppy mustache. Lack of sleep seemed to be catching up with her, for the curiously wrong image had started haunting her days too.

A fragment of melody surfaced and then submerged again. . . . The name escaped her.

"Piol?"

"Mm?"

"Do you know a play called *The Poisoned Kiss?*"

The old man blinked at her. "No. Who wrote it?"

"I have no idea. Perhaps there isn't one. I just thought it sounded like a good title. Um . . . Where does one start looking for a Liberator?"

"Don't know. There is only one road, so we may as well stay on it until it forks. Then we ask someone, I suppose."

"Who will let you near them?"

He chuckled toothlessly. "I can stand downwind."

True. She looked around. Niolwall was retreating behind them. To the east it disappeared completely and the bottom of the sky was flat. Niolvale was the largest of all the Vales, rich and prosperous—as was only to be expected of a vale whose patron god was the Parent. There was a village ahead, with a high-spired temple. It must be Joobiskby, and the road would certainly divide there.

After a few minutes, Piol began to cackle softly to himself. She demanded to know what was so funny.

"Remember the time we were playing *The Fall of the House of Kra* in Noshinby? Trong was playing Rathmuurd and he went to draw his sword—"

"No!" Eleal said firmly. "I do not remember that and I certainly do not know who had put the molasses in his scabbard. She must have been a real little horror, though!"

They laughed together. They had been doing this for days—reminiscing about the old times, the good times, the plays, the actors, the places, the crowds, the triumphs, the catastrophes.

After a moment, she said, "Do you remember Uthiam doing *Ironfaib's Polemic?* She won a rose. . . . That was the year I missed the festival, but I shall never forget her in rehearsal. Oh, she was marvelous!"

"That she was," Piol agreed sadly. "Do you know it?"

"Most of it, I expect." Every word!

"Let me hear it."

"Oh, you don't need to suffer through that," Eleal said hastily. She had just remembered that the reason she had missed seeing Uthiam perform at that festival was because she had been away tending D'ward, which was probably why the lines had come to her mind.

"Look!" she said. Two ancient, harmless-seeming peasants were tottering along the road ahead of them, moving even more slowly than the sloth. "Why don't you go and ask them if they've heard any news of the Liberator?" When she thought Piol might argue, she added, "You can easily catch up with the cart again if you run hard."

This was taking too long! She felt an itchy-scratchy urgency to meet D'ward again.

⟅ᔕ⟆ 23 ⟅ᔕ⟆

" ' **A** JUG OF WINE BENEATH THE BOUGH,' " JULIAN INTONED. " 'A LOAF of bread and thou/Beside me singing in the Wilderness/Oh, Wilderness were paradise enough!' That last rhyme needs *work*! I mean, it *looks* all right—"

Ursula peered across the table skeptically. "You left out the book of verse."

"Would depend what's it's printed on. Might make good bumf."

She laughed. Ursula's laughter had all the innocent gaiety of a child's, quite out of keeping with her normally gruff manner. "You're impossible!"

"I'm extremely easy, as you well know!" He raised his glass and she clinked hers against it. They sipped in mirror image, smiling the contented smiles of lovers.

The sun had set; the red moon, Eltiana, hung amid the wakening stars. Location? The side of a small, unnamed, and apparently uninhabited valley somewhere south of Niolvale. The air was cooling rapidly, but the campsite lay well below the snow line, and the weather had cooperated splendidly. For several days—Julian was deliberately not keeping count—they had ridden their dragons over glaciers, icefields, ridges, plateaux. They had gone up and down vertical cliffs. It had all been thumping good fun. The days had been thumping good fun, and the nights even more so. Spiffing!

This was how to rough it. This was how fieldwork should always be. Just the two of them, face-to-face across the little table, sitting on their folding chairs, eating off china with tableware that was a very good imitation of sterling silver. The wine was chilled. The turkey-shaped thing that T'lin had run down had been expertly fricasseed by the indomitable Dommi. The campfire crackled and blazed cheerfully nearby, its smoke drifting upward in a breeze so gentle that the flames above the candlesticks hardly wavered. Doubtless there would be cheese and coffee in a few minutes, as soon as Dommi finished erecting the tent. T'lin was a few hundred yards off, still polishing his precious dragons.

Meanwhile, a man and the woman he loved, the stars, the jagged peaks, the trees . . . Odd sort of trees, not quite conifers. They looked pinelike at a distance, but their needles were tiny stars and the fragrance they put out smelled more like incense than pine. No matter, they would do.

Wary of tearing their frills, dragons shunned forest, but T'lin had found a convenient avalanche path down from the icy highlands to a meadow beside the little river. Ursula had fretted that the woods might be inhabited by the nasty cat things called jugulars. Julian refused to worry about them, on the grounds that if you had to worry about a jugular, it was already too late.

She looked up and caught him studying her. Her chin was too square to be classically feminine, yet it suited her. She wore her hair shorter than he usually liked to see, but that, too, suited her, and it shone like jewels in the firelight. Her eyes were very large and all womanly mystery. She was more Venus de Milo than Mona Lisa, but beautiful in a way all her own. And she was a herd of tigers at lovemaking. Tigresses?

He thought of Euphemia and wondered for the thousandth time what he'd ever seen in the slut. It wasn't just that she fulked with Carrots—she just wasn't good for anything else. His Omar Khayyam joke would have floated clear over her pretty head, whereas Ursula knew a hawk from a handsaw and probably what act and scene they came from. She understood that John of Gaunt wasn't necessarily very thin. . . .

"Happy?"

He jumped and glanced around. "Ecstatically. Night is my favorite time of day. I'm ready for my coffee now, though."

Dommi was still tightening the tent ropes. He wouldn't be long.

"Perhaps we should have coffee in the lounge?"

Julian frowned at the dark mass of the trees around them. "I think we forgot to pack the lounge. How about the palm court? Or the croquet lawn? I'm sure Dommi brought the hoops and mallets."

"It's the Service makes it possible, love," Ursula said softly.

"Makes what possible?"

"All this. Dragon rides and servants. A touch of civilization in the bush—lady and gentleman on safari. Without the Service and its mana, you and I would be hacking our way through jungle and eating roots and sleeping under bushes."

Wanting to talk business, were we?

"If it wasn't for the Service," he countered, "we wouldn't be here at all, my little turtledove. Would we?"

"But we mustn't let Edward Exeter mess it all up, must we?"

He sighed. The moment was too precious to spoil with reality. He did not want any pikes in his millpond tonight.

"Is that the nub? 'I say, old man, you've got to put a sock in this Liberator prank, you're queering our pitch with the natives!' Is that what we tell him?"

Ursula placed her glass down carefully on the spotless white tablecloth. "Yes, that is part of it for me. We live well, I admit. But we work hard for it. You know how bloody rough the missionary cycle can be at times—rough and dangerous, too. You know how boring it can be, studying the language, learning all those sermons, spouting them. You know what homesickness is. We do good, dammit! We don't get paid in pound notes, but we are entitled to compensation, and I don't feel one damned bit guilty about it. So, yes, that's a consideration for me. Isn't it for you?"

Julian shrugged and evaded the question with a mental image of a toreador and his cape. "I don't think that argument will impress Exeter."

"Which one will?"

"Dunno. I'll decide when we've talked with him and I know how his wheels are turning. Do we have to discuss it now, when I'm halfway through composing a sonnet to your eyelashes?"

"We'll be in Niolvale tomorrow."

"And he may still be in Joalland. Or he may be bloody dead already."

She nodded. Dommi materialized in the firelight like a ghost. At some point during his preparation of dinner, he had contrived to change into his white livery. He removed the plates.

"That was delicious," Ursula murmured, although she kept her eyes on Julian.

"Thank you, *entyika!*"

"Listen," Julian said. "Let's not argue. Let's not even talk about it until we find out more facts. When we've heard Exeter's reasons, then we can see whether or not we agree with them. If we don't, then I'll try to talk him out of the whole business, I promise you." Offhand, he could think of no one less likely to be talked out of anything once he had made up his mind than Edward Exeter, Esquire.

"And if you don't succeed?"

"You're jumping to hypothetical conclusions."

"Answer me." Her voice was soft, but there was a lot of power behind it. All sorts of power.

"Then what I think won't matter, will it?"

"No, it won't."

And what Exeter thought wouldn't matter either. That was a skin-crawly idea—using mana to change a man's mind. Nasty. Not nice. It was more or less what he himself had done to the troopers at Seven Stones, of course, but that had been self-defense. He didn't like to think of Ursula doing it to Edward . . . or to any man, of course. He wondered what it would feel like, and whether the victim would even know it had happened.

Dommi laid out cheese and biscuits and butter, poured coffee. When he left, the silence seemed to remain, hanging over the table like a mist. The night was cooling rapidly.

Julian said, "Darling? What exactly happens in a battle of mana?" He saw her mouth tighten and went on quickly, "I mean, if Exeter does go up against Zath, one-on-one—"

"Then he dies! Zath's been at the business for years. Whatever scheme Exeter may have concocted to gather mana, he can't possibly match what Zath has collected from those thousands of human sacrifices. It would be like you taking on the German army single-handed, armed with a penknife."

"I realize that," Julian said, knowing that Exeter must think otherwise, "but in the general case? Forget Zath. If two strangers have a magical donnybrook, what actually *happens?*"

Ursula drank coffee. Eventually she said, "They almost never do, because it would be a leap in the dark. You can't tell the flyweights from the heavyweights in that league without actually throwing a punch and seeing what comes back.

That's why the Five play the Great Game with human chessmen. They never go for one another."

Julian hacked savagely at a piece of cheese. She was being evasive. The Service must know the answer. Prof Rawlinson would have investigated, even if no one else had. The library had been burned when Zath's thugs sacked Olympus, of course; that was frequently offered as an excuse when the new boy asked too many questions.

The stars were coming out in thousands now, but the romantic aura had faded. "So you don't know?"

"No."

"I bet Exeter does."

"What?" Ursula looked startled, surprisingly so.

"He's very chummy with Prylis, the so-called god of knowledge. Didn't you know that?"

She stared hard at Julian while she dabbed invisible crumbs from her lips. "No, I didn't." She was narked at being caught offside.

He felt oddly smug and annoyed with himself because of it. "Read his report on his first two years here—oh, I suppose that got burned? Pity. He told me about it before we came over. He spent two or three days with Prylis. He may very well have gone back there when he left Olympus. I'm sure Exeter knows what a mana battle would be like."

Ursula had her demon-tennis-player look on. "I think I can handle Edward Exeter, no matter what he's been up to these last two years."

"You can certainly handle me all you want," he said happily. "You ready to start now? We ought to let Dommi get on with the dishes."

"You never stop, do you?"

"You want me to?"

She laughed. "No. It's what I like about you."

He jumped up and went around the table to her. "Then let's go, lover!"

24

"THEY ARE NO GODS, THEY ARE IMPOSTERS! ALL THAT LETS THEM ACT like gods is that fools worship them. I tell you that they are mere enchanters, fakes, evil people masquerading in the guise of gods . . ."

D'ward was nearing the end of his evening sermon, building to the usual climax where he would promise to bring death to Death and invite his listeners to join the Free and follow him.

Dosh had heard it all before. "Time to take up your stations, sisters and brothers!" His helpers looked around in surprise, some of them seeming to start out of a trance. Then they scrambled to their feet and moved off in pairs.

The Free had come to Niolvale. The sun was setting behind the ragged summits of Niolwall, painting the sky in lurid reds and orange, turning the leafless trees into arabesques of shadow and silhouetting the tall figure of the Liberator. He stood on one dominant rock with a thousand people huddled together on the grass below him, all spellbound. As he so often did, he had chosen a curious place to camp, a boulder-strewn slope. There was a much better site half a mile away, a level meadow alongside a river. Perhaps he had thought the noise of the water would drown out his preaching or that he would be less visible there.

As soon as he finished, Dosh's helpers would start moving through the throng, taking up the collection. Dosh had selected them all with care and always sent them out in pairs to keep watch on each other. He believed that nine tenths of the money the pilgrims contributed was being turned in as it should be. *Set a thief to catch a thief!* Tonight's take should be better than usual, for a large part of the congregation were newcomers, Niolians who had heard of this latter-day legend and wanted to see him with their own eyes.

Yes, the crowd had grown during the day. Just from where he stood, Dosh could tell that it was also becoming more varied. The ragtag poor were still there in droves—the old, the crippled, the penniless, women with too many babies, convicts snatched from the Rinoovale mines—but he could see sturdy, healthy farmers. He could see artisans and merchants from the city, escorting plump, well-dressed wives. Some had come by carriage or on rabbits. Mingled among them, of course, were the weird. Always the weird: the lost, the dreamers, the lonely, the failures, unworldly intellectuals, fanatics. Especially fanatics. At least ten members of the Free claimed to be reformed reapers who had been sent to collect the Liberator's soul for Zath but had changed their minds when they came into his presence. In Dosh's view those were the weirdest of the lot.

Or perhaps the Niolian soldiers were. Of the troop that had so dramatically failed to stop the Free entering Rinoovale, almost half had then enlisted in it themselves. Most of them were more fanatic than anyone, even the Warband. At least the Warband mostly demonstrated its loyalty with actions, not floods of words, while the Niolian deserters went around all day babbling their wonderful new vision of life and the universe to anyone who would listen. They seemed to have a need to justify their change of allegiance to every mortal in the Vales. Or were they just trying to convince themselves?

Most interesting at the moment was a nearby dozen or so men and women wearing the gold earring of the Church of the Undivided. They were taking a risk in flaunting their allegiance here in Niolland, but perhaps they felt safe within this multitude of heretics. Huddled in a circle on the grass, they were arguing in fierce whispers, and Dosh could guess why—the Liberator had his own brand of heresy. His theology was not Undivided orthodoxy. It was still all heresy to Dosh, though. He was D'ward's friend and a senior helper, but he was not a believer, and if D'ward chose to change his dodge and start touting Gramma

Oriilee's homemade herbal impotence potion, that would be all the same to Dosh.

"Now you have heard!" the Liberator proclaimed. "You have heard the truth, you have heard the call. Now is the moment when you must decide . . ."

This was the finale. Many of the listeners would hurry home now, but some would adhere. More followers would need more to eat, and that also was Dosh's responsibility. It was a sign of the Liberator's continuing success that Dosh now needed assistants, and the Warband was run off its feet trying to keep so large a throng organized. Prat'han had begun enlisting locals to help with the crowd control. Niolvale was large and heavily populated; the numbers could only continue to grow in the next few days.

Unless the queen intervened. Monarchs did not approve of mass gatherings raised by anyone but themselves. The court in Niol must be hearing tales of invasion and uprising, which it could never tolerate, and D'ward had not only spurned Elvanife's warrant, he had subverted half her army. No official welcoming party had graced the mouth of Thadrilpass this morning as the Liberator led his band into Niolvale. There had been no phalanx of warriors, either. Possibly the military had learned its lesson, but more likely it just needed time to muster larger forces.

The sharp swords shall drink, spilling blood into the sands. Young men leave their bones where the Liberator has passed.

Who needed the dread forecasts of the *Filoby Testament* to know that trouble must be brewing? Think of the gods and the priesthood! So far they had ignored this rampant heresy, but he was preaching rank blasphemy not a dozen miles from the temple of Visek, greatest deity of all the Vales.

The sermon ended as the Liberator touched his hands together overhead in the benediction of the Undivided. The crowd sighed like the sound of wind in a distant forest.

Dosh's bagmen moved in. He watched to make sure that they were following the drill D'ward had stipulated—no entreaties, no harassment. Just hold out the bags and keep smiling. If asked, explain that the money goes only to feed the pilgrims. Above all, give thanks for every coin, no matter how small. If offered only rags or scraps of food, accept them as gratefully. Strange man, D'ward!

The Liberator departed, heading for his tent within a group of the Warband. The congregation was rising to its feet, stretching, muttering incredulously at what it had heard. Dosh was about to scramble up on a rock to gain a better view of his collectors, when he saw Prat'han approaching, towering over heads.

He waited.

"What're you grinning at?" he demanded.

"You. You're smiling."

Dosh was disconcerted. "What's unusual about that?"

"Lots. You never used to."

"Well, I'm planning to run off with the loot tonight." He felt himself grin as widely as the big lout. "You think I'm lying?"

"Not seriously." The big man leaned on his shield and glanced around. He lowered his voice. "The Liberator wants you to meet him at the pulpit rock when Trumb rises."

An odd thrill of surprise. "Why?"

"He didn't say. Just you, so far as I know. Said to leave the purse with one of us." Prat'han glanced down narrowly at Dosh; his mouth twisted. "I wouldn't get my hopes up too high if I were you."

Dosh pulled back an angry retort as he noted the twinkle in Prat'han's eye and recognized that the mockery held no real intent to hurt. Even stranger, his own face returned the grin. "A man can dream, can't he?"

Prat'han laughed and jabbed a friendly punch at his shoulder, then turned and stalked away. Fornicating porcupines! Where had that big ox learned sympathy for others' problems? Or had Prat'han developed a sense of humor? The Liberator had certainly taught him a thing or two.

And Dosh also, perhaps. What did he want with him tonight?

25

"Nobody knows what's happened to the Czar and his family," Alice said. "The Bolsheviks have been running a reign of terror since the attempt on Lenin's life last year, so they may well be dead. Britain and France have troops in the north and some in the south too. We're very much afraid that we shall be drawn into the civil war in earnest."

Mr. Rutherford said, "Good God!" loudly. He was usually loud, a heavyset young man with the bemused air of a bull that genuinely liked china and wasn't sure what he was doing wrong.

All around the table, faces frowned at the terrible tidings from Home. Alice felt as if she had not stopped talking for three days. The newly returned Peppers were probably being subjected to the same intense interrogation, but their knowledge would be scanty compared to hers. The Olympians had an insatiable appetite for news of Home and accounts of the war. Their incredulous reaction to her stories made her appreciate how much the England and Europe they knew had changed.

Realizing that everyone else had finished the soup course, she set to work on hers hurriedly. Yet another dinner party! The faces and the houses varied, but she seemed to repeat the same words every night and all day too, on an endless circuit of dinners and tea parties. When she wasn't being wined, dined, or pickled with what passed for tea here, she was being escorted around the station on sight-seeing strolls, answering interminable questions. A thousand times she had cursed

Julian Smedley, who should have brought the Olympians up to date on events prior to his arrival in 1917; but Julian had been unable to talk about the war. He was over his battle fatigue now, she gathered, but every audience wanted her to start at the beginning, 1914, and deliver an intensive history lesson on the worst four years the world had ever known.

She laid down her spoon. Footmen paced forward to remove soup bowls and serve the fish. Euphemia had described Olympus as an imitation outpost of Empire—Alice had not seen Euphemia since the day they arrived—and, yes, Olympus did bear a slight resemblance to Nyagatha, where she had spent most of her childhood, and even more to some of the neighboring stations that she had visited a few times. There were overtones of British India, which she could vaguely remember. The formal evening wear and the innumerable liveried servants were familiar, although the natives were as white as the sahibs.

But there were differences also, not all of which she could quite identify. One was certainly the era. The residents seemed oddly old-fashioned, Edwardian or even Victorian. The women's gowns were historical, the manners stilted. The wealth was overdone, too. Even in India, few Imperial Government officials would live as well as these people did, every one of them. They all seemed about the same age. Scanning the Chases' dining room—"banquet hall" might be a better description—she could see no one she would classify as junior recruits and no middle-aged seniors either. It reminded her of a rugby club dinner that she had been taken to once, before the war.

"Do tell us about these tank things!" demanded Prof Rawlinson from the far end of the table.

Obediently, Alice began to talk about tanks and aeroplanes and poison gas. They were an unsuitable topic for polite dinner conversation, but she had been seated between Foghorn Rutherford and Pinky Pinkney, with Jumbo Watson opposite her. She was beginning to learn who turned knobs and pulled levers in Olympus, and she suspected those three intended to bring up the purpose of her being here: Edward. She did not want to talk about Edward.

If this was a relaxing vacation, it had not achieved its purpose yet. She had been billeted on Iris Barnes, whose husband was off on the missionary circuit somewhere, enlightening the heathens. Iris was pleasant enough, in a prudish sort of way. Her house was extremely comfortable, although the walls were not totally soundproof and the lady entertained gentleman visitors at unconventional hours. No matter—the hospitality could not be faulted, and it was certainly pleasant to have an army of servants eagerly satisfying one's slightest whim. But relax? No, not yet. The crossing had been a gruesome experience of massive disorientation, followed by nausea and muscle cramps. For the first couple of days Alice had hardly been able to stay awake, only to discover that she could not sleep at night. The chronic exhaustion that had burdened her since her bout of flu still oppressed her.

The fish was delicious, a sort of trout. She was queried about food rationing in Britain. Red meat and red wine appeared. The wine had never known Bordeaux, but she had met worse. She was asked about the war in Palestine and the

charismatic Colonel Lawrence. Then came the sweet, a berry tart with cream—
she certainly should be able to recover the weight she had lost. It must be about
time for the U-boats.

No, not U-boats. Even before the footmen stepped back from the table, Mr.
Pinkney said, "By the way, Mrs. Pearson, were you informed of the latest news
about your cousin?"

"No."

The room fell very still.

"One of our agents arrived tonight. Just before dark. Exeter has left Joalvale
by way of Ragpass. That is the story. He is in Nosokvale." Pinky Pinkney was
a quiet-spoken, rubbery man, whom Alice had already identified as one of the
powers in Olympus. What his title was she did not know, but everyone else
seemed to defer to him, even the resonant Foghorn Rutherford, who was official
chairman of the committee that ran the Service—and whose tight-lipped expression hinted that this news was news to him too.

She could feel all eyes upon her. "He is in good health?"

"Oh, yes. Apparently. The news is a week or so old, of course. He is collecting
quite a following."

Alice decided she did not like Mr. Pinkney, his silky, self-satisfied manner,
or his center parting. She did not like his habit of smiling with his eyes closed,
nor his bombshell public proclamations. To have passed on news of a missing
relative in private would have been better form. If she did not like him, she need
not pander to his feelings.

"I never doubted he would."

Pinkney's smile was as polished as the silverware. "Oh?"

"Edward has always chosen his goals carefully and always achieved them."

"But what exactly is his goal this time, mm? This is what we should all like
to know. You understand?"

She shrugged. "I know no more than any of you, probably a lot less." She
caught her hostess's eye. "This tart is delicious! What sort of fruit is it?"

Mrs. Chase said, "Lobsterberry," in very flat tones and without a smile.

"It tastes much better than it sounds, then!" About to take another mouthful,
Alice realized that everyone else was just watching. Pinky had the floor, and
they were all waiting for him. He was apparently waiting for her. She put the
fragment of pastry in her mouth anyway.

"What we do not understand, Mrs. Pearson," Pinky said, "and what we hope
you may be able to explain to us, is why your cousin has declared war upon
Zath. The so-called god of death. The self-proclaimed god of death, mm? He
would have more luck trying to knock down the Tower of London with a
crowbar. What he is attempting is certain suicide."

Appropriately, a small pink butterfly swooped a few times around the nearest
candlestick and then plunged into the flame, vanishing in a brief flash. The dinner
guests remained silent. They were all very solicitous about Edward's well-being,
all of a sudden.

Alice swallowed her mouthful. "As I understand the matter, it was Zath who declared war on him, before he was even born. I don't believe Edward would ever be suicidal, under any circumstances. He might undertake something extremely hazardous if he thought the stakes justified it." She went on the offensive. "Explain to me how this mana affair works. I know that he can collect it from his followers and in large amounts it can act like magic. I know that Zath is supposed to have more of it than anyone else. Suppose Edward does challenge him to a duel? What happens? Do they toss thunderbolts at each other?"

Pinkney frowned, drumming fingertips on the tablecloth. "Perhaps, if he ever got that far. Strangers have certainly slain natives that way. It is, however, extremely rare for one stranger to assault another directly. A duel, as you put it. I'm not sure I can truly answer your question." He hesitated, then turned his head to peer along the table. "Prof? You're our expert in such matters."

The one they called Prof was slender and sandy haired, with a pedantic, donnish manner. Alice had already decided he was no leader, for men would trust his memory and intellect but not his judgment. He gave the impression that he should be peering at the world through very thick glasses, yet none of the Olympians wore glasses. Now he brightened at this invitation to pontificate.

"There isn't much known, just hearsay. I doubt thunderbolts, because it would take as much power to throw one as it would to block one. Both sides would lose mana. . . . I'm assuming that the contestants are rather evenly matched, of course, which would not be the case here. I think it would be more like arm wrestling—they both push until one goes down. Then the loser is at the winner's mercy."

Pinkney aimed an oily, I-told-you-so look at Alice. "One thing Zath does not have is mercy."

No one was eating, all waiting for her reply. They wanted her to say something like, "Oh dear, then I had better go and find Edward and tell him to stop it at once."

She was damned if she would. Whatever he was up to, he would have calculated the odds, weighed the ethics, and made his decision in ice-cold blood. It was none of her business and she would not interfere.

She spoke along the table to Prof Rawlinson. "How fascinating! Then where does the mana go? If I have— Say I have five pounds of mana, and you have seven, and I challenge you to a duel. Then you win, so I have none left and you have two? Pounds of mana, that is."

Prof blinked a few times. "No, I don't think so. I think you have none and I have twelve."

That remark elicited a few surprised glances.

The foghorn boomed out again. "Really? You sure of that, old man?"

"Fairly sure."

"Dammit! So Exeter is not just likely to die, he's liable to make Zath stronger than ever?"

Pinkney also seemed to doubt. "How can you know that?"

Prof shrugged. "I told you it was hearsay. Don't think of it as arm wrestling, then. Think of a tug-of-war. Winner gets the whole rope. It's the Great Game!"

he protested, apparently feeling his word was being doubted.

Alice detected an open goal and kicked. "Well, you admit you are not sure. Perhaps Edward knows something you don't?"

That remark provoked an ovation of sniffs and stuffy looks. The diners turned their attention to the lobsterberry tart.

"I think Prof is correct!" The voice came from a striking blond woman sitting across from him. Alice searched for the name. . . . Olga somebody. "Years ago one of Tion's flunkies changed sides, and Tion turned on him. He bragged to me afterward that he had *sucked the bastard dry.*"

This time the disapproval was even more general. Alice wondered why, and tried another broadside. "Tion's the one they call the Youth? I didn't realize that you were on social terms with the opposition."

"Talking of news," Jumbo Watson said loudly, "I suppose you've all heard about poor Doc? He's been arrested, you know. Blighters down in Randorvale raided a meeting at—"

A strange tremor seemed to strike the company. Every head turned to stare at the same corner of the room, like two rows of weathercocks in a sudden gust. Alice shivered as if cold fingers had touched her skin. Then everyone relaxed again in a buzz of comment, no longer at all interested in the Randorvale problem.

"What?" she said, annoyed at being the only one not in on the secret.

Across from her, Jumbo laughed. "Did you feel that, Mrs. Pearson? We are just inside the edge of the node, here. Someone just arrived."

"Arrived? From Home, you mean?"

"Where else? The node is a portal, of course. When people come through, it sort of shimmers. You felt it?"

"The Montgomerys!" Foghorn proclaimed loudly. "They're due back. Who's next on the roster?"

The Olympians were all on tenterhooks over the prospect of leave, like kids waiting their turns for a ride on a pony. Excited conversation had erupted all along the table. The unfortunate business in Randorvale was conveniently forgotten; even Edward was forgotten. Alice was happy to be offstage at last, but she was peeved at Mr. Jumbo Watson for so clumsily cutting off her question to Olga whats-her-name.

Furthermore, she thought the Randorvale incident deserved more serious consideration. She had heard the news the previous day, and no doubt everyone else had, too. One of their own, a Dr. Mainwaring, had been thrown in jail and at least a dozen native converts had been killed or injured. If she were a member of the Service, she would be demanding to know What Steps Were Being Taken. She had, in fact, asked that question several times, without receiving an answer. It was none of her business if she were merely a guest on holiday, but if they were going to drag her willy-nilly into their dealings with Edward, then she had a right to know just what sort of organization the Service was and what sort of protection it could provide for its own people.

In her books, "people" included natives.

She finished her sweet, dabbed her lips with a napkin, and waited until she could catch Jumbo's eye.

Edward had mentioned Jumbo Watson more than once. Charming, he had said, good company, a friend of Uncle Cam's many years ago, but possibly a traitor. Yes, he was charming. He was the only person Alice had yet met in Olympus who fitted that description. She enjoyed his humor. She could imagine being friends with Jumbo Watson, were she quite certain that he had cleared himself of the taint of treason, and she would trust nobody's word on that but Edward's.

He finished what he was saying to Hannah Pinkney and saw Alice looking at him.

"Tell me about Randorvale," she said. "What are you going to do about Dr. Mainwaring?"

Jumbo's long face seemed to lengthen even more. "Frankly, Mrs. Pearson, we don't know what we can do. We're not His Majesty's agents here, you know. We have no legal authority whatsoever. Quite the reverse, indeed. As far as the law is concerned, we're heretics, and that means we're criminals. We have no legal recourse, and illegal methods do not look promising. Our best bet may be to try to bribe the guards to let Alistair escape. We're going to try that first."

"Soon, I hope?" As soon as she spoke, she realized she was being presumptuous, but Jumbo just smiled.

"We have people on their way there already."

"And what about the natives who were—"

A thunderous crash from the direction of the kitchen sounded like a tray of dishes falling. Several voices screamed. Doors slammed. All heads in the room turned in unison once more.

In through the serving door strode a tall figure, swathed in black, too tall to be a woman. The hem of his robe swept the ground and long sleeves concealed his hands. He stopped and folded his arms. Although he held his head erect, his face was a mere blur within his hood. Yet he seemed to rake the company with invisible eyes.

After a first frozen second, pandemonium broke out. The red-haired servants shrieked and fled. One dived straight through a window, in a shattering smash of glass. Chairs toppled as diners leaped to their feet. Two or three men and at least half the women winked out of existence altogether. Crystal, china, and silverware clattered and danced on the parquet floor. Footsteps and screaming died away in the distance, leaving silence.

Alice stayed where she was, too astonished to move, the only person still seated.

"Leader?" demanded the newcomer. "Which one of you is leader?"

Foghorn was on the far side of the table, next to Alice. His burly face was ashen, but he lifted a fallen candlestick and set it on its base before it could start a fire.

"I am the current chairman, sir. Rutherford, Bernard Rutherford, at your service. I don't believe we have been introduced?"

"I am Zath," said the intruder harshly.

Hannah Pinkney slumped in a faint. Jumbo caught her with a remarkable display of reflexes and strength; he lowered her into a chair as if she weighed no more than a blanket.

"Good evening, Your Excellency," Foghorn said in unusually quiet tones for him. "Since you are here, will you take a glass of wine?"

"No."

Rutherford resumed his seat, and at once the others copied him, finding chairs still upright if they had knocked over their own. He leaned back and studied the dread figure. "Then pray state your business."

Still the face showed as only a pale smudge, the eyes as darker patches, and yet the creature radiated contempt. "I came to tell you to call off your dog or pay the penalty. I hold Olympus ransom for his behavior, and every soul in it."

"My dog? Would I be correct in assuming that you refer to Mr. Edward Exeter, commonly known as the Liberator?"

Beautiful! Loud and even obnoxious Rutherford might be in normal times, but he was hitting straight sixes now. Alice felt an insane desire to clap.

"Yes, you would!" Zath snarled. "Stop him any way you like, but stop him, or I shall blast this valley to embers."

Foghorn smothered a yawn. "I am frightfully afraid you have been misinformed, Excellency. Edward Exeter is none of ours. Not one of us has seen him in years, as I am sure your spies have reported. He is a free agent. Pray address your complaints to him in person."

"Then I may as well slay the lot of you now?"

Foghorn shrugged. His color was returning. "I am sure you can—but be warned that this is a node, sir, and every one of us will die believing we do so for Edward Exeter's cause. You wish to make us martyrs?"

Silence—as if that irrelevancy had somehow been a threat.

The god of death growled deep in his throat. "You have been warned. Heed my words!"

He wavered like a pillar of black smoke and wasn't there anymore. Alice felt the icy touch of the portal on her skin. For a moment the tension held as minds adjusted to this miraculous release, then everyone seemed to breathe at the same moment.

"Very nicely done, old man," Jumbo said.

"Bloody good show!" Pinkney agreed. He rose and hurried around to his wife, although some of the ladies had already reached her. "You wouldn't have a drop of brandy handy, would you, Larry?"

Their host opened his mouth and bellowed, "Tramline!"

Alice wondered why she had not felt more frightened. She could not recall being frightened, although she was a little shaky now. Had the whole charade seemed too unreal, or had she just gone into shock?

"Unmitigated bounder!" Foghorn said. His face was bright red now. "What do you make of that, Prof? Prof?"

Rawlinson was no longer present.

The butler swept in, his features as white as his starched shirt front, and his coppery hair askew. He bore a silver tray with a decanter and a dozen glasses, which rattled as he set it down.

"Good man, Tramline!" Chase said heartily. "We could all do with a snifter, I think. Anyone hurt backstage?"

"A few cuts, *tyika*. Nothing serious."

"Issue a noggin to all hands, then. Splice the main brace, what? I'll talk to you about a bonus for the staff in the morning."

Amid the general hubbub that now ensued, Alice registered Jumbo gazing quizzically at her. His eyes twinkled.

"Apart from that, Mrs. Pearson, how are you enjoying your holiday?"

She had been through the Great War; she would not let these bush babies outdo her in upper-lip stiffness. "It's interesting, Mr. Watson."

"Isn't it, though?" He reached over to the tray where Tramline was pouring brandy and passed Alice a glass with conspiratorial glee.

Alice laid it down carefully, hoping her hands were not jiggling too noticeably. She waited until Jumbo had obtained one for himself and then offered hers to clink. They smiled and sipped in unison.

Other people were chattering loudly, inspecting damage, picking up debris, gulping brandy. She and Jumbo sat opposite each other, ignoring it all.

"You probably didn't register it," he said, "but that little episode just vindicated Prof Rawlinson beautifully."

"Explain."

He smiled wryly. "When that blighter charged in here, we all thought it was a reaper. Most of us have managed to collect a little mana, as I expect you know. Half of us used the trapdoor—teleporting out, which is not too difficult when you're on a node, like this. The rest of us tried to clobber the bugger, if you'll pardon my Thargian."

She took another drink of brandy, feeling its warmth tingling in her mouth and down her throat. "And?"

He glanced around. "Don't know about the others, but mine just vanished. My power, I mean—it disappeared. That's when I knew we had more than a reaper to deal with. It felt as if Zath swallowed it, just as Prof said would happen. Interesting!"

"I hadn't realized that Zath was a fellow countryman. I find that rather disappointing."

"Why do you think that?" Jumbo drained his glass and somehow contrived to shake his head at the same time. "Oh, the language? Don't think he's one of us. Certainly hope not! He wasn't speaking English. He was speaking in tongues, glossolalia. It's quite a minor use of mana, making everyone think he's hearing his own language. Acts, Chapter 2, if I remember correctly. I've done it myself once or twice. But what are we to make of this curious event, Mrs. Pearson?" He quirked an eyebrow.

"I can't believe the Service will capitulate before the crude threats of an obvious bully."

"Not by a long chalk! Zath just made enemies out of allies, had he only known. More than that, Mrs. Pearson, wouldn't you say our deathly friend has got the wind up?" He narrowed his eyes in a smile that hinted at real excitement bubbling underneath.

"I received the distinct impression," Alice said solemnly, "that Edward scares the shite out of him—if you'll pardon my Joalian."

The rest of the room was still ignoring them. Foghorn was in full spate, drowning out two other men and the Olga woman in a ferocious argument. The Pinkneys had gone home, others had left in search of missing partners. Newcomers were pouring in, men in tails, men in dressing gowns, some carrying swords, all demanding to know what was going on, by Jove or by George. The servants had almost restored order, except for the litter on the table between Alice and Jumbo, which they had refrained from touching yet.

"What do you make of it, Mr. Watson?"

"I want to know what Exeter is up to that could so alarm his opponent. Obviously you were right. Zath doesn't see him as the pushover we all did." Jumbo fell silent, unconsciously rubbing his prominent nose. Was he wondering if he had been wrong all along about the *Filoby Testament?* What did it take to change a man's mind after thirty years? "Captain Smedley thought Exeter might have a trick or two up his sleeve," he muttered, more to himself than to her.

"So you're going to go and visit Edward."

He looked up with a gleam of challenge in his eye. "He should be informed of what happened here tonight. There are two dragons in the compound and the moon is bright."

"Only two?"

Jumbo pushed himself to his feet. "Only two. I'm going to change, pack a bag, and leave. No signed orders, no arguments, no good-byes."

No conditions, no questions, only challenge. She should have expected this from Jumbo. If he was a traitor . . . if Edward believed that Jumbo was a traitor, then he would not believe the message he brought. If he was not a traitor, then there was no danger. To her astonishment—perhaps it was the brandy—Alice stood up also. "Sounds like an excellent plan. Lead on, my dear Watson."

26

FOR SOME TIME, DOSH HAD BEEN LEANING AGAINST THE BOULDER, WATCHing great Trumb rise over the watery lands of Niolflat and wondering if he would eclipse before dawn. He had been studying the stellar twinkle of the pilgrims' fires in the meadow and wondering how many nubile maidens and lithe youths there were down there and how much longer he could maintain this unfamiliar chastity he had undertaken. He had been wondering why he did not have the sense to vamoose clean out of this peripatetic prayer meeting before it hatched into full-scale bloodbath and disaster.

"Dosh?" said a whisper, and he jumped like a cricket.

He had not heard anyone approaching. It was D'ward, of course, but he had discarded his priestly robe and wore nothing but a loincloth. His limbs and chest gleamed very pale in the lurid green light. D'ward in disguise must mean serious trouble. Had he decided to vamoose also, while the going was good?

"D'wa— Liberator?"

"How're your legs tonight?"

"Beautiful as ever."

A chuckle. "That was not what I meant, you scoundrel. Can you run as far as Niol and back before dawn?"

Once I could have done. "I can try."

"Then let's go!" D'ward turned and began loping down the hill.

That was tricky, stony going, but when they found the trail Dosh was able to move to D'ward's side. He was setting a mean pace, if he truly planned to keep it up all night.

"I didn't know you were a runner too."

"I may have to cheat a bit."

What did that mean? Dosh added another question to his already large collection, but before he could ask any of them, D'ward said, "This may be dangerous."

"I sort of thought it might be. Who're we going to call on?"

"Visek."

"Great gods!"

"No, they're not."

They jogged on for a mile or so while Dosh rolled this astonishing development around in his mind and wondered why he had not already turned on his heel and taken off in the opposite direction. Now he knew why the Liberator had not brought his bodyguards—the Warband could do nothing against the Parent. But dangerous? That was an understatement of enormous proportions. "Suicidal" would be more apt. The least the Liberator could hope for was to have his tongue cut out for blasphemy; his accomplice would be lucky to get off with a life sentence in the mines.

"This may be a turning point," D'ward said.

"Or an ending point!"

"Certainly. But it should be interesting. I thought you'd be interested. I'd appreciate your company, but turn back if you want to."

They kept on running. The farms they passed were dark. There was no one else on the road. Trumb lit the world with unworldly light and flashed off ponds, canals, and ditches, while the red moon was just setting at their backs. Niolvale nights had a heavy scent of damp vegetation that was all their own, very distinctive.

Dosh found his second wind. For once he had D'ward to himself and might get some answers. "According to the *Testament,* the Liberator was to arrive in this world five years ago and be tended by someone called Eleal—aided by a Daughter of Irepit."

"It happened."

"So you knew there was one god—enchanter—who was on your side?"

D'ward chuckled. "Go to the top of the class. No, you've always been top of that class. You're right. When I decided to stop fighting the prophecies and become the Liberator, I first went back to Thargvale, to call on our old friend Prylis again. He helped me shape my plans. Then I came north to Rinoovale and Irepit. She gave me her support. She sent me to Joal, to see her boss."

"You mean the Maiden?"

"Of course. Astina was not quite as supportive—she's the weakest of the Five at the moment, and nervous. But she did promise to deal with any reapers Zath might throw at me in Joalvale."

That explained a lot. Dosh jogged on, hearing only their breathing, the slap of their feet on the dirt, and distant nightingales. There were no clouds, and few stars could compete with Trumb when he was near the full.

"So those churn-brains who claim to be former reapers—"

"Don't mock them! Pity them. Astina de-spelled them—they're genuine. They have terrible, terrible memories to live with."

Their problem, Dosh thought, not his. "That was Joalvale. How about No-sokvale?"

"There too. Astina promised to keep me breathing in all Joaldom. Irepit did the same in Rinoovale. They gave me time to get the boat launched."

"And here in Niolvale?"

"Here I'm on my own. Remember I warned you we'd be playing with real money here? If you see any black shadows moving, speak up promptly."

Dosh felt the sweat freeze on his skin. He almost did turn back then.

"Can probably handle one"—D'ward panted—"or even two."

"No one can stop a reaper!"

"Not true. Killed one once . . . with a rock."

Impossible! but after that, D'ward saved his breath for running and would answer no more questions.

The greatest temple in the Vales stood a short way north of Niol, which was one of the three great cities. The runners approached from the southwest, slowing to a walk when they reached the holy grounds. They had not met a soul the whole way. The night was very still—ominously still, in Dosh's opinion. Trumb's great disk soared almost full through the sky and he would certainly eclipse before the sun rose. An eclipse of the green moon was a sure portent of reapers.

"You've been here?" D'ward was limping, panting, with sweat shining on his skin like silver, but Dosh was in no better shape.

"Course."

"Describe it."

Between puffs, Dosh tried to do justice to the temple of Visek. The innumerable minor buildings—shrines, barracks, libraries, colleges, refectories, dormitories, observatories—sprawled over many acres of tended parkland, interspersed with lakes and pools. There must be three or four thousand priests, priestesses, monks, nuns, and associated characters in residence.

"The main sanctuary is over there?" D'ward pointed a long arm.

"Probably. Yes, I think so. How'd you know that?"

"I can sense the holiness. What's it look like?"

"Columns. A rectangle of them supporting a lintel, but no roof. It's not like that hideous thing of Karzon's in Tharg, though! Visek's is bigger, white marble, breathtaking. One of the wonders of the world."

They trod along a wide avenue flanked by night-scenting shrubbery and tall statuary. To Dosh's nervous gaze, some of those mysterious figures tended to look very much like waiting reapers, although he was trying to assure himself that Zath would not dare seek out sacrifices in this place.

"How about an altar?" D'ward asked. "A holy of holies?"

"Don't know."

"Where's the god, then?"

"They're in the middle."

After a moment, D'ward chuckled. "The Parent—the Father *and* the Mother? You know, Joalian's a very handy sort of language! 'Visek' is abstract, so applied to a person it can mean masculine or feminine, singular or plural."

"That's true in all languages: Sussian, Randorian, Nagian, Thargian. . . ."

"I know some that won't work that way, but carry on. Where are they?"

"In the middle. On the throne at the top of the steps. Back to back. If you come in from this end, you're facing the Father. From the other end, you see the Mother." Dosh pointed. They had come around a curve, bringing the main temple into view, glimmering faintly in the moonlight. Even at this distance, its size was obvious, larger even than he remembered. It made the trees seem tiny.

D'ward muttered, "Mmph!" admiringly. "We'll deal with the Father, then. Or would you rather wait outside?"

Oh, no! Dosh was too conscious of the lurking shadows in the gardens. His skin crawled and he wanted to stay close to the Liberator. He just kept on walking, trying to match his companion's greedy strides.

As they neared the pillars, he made out a twinkle of lamps and vague shapes of people moving around just inside. There would be priests in attendance, even at this time of night, and they would certainly have some means of summoning guards. If they knew that the Vales' most prominent heretic was within the sacred precincts, they would take him faster than a fish snapped gnats. D'ward must know what he was doing, mustn't he? He must have plans or knowledge that he hadn't bothered to pass on, mustn't he?

Dosh worked a painfully dry mouth. "Does he know you're coming?"

"He claims to be the All-Knowing, so I didn't bother to write. We have no choice but to walk in the front door? We can't sneak in through the side pillars?"

"Not unless you're totally crazy. Nothing attracts attention like furtive."

"I'll trust your judgment and experience on that, Brother Dosh."

"And we'll have to make an offering, you know! Why didn't you warn me to bring some money?"

"Because that money was not given for that purpose."

Crazy! "They'll still demand an offering," Dosh muttered. His feet were sore and his legs ached.

Somewhere far off, someone was singing. There was no accompaniment, just a single voice in the night, soaring high in a lonely, wistful anthem, a woman or a boy caroling praise to the greatest of the gods. Or the greatest of the evil enchanters, if you believed D'ward. Dosh didn't—not here, where the sanctity was as palpable as rock. Even the air felt old and holy.

Side by side, the newcomers mounted the steps—long, shallow steps that did not fit a man's stride, with uneven risers so he had to watch where his feet were going and could not move with grace or ease. The marble was cold on bare feet, the night air even colder on bare skin and sweat-soaked hair. They reached the bases of the great pillars and entered a black puddle of shadow cast by Trumb. The lamps were obvious now, revealing turbaned, white-robed figures waiting within the entrance. The visitors would be questioned or at least asked to define their business.

Suppose the priests became suspicious? Suppose they began serious interrogation or called in the guards? D'ward would certainly give a false name, so what if poor Dosh were asked to confirm it? Then he would have to decide where his loyalty was and which side he believed in. *In Nosokslope they shall come to D'ward in their hundreds, even the Betrayer.* This might be where he discovered if he had ranked a mention in the *Filoby Testament.*

They passed between two marble piers, each larger than a house and taller than a tree. A white-ghost priest took a step toward them, touching his forehead. Dosh automatically responded with the same gesture. He did not quite see what D'ward did, but he thought the movement was not exactly orthodox—more like rubbing an eyebrow. The elderly priest could not have noticed the difference, for he held out his leather bag expectantly and his expression was benevolent . . . so far.

"Your troubles must be great, my sons, if you seek solace at this hour."

"Our labors by day make us keep strange hours, Father." D'ward spoke in Niolian, just as he had in his evening sermon. He never slowed his pace, striding past the priest and onward into the sanctuary.

Dosh sweated along at his side, resisting the temptation to look back. He could not believe it had been that easy!

"I just rang the doorbell," D'ward murmured in Nagian, which was his preferred dialect.

"What do you mean?"

"Visek probably heard me get by that old fellow. . . . Never mind. I'm just whistling in the dark."

He was not whistling and it was not dark! It was not bright either, of course, but Trumb was flooding the great space with light, and large candles burned around the holy figure ahead. They did not look large at this distance, but they must be. The great rectangle of white pillars and polished floor contained nothing except the plinth in the center, a truncated pyramid about half the width of the enclosure and not much over head height. On the top sat Father Visek, a marble god on a marble throne. Dosh had seen other gods much larger—the grotesque colossi of Karzon and Zath in the temple of the Man in Tharg, for example. Visek, he knew from memories of past visits, was scarcely more than life-size, or at least did not seem so from ground level.

The singing came from a boy at a corner of the pyramid, kneeling on the lowermost step. Then another boy walked out of the shadows to kneel at another corner. The first rose, touched his forehead in obeisance, walked away, and the second began to sing. Kids that age ought to have been in bed hours ago. There was no sign of anyone else nearby, but there must be at least a choirmaster skulking in the shadows and doubtless more singers awaiting their cue. The second singer was not as tuneful as the first, unsure of his key.

D'ward continued to stride forward. Dosh shuffled along at his side, wishing he had even an inkling of what was going to happen. He knew the Liberator provoked strange reactions from gods. With his own eyes, Dosh had seen Irepit appear to lend him a hand in Nosokvale only days ago. In a past that now seemed almost historical, Prylis had hailed D'ward like a long-lost friend. Karzon, the Man himself, had punched him on the jaw. That did not mean the Parent would not smite him with lightning or burn out his tongue and cut off his hands, which was the standard penalty for blasphemy.

The Father loomed above them, a majestic seated figure, hands on knees, flowing beard. If the marble had ever been colored, the tints had long since weathered away, but the features were still discernible, stern but loving in the warm glow from the tall gold candlesticks. Reaching the base of the steps, Dosh prepared to kneel—and D'ward kept moving. Dosh grabbed him and hauled him back. "You can't go up there!" he whispered. "Only the high priest—"

"Come along!"

D'ward seized Dosh's arm in a painfully powerful grip and urged him up the stairway. The singer missed a note and then continued. Oh, gods! This was forbidden. The priests must be able to see. They would call in the guards. Dosh tried to look around and stumbled when the next step wasn't where he expected. . . .

Moon and candles had disappeared. He was in a tunnel. No, not a tunnel, for there was carpet under his feet. Somewhere indoors, though, being hurried along a level floor. Where had the god gone? The throne? The temple?

"Where are we?" he squeaked.

"Damned if I know," D'ward said cheerily. "Watch out!"

Dosh sensed a very large place, a hall. The only light was a faint glow from up ahead, and D'ward released his grip to lead the way along the narrow path, twisting through a maze, a forest of miscellaneous objects, curved or angular, some very large, others small and heaped on top of one another—statues, tables, huge jars, candelabra, chairs, cauldrons, musical instruments, rolls of fabric, piles of what might be clothes, suits of armor, and thousands of other things, all pushed in together in no sort of order and in many places stacked higher than head height. The air was dry and musty. It was a gigantic storeroom, a junk merchant's cellar run riot.

"What is this?"

"Damned if I know that, either. A museum? A kleptomaniac's hoard? Offerings, I suppose. People keep bringing things, one must collect a lot of stuff over the centuries."

Trying not to whimper, poor Dosh followed his guide. Why had he ever let himself get involved in whatever this was he was involved in? He needed to pee.

The light came from a wide doorway. D'ward walked through it. Dosh crept in behind him, trying to be inconspicuous. D'ward stopped.

Dosh peeked over his shoulder. The light would be too dim to read by. It cast no shadows and he could not see its source. The room was large, as big as Bandrops Advocate's study, and just as cluttered and heaped as the antechamber. The only clear space was roughly triangular, its corners being D'ward himself and two huge chairs, angled toward each other. Everywhere else was packed with the same mindless jumble as the antechamber: furniture, figurines, boxes, pottery, birdcages, crystal, scrolls, weapons, and just about anything else a man could think of or ever want. Gold and gems glittered dimly under layers of dust. The air was stuffy, with the stale, acrid smell of a tomb.

The chairs were occupied. One held a man, the other a woman, both lying back motionless, with their hands folded in their laps. Their hair fell in frozen white waves to lap on their shoulders, their skin was as smooth as vellum, and their robes had long since faded to an indeterminate gray. The man's beard reached to his waist. He rested his chin on his chest, seeming to stare at the woman's feet, while she had her head back, gazing fixedly into space above him. Neither was heeding the visitors at all.

Silence. Dosh shivered violently. These could not be real people, of course, merely more images of the Father and the Mother, representations of the same dual god. They must have lain there for years, gathering dust, although they seemed to have escaped the film of cobweb that coated all the hodgepodge and bric-a-brac. Yet what sculptor could shape so convincingly and in what medium? Hair rose on the nape of his neck.

"Who is it?" muttered the man, not looking up, moving nothing but his mustache. His voice creaked, as if it had dried up from disuse.

After a long moment, the woman muttered, "A stranger. Come looking for a job, I expect." She continued to stare blankly at nothing.

Pause. "Have we any vacant aspects now?"

Longer pause. "Don't remember." Very slowly she turned her head to stare at D'ward. Her face was unwrinkled, yet it conveyed a sense of age beyond imagining. Her eyes were dull—not filmed with cataracts, as old people's often were, just lifeless glass. "Go away. . . . We are busy. . . . Come back in a hundred years."

"I am D'ward Liberator, the one foretold in the *Filoby Testament*."

The woman's head drifted back to its original position.

Even D'ward seemed nonplussed. When nothing more was said, he bristled, putting his fists on his hips. "I am the Liberator! It is prophesied that I shall bring death to Death."

"A reformer," the woman muttered.

"Another? It never works. Send him away."

Dosh's teeth were trying to chatter. He took hold of his jaw with both hands and held his mouth open. His bladder felt as if was about to burst from sheer terror.

"I am D'ward Liberator. You two are Visek? How long have you been sitting there?"

"Go away," the woman murmured.

"You are dying of boredom! I offer you a little excitement for a change, something new. I am going to slay Zath."

The man sighed, stirring the silver hairs of his mustache again. "Who?"

"Zath!" D'ward was not even trying to hide his exasperation. "The one who calls himself the god of death. He sucks mana from human sacrifices. He is evil, a blot upon the Vales and your religion."

Long pause. With glacial slowness the man looked up, his eyes showing the same dead indifference as the woman's. "Then go and do it and stop bothering us."

"I do not yet have the power. I need more mana. I go from node to node, recruiting followers, preaching my purpose, but I need help. Will you aid me? Will you lend me mana?"

Another sigh. "No."

"Will you at least grant me protection while I am here in Niolvale, so that Zath's minions cannot—"

"No. You are intruding. Play the Game like the others or pay the penalty. Begone." The man closed his eyes and lowered his chin again.

"*Strewth!*" D'ward said angrily. "Play the Game? Zath has more mana than you do! He has more power, probably, than the whole Pentatheon together! What if he decides he would like to be Visek? He'll kill you and take your place! What do you think of that move? Or don't you care anymore?"

The awful, stuffy room swayed around Dosh. His blood hammered in his ears. These talking mummies could never be divine, so D'ward had been right all along, and the gods were merely human enchanters who had stretched out their lives for untold centuries. Spiders caught in their own web, dying of boredom! Everything he had ever believed was totally false, criminal rubbish. His stomach heaved.

It was the woman who reacted first to D'ward's taunts, although reluctantly and with irritation. She peered at him. "You blaspheme against Visek."

"It is the truth! Talk to Karzon or Eltiana or Astina! Damn, talk to crazy Tion if you trust him! Every night more people die so that Zath can suck mana from their deaths. Prylis told me that it was Visek, three thousand years ago, who

banned human sacrifice in all the Vales—was that you or one of your prede-
cessors?"

"It was us, I think," the man mumbled, with the first hint of interest that he
had shown. "Wasn't it, dear?"

D'ward snorted. "Then Zath defies your edict! He is evil and deadly and
dangerous to you. The prophecy—"

"We are god of prophecy. Among other things."

"Others also prophesy. The prophecy says that I will bring death to Death.
If the one who calls himself Zath were to become Visek, then he wouldn't be
Death anymore and he would be safe, wouldn't he?"

"Blasphemy!" the woman quavered. Both of them were looking at D'ward
now. Both were showing signs of anger, or at least disapproval.

"Astina will confirm what I say."

"We must talk with the Maiden one day, dear," the man mumbled.

"Yes, darling, we must."

They would never get around to it. . . .

D'ward thumped his fists against his hipbones. "I ask from you only what
Astina granted me: first, that she would defend me from his reapers within her
domain, second, that she would issue a revelation to her priests to hold back the
civil—"

"No," said the man, closing his eyes again.

The woman uttered a creaky chuckle. "If you can't defend yourself from
those, how can you hope to handle a god?"

"But it will waste mana! You know that the more I have, the faster I will be
able to garner more. I need help to build my—"

"Revolution?" The man yawned. "It doesn't work. We built too well."

D'ward swore under his breath, words Dosh did not know. "No one has ever
managed to preach rebellion in more than two vales, so Prylis says."

The woman moved her lips for a moment. "True."

"I am in my fourth! I have lasted almost two fortnights already. I am something
new, do you hear? Something you have never seen before! I am foretold by a
chain of prophecy Zath has not broken in thirty years of trying. If you won't
guard me in Niolvale, will you at least watch my efforts? Will you watch to see
how far I get, when and how I die?"

With glacial slowness, the man raised a hand and scratched at his beard with
nails like small horn daggers. "That might be amusing," he conceded.

"Haven't seen anything new in a thousand years," the woman muttered.

D'ward released a deep breath, as if he had won a victory. "Astina promised
me one more thing. If I do survive to confront Zath on his node, then she will
lend me some mana for the final—"

"Oh, no!" snapped the woman, and this time she actually stirred in her chair.
"How could we ever trust you to pay it back? You say that Zath is a threat to
us, but if you won, you would be stronger than he."

"I gave my solemn word that—"

"Dragonshit." Her pebbly eyes shifted to stare at Dosh, peering around the

Liberator, and they seemed to come to life. "Who's he?" Her voice rose to a screech: "You brought a *native* into our sanctum?"

The man heaved himself erect in his chair to glare at Dosh, and his robe crumbled away to dust.

Without turning, D'ward whispered, "Go!"

Dosh spun around and shot out of the chamber.

ᏍᏃ 27 ᏁᏍᎨ

IN PANIC, HE FOUGHT HIS WAY THROUGH DARKNESS, FINDING THE TUNNEL by ricocheting off furniture, bouncing against tall urns, stumbling over chests, tripping on goblets and vases, knocking down giant candelabras and suits of armor. Debris cascaded to the floor behind him, and his flight must have sounded like an earthquake. He had no idea what sort of a door he would find, or if he would be able to open it. In the end there was no door—he flailed out into moonlight and rolled head over heels down the steps.

That was not the last of his troubles. Evidently the trespassers' violation of the sanctuary had been observed and all the available clergy had assembled to beseech Visek's forgiveness. At least forty white-robed priests and priestesses were on their knees there, chanting a lament. Dosh plowed into them like a runaway snowball, bowling over seven or eight before he came to a stop.

The green moon whirled in the sky above him, accompanied by flashes of flame and more stars than he had ever seen before. Three or four men threw themselves on top of him to restrain him, although he would not have been capable of even sitting up, let alone making a run for it.

The singing ended. People shouted. Order of a sort was restored.

Dosh found himself lying on the floor, with his arms and legs pinned. A burning agony in his nose was spraying blood. He peered up groggily at a ring of irate faces. Several tried to speak at once before one elderly man established his seniority.

"Where is your accomplice?" he screeched. He was standing between Dosh's widespread legs and looked dangerously liable to start kicking if he did not receive a satisfactory answer.

Dosh licked his lips, choking on blood from his nose. His left ankle throbbed. "With Holy Visek, of course."

The old man hesitated, considering the implications.

Poor Dosh had been in tight spots before, although probably none tighter than this. He groped for self-confidence, which was not readily accessible in his present condition. "He will be along shortly. Is this how you normally treat the Great One's guests?"

Amazingly, it worked—or at least the old man did not lash out with his feet, which was the most immediate danger. He scowled uncertainly and then stepped back. "Get him up!"

The hands holding Dosh's legs were removed. Those on his arms heaved him erect. The whole temple swayed vertiginously and a spasm of agony shot through his ankle. He stumbled and was held upright, balancing on one foot, nauseated by the battering and the blood he had swallowed.

"Who are you?"

That was a very good question, but it did not seem to have a suitable reply. "Tion," came to mind. No one would question a god's right to come calling on another, but a god would not fall down a flight of steps; a god would not arrive cut, bruised, and unable to put any weight on his left foot.

"A friend of the Liberator's," was another possibility. It had the advantage of being the truth, but it would lead to extremely unpleasant consequences.

"I am not at liberty to answer that," Dosh said.

Someone struck him and the temple rocked again. This time he did throw up, which at least made the senior priest back away and held off further questioning for a moment.

But not for long.

"Guards!" squealed the old man, almost gibbering in his fury.

The cordon of priests and priestesses parted to admit a squad of armed men, moonlight glittering on blades and armor and reptilian eyes.

"Interrogate this criminal!" the high priest quavered. "Find out who he is and what he is doing. Get the truth out of him."

The shiniest guard looked around uneasily. "Here, Venerable One?"

"Yes, here! Now! Immediately!"

As soldiers replaced the priests holding his arms, Dosh braced himself for unpleasant experiences. Oh, poor, poor Dosh!

"What are you doing?" demanded a voice from the throne. D'ward came striding down the steps. "Release that man!"

He wore nothing but a peasant's loincloth, but his voice rang with the brazen prestige of bugles. The crowd opened, men and women and even soldiers backing away. Dosh swayed and steadied, teetering on one leg.

Blue eyes seared the onlookers. "Stand back!" They all retreated one more step. "Farther!" The clearing widened. Then D'ward turned to Dosh and pulled a face at what he saw. He reached out and touched his throbbing, burning nose. The pain stopped instantly. Dosh wiped off the blood with his arm.

"And what's wrong with your foot?"

Dosh felt better already. This breather might not last, but every minute he was not being questioned by those thugs was an improvement. "I broke my ankle." He thought it was only sprained, but that was a mere quibble.

"Who are you?" The high priest had lost much of his screech.

D'ward turned and studied him for a moment. "Who do you say is the god of prophecy?"

The old man twitched in indignation. "Holy Visek in their avatar of Waa-tuun."

"And I am D'ward Liberator, the one foretold."

Screech became scream. *"The heretic?"*

Without deigning to answer, D'ward dropped to one knee and took Dosh's ankle in his hands. His fingers felt ice cold on the hot swelling. He pulled the foot down to the floor.

"Try that."

Dosh put his weight on it and nothing nasty happened. "That's fine now," he said calmly. "Thank you." He must have banged his head harder than he realized, for obviously this could not be happening. On the other hand, there was not a closed mouth in the audience.

D'ward rose and regarded the onlookers as a proud housewife might inspect cockroaches in her larder. He was taller than almost all of them, which helped. "I am the Liberator. I had business with Visek. Is that any concern of yours? It is prophesied that I shall bring death to Death. And it is written, 'Hurt and sickness, yea death itself, shall he take from us. Oh rejoice!' "

The high priest's knees began to buckle, but a younger, larger man beside him caught him by the elbow and held him upright. "The Liberator preaches foulest heresy against the Holy Gods!"

D'ward's eyes spat contempt at him. "How often have you heard the Liberator preach?"

"I would not let his lies foul my ears!"

"Then let his deeds open your eyes! 'Rejoice!' the prophecy says. You have just seen a wonder. What does it take to save you from your ignorance and error? I tell you to rejoice!"

The man looked at Dosh's nose, down at his ankle. Then he sank to his knees. The high priest followed more circumspectly, and all the rest also. Bronze helmets and white turbans dipped to the floor. Oh, that was much better!

"Rejoice!" D'ward snapped. "Rejoice until the sun rises to warm your cold and unbelieving hearts." He nudged Dosh and strode away.

Amazingly, no one tried to stop them. Soldiers and clergy cowered on their faces and the most notorious heretic in the Vales walked away unchallenged, his companion at his side. As they trotted out between the pillars and down the steps, he remarked casually, "You know, that was a lot closer than it looked."

But the priests were not the only ones troubled by ignorance and error. Dosh's eyes also had just been opened. "I have been a fool!" he wailed. "Lord, forgive—"

"Never mind that now! Can you run? Because I haven't got anything left! We'll have to manage on honest sweat and muscle. Can you run?"

"Yes, master."

"Good man. Then let's get out of here before they change their minds."

★　　★　　★

They ran. The way back was a thousand times longer than the way there had been. Trumb dipped to the west and duly eclipsed, becoming a black moon against a glory of stars, and only the cold blue glow of Ysh lit the road. Dosh should have worried about reapers then, but he was beyond such trivia. As the eclipse ended, clouds moved in; rain began to fall, slowing the pace even more.

He was tortured by both remorse and fury at his own blindness. He had known D'ward for years and identified him as the Liberator earlier than anyone else. He had seen him perform miracles before—they had all been unobtrusive, deniable miracles, but they should have been enough. Lack of morals never bothered him, but he hated to think of himself as lacking brains. In the last half fortnight he had heard D'ward preach about a dozen times, and yet he had let the words roll off his mind like water off a candle. Now he tried to recall all those words, to understand just how much he had missed.

What was D'ward, then? Was he a man sent by the gods, or was he a god himself? Surely only a god could have healed that ankle? Yet D'ward denied the gods. There was only one god, he said, a god Undivided, indivisible. The puzzle was too great to solve on a cold, wet night, jogging along in the mud. Fatigue blurred his mind until he could not think, could only slog along, following the pale glimmer of D'ward's back in the darkness.

The first time they stopped at a stream to drink, even before he had washed off the dried blood, he tried to ask for guidance and forgiveness.

"Don't worry about all that now," D'ward said. "There is time yet to straighten it all out. How are your bruises?"

As the hours passed, Dosh began to stumble more and more often. D'ward would hear his steps falter and come back and help him up, plastered with mud, and get him moving again. And then even D'ward seemed to run out of strength—although his strength was much more strength of will than of body, for he too was reeling on his feet. And the rain was becoming a downpour.

They took shelter under a bridge at a place where the road ran straight, a low causeway crossing marsh and lakes. At intervals it rose on timber bridges to let the wandering streams drain through, but at this time of year the water was low, exposing sand. The two of them crawled underneath and stretched out between the weed-furred piles with groans of contentment. Rain drummed on the planks only inches above them, but they were out of it.

Almost out of it—Dosh eased away from a dribble.

"Sleep awhile," D'ward mumbled.

"One fortnight or two?"

"Just one. When Prat'han wakes up and finds I'm not there, he's going to murder me."

After a bemused moment, Dosh worked out why that sounded funny, and surprised himself with a chuckle.

"Mm?" D'ward said. "Oh, well, when I get back he will. He'll have to manage somehow, won't he? Trouble is, we have a long trek to do today."

"Skip it," Dosh murmured. The Liberator had told Visek that he went from node to node. He wondered what a node was. "Rest today, go tomorrow."

D'ward began muttering about winter being due and the problem of finding enough food if the Free stayed in one place, but his voice came from a long way away. . . .

"Watch it!" A warning hand caught Dosh's head just before he jerked it up and cracked it against a beam.

He blinked in alarm, wondering where he was, why he was so confoundedly cold, wet, and sore, and who the bastard was who was sprinkling water on him. Then he heard the noise, and registered the vibration in the timbers above him that was shaking off the moisture. Green moonlight shone on the stream beyond the bridge, so they had not slept very long. An hour, perhaps, not as much as two. The rain had stopped.

"What . . . ?"

"Soldiers!"

Many hooves tramping across the bridge.

Dosh heaved himself up on an elbow to peer over his companion and study the shadows on the water. He saw shapes of lancers on moas, heading west. He looked at D'ward, two eyes shining in the darkness, and asked, "They're after us?"

"Not us two, I think. The Free. We'll have to wait until they're gone, and then go back and try to cut around the lakes."

"No!" Dosh said. "Once they're off the bridge, they'll speed up again. We'll never get there before them, no matter what way we go."

D'ward groaned. "Suppose you're right."

The rear guard passed and the noise faded into the distance.

Why go on? If the Niolian cavalry was moving against the Free, then the Liberator would return to find his followers massacred, arrested, or scattered. But of course D'ward would go back. There would be no talking him into deserting. And if he were there, then he might work another miracle, even without the help of Irepit. He was the Liberator.

Dosh thought back to his servitude with Tarion, the Nagian cavalryleader. "It may be possible. They'll bivouac before dawn to rest their mounts. We may get in front of them then."

It sounded impossible. It was impossible, for two exhausted men on battered, bleeding feet. But they did it.

As dawn was painting rosy tints on Niolwall ahead of them, they trotted past a field where moas were grazing on stubble and men huddled around campfires. Those proud lancers showed no interest in two peasants going by on foot and did not challenge. As soon as they were out of sight, D'ward quickened the pace. Somehow Dosh kept up with him on his shorter legs.

The campsite of the Free was much less organized and covered a far greater area. The pilgrims were awake, most grouped along the riverbank, washing, rolling up bedding if they had any, singing hymns, or eating whatever scraps they had saved from the evening meal. Few of them noticed the two bedraggled, mud-splattered young men walking along the road, and probably none recognized their leader without his priestly gown.

On the other side of the trail, on the boulder-strewn slope with the Liberator's tent near the pulpit rock, the Warband with shields and spears was moving over the ground like foraging ants, as if searching for bodies. Prat'han was the first to recognize the newcomers. The big man shouted and came leaping down the hill to greet them, looking ready to weep with relief—and also about ready to run his spear through Dosh for having abducted the Liberator. The rest of the warriors came running in to cluster around. Dosh flopped down on the grass.

D'ward remained standing, drooping with fatigue. "Water, please, food if there is any. I've got to clean up and dress. Pass the word that I will not preach this morning and get them moving. We're going to have trouble."

Teeth shone. "We can sharpen our spears now?" Gopaenum demanded.

"Yes. Yes, you can sharpen your spears. And I fear you may blunt them, too, before the day is out. A troop of lancers'll be here very shortly." D'ward rubbed his eyes wearily. "We mustn't lie around here like fish on a slab. Get everyone moving." He pointed.

The trail ahead crossed the river at a ford and then wound off through a watery morass of lake and sedge.

"Can't ride moas through that!" Part'han said, sounding disappointed.

"Can't follow us more than two or maybe three abreast, either!" crowed little Tielan Trader, who had more brains than was thought seemly back in Nagvale. "You want us to hold the bastards off, Liberator? Hold the road?"

"No. I'd rather we got ahead of the crowd. Or as much of it as we can." D'ward limped off toward the tent. Prat'han snapped orders and then followed him.

Suddenly alone, Dosh lay back on the grass. In the last horrible hour he had been unable to think at all. He had almost forgotten the lancers. Now he had arrived, the Liberator had arrived, and the Niolian cavalry would doubtless arrive very soon.

He ought to go back down to the river and clean up, but he did not think he could move another step. He could just curl up where he was and hope the lancers did not notice him or care about one heretic—or would at least not wake him before they skewered him. A loud jingling . . . He forced his eyelids open. Prat'han Potter was squatting beside him like a small mountain, shaking the money bag and grinning like a rock eater.

"Don't you want this back?"

Dosh's mouth felt full of sand. "Not especially. You hang on to it. I'm in no fit state to guard it."

The big man chuckled and produced a hunk of bread as big as two fists. "How about this then?"

Instantly Dosh was aware of a monstrous hunger raging inside him. He heaved himself up on an elbow. "Now that does look interesting!"

"Cheese? Pickles? Smoked fish?"

Afraid he might drown in his own saliva, Dosh sat up. "Brother Prat'han, you have just earned a place among the stars of heaven." He bit greedily. "I mean, you will be united forever with the True God," he corrected.

His companion grinned approvingly at this declaration of Liberator creed.

Already D'ward was striding down the hill to the river, conspicuous in his hooded gray robe, surrounded by the Warband. Perhaps a hundred of the Free had already crossed the ford and were moving off along the road into the marshes. All the rest would follow the Liberator and the lancers would come and that plan seemed totally wrong. Dosh thumped his sleepy brain; he had just worked out the answer when Prat'han put the question, frowning.

"What happens when the troopers get here?"

What he meant was, "D'ward doesn't usually hide behind his friends."

"They'll use a lot of military jargon," Dosh said, munching. "Technical terms for *feces* and *impregnation* and *unnatural sex* that god-fearing people like you don't know. They won't fancy charging two or three abreast along miles of track with swamp on both sides and lots of cover for archers or spearsmen, not to mention a thousand pilgrims getting in the way. If they do try it, the pilgrims can jump into the water and escape."

Prat'han grinned, a mouthful of ivory. "So they'll have to go the long way round and catch us at the other end? Wherever that is?"

"Probably." Dosh groaned and began to rise.

Prat'han offered a hand and hauled him upright. He handed over his spear. "Take this. Your feet look like raw meat. We get down to the river, I'll clean them up for you. Wrap them, too."

Dosh mumbled thanks, eating with one hand and leaning on the spear with the other. He hobbled down the slope, feeling every muscle, every joint. And a long way to go today, D'ward had said.

"Food? Can you organize the food? Someone'll have to get out ahead and buy— How much money is there?" Shamedly, he said, "I'm all in, brother! I need help." He mustn't let D'ward down, but asking for help was not something he was good at.

"Course. Soon's I've seen to those feet."

Giving thanks wasn't something Dosh was good at, either. He tried.

As they neared the trail, "While we're at the river, Brother Prat'han, would you do me that water thing you do with converts?" He received a thump on the back hard enough to knock his knees together.

The big man laughed delightedly. "I think D'ward would like to baptize you into the Church himself, Dosh."

"He won't mind, and I'd sort of like it from you, I think."

"I'd be honored to! Can—can you tell me even a little?"

Little what? Then Dosh saw the torture of curiosity in the Nagian's dark eyes. Oh, that!

"We went to Niol, to the temple. He announced who he was, but they didn't even try to arrest him. They didn't *dare!* Wonderful things . . ." Where could he even start? "I saw *Visek!* Not a god, just two old mummies. Oh, Prat'han, he's right! Everything he says is true! I was so wrong and all of you weren't. You believed and I didn't. I do now. I've been a fool, a terrible fool!"

The potter laughed and squeezed his shoulder. "I asked D'ward about that a couple of days ago. He said bigger brains need more evidence and I ought to mind my own business."

"Bigger *fools* need more evidence, you mean."

"True. But that's not what D'ward said."

They looked at each other and grinned. And then they laughed.

28

JULIAN AND URSULA HAD ARRIVED IN NOSOKVALE THE PREVIOUS EVENING, only to learn that the Liberator had already passed through. They had followed his trail over Thadrilpass, and now they were descending into Niolvale.

An hour or so ago, Julian had been greatly impressed by his first glimpse of it. For one thing, it was much larger than any Nextdoorian basin he had seen so far, its encircling walls dwindling away to vanish over a flat horizon. For another, it was superbly fertile. The bare, dry foothills of Niolslope plunged abruptly into a flatland symphony of green and silver. To the north many little white villages shone like pearls in the morning sun, and from higher up he had seen a city that T'lin said was Niol itself. Southward lay lakes, swamps, and rivers, with only scattered islands cultivated.

Now he was less concerned with geography than demographics. Just how many people were in that crowd down there? It wasn't a full battalion, he decided—closer to three companies, say seven or eight hundred. The vanguard was almost out of sight already, advancing into the marshlands along a narrow, winding track.

Dragons disliked traveling in close order, so conversation was rarely possible except at halts. While still a thousand feet or so above the road, T'lin Dragon-trader shouted, *"Zappan!"* Starlight stopped obediently. The other dragons closed in around him, puffing and belching, peering at one another and their riders with their intelligent, jewel-bright eyes.

"Dragons do not like water," T'lin said, scratching at his coppery beard and scowling.

Why should that be a problem? "I don't suppose there's any doubt that's *Tyika* Kisster's band, is there?"

"No, Saint Kaptaan. I have never seen a gathering like it before. It must be."

"But larger than it was in Joalvale?"

"Oh, many times, Holiness."

"Where are they going?" Ursula sounded grim and looked grimmer.

"The Thadrilpass road divides here, Holiness. That way leads to Niol. I think the other must go to Shuujooby. That would be the shortest road to Lospass and Jurgvale. . . . I am not sure. I have been to Shuujooby, but not by this way. Dragons do not like water."

"Probably stiff with mosquitoes," Julian suggested cheerfully. He did not see why Ursula should be in such a sour mood all of a sudden. She had been enthusiastically playful in the tent before they emerged for breakfast, which might be one reason he was feeling so jovial himself. Was she piqued that Edward had collected so many followers so quickly? That seemed rather petty of her. Bloody good show and more power to him!

"Exeter will be out in front," she said crossly.

"Can't imagine a prophet not leading the chosen people in person, certainly not Edward. Let's amble on down and find out."

T'lin rolled his eyes, clawed at his beard with both hands, and growled, "Dragons do not like water!"

Oh. Now Julian had caught up with the parade. "You mean we should have arrived a little earlier and cut him off?"

Ursula shot him an exasperated look. "A brilliant observation." She turned to survey the ridges of Niolslope behind them and then addressed T'lin again. "What is there at that Shuujooby place?"

"Just a village, Holiness." T'lin thought for a moment. "There is a ruined temple, half buried in sand."

Ursula nodded to herself. Julian could guess that she was thinking *node!* If Exeter was gathering mana and followers by preaching, then he would certainly do so on nodes whenever possible.

"But we can cut back through the hills and get in front of him?"

"Certainly, Holiness."

It was a reasonable suggestion, for dragons were the ultimate in cross-country transportation and the barren hills ideal terrain for them, but Julian was damned tired of sitting on a Brobdingnagian lizard all day, strapped in place like luggage with nothing to do except shout the occasional "*Zaib!*" or "*Varch!*" or "View halloo!" "Let's send T'lin and the mounts around that way. I wouldn't mind a chance to ride shanks' pony for a change."

"Walk?" She snorted. "In the middle of that rabble? You'll get your wallet lifted and fleas in return."

Julian refused to be nettled. "I haven't got a wallet. We came to find out what Exeter's up to, remember? Be a jolly good idea to hear what his crusaders think of him first."

She pouted, apparently unable to refute his arguments. The more Julian considered what he had just suggested, the wiser it seemed, but obviously Ursula would not back down and agree with him. She just did not want to walk and he did, and he could profitably investigate what Exeter was up to. Language might be a problem. His Joalian was still sketchy and there would be no Randorian-speakers this far from Randorvale. He knew someone who could get by in Joalian, though.

Dommi was sitting impassively on Bluegem's back, waiting for the *votyikank* to issue orders. His copper hair shone in the morning sunlight because he had removed his hat, but his face glowed almost as redly, because he had refrained from removing anything else. Which reminded Julian that he too was clad in mountain furs and liable to melt at any moment. He unbuckled his saddle belt and called over to his valet.

"The blue Joalian breeches, if you please, Dommi. And the orange smock. Or do you think something more conservative for a religious convocation? Possibly the forest green?"

Dommi was already standing by his stirrup to help him dismount. "The orange might be an overly brightness, *tyika*, if you wish to remain inconspicuous. And may I suggest the bubblerskin half boots? If I might have a moment, I could give them another coat of wasp oil, although I believe they are watertightest already."

"Oh, I'm sure they are. And I trust you to tie me a hanky-spanky turban."

As his batman headed for Bluegem's panniers, Julian began loosing a few buttons and eying the nearby boulders to decide which one was the gentlemen's changing room. "A snack for me to take with me, too, Dommi? And one for yourself if you want to come along."

Dommi looked around, beaming. "I shall be most honored to accompany you, *tyika*."

Ursula was still mounted, still scowling, staring down at the disappearing multitude. If Exeter had been drawing mana from so many for the last few weeks and not spending any of it on miracles, then he might not be the pushover she had anticipated. Then there would have to be honest negotiation, not any Svengali-type mesmerism.

"Look, old girl," Julian said, "I'm not trying to queer your pitch. I swear I won't even mention you, all right? No hints, warnings . . . I just want to sound him out. Dommi and I will walk. We'll meet you at Exeter's headquarters this evening. At Shuujooby or wherever."

She surrendered with a shrug, as if it didn't matter what he did. "Don't bring the fleas with you."

Dommi had produced the required clothes, all seeming new-washed and freshly pressed. Time to change.

"You could ride as far as the river, Holiness," T'lin suggested, looking worried at this sudden change of plan.

That was only half a mile or so, and by the time Julian got there the stragglers would still be crossing. "No, I'd attract too much attention. You'll take good care of Saint Ursula, won't you? What's that striped thing? Not my turban? For crying out loud, Dommi, you don't expect a gentleman to appear in public in that, do you?"

★   ★   ★

An hour or so later, Julian began to wonder if his decision to walk had been unwise. Two hours later, he was sure of it. The steamy air reeked of wet vegetation and was every bit as well supplied with mosquitoes as he had predicted. Reflecting off the water, sunlight came at him from both above and below. His sweat-soaked smock and breeches clung to him like leeches. So did the leeches. The track was narrow, muddy, winding, and crowded; he could make little progress in his efforts to work his way to the head of the line and steal a private word with Exeter. Here and there the trail would cross an island, and then he could speed around the other travelers, except when the adjacent land was planted in crops. The inhabitants had emerged from their bushy little shacks to stare at this mysterious migration passing through their lonely little world. It must seem like a strange dream to them.

Still, he was moving faster than any, so he would catch up with the leaders sooner or later. The only people who passed him were two men running, both carrying spears and shields. They shouted to clear the way and trotted through, dribbling sweat in the sticky heat but soon vanishing beyond the crowds ahead. No one else seemed to be armed, and yet no one had reacted to them with surprise or alarm.

"Interesting!" Julian said. "Wonder who those jokers are?"

"I saw them when we started, *tyika,* up a tree. I am believing that they may be Nagians, *tyika.*" Dommi's face bore no expression at all, only freckles. He must know as well as Julian did that Exeter had spent his first year on Nextdoor in the Nagian army.

Scouts, perhaps? Left behind to watch where the dragons went?

By and large, the pilgrims were not nearly as helpful as Julian had hoped. Their Joalian was more idiomatic and very much faster than the Joalian he had studied at Olympus—even Dommi often failed to understand their accents. When he could, the halting translation made the conversation stilted and awkward. Most of the crowd seemed to have very little idea why they should be part of this strange expedition, except that Holy D'ward was the prophesied Liberator, he would bring death to Death, he had called on them to join the Free and follow him. It was a perfect example of charisma at work. They were following Exeter because he was a leader, which Julian had known already. Most of the strangers in Olympus could have achieved the same effect as easily, had they ever had cause to risk the wrath of the Pentatheon and the civil rulers of the Vales.

The congregation was a curious cross section of Valian society. Some were in rags, others plump and prosperous. Julian saw ancients staggering along on canes and the arms of younger folk, sturdy young adults with children, babes at their mothers' breasts. He began to have misgivings that had not occurred to him before. Did Exeter have any ideas of how drastically he was disrupting the lives of all these hundreds of people? Where was he leading them and what was going to happen to them? Whether he won or lost his insane gamble, he was creating social chaos. However one regarded the justice of his cause, he was being blasted unfair to the participants. Damn it, they were more victims than participants! Julian could not recall anyone at Olympus offering that argument.

Around the middle of the day, many of the pilgrims settled themselves in the shade of trees or bushes to rest. That thinned out the crowd on the road considerably. Musing that mad dogs and Englishmen could take the same attitude to the noonday sun on this world as well as any other, Julian increased his speed. Dommi produced lunch from his pack, and the two of them ate as they went.

Then Dommi suddenly whispered, *"Tyika?"* and stopped. Here the road ran over a low, rocky island, too small to cultivate. It was graced with some willow-like trees, though, and a group of ten or twelve pilgrims had halted there to rest. There was an argument in progress. Julian could not follow the jabber, but apparently Dommi was picking up at least some of it. He was frowning.

The center of the squabble was a short, blond youngster perched on a boulder. He had no turban; indeed, he wore only a loincloth and sandals, and his feet were bandaged in bloody rags. The others were clustered on the ground around him, like pupils around a teacher. The class was definitely unruly, though, shouting objections. Then Julian saw what Dommi had perhaps noticed right away— most of the audience wore the gold earring of the Undivided. They did not like what they were hearing.

Obviously the kid waving his hands and bellowing was a native; if he had the charisma of a stranger, his message would not be meeting such resistance. Equally obviously, he was sincere in whatever he was saying, growing louder and more flushed by the minute with the righteous anger of a fanatic. He was not really a kid, although his small size and fair coloring made him seem boyish, a slightly balding cherub. A very angry cherub! He might be a Pentatheon believer denouncing the Service's imported theology or perhaps a Liberator disciple. The hitherto simple theology of the Vales was starting to become complicated.

After a few minutes Dommi jerked his pack higher on his shoulders and shot Julian an apologetic glance to indicate that he was ready to move on.

"Stay longer if you want."

"I have heard it all, I think, *tyika*. They are repeating themselves."

"Right-oh!" As they resumed their march, Julian waited for enlightenment. Dommi remained silent.

"What was the argument all about?"

"I think it was theology, *tyika*."

"You astonish me. Actually, you don't surprise me at all. Who was arguing what?"

"I only caught a few words, *tyika*."

"Let's have those, then."

Dommi became surprisingly reticent, his English even more convoluted than usual. Eventually he admitted that the little preacher had claimed to be a close follower of the Liberator and the bone of their contention had been the nature of the afterlife. Until now the Church of the Undivided had followed the Pentatheon's example in promising that the faithful would find eternal bliss among the stars of heaven, while the evil would linger alone forever in darkness. The Liberator apparently had other notions of what the Undivided intended, although Dommi seemed genuinely uncertain what those were.

That explained his troubled frown. The *tyikank* were now disunited, so his loyalties to the Service and to Exeter, his former master, were being put in conflict. Certainly Olympus would not be happy to hear that the Liberator was splitting its Reformation into rival sects. The Pentatheon might be very pleased.

"It's probably just a misunderstanding," Julian said airily. After trudging along for a while, hearing nothing but footsteps squelching in the mud, he decided that the contention he had witnessed required a bigger bone. And obviously Dommi still had misgivings.

"There was more to it than that, though, wasn't there?"

More hard work on Dommi eventually extracted an admission that the afterlife had been a side issue. The main debate had concerned the nature of the traditional Valian gods. According to the Church of the Undivided, Visek and Co. were demons. The Liberator was teaching that they were human enchanters.

That was the truth, of course. It was also a major difference in doctrine.

Julian said, "Damn!" This was much more serious. Prof Rawlinson and the others who had written the True Gospel had thought hard and long before introducing a deliberate falsehood, but they had eventually concluded that it would be simpler and safer to invoke demons than try to explain charismatic strangers, because demons were evil by definition. That was the official explanation. Julian was quite certain that their real reason had been that the apostles themselves were charismatic strangers. To equate the leaders of one side with the leaders of the other would provoke questions about the difference between them. Better to brand the opposition as demons than to argue that they are the baddies and we are the goodies. The obvious answer to that was: "Sez who?"

"Damn!" he repeated. "What the blazes does Exeter think he's up to?" He did not realize that he had spoken aloud until Dommi gave him an answer.

"He is taking help from them, *tyika*!"

"He's *what*?"

Dommi nodded miserably, his face so wobegone that it seemed surprising all his freckles did not jump off and run for cover. "The man on the rock said that the Demon Irepit appeared in Rinoovale at the side of the Liberator. She dispersed a troop of the queen's soldiers for him. And he said that he himself went with the Liberator last night to Niol and saw the Demon Visek in the temple with his own eyes, *tyika*!"

Julian used some words he had not uttered since the Battle of the Somme. Had Exeter sold out to Zath's opponents in the Pentatheon? Foghorn and the others had been absolutely right. The Liberator was going to bring the Church of the Undivided crashing down like Samson's temple.

Ursula would have forty purple fits.

℘ℛ 29 ℘ℛ

T HE TRAIL ROSE OVER AN ISLAND, WHICH BORE A SMALL FARM AT ONE END, the rest being upholstered in shoulder-high bushes. Five men with spears and big round shields stood guard along the west side of the trail. No napoleonic genius was needed to surmise that Edward Exeter might be taking a siesta in the shade somewhere at their backs.

Julian arrived in the company of Dommi, Garhug'n Papermaker, Garhug'n's wife, and their three children, the youngest being around four. Garhug'n spoke a Joalian that Julian found intelligible—most of the time. He had recounted at length how they had been returning home to Niol from visiting his elderly mother, how they had seen the unexpected assembly at the mouth of Thadrilpass the previous evening, how they had stopped to listen to the Liberator's sermon, how their eyes had been miraculously opened to the truth. Garhug'n had at once decided to follow the Liberator, bringing his family with him. He was floating on a cloud of religious ecstasy. His mousy, unassertive wife looked worried out of her mind. The children were muddy, hungry, tired, and bewildered.

The first guard was a stocky young man with dark hair and beard. His skin had been burned to walnut by the sun, about the color a Spaniard or a high-caste Hindu might be, had either ever condescended to live outdoors in a leather loincloth. His spear was a wrist-thick pole about six feet long, topped with a shiny metal blade that looked both sharp and deadly. He bared an excellent set of snow-white teeth in a cheerful smile and recited a formula greeting in the pidgin Joalian that served as lingua franca of the Vales.

"The Liberator will preach tonight at Shuujooby. Food will be available. Please move on and let him rest. The blessings of the Undivided be with you."

Garhug'n complied immediately, chiding his youngest to stop that wailing, urging the rest of his family along.

Julian returned the smile. "He will wish to see me. We are old friends. If he is asleep, of course—"

The smile shrank. "Move along please, brother."

"I assure you that I have known the Liberator since boyhood and he will be very pleased to see me." Julian took a step forward and found his way blocked by a large bullhide shield.

The teeth above it were no longer smiling. "Move along, I said."

Julian was momentarily shocked speechless. Even at Home, a former army officer could expect to bluff his way past a naked savage without raising more than an eyebrow. On Nextdoor his charisma ordinarily gave him the persuasive power of a charging tank.

"Now look here, my good man—"

The guard twirled his spear around in his fingers as if it were a twig and rammed the metal blade into the ground at Julian's toes. He jumped back instinctively, bumping into Dommi.

"Tonight, in the ruined temple at Shuujooby." The guard pulled his spear free and aimed the point at Julian's belt. His teeth smiled again. His eyes did not.

Another Nagian, if that was what they were, strolled over to reinforce him. He was considerably larger. Saint Kaptaan's charisma was not going to work here. These warriors had been exposed too long to Exeter's, and he had left orders.

Dommi cupped his hands to his mouth and bellowed, in English: *"Tyika Kisster! It is me, Dommi Houseboy, from Olympus!"*

The warriors frowned at each other, momentarily nonplussed. The first raised his spear as if he were about to use it as a club; the second snapped a word and stopped him.

Julian drew himself up, although he could not meet the taller one eye to eye. "Go and inform the Liberator that Kaptaan Smedley and—"

A voice called out from the bushes, not fifty feet away. It began, "Dommi?" and then became unintelligible. Whatever the language, the guards reacted and Dommi seemed to understand. With an enormous grin, he hitched his pack higher on his back and plunged into the undergrowth. The guards made no move to stop him.

Julian took half a step and was again blocked by a shield of wood and bullhide.

"You were not summoned."

Ridiculous! Absurd! That had been Exeter himself calling. So now Julian was going to have to yell out his name also, hawking like a bloody peddler selling fish? He would be damned first. The alternative was obviously just to cool his heels here on the road, and that was almost as bad. He felt his temper rising. He wished he had a store of mana, as Ursula and the others did. It would not take much to jerk these flunkies' chains, but his magical resources were precisely zero. Dommi would presumably inform Exeter that he was here right away.

Or very soon.

The warriors were starting to grin.

"Move along, please," said the taller in the exact tone used by London bobbies.

An instant before Julian began bursting blood vessels, Exeter's voice called out again.

The guards stepped aside at once.

"The Liberator summons you!" snapped the big one. "Move!"

For a moment Julian was tempted to tell them that Edward Bloody Exeter could come and deliver the invitation in person, but then common sense prevailed. He stalked into the bushes with as much dignity as he could muster, going where Dommi had gone.

The ground dipped abruptly to a small pond. Shrubs overhanging a low wall of rock threw narrow shade on a sandy beach, where a dozen or so of the Nagians were relaxing, some sitting up, alert, others lying down and apparently snoozing, although they all had their spears within reach. In the middle of the group, Dommi was on his knees with his pack beside him, chattering excitedly to Edward Exeter. Julian scrambled down the little slope and picked his way over outstretched brown legs. He sensed a faint tremor of virtuality. This snug retreat was a very minor node.

The Liberator wore a gray robe, which might be uncomfortably warm in the sticky heat but would at least keep the sun off. He had the cowl back, revealing a shock of wavy black hair in desperate need of a barber. He was jabbering at Dommi, the two of them grinning and talking all over each other like bosom friends, but speaking Randorian so fast that Julian could make out little except proper names. Seemingly Exeter was being brought up to date on events in Olympus since he had left. Almost all the names being bandied to and fro were names of Carrots, not strangers.

For a moment neither paid any heed at all to Julian standing over them. Then Exeter looked up. His brilliant blue eyes studied the newcomer warily before his mouth quirked in a smile.

"Dr. Livingstone, I presume? Or is that your line?"

Feeling oddly at a loss, Julian said, "Cheers!"

"Good to see you, old man." Exeter reached up a hand to shake. " 'Scuse me if I don't leap up, won't you?"

His eyes were bloodshot and sunken. His beard was better trimmed than his hair, but the cheeks above it seemed pale below their tan. His feet were bandaged—just like those of the blond man they had seen earlier who had claimed to have visited Niol last night. . . .

Julian sank down on one knee and accepted the shake with his right hand. Exeter had momentarily forgotten, obviously. He reacted with shock. Then he kept hold of Julian's flipper while he inspected it.

As he let go, he smiled approvingly. "Bloody good show! Nextdoor agrees with you, I'd say."

"It's an improvement." Julian sat down, crossing his legs and pushing Dommi's pack out of the way. "What the blazes is the matter with you, though?"

Exeter shrugged. "Too many late nights." He yawned, and then yawned again, even longer.

Assume a man walked all day, day in, day out. Assume he left his followers one evening and went on foot to Niol and back. . . . Any man might justifiably look all-in after thirty hours on the road. But Exeter was not any man. He was the Liberator.

He was also memories—school days at Fallow in the golden glow of youth, the too-brief trip to Paris that the War had cut short, the frantic few days in 1917 when Julian Smedley had rescued him from a mental ward and he had opened the door to another world for Julian Smedley and thereby saved his sanity. Was that still less than two years ago?

Julian pulled himself together. "No mana?"

"Not just at the moment. So it was you they sent. I rather expected Jumbo or Pinky." There were questions hidden in that remark, questions about loyalty and old friendship.

Why had Julian ever promised not to mention Ursula?

"They asked me to come and find out what you're up to."

"And *Entyika* Newton also," Dommi said quietly.

Whoops!

Exeter compressed his lips so that they vanished briefly between beard and mustache. He said, "A formidable lady, Mrs. Newton, as I recall." Again there were hidden queries in that steady stare.

Relieved that the cat was out of the bag—although he would not use those exact words to Ursula—Julian said, "Ursula will be waiting for you—us—at Shuujooby."

The reply was another cavernous yawn, which effectively masked any reaction the information might have produced.

Damnation! Exeter *must* have been collecting mana these last few weeks. He should be able to banish his fatigue and heal the blisters with a snap of his fingers. Surely he could not have been crazy enough to squander it all on fancy miracles to impress the peasants? Or had he spent it fighting reapers?

Ursula would see right away that he was vulnerable. She would eat him alive. The toughs with their spears and shields would be no defense against her, for Exeter would order them all to go home, dismiss his crusade, and follow her back to Olympus like a pet dog. Hell!

No mana at all? Had it been stolen from him?

"I understand you dropped in on friend Visek last night."

"Oh, blast!" He rubbed his eyes wearily. "How did you hear about that?"

Touched a nerve, have we? "A little bird told me."

The warriors sprawled nearby were frowning at their inability to understand the conversation, but Dommi knew English. He was gazing at Exeter with idiotic adoration. "We overheard a fair-haired man narrating this incident, *tyika*. He had sore feet likewise."

Exeter said, "Thanks!" without taking his eyes off Julian, and smothered another yawn. "Remind me to invent taxicabs sometime. Yes, it's true. His name's Dosh Envoy. I should have told him to keep his mouth shut. He usually makes oysters sound like starlings."

"He was babbling brookily this morning. So is Visek male or female?" Julian could win a sizable bet or two in Olympus with that information. Even Olga claimed not to know for certain.

"They're both—Jack and Jill. So where's Mrs. Newton?"

Julian's gaze wandered to the brown-leathery hills, which must be five miles away now, or more. From this distance, bluish ice-clad crags showed above them. "Riding around."

"Who else is with her?"

"Just T'lin Dragontrader. We came to—"

"That's all right then. Good."

"What do you mean, 'good'?"

A gleam showed in the tired cornflower-blue eyes. "I mean T'lin's dragons can probably outrun Queen Elvanife's moas, as long as he doesn't wander too far into the plains."

It was Julian's turn to jump. This was the meanest game of verbal tennis he'd played in years. "That's why you left two of your Trojans up a tree? You blocked the road with disciples and forced them to go around another way?"

"I detect the mind of a professional strategist."

Which was no answer. Julian shrugged. "There's a nasty prophecy about young men's bones in Niolland."

Exeter nodded, stretched his arms, yawned some more. He glanced briefly at his entourage, smiled at Dommi, turned his calculating gaze on Julian again. "Time to hit the road. It would be gentlemanly to be there to greet Mrs. Newton when she arrives, wouldn't it?"

Julian rolled a few curses around in his head. He had promised not to issue any warnings. . . . If only Exeter didn't look so damned played out . . . Hell! He could drop a hint. "Why don't you take a break, old man, and go on tomorrow, when you're fresher?"

Exeter seemed to understand, because his smile depicted gratitude like an illuminated vellum scroll. Then he shook his head. "I'd best be on my way. I'm expecting a squad of Niolland's finest, and it wouldn't be fair to let them run into Ursula without warning them, would it? Tell me, is it only Mrs. Newton I have to fear, or have the others loaded her up with their mana, too?"

Julian gaped. "Is that possible? You can *give* mana to someone?"

"Yes, it's possible. That's how the little gods pay their dues to the Five." He reached stiffly for his sandals, and his bodyguard scrambled to their feet, even the ones that had seemed to be asleep. "There's a whopper of a node at Shuu-jooby. I want to get there before the troopers do."

A node would be a fortress for him, but only if he had a store of mana to exploit it. Julian had no mana either, so he couldn't help, whatever happened.

ᖪᕈᕐ 30 ᕋᕈᖬ

EXETER LIMPED BACK TO THE ROAD, OBVIOUSLY FINDING WALKING AN OR-deal. His praetorians fussed around him like mother hens, but he ignored them, pulling up his cowl to hide his face. They would gladly have carried him shoulder-high, of course, but what sort of prophet would he seem then? Soon he called Dommi to his side. The road was narrow and crowded again, now that the sun was past its height, so Julian found himself excluded, walking behind his own houseboy and hemmed in by the armed escort like a felon being led to the gallows.

He tried to make conversation with the spear carriers on either side of him, but he could understand little of their heavily accented Joalian. They were loathe to speak with him anyway, being uncertain just who he was or how their leader regarded him. The red-haired one was obviously the boss's favorite.

Julian had made no progress with Exeter so far. He still had no idea why the man had changed his mind about the *Filoby Testament*, nor did he know what could be done about Ursula. He had been expecting to find the Liberator all charged up with mana, capable of at least putting up a fight. Watching the gray-robed figure striding along in front of him, though, he could see charisma at work. Even though they were not on a node, Exeter was bearing himself straighter already, drawing strength from the devotion of his bodyguard and the adoring pilgrims he passed. That would doubtless carry him as far as Shuujooby. It wouldn't help much with Ursula, or Queen Elvanife's lancers either.

For a sweaty, mosquito-laden hour, they trudged through the swamp, looping around toward the rocky gullies of Niolslope again. Finally Exeter remembered his manners. Leaving Dommi to walk alone, he dropped back to partner Julian.

"Dommi tells me the war is over." He looked fitter than before, his blue eyes twinkling again. Perhaps he felt better able to battle wits.

"Apparently. The Huns lost. We haven't heard much detail yet." Julian told what he knew, marveling how little it touched him now. He rarely even dreamed of the hell he had known in Flanders anymore. "And you've started another," he concluded. "Another war, I mean."

"Dear me! The Service is upset?"

"Very. When they hear how you're changing their doctrine, they'll all spit fire and brimstone."

"Their own fault for inventing the demons. What sort of religion is based on lies and slander?"

"Try telling that to Ursula."

Exeter did not answer. His cowl concealed his face. He had been a devilish-good bowler back at Fallow, never much of a batsman. When he was on bat, he had consistently stonewalled. He had not lost that ability, for he now proceeded to stonewall every question Julian threw at him.

"You don't hand out gold earrings to your converts?"

"Ain't got no gold."

"But you've imported baptism!"

"Water's cheap."

"I suppose every cult needs some sort of initiation," Julian mused. "And circumcision would be messy?"

Exeter shuddered. "Please!"

"So you went into partnership with the Pentatheon?"

"They're not all monsters."

"And they deal with any reapers Zath sends after you?"

"They have so far."

If the Five were frightened of upstart Zath, they might accept the Liberator as an ally or use him as a stalking horse, although only a congenital idiot would ever trust any of them. What promises had Exeter made to win that cooperation? How long a spoon was he using? How far had he bent his principles? To ask those questions would be to end the conversation and trample the fragile re-awakening of friendship.

"I thought Zath was stronger than any of them, perhaps even stronger than the whole caboodle?"

Exeter shrugged. "Who knows? Who can possibly know, without trying? No one plays the Great Game with his cards showing."

Julian persisted. "So why doesn't he come and get you, now that he's aware where you are?"

"You're the military man. You send out skirmishers and they fail to return. Do you march your whole army after them?"

"No. I send a stronger force to reconnoiter."

"I expect he'll get around to that."

Reapers were only natives, enslaved by mana. They were armed with rituals that could direct the power of their god, but all their strength came from Zath himself.

"If he sends that stronger force, will you be able to detect them? Will the spells show?"

Exeter took a while to reply. Julian could not tell whether he was thinking over the question or just delaying.

"If I have mana of my own, I may be able to detect them."

"Why don't you have any mana now?"

"Used it up."

"Doing what? Turning rods into serpents?" He knew he was prying danger-ously, but he got a civil enough answer.

"Running. I did heal an injured ankle, but it was on Visek's node."

"Why did that matter?"

"All the witnesses were Visek's clergy. They gave all the credit to Visek."

"You'll gain some back tonight, when you preach at Shuujooby?"

"Hope so."

Ursula might get to him before he even opened his mouth, unless Julian himself could distract her somehow. To a large extent, mana was its own fertil-izer, like money—the more one had, the easier it was to gain more. Physical exhaustion was not the best state in which to preach a religious revolution. Bloody idiot!

Julian realized he was starting to lose his temper, which was the worst way to deal with stonewalling. "You're heading for Tharg? You're going to knock the chip off Zath's shoulder, aren't you? Where the hell are you going to get the mana from?"

Exeter hit that one for six. He turned his head and flashed a smile at his tormentor. "From the *Filoby Testament,* of course."

Julian said, "What?"

"The prophecy itself has mana, old man. Haven't you realized that yet? It takes a ton of mana to prophesy—so where does it *go?*"

"Haven't the foggiest."

"Into the words! Every time the prophecy is vindicated by events, it collects more mana from all the people who know about it. Zath's been trying since before we were born to break the chain. He fails every time, and every time the prophecy grows stronger."

Julian stepped in a pothole and stumbled into a leather shield, which helpfully thumped him back to the vertical again.

"That's bizarre! I never heard that theory before. Who told you that?"

"Thought it up by myself," Exeter said with a shrug.

"I don't believe it!"

"I'm not sure I do, actually. But perhaps Zath does? I thought there was at least a fifty-fifty chance he'd come after me right at the start—nip me in the bud in Joalvale with *donner und blitzen* and fiery whips. He didn't. So perhaps he's learned his lesson."

"He'll just let all those things happen, you mean? Let the play be acted out? Hell's bells, man, the finale is his own death!"

Exeter chuckled. "Which means that he won't have dared do a foreseeing of his own. Did you know that, old man? Foreseeing your own death is fatal. He may have had someone else do it for him, of course. No, I'm sure he'll fight at the end. Now he knows I'm coming for him. He knows I have allies, but he doesn't know how many or who, and he'll want to know that for settling scores later if he wins. He may try another jab or two, but I do believe he'll save his strength for the final innings."

The idea of the *Filoby Testament* as a sort of active participant did make a wildly improbable sort of sense. Julian himself had postulated that Exeter might have seen something nobody else had. Was this it? More important, would it deter Ursula from meddling?

"That valley?" Exeter was pointing a long, gray-sleeved arm at the hills that now loomed over them, surprisingly close again. "Shuujooby's at the mouth of that."

"You've reconnoitered the whole route, haven't you? That's what you've been doing these last two years?"

Exeter just smiled.

~ 31 ~

W HERE THE RIVER EMPTIED OUT OF THE HILLS TO FEED THE LAKES AND marshland, its course was almost a mile wide. At that time of year it was all sand, brilliant white quartz, with only a few silver pools and shallow braids holding water, and nothing flowing except an invisible, tangible torrent of air, the breath of the mountains pouring out of the gorge to blow grit in men's eyes. The only relief from the glaring whiteness was a speckle of shadow under isolated dead trees, stark bleached skeletons.

The trail ended on the northern bank at a rickety jetty and a couple of stranded ferryboats. The celebrated metropolis of Shuujooby was a cluster of driftwood hovels cowering low in the long, rank grass, each hoarding a snowy drift of sand on its leeward side. About a score of ragged villagers stood gaping at the Liberator's crusade going by. They must have been puzzled by the pilgrims who had already passed and dwindled to specks in the distance, trooping over the shining white desert to reach the designated stopping place. The Warband with their spears and shields were an even greater wonder, and there were hundreds of followers to come yet.

The far bank was a faint green line of brush and woodland, before which stood the remains of the temple, half buried in the sands of the floodplain. Even at that distance, Julian could see that it had been picked clean, as if by giant vultures. Every stone must be burnished smooth, and few seemed to be standing in their original positions. It would have been built on a node, though, and the virtuality would remain. A whopper of a node, Exeter had called it.

He had gone forward to rejoin Dommi, so Julian was alone again. He did not mind, for he had much to think about. Ursula would certainly try to block Exeter's revolution. Julian found that he was hunting for arguments to stop her, so he must want it to continue. Why? Could he really believe that it had any chance of success? It seemed horribly like a children's crusade, a massacre of innocents. Whatever damage it was going to do to the Church of the Undivided was probably inevitable now. Whether the heretic sect was smitten by Zath in Thargvale or just discredited and dispersed when Ursula betwitched its leader, the Pentatheon and their traditional religion would be seen to have triumphed.

That was a very cynical attitude! At the rate Exeter was going, he would have gathered a huge following by the time he reached Thargvale. Better, surely, to abandon a few hundred people here than let thousands be slain there? Unless Julian could convince himself that the circus held some reasonable chance of success, he would never convince Ursula—and should not even try.

Ignoring Shuujooby and the watching Shuujoobyites, the Warband arrived at the riverbank and the jetty. The lead warriors jumped down from the spiny grass to the white plain. Exeter and Dommi followed, then Julian himself slithered after them in a shower of hot sand. As he recovered his balance, he saw Ursula a hundred yards or so off to his right, beyond the hamlet. For a moment he felt a strange reluctance to speak with her. He had sworn not to warn Exeter and then broken his word.

She saw him and waved. She ran down the bank, wheeling her arms for balance, and then stood waiting. He slipped neatly between two of the Nagians and started to run. If anyone tried to follow and was called back by Exeter, the wind stole away the words. He staggered and stumbled in the soft sand, his aching feet reminding him how far he had walked that day.

As he drew close, he saw that she was barefoot, clutching her shoes in one hand; the other held her wide-brimmed hat in place against the mischief of the wind. She was wearing a white dress of the flimsy Nextdoorian fabric the Service called cotton, although its fibers came from a tuber. Her arms were bare and the billowing of the material revealed her ankles and half her shins. It also displayed the curves of her hips and thighs and breasts, the unusual width of her shoulders. He had never heard of such a garment in the Vales, but he would not complain about it. She looked for all the world like a girl playing on a beach at Blackpool or Frinton, and must feel like that, also, for she was laughing as she watched his labored approach, her face flushed by the wind.

Instinctively he reached up to remove his hat and remembered that it was a turban. Good Lord! Kiss a woman with his hat on?

He did. She folded into his embrace and returned the kiss willingly, thumping her shoes against his flank in a one-armed hug. Then she applied her other arm as well, and in seconds the wind stole her hat. She swore. He broke loose and ran to catch it, noting that the Warband was tramping along in the same order as before, heading for the distant ruins. Had Exeter observed the meeting and drawn the appropriate conclusions? No matter—Dommi would certainly have told him how the land lay.

Julian brought back the hat and kissed her again.

"Mm! Walking must agree with you," she said breathlessly.

"Actually, I was dead on my feet until I saw you." And now he wasn't. Ursula Newton intoxicated him.

He exchanged the hat for her shoes, which he held in the crook of his right arm. Hand in hand, they plodded over the riverbed, heading for the ruins. He could think of no reasonable excuse not to.

"Those Zulus are Nagians, I suppose?" she said.

"Right on. His old comrades from the Lemond campaign."

"And how is General Exeter?"

"As well as can be expected." He was lying already.

Ursula glanced up at him quizzically. Her eyes were hazel with tiny golden flecks in them. "Did you discover the argument that will convince him to stop this madness?"

He hoped he had found an argument to stop *her*. "Not really. I— We really had no chance for thorough discussion."

She made no comment. The brim of her hat concealed her expression.

"Remember that night at the Pinkneys'?" he said. "I suggested that Exeter might have seen something the rest of us had missed?"

"Do tell." She sounded skeptical already.

"Well, he's got an interesting theory that the *Filoby Testament* itself may be a reservoir of mana. We know it was an accident; we know it drained Garward so he almost died of it. Mana certainly went into its making. Exeter thinks that every time it's been proved right, it's grown stronger."

"You believe this?"

"I don't know. I think we ought to get back to Prof Rawlinson on the subject before we take any action." Hearing no wild cheers of agreement, Julian pressed on. "I was sent out to reconnoiter, remember. We're scouts, not an assault party."

He was a scout. Ursula might think of herself otherwise.

"Fiddlesticks! It's enough to send Prof into delirium. You honestly think that a prophecy can somehow take on a life of its own and then gather strength from its own success? You're anthropomorphizing an idea!"

"I'm not the first to do that, old girl. A faith is an idea, and lots of faiths have been anthro-whatever-you-said. Religions and nation-states are ideas." Then Julian thought of something else. If he wasn't convincing Ursula, he was at least beginning to convince himself. "Look at it this way—if Zath had never tried to invalidate the *Filoby Testament*, then a lot of things wouldn't have happened. D'you see? Such as Exeter's return Home. That wouldn't *dis*prove anything, because the prophecy gives no dates or order. As far as the world's concerned, those things just wouldn't have happened *yet*, see? But Zath meddled and they did happen, and everyone says, 'Oo! There goes the *Filoby* thing again, ain't it wonderful?' People talk. Its reputation gets boosted. Fame is a source of mana—you've got to admit that."

"Pull the other one! Trafalgar Square's famous. You think it's got mana?"

"It may," Julian protested. "It makes me feel pretty proud to see old Horatio up there on his bally chimney. It's at least got virtuality." Was virtuality in places the same as mana in people? Did a place gain virtuality from worship as people gained mana? That was an intriguing idea, by George! When he got home to Olympus, he wouldn't just ask Prof about it; he'd work it all out in a paper and present it for discussion. But the problem at the moment was Ursula. "Besides, mana doesn't obey the laws of logic. Nor does charisma. Or nodes or portals."

"Or Captain Smedley."

They were halfway across already. The Warband had almost reached the temple, trailing a snake of pilgrims in its wake. The broken walls and stark, tilted columns were a pale yellow stain on the whiteness of the sand. Julian thought of streaky yolk in a fried egg and realized that he was hungry.

The Nagians might keep visitors away from the Liberator until he had delivered his promised sermon. He doubted they could stop Ursula from gate-crashing if she wanted to.

"What else did you learn?" she asked, not looking up.

"Not much. Well . . . he has allies. Astina and Irepit have been helping him. Apparently he had an audience with Visek."

Now she tilted her head and her eyes glinted angrily. "Is this common knowledge?" She had seen the asp in the basket already.

"Some of it," he admitted.

"And how does he rationalize consorting with demons?"

"Um, you'll have to ask him. Look, darling, just promise me that you won't do anything hasty, because—"

"I won't promise a blasted thing!"

"Dammit, Ursula, it's dangerous!"

"What is?"

"Tampering with the prophecy! Zath's been trying for years. All he ever managed to do was kill a lot of innocent bystanders—Exeter's parents, Julius Creighton, poor old Bagpipe. . . . You're likely to get your own fingers burned if you start meddling. All I'm asking is that you— *Oh, Hell!*"

Never mind Ursula. A column of lancers on moas was pouring down the far bank and across the sand, heading for the Liberator and his Warband. There were at least a hundred of them.

32

BACK IN 1916, ON LEAVE IN LONDON, JULIAN HAD VISITED A MOVING-pictures theater. This was just like that. There the screen had been canvas, here it was a glare of sunlit sand, but he saw the same black-and-white images—jerky, silent, and hard to make out, varnished in the same unreality. Only the thundering pipe organ was missing.

Moas stood ten or twelve feet high. They were bigger than ostriches and even faster, which meant they made a terrestrial horse seem like an arthritic Shetland pony. A man on a moa's back was out of reach of a foot soldier and his fifteen-foot lance was tipped with a triangular blade of razor-sharp steel. In full charge, he moved at around fifty miles an hour, a bloody near impossible target for bow or javelin.

This was a charge. Riding three abreast with pennants waving, the column swept across the riverbed like an express train, undulating over the low dunes and ridges. A cloud of dust from the hooves floated away in the wind, adding to the train illusion. The three files began to spread out, opening like talons, bearing death to all in their path.

Julian stood rooted. The Warband was sprinting to the temple—a man with solid rock at his back would be a harder target, although he would have little room to handle his own weapon. Within the ruins, the lancers would lose their advantage of speed, but not that of height, and moas were as nimble as men at dodging and cornering. The odds were five or six to one anyway. Two files were moving to encircle the temple. The third was heading for the long rope of pilgrims, which began to disintegrate as the prudent took to their heels, fleeing back toward Shuujooby. The procession became a rout.

"This should be an interesting test of Mr. Exeter's abilities," Ursula remarked acidly.

That broke the spell. Julian almost screamed as he realized their peril. He and Ursula were just standing there, two isolated onlookers in the middle of the empty field of sand. They could never be mistaken for ragged Shuujoobian peasants, so they would be assumed to be Liberator supporters. They were sitting ducks. He dropped Ursula's shoes, grabbed her wrist, and began to run. She must have come to the same conclusion at the same instant, for she did not resist.

Running in the hot, soft sand was pure nightmare. The hamlet seemed a million miles away, and it would provide no real cover anyway. The moas would move on the grass as easily as on the riverbed. Julian could not recall how far beyond Shuujooby the edge of the swamp was—he just knew that it was too far, so running was useless. No matter, they had no alternative. The shell burst of pilgrims was throwing fragments in their direction, a few agile youngsters overtaking them. So now they were within the fleeing mob itself, part of a designated target.

Out of the corner of his eye he saw a long shadow hurtle over the sand. He turned his head in time to see a boy die—a lad of about fourteen, a brown, skinny adolescent flailing his long legs, floundering as fast as he could through the powdery sand. The moa flashed in from behind him and past him and was gone before his corpse even hit the ground, hosing a crimson jet. The lance blade had severed the kid's neck. One of the flashing hoofs struck the falling head and hurled it in a long arc like a soccer ball. There was no sound at all.

The moa spun around ninety degrees and accelerated straight for Julian and Ursula without missing a stride. Mount and rider seemed to explode out of the distance, from small to huge in an instant, filling the sky. Julian pushed Ursula behind him. He caught a brief glimpse of the trooper crouched alongside his mount's long neck: bronze helmet, leather tunic, shiny boots in stirrups. He saw the moa's yellow eyes and teeth and the froth around its bit, saw human eyes slitted and teeth bared as their owner aimed his bloodstained lance straight at Julian's chest.

Shells and bombs he had survived, bullets and poison gas, and he was going to be stuck like a pig by this medieval nightmare, this anachronistic cowboy. He closed his eyes.

He felt the wind of the beast's passing; he caught a whiff of its animal scent. Hot sand sprayed against his shins.

He opened his eyes and looked around. The lancer had just caught an elderly, silver-haired woman. His blade took her in the back, lifting her bodily off the ground like a rag, then cutting loose through meat and bone. The body dropped free and the rider changed direction slightly, aiming at another target.

Julian peered at Ursula's chalky face. His mouth felt drier than the sand. "You did that?" he croaked.

She nodded.

"Thanks!" He wrapped a shaky arm around her shoulders, and she huddled in tight against him. Most of the fleeing peasants had been run down now. The last few were being skewered as they tried to scramble up the sandy bank. Some had taken refuge under the jetty, but the troopers had seen them.

There was still activity at the temple. There the butchery had not been so easy. Several dead moas lay in clear view and more wheeled around riderless. That would be the Nagians' work, of course, but spears were shorter than lances; they would have had to throw their spears. Even if you were good enough to hit such a target, what could you do for an encore?

The numbers had been impossible from the start. Even if every Nagian managed to kill one lancer, he would then be left with no weapon except a knife, facing three or four more. How many civilian pilgrims had gone to the temple ahead of them? A hundred? Two? Julian could see people scrambling up the walls in search of shelter, swarming ants. He supposed that the troopers would now draw their swords and go after them on foot. Exeter would certainly be dead, of course—prime target. Dommi was in there somewhere, poor sod.

He stood with Ursula on a white desert blotched with corpses. He supposed they should be moving, but shock had addled his wits. He couldn't decide what to do, which way to go.

"How long can you hold that invisibility trick?"

She shivered against him. "We're not invisible. I just distracted that one. It won't work if there's more than one or two of them. Besides, there aren't any more decoys to use."

"You mean you—" Don't ask! The old woman would have died anyway. "Then we ought to . . ." He looked around again to make sure no murdering Lancelot was heading their way. He could hear faint screams from the jetty. Some of the troopers had dismounted and gone in after the refugees. He looked away.

He blinked. He looked again and blinked again. It was real. "By Jove, I do believe that's our bus coming!"

Four dragons running over the sand, coming from the gorge mouth. T'lin's black turban and copper beard on the lead dragon. Julian waved and T'lin waved back, so he had seen them. How long had Ursula known? Never mind. Saved!

Well, perhaps saved. In a race on this terrain, the smart money would back the moas. Fortunately, dragons were hellishly expensive. No trooper was going to mistake a gentleman on a dragon for a penniless vagrant pilgrim. It would be like driving up to the scene of the crime in a Rolls—the bobbies would salute you and call you sir.

He saw the woman's body, and the boy's head lying in a puddle of water, a long way from the corpse. Murdering swine! Yes, artillery killed people too, but that had been on a battlefield, those had been soldiers. This was deliberate slaughter of unarmed women and children. *Damn Edward Exeter and his bloody peasants' revolt!*

Their butchery at the jetty complete, the Shuujooby troopers had formed up and were coming across the plain at a slow lope. They would certainly pick off the two they had missed on the first pass.

T'lin and Starlight came racing over the sand, with Bluegem, Blizzard, and Mistrunner spread out behind. Julian bellowed a wordless welcome as the dragontrader went by, barking commands that hardly seemed needed. Dragons often showed surprising intelligence, and Mistrunner was already heading for Ursula. Blizzard came straight to Julian and skidded to a halt on his belly, ready to be mounted. He was obviously suffering from the heat, puffing hoarsely, his long neck frills flapping like wings.

Julian threw himself across the saddle and scrabbled wildly until he could grip the pommel plate with his good hand and swing his leg over. *"Wondo!"* But Blizzard was already heaving himself to his feet. Now where? Stand and face down the troopers or make a run for the hills? While Julian was still trying to make up his mind and find his left stirrup, he heard Ursula's voice raised in command and a cry of protest from T'lin, "Dragons cannot *zomph* in this heat!"

But Mistrunner shot off in a shower of sand—heading for the temple.

"Dommi!" Julian shouted in sudden understanding. "Dommi's in there. *Zomph!"* Good for Ursula!

Blizzard's game leap forward hurled him back against the baggage plate. To make a run for it would likely have brought on pursuit anyway, and Dommi certainly deserved rescue if he were still alive. Edward Bloody Exeter did not! His crazy messiah delusions had provoked this bloodbath. Jumbo and the other antis had been right all along.

Ursula and Mistrunner were drawing out ahead. Poor Blizzard was managing no more than a *varch* and probably could not keep even that up much longer; he was blowing out more steam than the Flying Scotsman. T'lin drew up close on Starlight, the unladen Bluegem following.

"This will kill them!" the Dragontrader howled.

"It may kill us too," Julian said cheerfully. Though he still had no weapon, there was something about being mounted that stiffened a chap's spirit. Being the man on the ground when the cavalry charged was a ruddy poor show. That was what the Middle Ages had been all about, of course.

He passed the first dead moa, its rider sprawled nearby with his throat cut. The footprints showed where the Nagian victor had departed, taking his spear with him and apparently the trooper's lance also, for it was missing, but one down did not change the odds very much.

He went by more bodies: men, women, even small children, many of them horribly ripped by the force of the lances; blood-soaked sand. The fighting was still going on—he could hear shouts and screams from the ruins and he wanted to scream. There was nothing he could do to help. Now, if only Nextdoorian dragons were real fire-breathing monsters instead of hay-eating softies . . .

A whopper of a node, Exeter had said, and already Julian could feel his skin prickle at the awesome touch of virtuality. A great holy place, an ancient sanctuary . . . The temple remains were bigger than he had realized, so scattered and shattered that he could form no clear image of its plan. In places the original carvings still showed; in others the stones had been fretted into grotesque shapes; yet others had been polished smooth. Centuries of wind had pushed the sand into waves, leaving columns and walls sticking up at random from the dunes, many of them now bearing bizarre headdresses of refugees. There were people perched on every high surface. He saw one canted column with two women and a man on the top of it. How had they climbed up there? They looked as if one sneeze would hurl them all off. He sought vainly for a sign of Dommi's red hair.

T'lin had disappeared. Blizzard was following Mistrunner through the labyrinth—around a corner, then another, over a dune, and almost into a squirming, bleating herd of moas, which had been packed into a dead-end corridor and were being kept there by two mounted lancers. Their job had probably been hard enough even before the dragons appeared, but then the moas began to panic. The soldiers reacted with roars of anger. Ursula turned Mistrunner and put her straight at a wall. Blizzard followed without waiting to be told. Julian's hill straps dangled unfastened and useless behind him—he grabbed at the pommel plate with his good hand just as he was tilted onto his back and almost tipped off.

No human could have climbed that stonework and even the dragons took it slowly, their long claws scraping and scrabbling for purchase. He twisted his head around to see if he was about to be skewered, but the troopers had their hands full with the moas.

Then Blizzard reached the top of the wall, balancing precariously on the stony ridge at Mistrunner's side and belching clouds of steam. Ursula did not even look around. She was watching the drama in what must originally have been a great hall and was now a shadowed courtyard. The sandy floor sloped down to a slimy green pool at the far end, making a sort of amphitheater, and above the pool rose a high wall, bearing a few stumps and buttresses that had once supported a ribbed roof. The rest of the walls were a jagged sawtooth, all the higher points loaded with Exeter's pilgrims, feet dangling. More were perched on any ledge or sill that had a chance of being out of reach of lances.

The entrance was an archway blocked with drifted sand almost to its keystone. No moa could pass through that. Even men on foot would have to crouch to enter, so there the Nagian spearmen had been able to hold off the Joalians' greater numbers. At least three had died doing so, yet all their lives had bought was a little time for their friends, for now they had been outflanked. Now the troopers were swarming in through window apertures and breeches in the walls. The

Nagians had shields, but their spears were much shorter than the lances. They were hopelessly outnumbered. Brave defiance became instant rout. Soldiers yelled; onlookers howled; dying men screamed. It could not compare with the Western Front for sheer horror, but it was still bloody murder.

And there was idiot Exeter in his monk's robe, floundering and splashing through the water of the pond, accompanied by two of his henchmen. The others were trying to cover his retreat and being cut down. Running away? Being unharmed, Exeter had little choice but to run away; even so, it was not what Julian would have expected of him. He watched in grim despair as the trio reached the wall, assuming they would now turn at bay. Instead, the larger, brawnier Nagian dropped to hands and knees in the water, the other jumped up to his back and pulled his leader up after him. He cupped hands; Exeter scrambled to the man's shoulders and reached for a ledge overhead. There was a window opening higher up. He might even reach that, but did he really think he would be allowed to escape so easily?

The top half of his human ladder jumped down, the other man stood up. They had just time to grab up their spears again before the last surviving half dozen of their companions fell back and joined them in the water. Then the Joalian pack was upon them. The troopers came in a bristle of blades, offering no quarter. The pond became a bloody froth as the victims fell, most of them stabbed by four or five lances simultaneously.

Julian shuddered and looked away. Ursula's face was haggard, her lips drawn back in a grimace. He glanced quickly around the watchers on their perches, hoping for a glimpse of Dommi's red hair, but could not see it. He looked down at the cavorting, cheering victors and felt the cold familiar breath of mortality on the back of his neck. The civilians would be next, for the carnage at the jetty showed that someone had ordered a massacre.

"Think we'd better get the devil out of here. The show's over for the Liberator now."

"Wait!" she said.

Exeter had reached his objective, a circular opening about fifteen feet above the pool. It must once have been a great window. He stood within it, outlined against sunlight, balancing himself with outstretched arms and feet. He had his cowl back. The wind was billowing and tugging his gray robe, as if trying to dislodge him. He was a perfect target, an X in a circle. The Joalians had seen him.

An officer began shouting orders, calling upon his men to clear a space and give him a fair shot. It would not be a difficult one, for although a lance was too heavy to be thrown far, in this case it need go only a few feet. He hefted the pole and prepared to run.

"Stop!" Exeter roared. "Don't you realize what you have done, you fools?"

The scene shifted and shimmered as if a stone had fallen into a reflecting pool. Suddenly he was not a target anymore.

"Even Karzon forbids the slaughter of penitents and pilgrims! Have none of you read scripture? Have you forgotten your oaths?" His words echoed and reverberated, magnified into a knell of doom by strange acoustics and the intense virtuality. He loomed over the assembly like an avenging angel. The captain dropped his lance in dismay, staring up openmouthed at his accuser.

"Repent, repent!" Even Julian, perched on a puffing gargoyle atop the far wall, could feel his scalp prickle at the power of the call—and he was only a bystander. Exeter lambasted the lancers, berating them for the massacre. He quoted their own Valian gospels at them: the Green Scripture, the sacred words of Karzon, god of war; the Blue Scriptures of Astina, goddess of warriors. He reeled off passage after passage to show the sinners how they had sinned, the laws they had broken. He even quoted the secret oaths of the soldiers' Karzon cult, the Blood and Hammer. How did he know all that?

Julian glanced again at Ursula, but she was intent, as mesmerized as any. He ought to be making his escape or searching for Dommi among the living and dead, yet he could not move. The waves of charisma and authority streaming from Exeter were mind-numbing.

"So if those misguided teachings denounce your conduct, what then must the One True God think of you? The Undivided, the one who must not be named? Open your ears to the truth and tremble! Hear his commands. . . ."

Why was the idiot speaking English to Niolians?

· No, he wasn't. It was Joalian. No, Randorian . . . Whatever it was, the audience understood. Julian watched the soldiers cringe lower; he heard them sob. He felt his own eyes prickle with tears, and still Exeter lashed the guilty. The rest of the troopers, the contingent from Shuujooby, came filing in through the arch, falling to their knees as they, too, heard this awful judgment. At last the anathema ended.

"Yes, there is forgiveness! Yes, you still have hope! If you truly repent, the Undivided may yet turn aside his wrath. . . ."

This was the most incredible display of mana Julian had ever heard of. An hour ago—nay, much less than that—Exeter had been exhausted, able to walk only because he could draw strength from his devoted supporters. Now he blazed within that window like the sun at noon. He thundered with the authority of God.

"Will you accept my judgment?"

"Yes! Yes! Tell us!" The troopers howled agreement, reaching up their hands in supplication.

"Are there any among you who did not shed blood today?"

Six or seven men timidly raised their arms. The rest subsided.

"Then this be your penance. Go now. Find your mounts and ride with all haste to Niol. Take word to Queen Elvanife herself. Tell her to her face how she has offended against the people who were her children. Tell her that she must come here at once to weep on their graves—walking, barefoot, with her hair unbound. Tell her that only thus may she have hope for her soul. Go!"

The half dozen men reeled to their feet and fled from the courtyard, stumbling over the sand. The rest remained, waiting to hear their fate.

The Liberator had cowed a victorious army into a pack of sniveling penitents.

"And when you have gathered them up and prepared the graves . . ."

He was ordering the rest of the troopers to bury the dead.

But the greatest concentration of corpses was directly below him. There, in that scummy puddle of water, the last of his Warband had made their stand, defending their leader. There the Nagians had bled to death or drowned, and now only a few shields and lifeless limbs protruded from the bloody surface.

The bubble burst. Julian clapped his hands over his ears. His throat knotted in waves of nausea. Monster! Contemptible murderer! Hypocrite! The prophecy had warned Exeter that there would be killing in Niolvale. He had foreseen the carnage, and he had used it for his own ends. He had sacrificed his followers, the peasants—men, women and children—and especially his old comrades from Nagvale.

There was the source of his new mana.

The Liberator was no better than Zath.

No, he was worse. When Zath wanted human sacrifice, at least he did not slaughter his friends.

ℰℛℴ𝓇 33 ℴ𝓇ℰℛ

THE WIND DROPPED SOON AFTER SUNSET, LETTING THE MUGGY AIR OF THE swamps drift in with its bugs and pungent leafy scents. Julian had wandered off alone, away from the ominous virtuality of the node. Having found a trunk of driftwood on which to sit, he watched unseeing as the sky turned bloody above Niolwall and then dimmed to black, and stars came out like a million shiny tears. The green moon would not rise for hours yet, but Ysh, Kirb'l, and Eltiana shed enough light to reveal the activity on that plain like a stark etching, ebony on silver. The troopers labored to gather the bodies and dig graves. They toiled in silence, dark gnomes in a milk-opal world, anxious to work the bloodstains off their souls.

T'lin and the dragons had been sent off to high ground, where the poor brutes could rest and graze, and would return in the morning. Ursula was still somewhere around the temple. Dommi was alive and well.

Exeter must have dispatched messengers to tell the rest of his followers that it was now safe to continue the pilgrimage. Probably some had chosen to flee back through the marshlands, but an amazing number had trusted his word, and they came trudging in over the riverbed—hundreds of them, hour after hour.

At dusk, two Nagians had appeared with their spears and shields, driving a small herd of sheeplike animals. Julian had wondered how those two lone survivors must feel, then realized that he knew exactly how they felt, because he had felt the same way on the Western Front every day for two years. They would be feeling enormously relieved to be alive when their chums were all dead, and guilty as hell because of it.

How did Julian Smedley feel? He could not put words to his disgust, his sense of betrayal, his shock, anger. . . . Power could corrupt, but the greed for power corrupted more. He would not have believed that any Old Fallovian could have sunk so low to gain it, let alone Edward Exeter. He wished he had left his former friend in the psycho ward at Staffles, back in 1917. A cell in Broadmoor would be even better, beside the rest of the criminally insane.

His reverie was broken by singing. The funeral service was under way. Irony! The last time he had seen Exeter before today, he had been conducting a funeral for some of Zath's victims. Now he was burying his own.

This time Julian Smedley would not attend.

The service was brief. As soon as it ended, campfires flickered into life all around the ruins so the sheeplike things could furnish the funeral feast. Reluctantly admitting to himself that he was giddy from lack of food, Julian hauled his weary bones upright and set off in search of charity, but the scent of charred meat at the nearest campfire turned his stomach and he went on without stopping. Shunning the crowd, he wandered into the temple. He found the big courtyard, deserted now. The bodies had gone from the pool and only stars filled the empty window where Exeter had stood. The stonework was still warm, the air cool. Somehow the virtuality seemed even greater by moonlight, stark walls against the sky, black velvet shadows on the sand. It made his flesh crawl. Even the natives had sensed it and stayed away.

Except one. Tracking a flicker of light, he discovered a smaller courtyard and a man alone, lying prone before a small fire. He was obviously alive and conscious, because one of his feet scuffled busily in the sand, but his head and shoulders were hidden by a boulder. Curious, Julian walked over to him, silent on the ever-present sand. He recognized that what he had thought was a boulder was Dommi's pack at the same instant as the copper glint of Dommi's hair came into view. He was writing busily, his paper and writing board so close to the fire that they might become part of it at any minute.

"Hello."

His houseboy let out a gasp of surprise. Then he recognized Julian and showed all his teeth in a beam of welcome. "*Tyika* Kaptaan!" He squirmed around and sat up cross-legged, clutching his writing board to his chest. "I am most joyful that you and *Entyika* Newton escaped the villainous event."

"And I'm very glad that you did." Julian wanted to know what was so important that it had to be written by firelight and could not wait until daylight. "I expect we'll be returning to Olympus in the morning."

Dommi's face did not react and that very blankness was a reaction.

"We've done what we came to do," Julian added.

"Yes, *tyika*."

Oh, blast! "You want to stay, I suppose?"

Dommi nodded and bit his lip.

Julian stepped closer and sat down. He leaned his arms on his knees. "Tell me. You can't expect *Tyika* Exeter to need a valet when he owns nothing but a gown. Your wife is very near her term. Tell me why you want to stay."

"It is most difficult to describe in words, *tyika*."

There, for a moment, the conversation rested. As a stranger himself, Julian was almost immune to Exeter's charisma—he could feel it, but he understood it and could resist it in ways that a native could not. To explain the mechanics of charisma or mana and what had happened in the temple that day would not cure Dommi of his enchantment, any more than a child could believe that the rabbit had come out of the conjuror's sleeve. Did Julian feel like this just because he didn't want to lose a damned good houseboy? No, he was honestly concerned for Dommi himself, and Ayetha. The Liberator's cause had always been doomed to failure, and now its black heart was cursed by a terrible crime.

"You realize that there may be more danger, don't you?"

Dommi smiled. "Not from soldiers, *tyika*! Twice Queen Elvanife has sent her warriors against him, and twice they have failed her. What army will challenge the Liberator now?"

"I suppose you do have a point there." The tales of haughty cavalry officers weeping in contrition and digging graves for their victims would sweep through the Vales. The kings and magistrates might still try assassins, but they could send no more armies against Exeter's crusade. "Writing to Ayetha, are you?"

Dommi clutched the papers closer. "I am making some notes, *tyika*."

"Sorry. None of my business. I'll leave you to your task, then. We can talk in the morning, when *Entyika* Newton and I have decided what we're going to do." Julian began to rise.

Dommi looked up. "I am recording the words of the Liberator, *tyika*. While they are remaining green in memory."

Julian subsided again. The Gospel according to Saint Dommi? With his appalling spelling? But Julian had seen enough of the paper to know that Dommi was not writing English. He was using the Greeklike alphabet of the Vales.

"In what language?"

The question produced surprise. "In Randorian, *tyika*, of course. As he spoke. He numerously revealed things about the Undivided that are not told in the True Gospel."

Of course! Exeter had been making it all up as he went along, and he had been speaking in tongues, not Randorian. Among other things, he had completely scuppered the Service's teaching on the subject of the afterlife and the nature of the Pentatheon. The Undivided Reformation was now split into two opposing sects.

There was one question that Olympians never put to Carrots. Prophets had no honor in their own country and no man was a hero to his valet—except perhaps Edward Exeter. The Carrots knew that the apostles were only human and did not practice their public religion in the privacy of Olympus. Now, on impulse, Julian asked the forbidden question. "Dommi, what do you believe in? What god or gods do you follow?"

The freckled face glowed in the firelight. "I am believing in the Undivided, *Tyika* Kaptaan, although it is admissible that my faith was a most frail wisp until this afternoon when the Liberator spoke to my heart."

Which was to be expected. Exeter had a hell of a lot to answer for!

"Good," Julian said, and this time he did stand up. "I understand, and if you wish to remain with him for the time being, then I don't mind. You have been an exemplary houseboy, Dommi. I could never hope for better service. I shall miss all that you do for me at home very greatly, but I shall keep your position open. It will be yours again any time you wish to return. And if you do want to write a letter to Ayetha, give it to me and I will see she gets it."

"That is most kindly of you, *tyika*!" Shyly, Dommi released his writing board so that he could raise his arms and touch his hands together in the sign of the Undivided.

Julian nodded and turned away.

"*Tyika?*"

"What?"

"What god do you follow?"

The question left Julian at a loss. Certainly not Edward Exeter! "I'm not sure, Dommi. I'm still thinking." He beat a fast retreat.

He began wandering between the campfires, looking for Ursula, but it was she who found him. Shimmering like a white ghost in the darkness, she caught him by the arm and pulled him close.

"There you are! Have you eaten?"

"Not hungry."

She leaned back to study his face and said, "Mm!" thoughtfully.

"You can't stop him now, can you?" he snarled. "If we'd arrived here a day sooner . . . but not now?"

"No, not now. Come along, he wants to see you."

"I want nothing to do with him!"

"Now, now!" She sounded like a nanny. "Every man is entitled to face his accusers. Come and tell him what you disapprove of." She was urging him forward, over the sand.

"Disapprove of? Ursula, don't tell me you're on his side now?"

She squeezed his arm. "Not on his side, exactly, but now I don't think we can stop him. Zath probably can . . . but I'm not even quite certain of that anymore. I want to learn more of what he's up to. I underestimated him."

"I overestimated him. Christ, did I overestimate him!"

She pinched him. "Stop that!" They were heading back to the temple, back into the virtuality. His scalp prickled and sweat trickled down his ribs.

"What do you mean you underestimated him?"

She took a moment to answer. "He's done some things I never thought were possible."

"Such as slaughtering his friends? God! Don't you feel that's letting the side down a bit?"

"I wasn't thinking of that. He's won the support of the Pentatheon, or some of them, or at least he's won their neutrality. That's clever, darling! He must have impressed them. We know they're frightened of Zath, and Exeter's managed to capitalize on that."

"The devil you know is better than the devil you don't. The Pentatheon may decide Zath's a better bet when they hear how the Liberator treated his own supporters today."

Horrors! Obviously Ursula had switched sides—did that mean Exeter had bewitched her as she had planned to bewitch him? Would he now twist Julian's mind in the same way? For a moment, Julian considered doing a bunk, and then pride stiffened his spine. If he had not run from the Boche guns, he would not run from this.

They walked around a tent and there was the messiah, safely hidden from prying eyes in a private little sanctum. The tent and a fallen pillar and two ruined walls formed its sides; a fire of driftwood crackled and sparked on the sand in the center. The Liberator sat well back, in the corner of the two walls, his head bare and yet tightly hunched in his robe as if he were cold. Julian had seen that look on strangers before and knew it came from too much exposure to virtuality.

About a dozen Nagian shields had been laid out around the fire like hour markers on a giant clock face, with a disciple sitting by each—a new Round Table to replace the slain Warband. The two surviving Nagians were there, with their spears beside them. Another was the blond boy with the bandaged feet, Dosh Somebody, who looked as if he had been weeping. The rest seemed to be equally divided between men and women. They had been listening to their peerless leader talk, but he broke off when he saw the newcomers, and all eyes turned to study them.

There was a gap opposite Exeter, and Ursula's hat lay there—but no shield, Julian was relieved to see. The women on either side moved to make the space wider. Ursula sat down, adjusting her white dress, leaving room for him, but he remained on his feet and folded his arms, scowling over the campfire at the man he had hitherto called friend.

Exeter did not even appear weary. The exhaustion he had displayed so many hours ago had been washed away by his gluttonous feast of mana. Charisma and authority had replaced it.

For a long moment the two stared at each other. It was Julian who looked away first, of course.

"Tell me what troubles you," Exeter said, in English.

"Murder. Betrayal."

"Be more specific."

Julian glared at him. "You knew from the *Filoby Testament* that there would be bloodshed in Niolvale. You deliberately let it happen—hell, you invited it! You offered up your own team as human sacrifice, you sucked mana from the deaths of women and children and innocent men. You are no better than Zath himself!"

Exeter pulled a face, as if he felt the acid burn. "I knew there would be bloodshed, yes. 'Young men's bones,' was what the prophecy said. I told them that back in Sonalby. Some of them must die, I said. They knew."

Julian shuddered and swallowed against a surge of nausea. "A few days after you went away, Prof Rawlinson gave me the standard welcome-aboard pep talk in Olympus. I'm sure you had it, too, once. The source of mana is obedience, he said—the greater the pain, the greater the sacrifice, the greater the mana. And I said, 'And human sacrifice is the greatest of all?' He told me there was one much greater."

The blue eyes were steady and unreadable. "Martyrdom."

"Yes, martyrdom! The greatest source of all. 'Greater love hath no man.' . . . You let them die for you, so you could have their mana!"

The onlookers were frowning at this unfamiliar tongue and at the heretic who used so disrespectful a tone to their leader. Ursula was studying the fire. Standing over her, Julian could not see her face.

Exeter sighed. "I knew some of the Warband must die. I honestly did not expect so many. I honestly did not expect the others—the prophecy did not mention them. But"—he spoke quickly, before Julian could interrupt—"but I have been hearing tales recently of the Church of the Undivided coming under attack. Will you swear to me that the Service makes no use of martyrs?"

Unfair! "We try to defend our own. I never took mana from a killing. I never—"

"No." Exeter smiled grimly. "You aren't one of the inner circle, are you? But you aren't guiltless. You live your parasitic life in Olympus on the fruits the others gather. You eat with your silver spoons in your fine houses, tended by your servants. Very fine houses! What exactly has the Service achieved in fifty years, apart from that cushy little settlement at Olympus? I'd ask you to explain to me just how the strangers of the Service differ from the strangers of the Chamber, but I know the answer already. It's a matter of degree—that's all, isn't it? None of you are virgins, some are just more pregnant than others. And the martyrs are all on your side, aren't they? The Pentatheon doesn't dabble in that. Never mind. Swear something else to me, Captain Smedley. Swear that your guns in Flanders never killed a civilian."

A jolt of fury made Julian break out in cold sweat. "If they did, I never benefitted from the death!" he yelled. "I took no blood money!"

"You took your pay! You took your medals. Your side benefitted, your team—your cause, dammit!"

Julian opened his mouth and was shouted down. The blue eyes blazed brighter than the fire.

"I know you weren't in the trenches with the infantry. You never ordered the lads to go over the top, did you, but—"

"British officers don't order their men to *go* over the top, you bastard! They *lead* them over the top!"

"Like Field Marshall Haig, I suppose? Like Asquith or Lloyd George?" Either mana or the walls behind him made Exeter's voice thunder. Even the fire seemed to bend away from the blast. The disciples gaped, aghast at this quarrel. "The real leaders stand well back and *order*, Captain."

"If you're content to be compared with them, then may you rot in hell with them! I'll ask some questions now! I saw you in that circular window. I know a symbol when I see one. . . . Chose that in advance, didn't you? Scouted out this node and decided this was a good place to hold your bloodbath, didn't you?"

Exeter's lips vanished into his beard. He nodded to concede the point. Bastard!

"And your god is undivided?" Julian roared. "But you're not claiming to be a saint, Mr. Exeter. You're not quoting ancient prophets. You're issuing wisdom on your own authority! 'Verily I say unto you,' and all that. Where does your authority come from? If you're not a saint and your god is undivided, then what does that make you—*Christ?*"

"I am the Liberator."

"But are you human or divine? Are you god or prophet? Buddha or Mohammed or Jesus or Zarathustra or Moses?"

He had scored again. Exeter said, "I am human, Julian, you know that." But he had hesitated.

"Have you told them that? Go ahead and tell them now. I want to hear it. Speak nice and slow, in Joalian."

Exeter stared at him for a moment and then said, "No."

"Ha! Then I rest my case." Suddenly all Julian's anger drained away in a rush, leaving bone-aching weariness and a sick regret like the pain of bereavement. That it had come to this! "Remember that morning at the Dower House at Greyfriars? Two years ago. At breakfast. You explained all this to me. You swore you'd never become the Liberator. You asked what it would do to you. 'What would I have to become?' you said. Well, you did it and it happened, damn you!"

The onlookers could not be following the words, but they must be reading the tones and the expressions. They all turned to hear what their tin-pot deity would say next. He spoke very quietly, as if his anger, also, had turned to sorrow.

"The game isn't over yet, Julian. It's hardly begun. All I've done so far is jostle the board."

"And Zath will burn you in the end."

Exeter shrugged. "I have to trust the *Testament*. Remember it said that the dead would rouse me?"

"Ysian?" Julian laughed his scorn. He wanted to hurt, to wound. "Have you avenged her yet?"

"No, not Ysian. Not even the Carrots you helped me bury. Well, maybe a little. But mostly it was Flanders, that hell at Ypres. I saw a few hours of it. I saw fields turned to mud by human gore. I saw boys blown to bits or blinded by gas or driven insane by terror. I passed out cold from the shock of it. You must have seen a million times more than I did. You were there for two years. What can excuse that, Captain Smedley?"

"Nothing! Absolutely nothing!"

Softly, gently, Exeter drove in the dagger. "So the war was wrong?"

"You bugger! Wrong for the side that started it, yes. Not wrong for those who resisted the evil!"

"Then I, too, rest my case."

Julian turned and walked off into the night.

Ursula did not come after him.

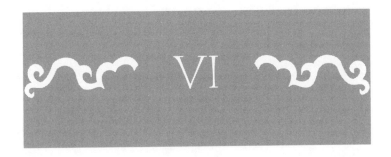

VI

And he goeth up into a mountain, and calleth unto him whom he would: and they came unto him.

THE NEW TESTAMENT: MARK, 3:13

34

ELEAL AWOKE WITH A START. FOR A MOMENT SHE JUST LAY AND STARED at the roof overhead, heart pounding, soaked with perspiration. She had been dreaming about D'ward again. Rather, she had been dreaming about that mouth-wateringly romantic admirer whom she knew to be D'ward although he did not look in the slightest bit like him. He might have grown broader in the last five years, might have grown a mustache and hairs on his chest, but he could hardly have grown shorter. Nor could he have changed the color of his eyes. And why, when they were locked in a passionate embrace, had she been *singing*? Oh, dreams were stupid!

It was very nice to wake up in a bed again, and even nicer to know that the stench of sewerberries had gone . . . almost gone. Never mind. She was awake now. Close above her hung a gable ceiling, with sunbeams angling through the dirty little skylight. From the street below came a faint racket of voices, wheels, and hooves as the world roused itself for business. This was not a luxurious inn, but it was not a slum, either. And she was in Niol! Today she would be able to explore a city as big and grand as Joal, one she had never visited before. She raised her head to peer over the edge of the blanket and make sure Piol Poet was still asleep, so that it would be safe for her to get up and dress.

Piol's bed was empty. That was exceedingly annoying. He must have risen and departed without waking her, and who knows what he might have learned by now? She threw off the blanket and sat up. Why, he might even have solved the Liberator puzzle already! She reached for her dress.

There had been no shortage of news of the Liberator in Niol last night. The rumors were thicker than flies in a butcher's, but no two of the stories agreed. She had dragged herself off to bed without reaching any conclusion.

With the inevitability of a glacier going downhill, the sloth's snail-slow progress had brought them to Niol itself, the only place in the world where sewerberries were used or bought, so that a cartful of them going in any other direction would have provoked questions. Here, they had sold the stinking mess, cart and sloth and all, making quite a good profit. They had spent about a third of it replacing their ruined clothes and getting cleaned up, as no bathhouse had wanted to admit them, and the rest she had shared with Piol, since it had been all his idea.

Clip! Clop! She lurched down the steep little staircase to the barroom, which was gloomy and deserted. It stank strongly of wine, with lesser odors of urine and vomit. Deciding that she was not quite ready for breakfast yet, she clumped over to the big door and heaved it open, blinking as the sunlight caught her in the face. Niol was famous for the width of its streets. Porters trudged past in twos and threes, carrying bales on their heads and moaning away in their lazy Niolian singsong. A few smelly, humpy bullocks crawled by, hauling wagons. She could hear peddlers hawking their wares in the distance, and the shutters were coming off the little shops opposite. Half a dozen juvenile beggars flocked around her at once, shouting for alms. She cursed at them and slapped them away before their prying little fingers could discover her money belt.

"The gods be with you, my lady," said a Joalian voice.

She spun around. Piol Poet sat on a bench outside the inn door, legs outstretched, back against the wall. He was munching on a roll.

"And with you, my lord." She smiled at him and joined him. The journey had done wonders for Piol, but whether it was rest, food, or just a sense of purpose that deserved the credit, she did not know. His eyes were brighter, his skin less jaundiced. A clean new robe certainly helped, and his turban was neatly bound.

He tore the doughy bread in two and gave her half. "Lots more where this came from. Be off with you!" he snapped at the beggars.

She bit, eying him thoughtfully. "You've got news."

He pouted. "Am I so horribly transparent?"

"No, I am excessively perceptive. Tell me."

He finished a mouthful with the patience of the toothless. "I have ascertained that the Tion Champions are in town, and there is to be a festival next fortnight in commemoration of—"

"Never mind all that! What have you learned about the Liberator?"

He raised a silvery eyebrow. "I thought you wanted me to be your manager in the furtherance of your artistic career?"

"Later. First, what news of D'ward?"

He sighed. "Eleal, *why* are you so concerned about him?"

"He's an old friend! I mean, those days in Suss were the most exciting time of my life. There's nothing wrong in wanting to meet up with an old friend, is there? Now, what's the news?"

He frowned at her doubtfully. "It makes sense now. The winds of truth have winnowed the chaff of rumor."

"Spare me the poetry." She caught his hand as he moved to take another bite. "Talk first."

He chuckled at her impatience. "He's been here, in Niol! He was seen in the temple. He's also been reported in the queen's palace, but that story seems altogether too far-fetched. It does sound as if he came into the city three nights ago, went to the temple, and pulled the priests' noses. Then he ran away before they could catch him. The next night he was at Shuujooby."

"Doing what?"

"Preaching heresy."

"Oh!"

Piol shook his head sadly. "Can't say I'm surprised, not really. He was never a strong supporter of the gods, you know. Remember, he wouldn't go to the temple with you when you went to give thanks to Tion for your safe deliverance?"

That's right, she thought, he didn't. And when the high priest summoned him to the temple, he ran away altogether, so her leg didn't get cured. But to support those awful heretics! T'lin Dragontrader had joined them, too, she remembered. The last time she had met him, they had quarreled over that.

"Well, I certainly will have nothing to do with heresy!" she said firmly. "I believe in the gods!" After all, her father was one.

"So we can forget about D'ward?" Piol beamed with relief.

"No!" Again she waylaid the bread on its way to the old pest's mouth. "If he's a heretic, why isn't he being thrown in jail?"

"Well, that is an interesting question! The queen sent her household cavalry to arrest him at Shuujooby. Apparently there was some fighting, just as the *Testament* predicts, but the accounts vary from hangnail to hangman, as they say here. In the end the guard failed to obey orders and most of them threw in their lot with the man they were supposed to apprehend."

"That doesn't sound likely."

Piol shrugged his thin shoulders. "It sounds like a miracle. There are rumors of other miracles, too." He hesitated, then added softly, "They say he is healing sick people, Eleal—and cripples."

With professional skill, she suppressed an impending shiver and laughed scornfully. "But you don't believe such tales, do you?"

"I don't know." Piol frowned and bit on his roll. Mouth full, he mumbled, "We have seen miracles of healing in Tion's temple. . . . All these stories are incredible, yet they seem to hang together too well to be completely wrong."

She nibbled at her own hunk of bread. "So where is he now?"

"Yesterday he left Shuujooby on the road to Mamaby. . . . If he keeps up his progress, then today he'll be going on to Joobiskby, and tomorrow he'll head over Lospass to Jurgvale."

If Piol Poet wasn't adding that he'd advised her just to wait in Jurgvale until the Liberator arrived, that didn't mean he wasn't thinking it. Bother! It had taken them *days* to come from Joobiskby. If D'ward ever got ahead of her, she would have to chase after him, and he was obviously covering the ground much faster than a sloth did. Almost anything would, of course, and she did not own a sloth anymore anyway.

Eleal sighed. "Speak up, old man. You're my strategist. Advise me."

Piol chewed for a long time. She curbed her impatience until he was ready.

"My advice to you, Eleal Singer, would be to go on to Joal, as you said you would, or else let me arrange some auditions here. In some of the temples, perhaps. Niol also has many fine pleasure gardens where an artist may earn a good living with her art, not with—"

"Forget that. How do I catch the Liberator now?"

He sighed deeply. "You always were a wayward child, you know. Follow the crowds, I suppose. And they are heading for Lospass."

"Crowds?"

"Hundreds of people are going to hear the Liberator. They're leaving their jobs, their friends, their families. . . ."

"You have been busy, old man! How long have you been up and about? Never mind that. We can't go on foot, either of us. How?"

With his mouth full, Piol mumbled, "There are people organizing wagon trains. One silver star there. Two for a return ticket."

"That's daylight robbery!"

He chuckled wheezily. "I'd pay the two, I think. The return price may be a lot more when they've got you there."

"We'll pay for one-way trips," Eleal said firmly, "and worry about the future when it comes."

ᜒᜒ 35 ᜒᜒ

A TUSK OX WALKED FASTER THAN A SLOTH, BUT NOT AS FAST AS A MAN. All day Eleal watched in frustration as people on foot caught up with the wagon, passed it, and eventually disappeared into the distance ahead. Were it not for her deformed leg, she would be out there too, striding along with the best of them. It was all D'ward's fault.

Piol had been well-informed when he reported that hundreds were going to see the Liberator, for the southbound traffic was much greater than the north-bound—and not merely foot traffic, either. The wealthy swept by on moas or rabbits or in coaches pulled by them, spraying dust or mud. For the first time Eleal wondered if this legendary crowd-drawer might not be the same boy she had known. D'ward had always tried to avoid attention, not attract it. He had been retiring, almost shy—although a wonderful actor, of course. Among all these people, how was she ever going to get close to him for a private little chat about old times?

Having been queried to death by the mob ahead, the meager wayfarers head-ing back toward the city were mostly uninformative, responding to shouted questions with oaths or angry silence. A few reported that the Liberator had reached Mamaby yesterday and might either be still there or have gone on to Joobiskby and Lospass. One or two spoke briefly of miracles, but none claimed to have actually witnessed one.

The ox's name was Tawny. Its owner, shuffling along at its ear, was a grubby, somewhat battered-looking man named Podoorstak Carter. Eleal had seen his like around the Cherry Blossom House often enough to be very glad she had not prepaid her return journey. The lumbering, bone-rattling wagon had been smelly even when it set out. After a day of baking sunshine, packed to suffocation with fourteen people, it reeked. Its cargo included two elderly nuns, who spoke only to each other in whispers. A very loud matronly lady, whose son had been slain by a reaper, wanted to give the Liberator her blessings and wise counsel on his campaign to slay Death. An addlepated, hunchbacked young man babbled nonsense about prophecies, rolling his eyes and slobbering. A girl of thirteen who had seen a vision she must describe to the Liberator was accompanied by her proud mother. There was a very sick baby, clutched by an underfed, worried-to-death woman who hoped that the Liberator might bring death to Death before her child died. The baby coughed a lot and threw up everything the woman fed it. There were two overweight, green-robed priests of Padlopan, the Niolian aspect of Karzon, who indicated grimly that they were going to beat the heretical manure out of the Liberator as soon as they got their hands on him. Unfortunately, their neighbors were an elderly couple wearing the gold ear circle of the Undivided. Their conversation with the priests was strained.

Healthy, wholesome people had gone on foot or stayed home.

The priests and the nuns, of course, were intent on stamping out heresy, and therefore traveling on the gods' business. They regarded their companions as wastrels, sensation seekers, and potential heretics. When Eleal explained that she hoped to use her former friendship with the Liberator to recall him to the true faith, their manners improved a little. But not much. She did not mention that she was the Eleal of the *Filoby Testament*.

Lubberly lot though they all were, they were a potential audience, and no true artist could resist an audience. So Eleal sang for them from time to time. They all seemed to enjoy that, excepting the baby and the straitlaced nuns. Later, she and Piol performed brief excerpts from some of his plays, and everyone enjoyed those except the priests, the baby, and the girl with the vision, who had an epileptic seizure halfway through *Hollaga's Farewell*.

The wagon rolled ever more slowly as the tusk ox tired, but evening came at last, bringing them to Joobiskby. It had been a sleepy, peaceful little place when Eleal and Piol had slothed their way through it a few days ago, but now the only thing she could recognize was the spire of the temple. The inhabitants, male and female both, had built a barricade across the road and manned it, brandishing forks and mattocks to repel the intruders. It was fortunate that the harvest had been gathered in and the paddies, which in spring and summer had been thigh-deep in water, had dried to mere mud at this time of year, for the horde of visitors had trampled over everything, knocking down hedges and dykes, leaving a wasteland.

Podoorstak halted the wagon a cautious quarter mile or so away from the ramparts, at the end of a long line of parked carts and coaches. The bored drivers and servants left to guard them ignored these latest arrivals.

"Ain't going no nearer," Podoorstak announced. "We'll leave from here at dawn, them as wants to come. Fend for yourselves till then."

His passengers burst into complaint, but to no avail. Obviously the village was sealed and his ox could not drag the wagon through the soupy morass that surrounded it. Sighing, Eleal scrambled down and offered a hand to Piol. It was good to be out of the wagon at last, but she was not looking forward to the last stage of the journey. Her ultimate destination was obviously a small hillock to the north, for there the crowds had gathered. That must be where the Liberator was.

Piol wanted to carry their little pack; she insisted on taking it. Side by side, they clambered over the remains of a ditch and set off across the fields. They moved more slowly than most, faster than some, and still pilgrims were arriving behind them. The going was hard—red mud sucking at her boots with every step.

An old refrain was going around and around in her head: *Woeful maiden, handsome lad.* . . . She had not heard that song in years.

"How many?" She puffed.

"Thousands! Can't see them all from here." Piol chuckled wheezily. "Trong never drew a house like this one. We should have kept D'ward in the troupe!"

His good humor shamed her. "But are these people the audience or the extras, old man? Even Trong couldn't have directed so many."

The situation seemed more and more hopeless the closer she came to the hillock. There was a building on the crest of it, perhaps an old shrine. The flanks supported a few scattered trees, but whatever else they might have borne—grass or fences or berry bushes—had vanished under the human tide.

"This is madness! What do they all want? Just to see him or touch him?"

"The madness of multitudes," Piol murmured. His eyes were bright with a faraway look she could recall from her childhood, a sign of inspiration at work. "It will pass. Nectar-ants swarm so in spring. The Liberator is their queen and they must be as near him as they can."

"If he speaks, most of them won't even be able to hear."

"But he is something new in their lives. They will go home and tell all their friends. And when the world doesn't turn upside down in a fortnight, they will forget him. It will pass."

As they reached the trampled lower slopes of the knoll, and then the edge of the horde, Piol took hold of Eleal's hand. There they stopped, seeing that any attempt to push into the throng would be not only fruitless but dangerous. She could hear a menacing rumble mixed in with the normal crowd buzz as those higher on the hillock resisted efforts to displace them or pack them tighter. Already more people were jostling in at her back. She exchanged rueful glances with the old man—neither of them was exactly tall. They would not even see the Liberator, let alone hear him. She assumed that he would speak. He would have to do something or the crowd would riot.

"Sh!" said a few hundred voices all around her. Someone was making an announcement. She could not make out the words, but she sensed that the crowd was breaking up, somewhere off to the right.

A moment later, she heard the speaker again, and this time he was closer.

"There is food available around the other side. The Liberator will speak now, and later he will speak again for those of you who did not hear. Go and eat now, and come back."

Eleal and Piol exchanged questioning glances. They had thought to bring food, so they were not hungry. How many would be tempted away?

Then the speaker came in sight, walking around the outside of the gathering. He was a short, fair-haired youth, wearing only a loincloth, burdened with a leather satchel and a large round shield slung on his back. Slight though he was, he projected well. He made his proclamation yet again.

The crowd began to roil, some fighting their way out to go in search of the promised meal, others pushing in to take their places higher on the hillock. Dragging Piol behind her, Eleal lurched over to the herald. She banged a hand on his shield just before he disappeared.

"You!"

He turned around and regarded her with soft blue eyes. His face was drawn with fatigue and reddened by the day's sun; he was spattered with mud. She expected annoyance, but he spoke with surprising patience. "Sister? How may I help?"

"I need to speak with the Liberator."

He even managed a smile, although her request was obviously insane, and raked fingers through curls that might be pure gold on a better day. "We all do. I have been trying to get a word with him myself for three days. I wish I could be more helpful."

Eleal was impressed. He was really very cute. He would make an excellent Tion in the right sort of play.

"I am Eleal."

A guarded expression fell over his face like a visor. "Sister, I am very honored—"

"Really I am. The Eleal of the *Filoby Testament*. I cared for him and washed him . . . almost five years ago. I want to see him again."

A faint smile of doubt. "Do you know his name? Can you describe him?"

"His name is D'ward. He is tall. He has black hair, quite wavy, and the bluest eyes I have ever seen. When I knew him, he was very—lean, I suppose is the nice way of describing it. I expect he will have put on weight since then."

The boy clicked his teeth shut. "No, he hasn't. You are Eleal!" He fell on his knees in the mud.

"Er . . ." Eleal looked to Piol for guidance. He seemed equally astounded. The milling bystanders had noticed, and a ring of the curious was solidifying around them.

"Don't kneel to me!" she said firmly. She found that strangely disturbing. "Get up, please! But I would like to see my old friend."

The boy stood up, having trouble managing the big shield. He glanced around at the audience. "A moment!" He made his proclamation again, and again the people within earshot began stirring like vegetables in a boiling stew pot.

He turned back to Eleal, biting his lip. "I cannot get you to him now. After he has spoken the second time, he will bid the crowd disperse or sleep. Then we have a—" He smiled a rueful smile. "Well, usually we have a meeting. The numbers are becoming so great that I can't even count on that today. But look for me, or for people carrying shields like this. Tell any of them what you have told me, or tell them I said so. My name is Dosh Envoy. I am sure that they will get you to the Liberator then."

It was as much as she could have hoped for. "I thank you, Dosh Envoy."

He nodded. "The blessings of the Undivided upon you, sister." Then he eased his way off through the crowd.

She would have to be content with that, and she supposed she would not die of impatience. Her craving to meet D'ward again seemed to be growing stronger all the time. The closer she came to him, the more eager she felt.

᧒ 36 ᨆ

SOME OF THE PLACES D'WARD CHOSE TO PITCH CAMP WERE BIZARRE, BUT Dosh could not have faulted the knoll at Joobiskby. It was a natural theater, for the little ruin at the top made an excellent stage and the slopes could have held even more thousands than had turned up. The problem was not the campsite but the wind and the size of the multitude. Loud as D'ward could be, he could not make his voice carry upwind. Those who had heard the first sermon—a necessarily brief one—were reluctant to move away and make room for others who had not. The lower slopes were muddier than the top, an unsavory place to sleep.

Patience. Understanding. Tact. Above all, patience.

Even with a manageable crowd, the shield-bearers would have had trouble, for they were all new at the job, other than Dosh himself and the two surviving Nagians. D'ward had appointed the shield-bearers the previous evening to replace the Warband, naming four women and six men, promising to add more soon. He had chosen well, Dosh believed, but dedication was no substitute for experience. Even Prat'han and his brothers would have been out of their depth shepherding this multitude. In retrospect, the band that had followed the Liberator through Nosokvale and Rinoovale seemed like a family on an outing—already those were the good old days, fond memories shining through golden haze. Now the greater burden had fallen on shoulders unprepared to take it.

Dosh had not been off his feet since dawn; Tielan Trader and Doggan Herder were doing their best, but they were still numb with grief and shame at being alive.

Dosh had shame to bear also, for he had not believed in the Liberator until their audience with Visek, so he had never had a chance to tell most of the Warband that they had been right all along and he had been wrong. He had not appreciated their courage and loyalty. Now, for the first time in his life, he knew what guilt was.

Patience: "I know you are tired, brothers and sisters. There are many down there who have come just as far as you and have not yet had a chance to hear the Liberator. It would be a demonstration of the understanding he described if you were to give them a chance. . . ." And so on and so on.

As he repeated the same carefully phrased and reasoned request for the thousandth time, Dosh wondered where he had learned patience. Not just patience, either. If the Dosh who had left Joal a fortnight ago were to meet himself now, they wouldn't know each other. They wouldn't like each other much, either. Fortunately, he was too accursedly busy to wonder whether he enjoyed being this sort of person. He supposed he would eventually weaken and revert to lechery. Meanwhile, he must keep on being a good boy, because there were whiffs of riot in the night air. He had broken up three fights already.

The sun had set. There was not a single moon in sight, and D'ward had just begun his second speech. The wind was still rising, snatching his words away. The clouds that had been gathering at sunset over Niolwall portended the start of the winter rains—that would thin out the crowd in a hurry.

Dosh began to work his way up the knoll. He had done all he could down here. He moved quietly and with exceeding care, literally stepping between people's legs, being careful not to bang any heads with his shield. A shield was a great honor, but a demoniacally heavy and awkward honor. In his case the honor was especially great, because he had been granted Prat'han's. The hole in it marked the blow that had felled the big man and the stains were his life's blood. To carry such a relic was honor and privilege.

Dosh wondered if Queen Elvanife had obeyed the Liberator's edict and gone to Shuujooby to do penance. He wondered if D'ward would move on again tomorrow, as he usually did. He wondered how many of this horde would choose to join the Free and march with the Liberator. They would have to be fed, but his satchel was quite empty, although the collectors would soon have money for him. He wondered when he would get a chance to sit down.

He reached the crumbled walls of the old shrine just as Kirb'l flashed into view in the east, shedding a welcome yellow light on the hundreds of upturned faces paving the sides of the knoll. D'ward stood on the highest corner, lit from below by a bonfire, casting his message to the night air.

Amazingly, Kilpian and the others had managed to keep the crowds out of the shrine itself. Most of the walls had long since collapsed into heaps of stones, but even those were a barrier and gave a sense of privacy. Dosh climbed over a low spot and slithered down inside, spilling onto the grass. He detached himself from his shield and relaxed with a long sigh of wearied contentment.

A portly, gray-haired woman came to him, offering a gourd of water. He accepted gratefully, trying to remember her name. She was a friend. D'ward had appointed shield-bearers and friends. The friends were supporters not yet quite ready profess their faith or to assume authority, he had said, but they were to be admitted to the evening meetings.

Dosh drained the gourd and muttered thanks. The Liberator's voice rang out overhead.

"Food?" she asked, smiling at his woebegone manner. Hasfral, that was her name, Hasfral Midwife.

"Food? What's that? Has D'ward eaten yet?"

"No."

"Then I'll wait till he does."

She shook her head as if puzzled. "That's what you all say."

"Because we know there wasn't enough for everyone out there today."

"Lots of them brought their own."

"But some will go hungry, and D'ward won't want to eat if he knows that. The only thing that will make him eat then is if the rest of us haven't eaten either and he knows we'll do whatever he does."

"Will you? Will you go without if he does?"

Dosh sighed. "Let's hope we don't have to find out."

He glanced around the little group. Quite a few missing still. Doggan Herder was brooding in a corner by himself. No sign of Tielan Trader. Kilpian Drover and Kondior Thatcher and Bid'lip . . . Bid'lip Soldier had been one of the troopers who had defected in Nosokvale. He was a bear of a man, with the thickest eyebrows Dosh had seen since Bandrops Advocate's. He wasn't Prat'han, but he would be a strong arm for the Liberator. Half a dozen others . . . A red-haired youngster sitting close by the fire was writing so busily that he must be trying to take down the Liberator's words verbatim.

"Who's he?" Dosh whispered, pointing at the scribe.

"Dommi Houseboy. A friend."

It was becoming hard to keep track of everyone.

And there was Ursula Teacher. Dosh disliked her without quite knowing why. Perhaps it was a relic of his old days of lechery, when he had preferred women pliant and muscles on men. Her jaw was too square, her hair too short, her manner too domineering, but none of that should matter to him now. Or perhaps he just wasn't sure what to make of her—she spoke with the Liberator in a language unlike any he had ever heard. At least her insolent male friend had departed, heading out at dawn yesterday on a dragon; good riddance, whoever he was.

The sight of Ursula suddenly reminded Dosh of Eleal Singer. Bother! Well, it would be useless to go and look for her in that mob out there. If she really was the fabled savior mentioned by the *Testament*, then she would find her way here somehow. Must remember to tell D'ward about her . . . Screw it, but he was tired . . . !

The sky was clouding over. No matter—no deluge would keep Dosh from sleeping tonight. He eyed the baggage heaped in one corner. With a groan, he sat up and prepared to rise.

"Bid'lip? Give me a hand putting up the tent."

The soldier shook his head. "D'ward said to leave it. Said we can all use it as a cover when the rain starts."

Dosh sank back to where he had been before. He suspected that the Liberator rarely slept in the tent and it was only a decoy to deceive the reapers. There had been no reapers for several nights. What was the enemy up to now? While worrying about that, he almost dozed off. A jingling sound roused him when Kondior Thatcher dropped a cloth poke at his feet. The Liberator had just finished his speech and was clambering down from his vantage point, being steadied by Kilpian Drover. More shield-bearers and friends had arrived. The crowd on the slopes of the knoll rumbled like a great beast as it tried to make itself comfortable for the night.

Hasfral Midwife and Imminol Herbalist were handing out the evening meal: beans and tubers and some pieces of fruit. D'ward accepted his gourd, looking around his followers, studying each in turn. When everyone had been served and no one had begun to eat, he smiled as if he knew what they were thinking.

"Praise the food the Lord sends; may it give us strength to serve Him."

A chorus of amens became a fanfare of crunching.

D'ward made himself comfortable and nibbled on a pepperroot. "Well done, all of you! You've had a brutal day, and I appreciate how hard you've all worked. I think it will get easier now. Not many of those city folk will follow us over Lospass. Who has anything to report?"

Dosh remembered Eleal, but others spoke up first, complaining about problems sharing out food equitably, assigning toilet areas, dealing with troublesome delegations of priests.

Nothing to be done about any of those now, D'ward said cheerfully. Let tomorrow look after its own afflictions. Had everyone met Dommi Houseboy, a new friend? The youngster blushed in the firelight and beamed toothily.

More shield-bearers and friends came scrambling in over the walls. D'ward made more introductions, announced a couple of promotions. People brought money to Dosh and he began dumping it into his satchel. Even so, there would not be enough to feed everyone tomorrow unless the crowds thinned out considerably.

Then a loud, clear female voice cut through the mutter of conversation like lightning through a cloud: "D'ward?"

The Liberator looked up. He started violently, dropping his gourd.

Tielan Trader had arrived at last. He had brought the girl who claimed to be Eleal and the little old man who had been with her, who now carried her pack.

"D'ward? Slights live long in memory, but debts die young?"

"Eleal!" D'ward scrambled to his feet. "Eleal Singer! And Piol!"

She lurched forward a few steps to meet him. Kondior Drover moved to block her and she stopped.

Dosh had expected the stunned expressions on the rest of the faces, but why did the Liberator look so strange? There was something odd here. What did it take to bring such a pallor to D'ward? Everyone knew the prophecy about Eleal and the coming of the Liberator, but the *Testament* did not mention anyone called Piol. Was the old man the problem?

Eleal was a pretty enough young piece, certainly. Had he still been that sort of man, Dosh could have gone for that sort of woman. In fact . . . It takes one to know one. . . . Just what grade of woman was she? Studying her in the uncertain flicker of the firelight, he decided that if he had still been that sort of boy, he would have been prepared to gamble that she was that sort of girl. No blushing virgin, certainly. Younger than he would have expected, for "Eleal shall be the first temptation." . . . It was almost five years since the seven hundredth festival, when the Liberator had come into the world. She would have been only a child then.

"Eleal!" D'ward repeated. He shook his head as if breaking a trance. "I forgot how long it's been. The years have blessed you greatly."

"They haven't changed you." She smiled and held out her hands in greeting. "Aren't we still friends?"

D'ward did not order Kondior to move out of the way. "You are very welcome. Sisters, brothers, this is Eleal Singer, the Eleal named in the *Filoby Testament*. Piol, it is good to see you also. What news of the others?"

"Time enough for prattle and idle gossip later," Eleal said with a toss of her head. Her eyes were flitting around, appraising the group. "I doubt that your entourage would be interested in our bygones. Are you going to offer us hospitality or not?"

D'ward laughed. "You are still Eleal! And I am a boor. Come and join our feast by all means, both of you. Make room there for Eleal Singer and Piol Poet. Welcome to the Free." His laughter had not rung true, though. Dosh was very intrigued. He had studied the Liberator long enough to sense a mystery here.

Then the girl walked to the place cleared for her and her lurching gait drew all eyes down to her feet. The sole of her right boot was built up. Hasfral and Imminol moved apart to make a place by the fire. Eleal sat and the old man eased himself down beside her, wriggling out of his pack straps.

D'ward picked up his gourd and held it out to Bid'lip Soldier, his neighbor. "Pass that to our guests. We live simply, Eleal, as you see."

Bid'lip tipped in what was left of his own meal and passed the gourd.

The sharp-eyed Eleal had noticed. So had the old man, and he began fussing with the tie on the pack.

"Pray do not let us deprive you," she said haughtily. "As it happens, we have some provisions of our own remaining."

D'ward sat down without a word, and perhaps only Dosh noted his smile, for it was a brief and private smile. When his gourd returned, he shared out its contents with Bid'lip and began to eat again, without taking his eyes off Eleal.

"Excuse us if we talk business at mealtimes. Has anyone else anything to bring up?"

Bid'lip said, "I heard a rumor tonight, Liberator. I was told that Queen El-vanife remains in her palace."

"I'm not surprised." Still D'ward studied the girl, as if every mouthful she took was a revelation. "She is not our concern. The One God will deal with her—probably through her courtiers, would be my guess."

"Tomorrow, master?" asked someone else.

"Tomorrow we keep going. We can't inflict this torture on Joobiskby any longer. I hope the weather holds for the pass."

Fornicating scorpions! Where was Dosh going to find provisions for several thousand people marching over Lospass? It was at least a two-day trek to Jurgvale, so he could not run ahead and buy there. He would have to accost the Joobisk-bians on their barricades. They might demand totally unreasonable prices to compensate for the damage the crowds had done, but he could argue that the alternative was to have the Free stay where they were, starving. That ought to convince them. . . . The Liberator had spoken his name.

Without taking his eyes off Eleal, D'ward said, "I need you around. I want you to keep the purse, but we'll let someone else take over the commissariat. Any suggestions?"

Dosh tried not to show the warm rush those words had given him. To be needed, trusted, asked . . . "Doggan knows livestock—"

"No. I need him around too."

"Hasfral, then?"

"Will you take on the provisioning, Hasfral?" D'ward asked, still staring at Eleal.

"I'll be glad to, master," Hasfral said.

"Then I'll promote you to shield-bearer, if you won't mind carrying one."

"Anything to keep her from doing the cooking," said Imminol. Those two were old friends, so it was all right to laugh.

A drop of rain struck Dosh's leg.

D'ward must have felt one too, for he glanced up at the sky, frowning. "To-morrow we'll camp at Roaring Cave. At least we'll be dry there. It's a short trek. You can pass the word in the morning. Bid'lip, when we get near the tree line, see if you can get every able-bodied pilgrim to pick up a branch and take it along for firewood. Anything else?"

"Yes, Liberator," said a Nagian voice. Doggan Herder hauled himself to his feet like an old man, yet once he was upright he stood straight enough, holding his spear and shield in proper warrior style. "I wish to go home."

So it had come at last. Dosh had been expecting it for two days, and D'ward showed no surprise. He glanced at Tielan, and the trader's face was a blank slate. Assume that Tielan had known and D'ward had expected. . . .

"Go then, but nevermore count yourself my friend or brother."

Doggan had not expected *that*.

"I know what you're thinking," the Liberator said quietly. "They were my brethren too, remember. I threw my first spear at Gopaenum, then watched Gopaenum throw it back at me. Had I known then how much beef the butcher packed in that arm of his, I'd have turned and run straight up Nagwall. Burthash and Prat'han drew the lines on my ribs for me to cut when I earned my first merit marks. We were all brothers together. Side by side we marched and fought. When I came asking aid a couple of fortnights ago, they threw down whatever they were doing and came without question, as you and Tielan did, as brother should for brother. I told them there was danger and they scoffed. At Shuujooby they died, all of them except you two, but that was God's election, no shame on your heads. I underestimated the evil, so if anyone is to blame . . . No, hear me out. History will not judge me blameless. And now you feel it is your duty to bear the tidings back to Sonalby so the rest of our brothers can take up arms to spill the guilt blood. Against whom will you lead them, Brother Doggan? The lancers who did the slaying? But most of those men are out there now, shamed and penitent and doing whatever they can to aid our cause. Against Queen Elvanife, who gave the orders? I doubt very much that she will still sit her throne by the time you fetch the brothers to Niolvale. Against Zath, whose evil moved the queen? He is the true source of darkness, but what hope will you have against him? I have promised you that he will die when we come to Tharg. I need your help on the way, but if you will not trust my word—if you think that Sonalby has not suffered enough—then go. But do not expect my blessing."

Doggan stood in silence. His mental processes had never been speedy.

"He is right," Tielan said. "I told you. Sit down."

Doggan sat down. He laid his spear and shield on the ground. Then he doubled over, weeping onto his knees. Tielan put an arm around him.

No one spoke for a while. Embarrassed and mourning, they finished eating. For dessert, Dosh decided, he would really appreciate a thick, juicy steak. He had not overlooked the rolls and meat that Eleal and her elderly friend had been devouring, and he wondered what else might remain in their pack. He was not the only one watching the two of them with hungry thoughts.

Eleal gulped down her last few bites and licked her fingers. "Well, D'ward?" She smiled nervously. "Can we retire somewhere more private and reminisce about the old days? I can enlighten you about the fates that have befallen so many we held dear."

"No!" D'ward said sharply. Then he gabbled something in that strange other language.

The mysterious Ursula Teacher had been watching and listening in silence. She, too, had kept her attention on Eleal Singer. Now she nodded and replied briefly in the same tongue. Whatever the words, her frown made them a warning.

D'ward rose and walked over to the girl. He stood between her and the fire. Eleal looked up at him warily, then began to rise.

"Sit down!"

Surprised, she sank back.

"Take off your boots," he said.

"What? I certainly will not do any such—"

"Take off your boots!"

The order cracked like a cane on a tabletop. No one could resist an order from the Liberator when he used that tone. She paled and obeyed, and then looked up at him again with fury and defiance and shame.

It was cruel. Everyone could see the comparison—the deformed leg, horribly shorter than its companion.

D'ward glanced at Imminol and the old man on either side of her. "Hold her hands."

Eleal began to protest, but the others seized her hands. "D'ward! What are you—"

The Liberator raised his eyes as if studying the sky. He lifted his arms overhead in the circle. A flash of revelation told Dosh what was going to happen an instant before the girl cried out. She struggled against her captors.

D'ward lowered his hands. "Give thanks to the True God."

He turned and walked back to his former place, his robe swirling in the rising wind. Raindrops hissed in the fire. Imminol and Piol released their hold on Eleal. She had turned ashen pale, staring down at her feet.

"A blessed miracle!" Ursula said in accented Joalian. "Praise to the Undivided for this sign to us."

One or two voices muttered, "Amen!" Everyone else was too stunned to speak. The girl's legs were now the same length.

"It is written," Ursula continued. " 'Hurt and sickness, yea death itself, shall he take from us. Oh rejoice!' "

Then Eleal reacted. She screamed, "D'ward!" and scrambled to her feet. She started to move toward him and lurched, almost overbalancing.

"No!" D'ward snapped. "Come no closer!"

"But— You cured—" She looked down at her feet, as if unable to believe her senses.

It would feel very strange, Dosh thought. Even having a sprained ankle cured had felt strange, and she must have lived with her deformity all her life. It felt bizarre even to witness such a miracle. His scalp prickled, although he had seen the Liberator use his powers before. The effect on the others would be even stronger.

Ursula laughed, and the sound was as shocking as it would be in a temple. "That was foolish of you, Kisster. You should have done that where the world could see."

D'ward scowled at her. "I did not do it for that. It was recompense for an old offense. Tielan, can you take that extra sole off her boot? Eleal, I have repaid some of my debt to you. Go now."

Eleal's face glistened wet in the firelight, and that was not all rain on her cheeks. She trembled visibly. "D'ward, D'ward!" She took a tentative step.

"No closer! I am happy to see you again, and even happier that I could do what I just did, but you are not welcome here tonight. You must find a place outside. Piol . . . What do you think, Piol? Am I being foolish?"

The old man was pale also. He shook his head.

D'ward pulled a face, as if that confirmation of whatever troubled him was highly distasteful. "Bid'lip, Doggan . . . will you see that Eleal Singer and Piol Poet find a place to lie tonight?" He did not add, "Far away from me," but the implication was obvious.

Tielan had pried the lift off Eleal's boot with the blade of his spear. He handed the boot to her in silence. The rain was starting to sting on Dosh's shoulders.

"The rest of us," D'ward said, "will use the tent cloth as a blanket. It won't be very comfortable, but it will cover more of us that way, and we shall be a lot better off than most of the people out there. If you see any small children, invite them in. Farewell, Eleal and Piol. I wish you safe journey home."

ℰℛℯ 37 ℛℯℰ

SHOWERS CAME EVER MORE FREQUENTLY AS THE NIGHT PASSED, GROWING heavier, colder, and more persistent. The fires went out early, starved for lack of fuel or just drowned by the rain. Strangers huddled together, grumbling and muttering, sharing their misery. Few slept much.

Eleal slept hardly at all. She would no sooner start to nod than something would disturb her—if not a dream then rain on her face, a child wailing, or someone moving beside her—and instantly she was wide awake, thinking *my leg is cured!* She was no longer a cripple, a freak, a monster. Now she could plan a career as a singer or actor. She could dream of entering the Tion Festival. She could make plans for husband, family, children. She could imagine herself as beautiful, attractive to men, a complete person.

And it had been D'ward who had done this. Not Tion or any of the other gods. D'ward, who preached heresy. How could she reconcile this miracle with the terrible things he said? How could she tell evil from good anymore? Five years ago D'ward had betrayed her trust. Now he had granted her dearest wish without a word from her, asking no favor or service or pledge, repaying in one stroke everything she had ever done for him.

How? Who was D'ward? She had been thinking of him as man born of woman, and yet she had seen him come into the world, materializing out of empty air. If he was not mortal, then he must be divine or demon, and why should a demon grant such a blessing?

As the first faint hint of day began to seep through the sodden clouds, the multitude on the knoll stirred and crumbled. People rose shivering to their feet and headed for the road, jostling and disturbing any who remained asleep. From the angry mutters she had overheard around her in the night, Eleal knew that most would be heading straight back home to Niol. D'ward had dismissed her, refused to meet with her alone. She had saved his life once and yet he did not trust her! He had bade her leave.

Piol came awake with a paroxysm of wheezing and coughing. How could so few teeth chatter so loudly?

"You all right?" she asked.

"Apart from rheumatics and frostbite and double pneumonia, yes. How about you?"

"Mental confusion and moral uncertainty, mostly."

He turned to peer at her in the gloom and then chuckled. His bony hand found hers and squeezed. "A new life opens its doors?"

She hugged him. He was a bundle of faggots and cold as a fish. "I don't know, Piol, I don't know! Explain it to me."

He hacked again. "Wish I could. Where are we going now?"

After a long moment, Eleal whispered, "I want to follow the Liberator."

"I was afraid of that. Why, Eleal? What is driving you? You told me you wanted to go to Joal, but all you really seem to want—"

"D'ward cured my leg."

"That's no reason. Even before—"

"Yes, it is!" But was it? Her dream had changed. In the night it had really been D'ward in her arms, not that unknown admirer with the mustache— D'ward as he was now, with his trim beard. *Woeful maiden, handsome lad . . .*

Piol was waiting for more. What could she tell him? It was ridiculous to think of revenge now. However D'ward had harmed her in the past, he had made redress. But how could she ever be friends with a man who uttered such frightful blasphemies? Furthermore, he was leading his army to Jurgvale, and in Jurgvale was Tigurb'l Tavernkeeper. She had not told Piol about him, but he had guessed enough. There was absolutely no reason for her to join this crazy heretical pilgrimage.

There was no way she could not. "I never thanked D'ward properly."

"Yes, you did."

"Well, I'd like to talk with him. Talk about old times. He's an old friend, isn't he? I like him. He's nice. Let's eat something." She reached for the pack they had been using as a pillow, and he caught her wrist.

"Not yet. Too many eyes and mouths here. Let's start walking. It'll warm us."

The crowd was already flowing down from the hillock, dividing into two streams. The larger by far was the stream heading for the Niol road, but a surprising number were making for Lospass. Eleal and Piol moved more slowly than most—he because he was old, she because she had to learn how to walk all over again. As soon as her mind wandered, she tripped or staggered as if she were drunk. It was funny, really, and once or twice she laughed aloud.

Daylight came grudgingly, a drippy, gray morning. It must be Twenty-second Fortnight already, so bad weather was hardly surprising, even in Niol. Narshvale would be thigh-deep in snow by now. So might Lospass. She was not dressed for winter and neither was Piol.

The road wound across the flats. Rain clouds drifted overhead, trailing gray tendrils. Niolwall and most of Niolslope were hidden. Just as the marshy paddies began to give way to gently rolling pastures, she noticed that the Liberator and his bodyguard were coming up behind, and drawing closer. They moved in spurts. It seemed as if D'ward was hailing almost everyone he passed by name, sometimes striding on by, other times slowing for a few minutes' chat upon the way. Then he would lengthen his stride again and so would the shield-bearers, and he would move on to the next group.

Perhaps he would be in a better mood today—a hug and a kiss for old times' sake. . . .

Piol was managing well. He was slow but sure, he said; he could keep this pace up all day, just as long as nobody rushed him. They ate the last of their rations without stopping.

D'ward's party caught up with them before Eleal expected. The first she knew was a voice at their heels:

"Piol Poet?"

Piol was too unsteady to look around while walking. He stopped and turned to peer at the speaker inquiringly.

"I am Dosh Envoy. The Liberator asks a word with you."

Piol said, "Oh?" and "Oh!" and "Of course!"

"And I will keep you company, Eleal Singer." The little blond man smiled pleasantly enough, but he nudged her forward.

"Why Piol? Why doesn't he want to speak with me?" She allowed herself to be conducted along the road while Piol fell back to be immersed in the body-guard.

"I don't know, lady. I would love to know that. He granted you a miracle and then threw you out. I was sort of hoping you would tell me why. Are you a reaper?"

"A *what?* Of *course* not!"

Dosh was not the stripling she had thought. Seen by daylight, he was un-doubtedly older than she was, and while that might be innocence steadying the gaze of his baby-blue eyes, it was creepily like the cynical contempt she had seen so often in Tigurb'l Tavernkeeper's.

"I'm the Eleal of the prophecies. That's why I got the miracle."

"And I'm nosey. That's why I'm asking. Would you tell me what happened at the seven-hundredth festival, when the Liberator came into the world?"

"That's a very good smile—most winsome. Have you acted professionally?"

He laughed, not at all abashed, pushing wet hair out of his eyes. "Lady, I have done things professionally that would shock you to the core." His teeth gleamed. "Or would they?"

"I ought to slap your face for that."

"Go ahead. I deserve it. D'ward has shown me the light; I'm trying to reform and it's harder than I expected. I am sorry if I offended."

"Did he tell you to cross-examine me?"

Dosh nodded cheerfully, hitching his shield higher on his back. "He said I would find your story interesting, if you would tell it. I met him not long after you did, a few fortnights later, in Nagvale."

"Oh, that was where he ran to, was it?"

"Wouldn't you run if Zath were after you?"

Eleal walked at least a hundred steps on her new leg before she could answer that question. It opened doors she had never thought of. She had always thought of the Lord of Art as a defender, but he might not defend heretics. "Would Tion have betrayed him to Zath?"

"Very likely. I would trust almost any of them before Tion."

She shuddered at the blasphemy. "You are personally acquainted with gods, are you?"

"I thought they were gods, too," Dosh said calmly, "until a few days ago. I've met at least four, probably five, because I think I was Tion's pathic for a few years. There's a chunk of my memory missing. I'll tell you about them if you'll tell me how D'ward came into the world."

"You first."

"No, you first."

The trail rose gradually into the hills. Forest closed in. The rain became colder.

Dosh was granted a very brief account of the Liberator's arrival in Sussvale. Eleal was a shrewd little minx, and he had to hammer her with questions to obtain a reasonably full account of what had happened. She was astute and willful and pretty, he decided, but not as worldly wise or ravishing as she thought she was. He found himself almost regretting his present state of grace, for there could be no doubt who would have been ravished had she met the old Dosh in a mood for girl.

He eventually decided that she genuinely did not know how D'ward had managed to escape from Sussland. That was a nagging mystery, because the Youth must have known the Liberator was prowling on his turf. It was very much out of character for Tion to ignore a handsome young innocent, which was what D'ward had been in those days, and to let the Liberator leave in peace would have been rank defiance of Zath. Eleal had no inkling of Pentatheon politics, though.

When he was satisfied that he had learned as much as he was going to, Dosh picked up the story. He was just describing the army's escape from Lemodvale when a group of shield-bearers moved past them to take up station ahead. D'ward himself arrived, walking at Dosh's other side, using him as a barrier between himself and the girl.

She said, "D'ward!" Her smile was quite convincing. It didn't quite convince Dosh, though.

"Stay there, please," the Liberator told her. He had his hood back, and his black hair was sparkly with rain. "Why didn't you go back to Niol?"

"Aren't you pleased to see me again?"

"You I am delighted to see, and Piol too. What I don't welcome is your curse."

"*Curse?*" If that reaction was faked, then she was first-class.

"There's a spell on you, Eleal. I'm not quite sure how I know that, but I do, and my friend Ursula agrees. She is wise in such matters."

"I don't know what you mean! That's a ridiculous, horrible idea."

D'ward sighed. "Who did it, Eleal? Which of your supposed gods?"

She grew shrill. "You're talking nonsense! Curse indeed!"

"Piol says you were living in Jurg, so the most likely culprit is Ken'th, who happens to be your father, as I recall. Why did you throw up your job and come looking for me? Come on, Eleal, we're talking murder here. . . . Do you really want to kill me?"

"Of course not!"

"Would you let me kiss you?"

"Of course . . . I mean perhaps." Now she was certainly hiding something.

D'ward sighed. "We'll be in Jurgvale tomorrow. You can go home and resume your career."

"I can *start* a career, you mean! Didn't Piol tell you? I sang in a brothel. I was a whore, D'ward! That's what cripples do to eat."

There were other ways to earn a living, Dosh thought, although he had heard that they paid poorly. She was limping again, but he could not decide whether that was from habit or because her muscles were unaccustomed to an even gait. Or it could be just a ploy to win sympathy.

"No troupe would hire me. I was starving in the gutter, D'ward! But now that's all behind me, thanks to you, and you think I want to kill you?"

The Liberator had turned his face away and pulled up his hood against the rain. "I see why you would have wanted to."

"But I didn't understand!" she proclaimed. "I admit I felt hurt when you ran out on me, D'ward, but I was only a child. Now I am a mature woman and can see things more clearly. I didn't know Tion would have turned you over to Zath."

"Well, I thought he might. What do you think, Brother Dosh?"

"About what, master?"

"Can I trust her?"

"I'm sure you're going to. I wouldn't, of course. How does one recognize a curse on someone?"

The Liberator shrugged. "It isn't something you could ever learn to do. I couldn't have seen this one if it had been done properly—which is another reason to think that Ken'th is the culprit. He's quite a minor sorcerer." He nodded to the girl. "You can come as far as Jurg with us, Eleal Singer, and welcome." He strode forward very quickly, and the shield-bearers followed.

"Which brothel?" Dosh asked.

"Mind your own business!" Eleal spun around and limped back down the road to where the old man was following.

It wouldn't be the one Dosh had worked in.

Different clientele.

ᖇᖇᖇ 38 ᖇᖇᖇ

ALICE CAME AWAKE SUDDENLY, IN THE SHOCKED WHERE-AM-I? AWARENESS of a strange bed. The room was almost dark, with just a hint of light around the shutter, and the rattling of that shutter had wakened her. The weather had broken; she sensed a strong wind gusting outside and the dampness of rain. Unfamiliar scents of spice or potpourri added to the strangeness, and someone very close to her ear was breathing in a measured half-snoring rhythm. There was a man in her bed.

Then her memory awoke also and began supplying answers. She was in Boydlar Rancher's house in Jurgslope, the foothills of Jurgwall, and the man on the other side of the bolster was Jumbo Watson. Valian peasantry were always willing to offer hospitality to wayfarers, and Jumbo was not above using his charisma to obtain the best. The best in this case was Boydlar's own feather bed, for although Boydlar had a large rambling house, he had an even larger rambling family to fill it. Jumbo, always the gentleman, had announced that he would roll up in a blanket on the floor. Alice had told him to put the blanket between them, and she would trust him to behave himself. So here she was, bundling with a man she had met only a week ago.

Her affair with Terry had gone even faster, but that had been a wartime emergency. Jumbo Watson was not a terrified, doomed boy. Gentleman or not, he had taken more than his share of the covers. She pulled gently. He snorted, but in a moment he was snuffling regularly again.

Boards creaked overhead. Something mooed or lowed in the distance. The Boydlar family would be astir at dawn, she supposed, but there was no reason why she should not go back to sleep for an hour or so.

A week ago she had been hiding in her hermitage in the flats of Norfolk. Now she was roaming the ranges of another world on the back of a dragon. And loving it! Miss Pimm had been absolutely right. This impossible adventure had jolted Alice Pearson right out of her depression. If that rain she could smell was going to hang around—from the look of the clouds at sunset, Jumbo had predicted that it would—then future days might not be quite so much fun as the last few. But a little damp wouldn't kill her, whereas Norfolk might well have driven her loopy.

Jumbo rolled over. She could not have found a better guide or traveling companion than Jumbo. She wished she knew how old he was. He seemed about twenty-five and yet he told tales of Uncle Cam, who would be almost eighty if he were still alive. She wondered if Edward looked his age now. Trying to imagine the expression on his face when she turned up to meet him, Alice went back to sleep.

Breakfast was served in a huge, stone-flagged kitchen that could have belonged to any prosperous rural family in Europe. Kettles simmered on the great hob, metal pans hung gleaming on the walls, and the Rancher family swarmed in and out: husky workers, frail old crones, wet-mouthed toddlers. Things that looked like cats snuffled under the table like dogs. Boydlar's wife—named Ospita or Uspitha or thereabouts—was a red-faced, cloud-shaped woman, who seemed to be everywhere at once, tending children, dropping loaded platters on the table, pushing reluctant adolescents out the door to attend to chores, and talking all the time very loudly, mostly to Jumbo.

Alice understood less than nothing of what was said. On the first night of their journey, Jumbo had tried to pass her off as his sister from Fithvale, which was a long way away. That ploy had not worked very well, because everyone in the Vales spoke at least a few words of Joalian. Since then she had been his sister who had been deprived of speech by a sickness, and whom he was taking to the temple of Padlopan in Niol to be healed. So Alice communicated in gestures and everyone was duly sympathetic.

Three children were chased out. Two more appeared, followed by Boydlar himself, all wet and pink from the weather, with his scanty hair hanging in streaks. Ospita made a comment; he laughed and riposted, setting his listeners laughing louder. It was an idyllic scene of rural domesticity. Whatever the evils of the Pentatheon, this section of the Valian peasantry seemed happy and prosperous, and a great deal healthier than any working-class family back in England's city slums. No world wars troubled them, no clamoring traffic or industrial strikes. If she had to spend the rest of her days in rural solitude, she would prefer the Vales to Norfolk.

The food she had been given was delicious, even if it did seem to be the illegitimate offspring of an omelette and a meat pie. It was also four times as much as she could eat. While she was forcing down a few last mouthfuls in an effort not to insult her hostess too much, there came a stamping of boots outside. The door flew open to admit a swirl of wind and rain, plus a tallish young man in a leather cloak and hat. The usual jovial greetings flowed to and fro. Then he removed his hat, shaking the rain from it.

Alice realized she was staring and looked down at her food hastily, only to discover that her appetite had gone completely. The unintelligible conversation eddied around her without pause, so her rudeness had either not been noticed or was being ignored. The newcomer seemed to be conveying some news to Jumbo, speaking in a slurred gabble. Her eyes kept stealing furtive glances. She should have known that every Eden had its serpents—the young man was missing half his face, his left arm, and most of his shoulder too. In a nightmare leer, his mouth reached back to where his ear should have been, showing teeth and parts of his skull. The injury was not recent, but it was very horrible. Not high explosives, not machinery . . . The only explanation she could imagine was some sort of wild beast, some monster like the bears and wolves that Europe had killed off centuries ago.

What you gain on the swings, you lose on the roundabouts.

Clouds had settled in around the Boydlar house, reducing the ranch buildings to faint ghosts and the scenery to nothing at all. The rain was a steady fine drizzle but not as cold as it looked. Migraine and Apocalypse, who preferred their water solid, were belching and burping in disgust. They set off at a moderate run, but a mile or so along the trail, as soon as they were safely out of sight of their former hosts, Jumbo called a halt for talk.

"You going to be warm enough?"

"I shall be both warm and dry," Alice assured him from within her voluminous furs. "I cannot guarantee that I shall not smell abominably, though."

He laughed. "A hazard of the road, my lady! That one-armed chappie was Ospita's nephew, and he brought news. Your cousin was in Niolvale two days ago, with a large following. Thought to be heading for Lospass."

Alice released a long breath. She was surprised how welcome that news was, how much she had secretly dreaded news of another kind. "Then we should meet up with him tomorrow?"

"We should meet up with him this afternoon, I'd say. Jurgvale's quite narrow. Yes, easily."

"Good!" Nevertheless, Alice wondered how Edward was going to react. She would have to explain right away that she had not come to meddle.

Jumbo was eying her quizzically. He must guess what she was thinking. "Right oh? Ready to *zomph*?"

"Yes . . . no. One thing. What happened to that poor boy?"

"Which— Oh, Korilar? From the look of him, I'd say he'd had a very narrow escape from a *mithiar*."

"What's a *mithiar*?"

"Well, that's the Joalian name. Don't know the local term." Jumbo pulled a face. "If you can imagine a ten-stone tarantula, or a black panther with saber teeth and six legs, you'll be getting close. We call them jugulars. They attack on sight—grab you with their claws and tear you to bits."

Alice glanced around at the fog. "You never mentioned those before, Mr. Watson."

"They're not very common," he said solemnly. "I've never spoken with a man who's met one, except possibly Korilar just now."

She distrusted the twinkle in his eye. "I can guess why not. Have you spoken with people who met one later?" She realized she was inviting him to display his humor. Jumbo had a very good sense of humor and knew it. The fastest way to a man's heart was always through his vanity, but why was she playing up to him like this? She had caught herself at it several times yesterday.

"Of course. Seriously, you don't see jugulars very often—and never for long."

"Only when they spring at you?"

"No, only when they spring at other people!" Jumbo laughed and shouted to the dragons to *zomph*.

ᕔᕔ 39 ᕐᕚ

WHEN JULIAN SMEDLEY TOLD T'LIN DRAGONTRADER THAT HE WANTED to go home as fast as possible, the big man took him more literally than he intended. T'lin made a beeline for Olympus with very few stops, and four dragons could transport two riders much faster than four. Julian discovered that he was expected to eat and sleep in the saddle, but pride would not let him countermand his own orders, so he ate and slept in the saddle. The fine weather had broken at last, and the dragons raced joyfully through driving snow, over crag and crevasse. How they managed to stay in contact, Julian had no idea. Most of the time he seemed to journey entirely alone through a blinding white fog, but T'lin and the spare mounts always reappeared eventually.

He had leisure to brood on Edward Exeter's megalomania—the disease was obvious enough, the cure was not. *You call him crazy because he used to be your friend. You would label anyone else as straight evil and not beat about the bush.* Crazy or evil, he was a mass murderer and must be stopped before he did more damage. How, though? With all the mana he had sucked up by martyring his friends, it would take the entire Service to have any hope of overpowering and defanging him, but the Service had already tried and failed. There was no way to tell whether he had recruited Ursula to his team honestly or by using mana on her, and it did not matter. Obviously his Olympian opponents would not have sent her against the Liberator without giving her all the mana they had been able to supply. The Service had shot its bolt. Only Zath could stop the Liberator now.

Julian had never thought he might find himself cheering for Zath, but if there had to be one supreme homicidal maniac slaughtering innocents all over the Vales, he would rather it not be a former friend of his.

He also had time to meditate on his own folly. He had behaved like the crassest of boors to Euphemia, walking out on her in her distress, and then he had compounded his sins by bedding Ursula—whom he had never cared for, never lusted after, and now detested. Oh, what a muggins he had been! One little waft of mana and he had run to her side like a lapdog. She had used him all the way to Niolvale. He could not have resisted the mana, but he ought to have guessed what she was doing to him. He would never be able to hold up his head again. Euphemia had warned him, and he had forgotten her warning. He could certainly never look Euphemia in the eye after this.

It felt like a broken heart, but it was probably only wounded pride.

Groggy with fatigue, he did not realize that his journey was over until Blizzard, scrambling down a sheer cliff, emerged from the clouds directly above the paddock at Olympus—about a thousand feet above. Julian closed his eyes and kept them shut until he was safely delivered to the grassy valley bottom. Belching triumph, Blizzard raced to the gate, where Mistrunner and Bluegem were already gorging on hay and T'lin was stripping off Starlight's tack.

Julian tried to dismount with grace and dignity, but his legs failed him and he sat down abruptly in the mud. Green eyes glinting amusement, T'lin took hold of his arm and heaved him to his feet.

"Thank you, Seventy-seven," Julian said staunchly. "You made excellent time. Good show."

A broad grin of satisfaction split T'lin's ginger beard. "The dragons enjoyed it. A record, I believe, Saint Kaptaan."

"I really do not doubt that. I'll have someone collect my kit, if you'll just leave it here."

T'lin promised to have it delivered. Julian thanked him again and trudged off, already sweltering in his furs as the packed snow fell off them in handfuls. One of the joys of Olympus was the mildness of its climate, even in winter. While storms raged on the peaks all around, here only a faint drizzle was falling, but the sky was overcast and darkness not far off.

He reached his house by blind reckoning and had stumbled up the steps to the veranda before he remembered that Dommi would not be there to care for him. Still, young Pind'l and Ostian ought to be able to manage for a week or two, until Dommi came to his senses and returned. Throwing open the door, Julian bellowed, "Carrot!"

He marched through to his bedroom, fumbling one-handed with his buttons. Receiving no response, he bellowed again.

Still nothing.

That was definitely odd! Where were those two? Then he recalled that there had been no one but T'lin at the paddock, and he had met no one on the road, either, neither Carrot nor *tyika*. Up welled sinister memories of his first, disastrous arrival at Olympus, with Exeter. Oh, ridiculous! On that occasion the whole station had been burned to the ground. But still . . . He went over to the window and peered out. No lights showed in any house he could see. Well, it wasn't really dark yet. But still . . .

Hauling off his coat, he went through to the kitchens. Everything was tidy and spotless as if no one lived here, and the grate was cold. No hot water, not a crust in the larder. Feeling more and more uneasy, he returned to his bedroom and dressed in fresh clothes. Taking an umbrella from the stand by the front door, he tramped out into the dusk.

He had trudged halfway around the node before he saw any lights in windows, and still he had not met a soul—definitely odd! The first inhabited house was Rawlinson's, so he went up to the door and rang the bell. He heard it jangle in the distance.

After a minute or so, he pulled again.

At last bolts and chain clattered and the door opened. Prof himself peered out, wrapped in a black dressing gown. He held an oil lamp in his hand and had an open book pinned between his ribs and his elbow.

"God bless my soul! Captain Smedley?"

"Who else? What the deuce is going on, Prof? Since when have you locked your door? Where is everybody?"

"Oh, you don't know, of course, do you?"

Julian almost exploded. The maniac Seventy-seven had brought him all the way from Niolvale in three days. He was beat and in no mood for any of Prof's confounded puzzles. But all he said was, "I have news of Exeter and his crazy Liberator crusade."

Rawlinson coughed wheezily. "Excuse me. I've got the flu, though I think I'm over the worst of it. Wouldn't you rather try one of the others? The McKays, or—"

Julian pushed the door. "I must talk with you about Exeter. And I need a drink."

Prof retreated in disorder. "Well, if you insist . . ."

"I do insist," Julian said.

Five minutes later, he was stretched out in a leather armchair with a glass of spirits in his hand, staring in stark disbelief at his host. *Götterdämmerung?*

Prof's wife had died in Zath's assault on the station and he had not remarried. According to the Carrots, he was regularly consoled by the tender embraces of Marian Miller. His living room was a bleak, empty-looking place, because he had rebuilt it with an immortal's lifetime supply of bookshelves but had not yet had time to acquire books to fill them. His taste in furniture ran to London club style, heavy and dark. The single oil lamp within this barn cast an apologetic glow on a scattering of discarded clothes, books, dirty dishes. The fireplace held only ashes, although the winter air was dank. Prof, in other words, appeared to be just as bereft of domestic servants as Julian.

More surprising even than that was his fevered look and racking cough. Under his robe showed mauve pajama legs and green bedroom slippers. He had put a bookmark in his book and poured his guest a drink without taking one for himself. Now he was huddled in a corner of the sofa, looking wan and ill in the lurid light. The big house echoed with lonely emptiness.

"You're not well!" Julian said.

Prof scowled at him balefully. "I did mention flu, did I not? Does the simple term 'flu' not find suitable referents within your English vocabulary?"

"Well, then, cure it! Dammit all, man, you're a stranger. You're not even supposed to catch head colds." Julian looked down at his crippled hand. "I thought healing just happened."

"Not always." Prof coughed painfully. "Sometimes it requires conscious application of power. I think your suggestion is an excellent one. I do believe I might have thought of it myself, given sufficient time. The only trouble is that I have no mana at present."

"Then ask someone else. . . ." Julian realized that he was being excessively stupid and Prof's sarcasm was not unwarranted. He took a long draft, feeling the brew burn all the way down inside him. " 'Scuse me, I'm all in. What's going on?"

"There is something of a mana famine in Olympus just now."

"You gave it all to Ursula to use on Exeter, you mean?"

"Er . . . That is part of the trouble, yes. But then Zath came to call."

"*Zath* did?"

Prof greeted his astonishment with a gleam of satisfaction. "Indeed. You have missed eventful times, Captain. Zath transported in by the node one evening and gate-crashed a dinner party at the Chases'. He demanded that the Service restrain the Liberator, otherwise he, Zath, would take it out on our hides. Burn us to the ground. Then he transported out again." Prof pouted balefully. "I see from your bemused expression that I shall have to be more specific. I personally did not hear the intruder's words. I confess that when he appeared, what I should like to refer to as a reflex for self-preservation came into play. I hit the ground almost at the dragon paddock. It took me fifteen minutes to walk back. I am not proud of that, but I was certainly not alone in using the trapdoor. About half of those present did the same. The rest reacted by trying to subdue what they assumed was only a reaper—vainly, of course, because he wasn't. The long and short of it was that everyone who was present at that dinner party was totally stripped of mana."

Julian stared at his host. He certainly did look ill, but could he be delirious? Was any of this nonsense true? "But—but that can't have been everyone!" The Chases' dining room was not big enough to have held the whole of the Service.

"No. But we are extremely short-staffed now. That is another development you missed. A great many people were suddenly overcome by a fervent calling to minister to the benighted heathen. They did a bunk—vamoosed, scarpered."

"You mean they let Zath scare them away?"

Prof scowled. "No. They let the flu scare them away. This is no ordinary flu. Back Home they call it the Spanish flu. It's killed more millions than the war, and it especially strikes down young adults. It's incredibly infectious—it circled the Earth in five months, Betsy says."

"I thought only people could cross over! You're saying that germs can?"

"If by germs you mean bacteria, then influenza is not caused by a bacterium."

"What is it caused by?"

"A *filterable virus*," Prof said smugly.

"What's that?"

"No one knows. It can't be seen in a microscope but is infectious. And obviously it can cross over between worlds. The Peppers caught it, but they had recovered before they came back." His voice was becoming hoarser and weaker.

"That's why they were late. It must have been Euphemia. She went Home for just a few hours, to fetch Exeter's cousin. She noticed nothing herself, but her Carrots all came down with it, and it spread through the valley like a flash of lightning. Those who still had mana tried healing. They could not keep up with it." He coughed several times painfully. "I don't know how many Carrots have died, but a lot, certainly. And some of us, too: Foghorn, Olga, Vera, Garcia. Very suddenly, all of them."

"Good God!" Julian took a long drink. *Strangers* dying? Of *flu*?

Prof seemed to find his astonishment amusing, for he bared his teeth in an ironic smile. "Götterdämmerung, Captain? The Carrots are naturally somewhat disillusioned. Their idols have feet of clay. The immortals are mortal after all. They have withdrawn their services. Personally, I am surprised that they have not driven us out of the valley, lock, stock, and barrel. They may do so yet."

Julian drained his glass to help him digest this incredible news. Prof blinked blearily at his guest. Then he hauled himself off the sofa and shuffled over to the sideboard. He poured himself a drink and brought back the decanter, depositing it alongside Julian. He returned to his seat and was convulsed by a severe spasm of coughing.

"Alice is here?" Julian asked.

"She is on Nextdoor, yes. She's gone off to see Exeter. What news of the Liberator, then?"

"His belfry is jam-packed full of bats. It's every bit as bad as Jumbo and the others predicted. He thinks he's the messiah. He's marching on Tharg, dragging a ragtag rabble of peasants behind him. I was hoping . . ." But any lingering hopes of the Service being able to stop Exeter were now dead. "He's ripping up all your work on the True Gospel. He calls the Pentatheon and the others enchanters, instead of demons, and you know where that leads. He's in cahoots with some of them, so God knows what sort of bargains he's been making. He's invented some kind of reincarnation claptrap to replace the afterlife among the stars. He's issuing divine doctrine on his own authority. He's mad as a whirling dervish." Julian refilled his glass.

Prof rubbed his chest as if it hurt. "I shouldn't worry about him too much. I think Zath has his number." He smirked, which meant he thought he was being especially perceptive.

Fatigue and liquor were making Julian's head spin. "Let me get this straight. First of all, what the hell was Zath up to, coming here? That kind of threat is just the thing to get all our backs up and turn us into Exeter supporters!"

"Well, of course. You're quite right there. Bluster will work on natives, but Zath can't know much about the English. Even Pinky was sounding pro-Liberator next day."

"And second . . . why would he? Why try to stop the Liberator by threatening us? That's even rummer! It almost sounds as if Zath has the wind up!"

Prof nodded and leaned back, closing his eyes. "Of course. That's what we all thought. I'm afraid it was what we were supposed to think." Ill as he was, he was not beyond playing stupid games.

"What's missing?" Julian barked. "What haven't you told me?"

"Jumbo. Jumbo and Alice Pearson—Exeter's cousin—that's her name now, Pearson. She's a widow. They were present, of course. Later that night the two of them swiped a couple of dragons and took off."

The implications took a moment to register. Then Julian said, "Oh my God!" and drained his glass. *Alice, what have we done to you?* "This was not planned?"

"Not at all. Zath asked who was in charge and spoke only to him. He wasn't in the room more than a minute or two, I'm told. But Jumbo was there, and Mrs. Pearson was there."

"You think Jumbo's . . ." How could a man put it into words? "You think he's a traitor? You think Exeter was right all along?"

Prof rubbed his eyes without opening them. "I know he was. The Jean St. John story was a blind. It was Jumbo who tried to queer Exeter by dropping him in Belgium—he admits it. The point is that Jumbo couldn't help himself. He's been around a long time, so he's well known to the opposition. Zath trapped him, installed a compulsion, and sent him off to be Judas."

Julian shuddered. Much as Exeter ought to be stopped, there was something peculiarly repellent about a trusted friend turning Brutus, even if that friend was not responsible for his own intentions. Mana had not seemed like an utter evil when he had used it to convert the troopers at Seven Stones, but Ursula had turned him into a gigolo with it, Exeter had slaughtered his friends to obtain it, then used it to unman the Niolian cavalry—and now this tale of Jumbo being bent, at least once and probably twice. No one was safe when there was mana around.

"You think Zath chose Jumbo again? Seems odd. Exeter will be suspicious this time, won't he?" Then he shuddered a second time, feeling his skin crawl as if he had just fallen into an especially foul pit. "You don't mean Alice?"

"I don't know." Prof peered blearily at him. "Jumbo's more likely, because Zath would know he was a senior member of the Service. He shouldn't have known who Mrs. Pearson was—but I fear it is a great mistake to underestimate him. Hell, Captain, maybe he did come just to make threats."

"But you don't think so. You think he came to hex Jumbo again."

Rawlinson struggled with a cough and took a drink. "I think one of them's a poisoned pawn, probably Jumbo. He may not even know it himself, but I think he's a loaded gun, and when he meets the Liberator, he'll fire."

"And he took Alice along to allay suspicion? As a decoy?" Just as Ursula had taken Julian himself. "Exeter'll be so surprised to see her that he won't pay much attention to Jumbo."

"That would be Jumbo's thinking," Prof agreed in a whisper, "although not willing thinking, if you follow me. But it could have been Alice who talked Jumbo into taking her."

Julian cringed. "Exeter has buckets of mana of his own. Whichever one of them is the hemlock, he'll detect the hex . . . won't he?"

Prof heaved himself upright with a groan. "If you'll excuse me, old man, I'm going back to bed." He was swaying on his feet. "Stay and finish the bottle if you want. There's more in that cupboard. No, I don't think Exeter will detect the trap. With the kind of power Zath has at his disposal, he won't have left any fingerprints."

40

JULIAN SPENT THE NIGHT ON PROF RAWLINSON'S SOFA AND WENT HOME through a drizzly dawn to clean up as best he could. Even the water supply had failed, though. Exploring his own house in a way he never had before, he discovered that the taps were supplied from a tank in the attic, which was charged by hand-pumping from an underground cistern—how it arrived there was not clear, but he managed to fill a bucket from it without falling in. There was no firewood cut, and he could not handle an ax.

Clean but shivering, he had just conquered the last shirt button when he heard the doorbell jangle. On the veranda stood William McKay, unshaven and rumpled as a wet cat, beaming in his usual witless fashion and holding out a covered basket.

"Heard you were home, old man. Brought you some brekker."

Julian was nonplussed. "That's extremely kind of you."

"Oh, don't thank me, old son. Thank the Reformed Methodist Ladies' Good Deed and Morris Dancing Society, Olympus Branch. They distribute gin to the needy. I'm just the messenger boy. You can tip me a tanner if you're feeling generous. Need the basket back."

"Come in a moment."

McKay stepped over the threshhold and stopped. He was a tall, vapid man and the best linguist in the station, able to speak at least twelve of the Valian dialects without saying anything of substance in any of them. His only interest was fishing and he was of interest to Julian only because he was Euphemia's husband. She swore they had not shared a bed in years, but how did one cross-examine a man about his own wife?

Lifting a corner of the cover, Julian found fruit, bread that smelled newly baked, and a stoppered bottle hot enough to contain tea. His mouth began watering enthusiastically. He thought of Prof. "You do this gin-distributing to all us worthy poor?"

"Well, it makes sense to have a central mess. Got to ration the supplies, what? All hang together. Polly organized it." McKay's gaze wandered past Julian and back again. "You—you're alone?"

"Yes. Come and sit a moment. I need to talk to you."

"Oh. Should be getting back. Just wondered if you had news of Euphemia. We're a bit concerned, you know."

"What? Why? Come in here," Julian said firmly. Taking the basket, he led the way into his drawing room. It was small and rather sparse, for he had no skill at homemaking and rarely entertained, but he noted that it was at least tidy. He waved his guest to a chair and took one himself. He began emptying the basket. "Tell me."

McKay folded himself down into the chair and stared at the floor uncomfortably. "Well, she went back Home briefly to fetch Exeter's cousin. . . ."

"And brought the Spanish flu back. Yes, I heard. Where is she now?"

"Don't know. Just got back from Thovale myself yesterday. Haven't caught it yet, but I expect I will. She'd gone already. Thought you . . . Well, you know. Thought you might know."

Julian gripped the bottle between his knees and pulled out the stopper. An intriguing wisp of steam emerged. "No." He took a swig of tea and burned his throat satisfactorily.

"Ah. Seems she managed to sweet-talk the Carrots into supplying us with some grub a couple of days ago, when we ran out. Then she did a bunk. Didn't tell anyone where she was going. Left no note." McKay was looking everywhere except at Julian. "Unless you . . . ?"

"None here, I'm afraid. Look, McKay. . . . You know we're lovers."

The tall man shrugged at the fireplace. "No moss. We've gone our own ways a long time. You made her very happy, old man. More than—er, well, you know."

More than half the other men in the station in their respective times? How *old* was she? Pride would never let him ask.

"We had words. I'm deucedly sorry and I want to make up. You have no idea where she's gone?"

"Not a bally notion. She works Lemodvale, you know. She'll have contacts there. Or—" He bit his lip. "The Carrots may know, I suppose. She gets on better with them than most of us do."

"She told me about Timothy."

Suddenly it was eye-contact time, man to man stuff, stiff upper lips. McKay colored, then clasped his hands together so tightly that the knuckles showed white. "Long time ago. Look, I should be getting back. . . ."

"It makes no difference to me, what she did. Like to hear your side of it, though."

"Dang it all, old man . . . !"

"Please?" Julian said, feeling his own face burning but utterly determined to see this through. "For her sake? I love her, but I hurt her feelings without meaning to. Want to make up. I want to understand her."

"Don't we all! Men can't understand women, laddie. Women are a mystery in all worlds. Can't live with 'em, can't live without 'em." McKay stared at the empty fireplace, chewing his lip. "It may not have been entirely all her fault, actually. I suppose. One of those things . . . She didn't fit in, really. The women were pretty bad to her."

Idiot! What had he expected? How long ago? Twenty years? Fifty? Even now it was easy to imagine the ladies of Olympus snubbing the fishmonger's daughter from rural Ireland, a pride of cats sharing a mouse. It was also easy to see that such stupid class prejudice should mean a lot less to Julian Smedley, who had been through the Great War, than it did to all those Victorian fossils. If the war had decided anything, it had brought England together. Things would be different from now on. But even if Euphemia might still be a misfit back in Cheltenham, here on Nextdoor she was his woman and that was all that mattered.

"I may not have been as much help as I should have been," McKay said gruffly. "She went native. Moved in with a Carrot woodcutter."

Where else could she have gone? "She—they—they had just the one child?"

"Well, yes. Then her big buck Carrot got eaten by a jugular. A year or two later she came back to me, brat and all." He shrugged. "Took her in. Separate rooms, you know? We got along better like that. And Tim. Jolly good kid, actually. Brought him up as a gentleman. Taught him fishing. He went off Home a few years ago. Last we heard he was with Head Office. He's a stranger over there, of course. Well, mustn't point fingers, old man! I'm pretty sure I've fathered a few by-blows around the Station myself." McKay lumbered to his feet.

Obviously it still rankled that his wife had gone native, left him for a Carrot. He probably didn't even appreciate the courage it must have taken for her to come back to him and his precious friends. Well, what she had done or not done did not matter now to Julian. He'd rather think of the young Euphemia having a love affair with a young Carrot than of her being blackmailed into bed by slimy Pinky Pinkney. Nothing wrong with Carrots except that they were mortal. Dommi, for one, was a hell of a lot better man than Pinkney or even this bat-brained William McKay.

"What news of Exeter?" McKay asked, shambling toward the door.

"All bad." Julian told him the tale. "It's Alice Prescott I'm worried about. Pearson, I mean."

McKay nodded vaguely. "What are you going to do?"

Julian took a moment to digest what he had learned. If Euphemia was not in Olympus, then there was no reason for him to stay. With only one hand, he was limited even in the help he could give to the sick. "I think I'm going to head back to Exeter's crusade again. Alice is an old friend, and Exeter may be dead. I sort of feel responsible for her. If Zath bewitched her, then she may be dead, too, or crazy by now. Or Jumbo is, if he was the poisoned pill. The flu must be all over the Vales already. She doesn't know the language, she has no money." That bitch Ursula might not help her.

"Better you than me, old man. I must get back to Kingdom Hall. Good luck." McKay held out a limp hand. "Don't count on finding much here when you come back, what?"

"No. I won't."

Götterdämmerung!

41

A QUICK RECONNAISSANCE OF THE STATION CONFIRMED MCKAY'S REport. Polly Murgatroyd had organized meals and care for the sick, but the Carrots controlled the food supply and might cut it off at any time. There was nothing Julian could do to make things any better. He discovered that three quarters of the strangers had fled and not one of the remainder was able or willing to accompany Captain Smedley on a hundred-mile walk. All the rabbits had gone from the paddocks and when he continued on up the valley to the dragon compound, he found that deserted also. Seventy-seven must have discovered the situation and chosen the logical course of action.

He gathered a blanket, spare clothes, and some money, and walked out his front door with a pack on his back and an umbrella in his good hand. He could reach Randorvale before dark. He might be carrying the infection with him, but so many of the Service had preceded him that he was not going to make matters any worse. From Randorvale he would go by Lappinvale, Mapvale, and Jurgvale—none of those passes was beyond a man on foot. If necessary, he could carry on to Niolvale, but before then he ought to have news of the Liberator. He should also have learned just how badly the Spanish flu had struck Nextdoor. An epidemic that could circle the Earth in five months would have spread across the Vales in days.

Fifteen minutes brought him to the Carrots' village. His approach was noticed, and a delegation of three elderly men came out to meet him on the road. Two he could not recall ever seeing before, but the third had been the Pinkneys' butler, although Julian could not recall the man's name. When he was still about twenty or thirty feet away, that one shouted, "Stop!"

Julian stopped and stood there in the mud, facing rebellion while rain pattered on his umbrella. "How many of you have been stricken? How many have died?"

"Too many! Let the *tyikank* attend to their own sick and leave the Carrots alone. You are not welcome." Their green eyes were uniformly hostile.

"I do not understand. We have brought much prosperity to this valley, and done much good for your people. Just because a sickness comes, you suddenly turn on—"

"Go away, Kaptaan!" said another. "You have brought the wrath of the gods upon us. Many of us think we should burn your big houses and drive you out. Do not tempt our young men to rashness. Go!"

"I am trying to."

"Go by the river trail, then," said the former butler.

That was a sizable detour, but evidently charisma was not going to work.

"Is *Entyika* McKay with you?"

"No."

"I have two letters here—one for her, if she comes back, and one from Dommi for Ayetha."

"Leave them on that stump and begone."

Julian did so and trudged back to the turnoff. The Carrots' attitude was infuriating but understandable. It was only natural for them to attribute the pestilence to Zath and the anger of the Pentatheon. Perhaps the storm could have been weathered if the *tyikank* had stood their ground and not been so craven. As it was, the Service was wounded mortally. It could not blame Exeter or the Pentatheon, for it had brought götterdämmerung upon itself.

ᔓᔓ 42 ᔕᔕ

No one knew how Roaring Cave had earned so inappropriate a name, for nowhere contained more silence. It was a huge cavern in a hillside overlooking Lospass, much used by travelers. Eleal had overnighted in it and explored it a few days ago on her way to Niolvale. She was greatly relieved to see it again, for her muscles were not accustomed to her new leg; they throbbed as if tortured with red-hot pincers. Old Piol seemed to be in no worse shape than she was, but they were both chilled to icicles by the rain. They scrambled up the slope to the cave mouth in the company of a dozen or so other pilgrims, being met there by one of the Liberator's shield-bearing deputies. He wore a shabby, incongruous military tunic.

"We have just lit a new fire," he announced pompously. "Follow me and I will lead you to it. Try not to make unnecessary noise."

The floor was generally level, but littered with boulders of all sizes, which must have fallen in past ages from the soaring roof. The uneven path was tricky going in the gloom. At first Eleal could see nothing except Piol's back directly ahead of her, but gradually her eyes grew accustomed to the dim light of many fires, each one surrounded by several dozen people. The warning against noise had been given because everyone was trying to listen to D'ward himself. He was sitting with one group but speaking loudly, apparently not preaching as much as answering questions.

Led to a smoky, crackling heap—more fuel than flame as yet—Eleal huddled in as close as she could and shivered strenuously. Between the snapping of the twigs and the chattering of teeth all around her, she could not make out what was being said at all. The air smelled very strongly of wet people, but she was glad of the company. As the flames leaped higher and the heat penetrated, her bones began to thaw. It was then she realized that one of the men pressed against her was Dosh. His eyes shone in the firelight as he saw that she had noticed him.

"Are you keeping watch on me?" she whispered angrily.

He nodded and held a finger to his lips.

She looked around. More and more people were trickling into the cave. Another fire had been lit nearby, and newcomers were led to that one now. The overall silence of such a crowd was quite eerie.

D'ward had risen and was moving to another group. They cleared a boulder for him to sit on. Now he was closer, and she could hear better.

"Well?" he said cheerfully. "No questions?"

"I have a question, heretic!" The harsh voice came from a large man in a dark robe. Eleal would not have been sure of its color had she not recognized its wearer as one of the priests of Padlopan who had shared the wagon with her yesterday.

D'ward's voice was no softer. "You waste your life worshipping a false god of sickness! I doubt that mere words can penetrate so many years of wrongful thinking, but ask."

The priest rose to his feet, a massive dark shape against the dancing firelight. "You say you go to slay Death. Then tell us what happens after, when Death is dead! Shall we all live forever?"

The Liberator sighed. "Whatever I answer, you will not believe. Come with us and see for yourself what happens. Who else has a question?"

"I have not done," the priest bellowed. "Nay, I have many other queries!" The reaction was a roar of fury from the audience. The priest was clearly shocked but undeterred; then D'ward said something sharply to him and he sank down out of sight.

Eleal discovered she was on the verge of sniggering. She caught Dosh's eye and saw he was grinning as if he had heard such exchanges before.

The next query was inaudible.

"Ah!" D'ward said. "Not everyone heard that. You, priest, have an excessively brazen voice. Repeat for these good people what the lady asked."

The priest did not rise, but he made himself heard. "Gladly, I will, gladly! The woman said her babe is dying and can the Liberator slay death in time to save it? Yes, answer that, Liberator!"

D'ward did not reply for a long moment, and Roaring Cave was very silent. Only faint crackling from the fires disturbed the hush. Then he said, "Pass me this child."

Eleal rose up on her knees, hoping to see more, but there were too many bodies and boulders in the way and people behind her began hissing angrily until she sat down again. All she could make out was D'ward's familiar face, framed in a narrow gap, lit from below against darkness. He looked up from whatever he had been doing.

"There!" he said. "I think that will answer your question, mother, and answer yours, too, priest. The poor mite is hungry. Has anyone a scrap of food for a hungry child? Thank you, brother—a blessing upon you. And back to your mother with you, kitten."

Roaring Cave did not exactly roar, but a whirlwind of whispers seemed to sweep through it, and then some voices cried out, "A miracle!"

Eleal looked around, and Dosh's expression was as mocking as she had expected. "Like me?" she said. "He cures others? He does this all the time?"

Dosh nodded. She cowered down low, thinking furiously.

D'ward waited until the reaction died away. "It was a blessing from the Undivided upon our quest. Who else has a question?"

He kept it up for more than an hour, moving around from fire to fire. In that time he apparently cured a woman's paralyzed arm and another fevered child and gave a blind man back his sight. Sometimes he would laugh and joke, sometimes be solemn. Often his replies took the form of little stories that made a point but left no handhold for the priests wanting to contest it. He was unfailingly gracious to everyone except clerics, and to them he was scathingly rude. That was understandable, as they kept trying to trap him. None of them ever seemed to catch him out, although some of his answers were evasive, like the one he had given the priest of Padlopan.

His mastery was amazing. Eleal had seen audiences held spellbound before, but never for so long and never by an extemporaneous performance, for obviously D'ward was following no script. His progress would eventually bring him to her fire, and she waited with trembling anxiety lest he break off and go elsewhere.

By the time he arrived, dusk was falling beyond the great arch of the entrance—and not just dusk, for the rain had turned to snow. People squirmed out of the way to make a place for him. Instead of sitting, he remained standing, his arms folded. She remembered the time he had played Gunuu in *The Tragedy of Trastos*. Then he had not worn a robe, only a loincloth, and the magic of firelight had made him shine like the god he portrayed. Oh, what a triumph that had been! A lump arose in her throat, and she trembled with a fierce longing to jump up and throw her arms around him.

He glanced at her without expression, then looked around the group. "Who asks here?"

An old man beside him cried out in the loud, flat tones of the deaf. "There is a storm coming! My bones know it! My bones always tell me when there's bad weather coming. Will you lead us onward again tomorrow, young man, or stay here and wait it out, mm?" It was a good question. He looked even older than Piol, and he was wearing no more than the legal minimum. At a guess he was just a beggar who had joined the Free for the food.

D'ward shrugged. "We're warm here now, there's fuel in the woods, water in the stream, meat walking in our direction—why run to meet tomorrow's troubles?"

"Because I don't have many tomorrows left, young man! That's why!"

D'ward laughed gleefully and reached over to clap the man's bony shoulder. "You have all eternity to look forward to, grandfather! But if your bones are telling us the truth, then I think we'll have to wait out the storm. You're not the only one without proper clothing. I don't want to see anyone freeze. Now, if we have any rich people here who would like to contribute money or spare clothes to the Free, that would be a very meritorious deed in the eyes of the Undivided."

He glanced over the group as if looking for another question, but it seemed to Eleal that his eyes momentarily flashed sapphire at her. Could he know about her money belt? She must have more wealth to hand than anyone else in the cave. She would not let D'ward have that money to foster his blasphemies!

But if she did, would he forget his unfair suspicions? Would he accept that she only wanted to be his friend now?

Would he even give her a hug, just one brief hug, to say that he knew he could trust her?

"May I ask?" The voice was that of Piol Poet, who had somehow become separated from her and was now on the far side of the fire. "I fear it may be an impertinent question, master."

D'ward chuckled. "But coming from you it will be an astute one, old friend. Ask."

"You teach things that are not written in any scripture. By whose authority do you speak?"

The Liberator's dark eyebrows rose very high. He lifted his head to address his answer to the whole cave. "Piol Poet asks by what authority I speak. Oh, Piol, Piol, do you really put so much trust in books? You know how often a scribe will make mistakes when copying a text. You know that even the original was written by mortal hand, for gods do not stoop to writing their own scriptures. Is it not better to hear the words of the teacher at firsthand than at innumerable repeats? My authority comes from the One True God, who sent me."

Several voices began to speak at once. D'ward nodded at the loudest, a burly, sullen-looking man who had been sitting with his arm around a girl no older than Eleal. Perhaps she was the only reason he was here, for his manner did not seem at all respectful.

"You claim to be the Liberator foretold in the *Filoby Testament*. But according to the *Testament,* the Liberator was born less than five years ago. How then can you be the Liberator?"

D'ward did not take offense, although several of the listeners growled angrily. "That is not what the *Testament* said about me, and I can call a witness to what did happen. Eleal Singer is here, the Eleal prophesied, the Eleal who fulfilled that prophecy. Rise, Eleal, and tell the people what you saw."

Eleal had almost forgotten what stage fright felt like, for she had not experienced it since she was a child. Now she cringed away in shock, staring aghast at D'ward's twinkling blue eyes. She could not follow an act like that!

Dosh pinched her. "Up with you! Give them the performance of your life, Singer. But keep your clothes on."

She slapped him away angrily.

Then D'ward smiled at her. She had forgotten his smiles. The beard hadn't changed their impact. She rose unwillingly to her feet.

"Come and bear witness," he said. "Up here! Excuse us, grandfather."

He meant her to stand on the flat rock the old man was now vacating. She held out a hand so he could help her up, but he ignored it. Then Dosh gripped her waist and lifted her onto the makeshift podium. A great cavern, full of twinkling fires, bright now against the evening . . . innumerable intent faces. She had never performed before an audience this size before, and she did not have her lines memorized. Piol had not even written her part yet. The pounding of her heart seemed to fill the cave; something was building a nest in her stomach.

"Begin at the beginning," D'ward said below her. "Like you told Dosh." He smiled again.

She turned to the audience and drew a deep breath. "My name is Eleal Singer." She heard her voice echo back satisfactorily from the rocks. "Five years ago, I came to Narshvale with a troupe of strolling players. Innocent child that I was, I never dreamed that evil forces conspired to slay me, nor that I was destined to play a starring role on the stage of history. . . ."

After that it was easy. She told everything, or almost everything. She did not describe D'ward's hasty departure from Suss, but she included the first miracle, when he had cured Dolm Actor of his curse, and the miracle yesterday that had cured her leg. By the time she had finished, the sky outside was black. She expected an ovation, for she was sure that it had been the finest performance of her life. She was greeted by a numbing silence. Well, no matter! People did not applaud in a temple, and today this cave was a temple. Silence itself was appreciation; the cave was very still. Not a cough. She had preached for the heretic. She had no regrets—although she wondered what her father thought of her now.

She spun around on her podium, planning to jump down into D'ward's arms for a little hug and a whispered congratulation, perhaps even a quick kiss.

But D'ward had gone.

ᘒᕟ 43 ᕟᘒ

As ELEAL SINGER BEGAN WORKING UP A SERIOUS SWEAT IN HER HIGHLY dramatized version of *The Coming of the Liberator,* D'ward nodded to Dosh to follow him and slipped away the little group around the fire. Unnoticed by the intently listening pilgrims, he moved off into the dark. Doing the same was not quite so easy for a man loaded like a turtle with Prat'han's great shield, but Dosh accepted the challenge.

He reached the toe of the rockfall first. D'ward arrived, then turned around to look for his missing follower. Like an unusually silent shadow, Dosh stepped in close behind him and whispered, "Master?"

D'ward jumped rewardingly and then laughed. "You trying to frighten me to death?" In the faint glimmer from the many fires, his face was hardly more than a blur, but he was smiling, and if anyone's smile could glow in the dark, it would be his. "You know this cave?"

"Best lodgings in the Vales, for the price."

"True. So you know the little hollow back there?"

Dosh nodded. "It's called the Fleapit."

"Probably well deserved. I asked Kilpian to get a fire going. Try and keep everyone except friends and shield-bearers away, will you?"

Oh, blazes! The cave was fifty strides wide, and although the main path over the rockfall was well defined, there were other low spots. Dosh had spent days exploring Roaring Cave in his youth, for it was a favorite Tinkerfolk campsite. He knew six or seven passable routes to the Fleapit. Dusk was falling, but with so many fires burning, the cavern would not be truly dark. Intruders could manage the barrier without a torch if they took it slowly.

He sighed. "You always give me the tough ones!"

"I do," D'ward said solemnly. "That's partly because I can rely on you to tackle them better than anyone else. It's also because I know you like getting the tough ones." He grinned again. "Don't you?"

"No!" But then Dosh realized that he did enjoy the unfamiliar sensation of being trusted, which was probably the same thing. "Well, maybe. I suppose I do." He hadn't really known that, but it was true. Not for the first time, he wondered if the Liberator knew him better than he knew himself. "I'll see you're not disturbed, master."

D'ward squeezed his shoulder. "Good man. You never let me down, Dosh." He faded away into the gloom.

Dosh stood for a moment, savoring those final words. *Never let him down!* How good that felt! And how strange that he should think so—he, Dosh Envoy, who had never before cared for anything except carnal pleasure, the kinkier the better. Some miracles were less obvious than others. . . . Then he heaved Prat'han's shield straight on his shoulders, adjusted the (horribly light) money bag on his belt, and set off to locate some helpers.

He enlisted shield-bearers Tielan and Gastik, two friends, and also three Niolian youngsters he'd picked out earlier as promising recruits. Then he found Tittrag Mason, a new shield-bearer who was big enough to move the whole rockfall single-handed.

He posted them in pairs to cover the most likely paths over the pile. None of them was very happy at the prospect, thinking of reapers.

"Don't worry about them," he said. "A reaper can go by without being seen if he wants to, and in this case he won't want to leave bodies around to raise the alarm, right? The same thing's true of Eltiana cultists or Blood-and-Hammer thugs, or any other assassins the evil sorcerers may send against D'ward. Don't worry about them, because they won't worry about you, and you can't do anything about them anyway. If they do turn up, D'ward will deal with them. Your job is strictly pest control. Be polite and understanding, but firm. If you have any trouble, shout for me. I'll be going up and down the line."

Pest control. Some people just *had* to speak to the Liberator personally, to explain their problems, the gods' truth, or his mistakes. D'ward dealt with most of those during the day, but that sort could never understand that he might have more important business to attend to, such as sleeping. The worst pests by far were the priests. There were dozens of priests around now, every one of them determined to stamp out his heresy.

Dosh began patrolling back and forth across the toe of the rockfall, keeping both eyes wide open, watching anyone who headed deeper into the cave and also watching his helpers. He was annoyed to discover how easily he could work his way past them without their seeing him. He was a very good sneak, of course, after a lifetime's practice, but others might be just as good.

There was too much cover, too many people in the cave, too little light. Even if he had the fuel to build a chain of fires from one wall to the other, there would still be too many shadows. The job D'ward had given him this time wasn't just tough, it was an eyelash short of impossible.

℘℘ 44 ℘℘

"CRIKEY!" JUMBO SAID. "FOR A NATIVE, SHE'S QUITE A PERFORMER!" He was sitting near a smoky little fire at the far side of Roaring Cave, leaning his arms on his knees and looking as totally relaxed as if he were watching a cricket match on a village green.

Alice refrained from comment. He was referring to the famous Miss Eleal, who had certainly grown up from the child Edward had described in 1917. She had grown *out,* too, in conspicuous places.

Riding a dragon had been a very strange experience, but this cave was stranger yet. Never would Alice have believed that her next meeting with her cousin would take place in such grotesque surroundings. When she came in, she had known his voice at once, even reverberating in that huge, echoing space, even speaking whatever dialect that was. He had not been speaking in tongues, as Zath had, yet she had often been able to catch the gist of his words. Later she had seen him in the distance. He had not changed a bit, except that now he had

a beard. It did not suit him, but it might be required wear for the unlikely career
he had chosen. He was obviously doing very well in it. Hundreds of people
were grouped around dozens of twinkling fires under a blue haze of wood smoke.
It all looked rather like one of Uncle Roly's more lurid descriptions of Hell,
except that no one was screaming or suffering. Quite the reverse—this cavern
was a node, and the virtuality added an unnerving aura of holiness to the proceedings. She had been tempted to stand up and shout, "He's only Edward! I
knew him when he picked his nose and woke up crying from nightmares."

She hadn't, of course. Nobody would have understood her anyway. But it
was definitely an odd feeling to have a holy man in the family.

A woman with a shield on her back was shouting over the rising buzz of
conversation.

"Now what's going on?" Alice demanded.

"She says," Jumbo drawled, "that the train on platform four is the express to
Pontefract and Llandudno."

"I shall ask my cousin to turn you into a pillar of salt."

"Actually she said that there's food coming, that the ladies' room is over that
way and the gentlemen's that way, and could she have some volunteers to fetch
firewood?"

"Go ahead and volunteer," Alice said. "Shouldn't we be checking on the
dragons, anyway? Suppose somebody steals them?"

"Then we walk home. They'll be all right. I think it's time to go and have a
word with our esteemed Liberator." Jumbo sprang nimbly to his feet and held
out a hand to aid her. All over the cave, people were rising to stretch their legs.
The darkness seemed to move in as bodies blocked the firelight.

"I don't see him now," she said.

"I know where he went. Come on. If we get separated, I'll meet you underneath that molar, all righty?" Gesturing at a prominent stalactite, Jumbo took
her hand and set off confidently across the cavern floor. His strong left arm
cleared a way through the milling throng while he growled peremptory apologies. It seemed odd that he should be so little concerned for the safety of the
livestock he had left to graze unattended outside the cave. Until this evening he
had fussed over them as if they were prize racehorses. Still, he must know what
he was doing. All the way from Olympus, he had been a competent guide and
an enjoyable companion.

She was about to meet Edward. That was why she had come. Would he feel
she was meddling? That had been a danger all along. Now there was something
new. Now she had seen a blind man given back his sight and a feverish, whimpering baby come suddenly to life and start laughing. Faith healing might explain
the man, but not the baby, and she wasn't sure how far she believed in faith
healing anyway. Had anyone else staged those miracles, she would have been
sure that they had been faked, the "invalids" being accomplices planted ahead
of time in the audience.

Edward wouldn't do that. If he had worked miracles, then they had been
genuine miracles. Magic, of course—Miss Pimm could use magic and the rules

of the parallel worlds would give Edward on Nextdoor the powers Miss Pimm had on Earth. All the same, it was disturbing to see the cousin she had known all her life, her foster brother, deliberately playing Jesus. There could be no doubt that that was what he was doing. Although she thought of herself as a Christian, she liked to believe she was tolerant and broad-minded. His performance made her uneasy, but it could hardly be blasphemous in a world where Christianity did not exist—or could it? She must not jump to conclusions. Doubtless he would explain his reasons to her. Even if he wouldn't, she would trust him and not ask.

She felt a vicarious pride at the numbers he had collected. My cousin the messiah . . .

She followed Jumbo through the crowd, weaving between clusters of people, heading for the depths of the cave. Soon their way was blocked by a wall of rubble and megalithic blocks and frozen rivers of stalagmites. The ominous irregularities overhead showed where masses of stone had fallen off and crashed to the ground. This cave was old. The odds of another fall happening just as she was passing underneath were remote—remote but still hard to ignore. There was almost no light here, far from the arch and the fires. She had never suffered from claustrophobia before, so why start now? It was only virtuality making her skin crawl, wasn't it?

As she neared the foot of the rockfall, she heard voices raised in argument. Suddenly Jumbo halted, listening. In front of a wall of cyclopean boulders, three figures in gowns were confronting two men, one of whom bore a round shield and a dangerous-looking spear. Even without understanding the words, it was obvious to Alice that the three were demanding and the two were refusing. The subject of their disputation seemed to be access to an ominous dark notch.

"What's going on?" she whispered.

Jumbo said, "Sh!" In a moment, though, the three turned away and headed back to the main gathering, muttering angrily. The two stayed where they were.

"It appears," Jumbo said quietly, "that our reverend friend does not wish to be disturbed. Those monk-chappies were priests—Tion's I think. Let's see if we can do any better."

He led her forward again, passing the three grumbling clerics, heading for the two gatekeepers.

"They don't look much like a welcoming committee," she murmured.

"Just keeping the riffraff out. I'm sure they'll recognize a lady when they see one."

Alice did not feel much like a lady. The last few days had done nothing for her coiffeur or complexion; she was still bundled in heavy, waterlogged furs, smelling strongly of wet sheep. The guards did not spring smartly to attention at the sight of her.

Jumbo drawled an explanation as he went by—tried to go by. He stopped at the sharp end of the spear. His tone changed, but still displayed the blithe arrogance of strangerhood.

The spear did not waver. The other guard growled a response.

Jumbo tried again, in yet another voice. That one worked no better. He was obviously taken aback by this failure of charisma.

"You're not wearing the old school tie," Alice suggested and gave her knuckles a mental rap for tactlessness.

Jumbo shot her an acid glance. "I'm tempted to turn them both into pumpkins."

"An intemperate response . . . Can you?"

"Not until midnight." He launched into a longer, quieter speech. That one at least produced a civil reply. It even had hints of regret in it, but it was still clearly a refusal.

Then a third man drifted in out of the darkness. He was short and very blond, and at first glance Alice thought he was just a boy. Then she noted that he, too, bore a shield on his back. He had no spear, but he was obviously in charge.

Jumbo began again, and this time Alice heard her own name and others: "Ursula," "Captain," and "Jumbo." He was having to beg, and he would not like that. Something he said impressed the blond boy, who snapped out an order, and the guard who did not have a shield turned and disappeared into the opening between the two great rocks.

That was progress. It left four people standing in near darkness: two very vigilant and suspicious guards, one toe-tapping, heel-cooling, icily furious Jumbo, and one Alice trying not to let her amusement show.

"Where are we trying to get to, anyway?" she asked.

"*Hrnnph!* There's an inner cave here behind this rockfall. I've slept there many times. Travelers prefer it, because it's cosy. Tends to be warm in winter and cool in summer. Obviously that's where Exeter's hiding out."

Jumbo fell silent again. Minutes dragged by. In the outer cave, the pilgrims had begun singing. The tonality was strange, but the beat was rousing enough— possibly the Valian equivalent of "Onward, Christian Soldiers." Had Edward taught them the Fallow school song yet?

"There are other ways over this junk heap," Jumbo growled.

"Patience!" she said soothingly. "He's a celebrity, remember. He can't let himself be pestered all the time."

Light flickered. Out of the canyon emerged a flaming torch carried by a woman. She came to a halt and raised it to inspect the supplicants.

"Evening, Jumbo. And good evening to you, Miss Prescott. I'm Ursula Newton."

"Charmed," Alice replied, blinking against the light. "Actually, I'm Mrs. Pearson now." Why the devil should that matter here? "But still Edward's cousin, of course."

At that point, Jumbo should have spoken, or Mrs. Newton should have offered to lead the visitors to the holy of holies. Instead, she just stood and looked hard at each of them in turn. Alice felt twinges of apprehension. She had come so far. What could be wrong now?

"Is Captain Smedley with you?" she asked.

"No, he's on his way back to Olympus." Ursula Newton was a solid, powerful-looking woman, wearing a thick woolen robe of Valian cut. Her hair was unusually short and her manner definitely suspicious. "Forgive me if I ask you a couple of questions?"

"Dammit all, Ursula!" Jumbo said. "What's got into you?"

"Prudence." She turned her watchful gaze on Alice. "Who was Bujja, Mrs. Pearson?"

"Who?" Merciful heavens! "Edward's nursemaid at Nyagatha."

"And Spots?"

"That was a leopard cub we tried to domesticate once, without much—"

"Wrong answer!"

For a moment Alice just stared at the woman, quite unable to believe this was happening. Then she said, "Oh! It was also Julian Smedley, when he was national acne champion."

Ursula relaxed visibly. Her smile was not exactly winsome, though. "Thank you. The Liberator has to be extremely careful, you see, and news of your arrival here was a surprise."

Jumbo laughed. "Oh, he's 'the Liberator' now, is he? Have you changed sides, Ursula, darling?"

Her eyes narrowed. "Not really. I still think he made a serious mistake in launching this crusade. Now he's done so, I believe it must be carried forward as well as possible. And you?"

"Much the same. We didn't come to try and talk him out of it, whatever you may have told Exeter. We have some interesting news for him."

"Then Mrs. Pearson can pass it on. He prefers not to meet with you, Jumbo."

"I quite understand." Spoken like a gentleman, but even in the flickering light of the torch, Jumbo's flush showed. "Give him my regards, won't you?" He turned and stalked away before Alice could think of anything to say. How awful!

Ursula gestured for Alice to follow. Holding the torch overhead, she led the way up a steep, narrow trench. The rocks pressed closer, looming, threatening. Alice could feel them all around her and overhanging, grinning at her—claustrophobic! The floor was steep and uneven.

"I apologize for that inquisition," Ursula said over her shoulder. "The Chamber has been sending human time bombs after him. Your presence here was so unexpected that I insisted he take some precautions."

And Jumbo's presence was definitely unwelcome. Alice would have to have a word with Edward about that, and build some bridges. "Quite all right. Understandable. What exactly are human time bombs? I presume they don't have fuses dangling from their ears?"

"Not so easy, I'm afraid. They're people enslaved by mana to kill the Liberator. If it's any comfort to you, I can't detect any sorcery on you—nor on Jumbo, for that matter—but that doesn't mean much. Only a very clumsy curse would be detectable."

"Well, I assure you that I truly am his cousin. Fresh from England. I'm here on holiday, surprising as that may seem."

Mrs. Newton uttered a loud snort of laughter. "You have strange tastes in vacation spots! We have to squeeze through here. Watch your footing." She held the torch higher to illuminate the gap. Then the path led steeply downward, and Alice had to hold back to avoid the heat of the flames ahead of her.

Her guide stopped and turned around. "Almost there," she said quietly. "One final request, Mrs. Pearson—please do not go close to your cousin. His body-guards have been warned to block anyone who tries to touch him. They might not be overly gentle."

Alice was becoming very tired of this nonsense. "Is it necessary for a human time bomb to touch him to kill him?"

"Probably not, but that would be by far the easiest way to set up the sorcery. It is how Zath always primes his reapers. You might not even be aware that such a curse had been laid on you." Ursula Newton was obviously quite serious, despite the unbelievable words she was speaking. "You would be given an ir-resistible compulsion to touch him and then complete some deadly ritual, al-though whatever it was might seem quite harmless to you."

"I shall be extremely careful to keep my hands to myself, then."

"That would be advisable. Follow me, please."

As Jumbo had promised, the air was appreciably warmer here. Summer lin-gered on, deep in the bowels of the hill, and yet the virtuality seemed even stronger. Then a faint glimmer of light showed ahead, and Alice found herself stepping down into a hollow that could almost count as a separate cave. Obvi-ously it was a well-frequented campsite, its floor littered with old chips of wood and bark. In the center was a fireplace of blackened stones, surrounded by a circle of low rocks for sitting. Beyond that, in turn, lay heaps of frondy leaves for bedding and a miscellaneous clutter of gourds and logs.

Half a dozen people were grouped around the twinkling fire, their faces danc-ing in and out of the dark like ghosts. Edward was on the far side, speaking softly while the others listened—the king and his court. He looked weary but not as weary as might have been expected for an actor resting after such a performance.

Her arrival made them all scramble to their feet, but she had eyes only for the tall man in the prophet's robe. Yes, she wanted to run to him and hug him, but she did not think there was anything sinister in that urge, just normal affection for her only living relative after a long separation. She sensed the others' hair-trigger vigilance, watching to see if she would try it.

"Alice!"

"Edward! It's wonderful to see you!"

"And you. Er . . . won't you sit down?"

She moved to the closest seat, a flat rock upholstered with a scrap of fur. After a moment, everyone else sat down also, all except Ursula Newton.

Nobody spoke. Edward was just staring at Alice as if she were a ghost, the Holy Grail, or King George himself, and she was similarly tongue-tied. There were so many things to say that they could not even begin. She sensed an invisible wall of distrust between them.

Norfolk seemed very far away now.

She found her voice first. "I'm not here on business, Edward. Just on holiday. I'm not carrying any banners. Funny—you haven't changed a bit!" The beard was not all that bad at close quarters, hardly more than a heavy stubble. With a patriarchal bush like Tennyson's, he would look like a character in a school nativity play.

Behind her, Ursula coughed harshly. "Well, I'll leave you to have a private chat, shall I?" The guards, three men and one woman, would not understand English. She must have left, then, but Alice did not turn to see.

"Sorry about the cloak and dagger," Edward said. "Ursula . . ."

"It's a good idea. I don't mind."

"You're thinner. Keeping well?"

"Splendid, thank you." Under the circumstances, this was an absurdly banal conversation. It was wonderful to see him again. There was an extraordinary pain in her throat. "And you?"

He smiled wistfully across the fire at her. "I'm ever so homesick! Tell me about England."

⦚ 45 ⦚

THE FREE HAD BEGUN YET ANOTHER HYMN. ELEAL DID NOT KNOW THE lyrics to this one either, and she was not in a mood to sing the praises of the Undivided anyway. She was still struggling to accept the idea that the gods she had always believed in might be imposters. The fire was burning low, but she was not cold now. She was hungry, and the supplies in her pack had run out. A shield-bearer had come around promising that the food would appear shortly, so meanwhile she must just huddle in miserable solitude amid a crowd of tune-lessly chanting believers, wrestling with her faith and her conscience.

Old Piol squeezed himself onto the rock beside her. She glanced sideways at him, unsure whether she wanted his company.

He smiled—not the smile of the naive dreamer Piol Poet but that of the other Piol Poet, the genius who knew the human heart and could lay it bare in a carillon of silver words. "Talk it out," he said. "The first thing to do with problems is to list them in order of worrisomeness."

"They're all worrisome." And some she couldn't tell even to Piol. "Who is D'ward? What is he—human or god?"

"You told the crowd that he almost died once. If you believe that, then you must believe that he's human."

"Well, he was human then," she admitted. "But in those days he didn't go around performing miracles . . . at least, not like he's doing now."

Piol nodded, cannily waiting for her next problem.

She said, "I can't believe both him and the Pentatheon, can I?"

"Not both, no."

"But Tion heals cripples too!"

"D'ward calls that sorcery."

"And Tion would call what he does sorcery. Their words cancel out."

Piol rubbed an eyebrow. "Then look for other evidence."

That was obvious, but she had not thought of it quite that way. What was he hinting at? "Which of them do you believe?"

Piol was not to be trapped. He grinned, gap-toothed. "Tell you later. I won't make up your mind for you."

She pulled a face at him. "Their words cancel out and their miracles cancel out. What else is there to consider? Well? What other evidence is there?"

He probably wouldn't have given her a straight answer, and he was saved from having to reply at all, because a shield-bearer came by the fire with a bag, soliciting money. He didn't speak, because most people were singing. A few found coins for him, most just shook their heads sadly to show they had nothing to offer. Eleal declined too. She carried a fortune around her waist, but she was not about to expose it to so many curious eyes in this cave. The shield-bearer flashed her a smile and went on by.

He had reminded her of another problem: D'ward was worried by the weather. He needed money to clothe and feed his followers. She had money. Could she force herself to give away so much, even to D'ward?

Piol was waiting. "What will you do tomorrow, Eleal? You can be an actor now, a great actor. Frankly, you always had more talent for acting than for singing. Will you stay with the Liberator or set off to seek your fortune?"

"That's the whole problem, you silly old goose! What I believe doesn't really matter—I can take years to decide that. What I need to know is what to *do*!"

"Good! You're getting closer."

She debated wringing his scrawny old neck—affectionately, of course. "You? What will you do?"

"Me? Oh, I shall join the Free. Whether I believe D'ward or not, what he's doing is the most exciting thing I've ever seen in my life. I shall follow him to Tharg and witness the fulfilment or failure of the prophecy." Piol sighed and clasped her hand in his cold fingers. "But I am an old man, with few years left to me. In your place I might not make that choice, because it may be very dangerous. If I am spared, I shall try to write an account of it all." After a moment, he chuckled. "Maybe when I have done that, I shall know what I really believe, mm?"

He already knew, of course. He just wasn't saying.

Tharg would supply the answer, but Eleal could not wait for that. She could not live with this awful predicament. She had to make her decision sooner. Now! To follow D'ward or go her own way? D'ward had told her to leave. He had definitely not made her welcome. That was one point. She dare not return to

Jurg itself, and the clutches of Tigurb'l Pimp. That was another. D'ward seemed to avoid cities, so he would probably just cut across Jurgvale and carry on to Mapvale. She could risk that. Or she could go back to Niol and try for auditions there, as Piol had suggested several times.

"I can't decide!" she moaned. "*What* other evidence is there?"

"Actions, of course. Judge people by what they do, not what they say."

"Miracles? Sorcery?"

"What else do they do, apart from miracles?"

Eleal shivered. "Zath, you mean? Reapers?" She could never imagine D'ward sending out reapers to kill people. "Give me a clue, Piol!"

He sighed. "Girls with problems should ask their mothers. I'm afraid yours would not be much help to you, even if she still lived."

Eleal gulped. "You knew her? I thought that was before you joined the troupe."

"No. Just after. For a whole fortnight we searched Jurg for her, all of us and all our friends. She was nowhere to be found. Nowhere! Suddenly, out of the blue, she just wandered up to the door of the house where we were staying."

"Mad! Mad for love of the god?"

"Mad for someone. All she would ever say was, 'He kissed me!' "

"He did a lot more than that!"

"Perhaps he did, but the first kiss was what she remembered. From then until the day you were born, those were the only words she ever spoke. No matter what we asked her, or how your grandfather raged, all she would say was, 'He kissed me!' Dreamily. She wasn't really unhappy. She tended to wander away and hang around his temple, and of course we had to try to stop her doing that or fetch her back right away if she had eluded us. After you were born, she said nothing at all. It was not a hard birth, but it killed her. No, it *released* her. She had just been waiting for you to arrive, and after that she faded away, her job done."

"Ken'th!"

"Well, she never said so, and Trong would never admit that a god would do such a thing."

Eleal squeezed her eyes tight shut in case they started leaking. "D'ward would never—" Her voice broke.

D'ward would never do that sort of miracle, or that sort of sorcery. A shiver of revulsion racked her. Her mother: a woman starved for the love of a god or a woman enslaved by a poisoned kiss?

Lecherous Ken'th. Murderous Zath. Depraved Ois, with her holy whore-house. Or Gim Sculptor, whose beauty had won him the right to represent the Youth at the prize giving in Tion's temple? Two years later, his parents had still been hunting for him.

"Trust their actions, not their words!" Piol said firmly.

"Gods who kill people, gods who hurt people—those are not good gods." She gripped his hand in gratitude. "I choose D'ward. I believe him, not them!"

"I do too."

Eleal straightened up. Good! Then her choice was easy. She must go and find D'ward and tell him that she believed in him and his Undivided god. She would give him her money, every copper of it. Then, surely, he would let her stay and be one of the Free. A shield-bearer, even? She could help him, too! She could repeat her witness of his coming, as she had done today, to help convince others. She could imagine his astonished thanks, his hug of thanks . . . a quick kiss. . . .

She mumbled some words of thanks to Piol without thought. She rose and walked away, heading for the inner cave, for she had explored this place on her way to Niolvale and could guess where the Liberator would rest after his marvelous performance. The greenroom, she thought with a smile.

The fire had almost gone out, so her eyes were well adjusted to the dimness. As she reached the rock pile that divided the cavern, she saw the guards before they saw her. She stopped, unwilling to face an argument or make long explanations to underlings.

Well, there must be other ways around. She turned off to the left, moving with care, for the going soon became very tricky. She scrabbled up between the boulders, frequently bumping her right foot, for it was farther away from her now than it used to be. That did not matter, though. All that mattered was that she would be able to renew her friendship with D'ward. How could she have ever doubted him?

She need not dream of making love to him, though. Dosh had told her how the Joalian-Nagian army had sacked Lemod, and how every man had taken a Lemodian girl to be his concubine, all except D'ward. D'ward had taken a girl and never laid a finger on her, even when she begged him to, Dosh said, although Dosh had probably been guessing there, for how could he have known? Still, he was undoubtedly right when he said that D'ward was a very holy man, with strict standards.

So they would not be lovers, only friends.

No passion. Just a quick hug? And a little kiss, to let bygones be bygones?

She clambered over a smooth, rounded boulder and peered down at the drop. It looked about five feet, but she could not see the ground clearly enough to risk a jump, even with two legs of the same length. This little canyon led directly down to the inner cave, with its ancient ashes and its circle of rocks to sit on.

A pebble clattered. Someone was coming.

She hunkered down on the rock, willing herself to be invisible. And then, in the frail glow of reflected firelight, she saw him, working his way cautiously along the path below her. He wore a long robe with a hood. A gray robe! It was D'ward himself, all alone for once. The urge to leap down and surprise him was absolutely irresistible.

46

ONE OF THE SHIELD-BEARERS TOSSED A LOG ON THE FIRE, SENDING SPARKS swarming up into the dark. Alice felt as if she had been talking for hours. Any time she hesitated, Edward demanded more. She had described the horrors of war, the unexpected horrors of peace, the new war in Russia, the terrible flu epidemic, the changes that had come and would probably never go. . . . She had talked of the few acquaintances they had in common, like Mrs. Bodgley and Ginger Jones, and even, reluctantly, told him about D'Arcy and then Terry. He had responded with concern and no maudlin formulas.

There were a million things she wanted to ask him, but his need was greater. He had been trapped on a faraway world for five years now, with one brief break. He was starved for information. She could see that being a prophet must be a desperately lonely business, with a thousand followers and not a single friend. She forgot her doubts and was glad she had come, for she was uniquely able to be the confidante he needed. He hung upon her words, staring at her as if she were a dream who might vanish if he even blinked, but his face said everything needful.

Then the log went into the fire.

"I'm hoarse!" she said. "You talk now."

He glanced around at the four disciples, who had lost some of their coiled-spring alertness, doubtless bored to distraction by the newcomer's incomprehensible jabber. He turned a look of wide-eyed innocence on Alice. "What do you want to know, child? What wisdom would you seek from the master? How it feels to out-hypocrite Holy Roly himself, for instance?"

"Uncle Roly wasn't a hypocrite, he was a fanatic. You're not."

He pulled a face. "Don't talk to me about fanatics! I'm creating fanatics, Alice! My helpers—disciples, I suppose. They believe every word I say, and I see it happening to them, day by day. They're becoming fanatics, all of them, and I feel like a terrible hypocrite."

Surely My Cousin the Messiah was not suffering doubts? Was he asking for Alice's approval? That did not sound like Edward.

"What do you teach them? The Service's universal Unitarianism?"

He shrugged as if the question was irrelevant or the answer obvious. "Pretty much. Ethically it's the Golden Rule, the stuff that's common to all religions— concern for the sick, alms to the poor, smite not thy neighbor with thine ax.

. . . It's Christianity mostly, because that's my background, but I think any Moslem, Buddhist, or Sikh would recognize it."

"And theologically?"

"Monotheism." He paused for a moment, frowning . . . looking for all the world as though he had never really thought about it before. "And reincarnation."

"Why that?"

"Not sure . . ." He ran a hand through his hair and grinned. "Because Uncle Roly gave me a fixed picture of heaven as an endless ghastly Sunday morning of psalm singing. Because reincarnation seems a happier creed than hellfire. Why should God insist we get it right the first time?"

"And if we have only one chance to get it right, that gives the priests much greater power over us, doesn't it?"

"By Jove! You know, I hadn't thought of that. Jolly good! I like it. Besides, you can't prove I'm wrong, can you?"

"No. So why are you worried if you create a few fanatics? You don't encourage violence or persecution, do you? You don't tell outright lies."

His mood turned glum again. "Yes, I do. I use the magic they give me to heal babies and then tell them that this is a miracle sent by a god I don't believe in myself."

"What would happen if you told them the truth?"

"What is truth? That all my power comes from their belief? They wouldn't believe me. Even charisma has its limits."

No faith, no mana. No mana, no crusade.

"Are you quite sure God *didn't* send you?"

"Alice! *Please!* If I start thinking like that I'll turn into a total theomaniac."

"You're not the type. I'd say you're a pragmatist. You're doing the best you can in the circumstances. The object of the Game is to kill Zath, isn't it? And thereby rid the world of a monster?"

Again he ran a hand through his curls. He needed a haircut. "So the ends justify the means?"

Memories, memories! "You're playing devil's advocate, my lad. You always did that." She saw his shy grin flicker and that, too, was heart-stoppingly familiar from years gone by. "And you've had a lot more time to think up the answers than I have. You tell me."

He stared sadly into the fire for a moment. "I think that sometimes life forces us to choose the path of least evil. How's that for rationalization?"

"It sounds sound to me," she said loyally.

"It didn't convince friend Smedley the other day. It's not the way a saint thinks. A saint won't bend his principles no matter what the cost—to himself or anyone else. I'm just a political revolutionary masquerading as a prophet."

"You're more saintly than most. You've always had strict principles."

"So did Holy Roly. You know, I used to think the old bat enjoyed heaping brimstone on his wayward nephew's head? Now I'm not so sure."

"Good heavens! You really have been gathering insights, haven't you?"

He laughed, probably not noticing the surprised smiles of his guards. "Wonderful to see you here!" Abruptly he turned serious again. "Dear Alice, I don't doubt that you are the true, dear Alice. I don't doubt your motives in the slightest, and yet your arrival here leaves me a teeny-weeny bit suspicious still. Are you quite certain that the Miss Pimm you met was the genuine Miss Pimm?"

Alice opened and closed her mouth a couple of times. "Well, I suppose the answer to that is No! I mean, how could I ever be *certain*? She did seem younger than she was two years ago. I assumed that was because she'd been playing a role then, and wasn't now—or at least not the same role." She realized that she had not told him about Zath's appearance at Olympus, which was the reason for her coming here at all.

Edward bit his lip. "Doesn't really mean anything," he muttered. "So you went to Olympus. Whose idea was it for you and Jumbo—"

He was interrupted by shouts and a clatter of boots. His bodyguards sprang to their feet. The little blond disciple she had seen earlier came running into the hollow, waving a flaming torch. Right on his heels came Ursula Newton. Much singsong jabber was exchanged. Edward rose and began to move toward the exit. At once two of the guards set themselves between him and Alice. She stayed put on her nice, comfortable rock.

The torchbearer ran out again, probably taking word that the Liberator was coming.

"You'll have to excuse me a moment," Edward said. "There's a young girl out there having some sort of seizure, and everyone thinks she's about to die." He grinned ruefully as he passed her. "A god's work is never done."

"As I recall," she countered, "under similar circumstances, Jesus did not need to go to the centurion's house."

Edward's smile vanished. "But that was Jesus. This is only me." He disappeared, too, into the passageway. Well, at least he wasn't a total theomaniac yet.

The sound of singing was still drifting in over the barrier. Most of the Free must be quite unaware of the current medical emergency. The bodyguards all sat down, not following the Liberator. Did that mean they were now jailers? Ursula Newton had stayed behind also. She made herself comfortable on the next rock with a sigh of wearied satisfaction, like a schoolmistress after the final bell of the day, and fixed Alice with a gaze as steady as a recruiting poster's.

"I assume you're now certified as the genuine article, so may I start all over? I'm Ursula Newton, and I'm very happy to meet you." She leaned over to offer a hand. Her smile was more hearty than winsome, but that was because her face would never manage winsome. The smile itself seemed genuine enough. She had a grip like a blacksmith.

"No offense," Alice said. "You're quite right to take precautions. He's a pretty important man, now." The significance of her own words seemed to ricochet back at her from the megalithic walls. Important? Edward was working his way into the history books of a world. "I mean he will be if he succeeds, like Moses."

"He'll be Jan Hus if he fails."

Alice shuddered. "Meaning?"

"Martyrdom, murder, massacre, and mayhem. He knew the risks when he burned his first bridge. He had no choice, you know."

"Edward or Jan Hus?"

"Your cousin, of course!" Mrs. Newton glowered belligerently. "Julian has told me what happened back Home, how the Blighters almost caught him—and you too. Obviously Zath will never stop trying to kill him. He was forced to defend himself, and this was the only way open to him."

Alice was taken aback. She could not recall saying anything critical of Edward's crusade and did not see why Mrs. Newton need defend it to her so aggressively. Besides, she found the proposed defense repellent.

"I can't believe Edward would have involved so many innocent people just to save his own skin. I am sure he seeks some greater good than just his personal survival."

Her companion conceded the point with a faint pout. "He chose a more daring path than I anticipated. I expected him to begin by freeing the slaves in the Thargian mines."

"Being Moses?"

"Exactly. 'The Liberator,' you see?"

"But you don't have a Red Sea handy. I suppose the pursuing Thargians could have been buried in a landslide instead."

Mrs. Newton was not amused. "He elected instead to be Christ, which is a bolder concept altogether."

It certainly did not lack ambition, but putting it in words raised worrisome questions that Jumbo had not been able to answer. "What will happen when he reaches Tharg itself? I understand crucifixion is not a Valian custom."

Ursula grimaced. "They've never heard of it. Thargians execute criminals by dashing their brains out on an anvil. They'll have to catch him first, won't they? I don't believe your cousin has anything so barbaric in mind for Zath or so suicidal for himself, Mrs. Pearson. I do wish the cooks would hurry up. I'm hungry."

The guards had begun whispering, perhaps discussing the strangely ill-tongued intruder.

"But he may fail?" Alice said. "How do you rate his chances?"

"Impossible to say."

"You must have a better idea than I do, for I have no way of judging at all. If you thought he had no chance you wouldn't be here, would you?"

"On the face of it he doesn't, frankly." Ursula folded her arms and thought for a moment, scowling at the fire. "There are three unknowns. The biggest is the Pentatheon. If enough of them rally to Exeter's side in the final scrum, then they may tip the scales. They're scared of Zath, but they have no real reason to set up your cousin in his place, which is basically what they'd be trying to do if they intervened."

"I suppose they're fence-sitting at the moment?"

"Absolutely. Don't expect a peep out of any of them until the last possible minute. I expect every one of them has a spy or two within the Free, though.

They're watching. And there's no way to know how they're judging Edward's performance, which is what this parade is." She seemed to be warming to her lecture. "The second factor is the *Filoby Testament* itself. It hasn't hit a wrong note in eighty-five years. That's impressive! Prof Rawlinson estimates that three quarters of the prophecies have already been fulfilled."

"But there can always be a first time failure?"

"Oh, crikey, yes! And I'm a little bit suspicious of the way verse three eighty-six is worded. It doesn't say that the Liberator will slay Zath, or that he will win a fight. It just says he will bring death to Death. I only hope that isn't to be interpreted in some sort of mystical way. Nevertheless, I'd much rather have the *Filoby Testament* working for me than against me."

"It saved my life once," Alice said. "Or, rather, it saved Edward's and I was with him. The third factor must be his own mana?"

"Right. No way to measure that, either, of course. Can't stick a thermometer in a man and test his mana level. Drat them, I wish they'd bring the tuck basket around!" With a sudden show of irritation, Ursula grabbed up a log and hurled it on the fire. She was concealing something, or trying to detour the conversation away from something.

Alice prompted. "Edward's obviously collected great power if he can give a blind man back his sight."

"True."

"And the miracles inspire the crowd to provide more mana? He gets it back?"

Ursula nodded, beating her hands on her knees and staring angrily at the rocks as if trying to glare through them. "All that singing going on out there doesn't sound like anyone's doing much eating yet."

"What's wrong? Why don't you want to talk about it?"

"I never . . ." The doughty Mrs. Newton scowled at this frontal attack. She glanced at the wall around them as if looking for listeners. "You really want my opinion, no matter what?"

"Please."

"Well, I suppose you are his next of kin. I wouldn't say this to anyone else. You won't repeat my words to Jumbo or your cousin?"

"Certainly not."

"Rain, Mrs. Pearson! The rain's bad news. He's lost a lot of people since yesterday. If the weather continues bad, he's going to come a cropper. He can't travel as fast in the rain, he can't attract enough people. So he won't collect enough mana—or even enough money. If he can't feed his flock, it'll wander away. He's certainly not strong enough yet to do loaves-and-fishes miracles, not on that scale."

Ursula scowled at the fire for a moment. "And that's not all. I keep telling him he's not ruthless enough. As you said, when he uses mana to perform miracles, the resulting adoration should give him back more than he spent. That's the way it should work. But he's too softhearted. It begins that way, but it's astonishingly easy for people to become . . . um, saturated. Blasé. The first couple of miracles today, I could feel the whole node tremble with the surge of mana. Did you notice?"

"I felt something."

"That was just a whiff of spray we were getting—the waves were hitting the Liberator and they must have rocked him to his toenails. Did you notice how much less the response was the fourth time?"

"He overdoes it, you mean?"

"Absolutely. The Pentatheon's god of healing is Paa, one of Tion's. We estimate he grants about one real healing miracle a year, plus a few minor, show-offy things: squints or harelips or measles. Those keep the crowds coming. Tion himself does one miracle cure every year at his festival. By definition, miracles need to be rarities."

"I suppose Edward can't refuse suffering babies."

"He could tell them to wait until tomorrow," Ursula growled. "Listen!" She waved a hand at the dark. "They're still singing! He went out there to perform a miracle. He can cure an attack of epilepsy with a snap of his fingers, if that's all it is. But why do it that way? Why hasn't he ordered the singing stopped and made everybody gather round to watch? He's not enough of a showman! Oh, he does quite well, but he could do a lot better."

Showing off would go against everything he had ever been taught. "So you think he isn't gathering mana fast enough?" But if there was no way to measure mana . . .

"I'm very much afraid he's *losing* it. I don't think he has as much now as he did—"

She was interrupted by a scream. It began, very briefly, as a yell of outrage or anger. It immediately shot up to the unmistakable shrill note of mortal terror, four and a third octaves above middle C, the universal alarm cry of the human species. It came from somewhere very close, amid the encircling maze of rocks and stalagmites. It reverberated through the cavern, doubled and redoubled by its own echoes. It froze the blood. Alice and Ursula and the four bodyguards leaped to their feet, peering around, trying to locate the source.

Then the human scream was joined by a sound much greater, an earsplitting animal roar. The two swelled in chorus, alternating, combining, mingling with mighty cracks and thumps.

Alice clapped her hands over her ears. "What in the world is that?" she howled.

Ursula yelled back through the din. "A *mithiar*! What they call a jugular. It's killing someone."

Judging by the noise, it was tearing someone apart.

As suddenly as they'd begun, the sounds stopped. They were replaced by the blurred roar of a multitude of terrified people on the far side of the rockfall. Their screams, too, echoed everywhere, but at least they were not as close. Roaring Cave suddenly justified its name.

Alice uncovered her ears. Ursula was ashen. She could not possibly be more shaken than Alice, though, and the men looked no better, apparently torn between a desire to flee and a need to stay close to the light. One of them had hauled a burning branch from the fire, but he wasn't going anywhere with it.

Ursula snatched it from him and headed toward the source of the trouble. The men all yelled and tried to stop her. Shouting and shaking her head, she cleared them out of the way with her flaming brand and kept on going. Shamed, perhaps, they followed. Alice did too, determined not to be left alone in this nightmare.

They did not have very far to go, and then they all stopped dead, blocking the way and also Alice's view of what they had found. She scrambled up on a table-high ledge and peered over their heads. Steep walls rose to shoulder height on one side and even higher on the other, forming a narrow canyon that continued on, twisting out of sight. The rocks were pale gray, mottled and cemented together with oozings of white stalagmite like melted candle wax, but now all splattered with sheets of shocking red as if a whole barrel of blood had exploded. In places streaks of blood and blobs of flesh had splashed ten or twelve feet up, glittering wetly in the light of Ursula's torch. Surely it would have taken a dozen victims to produce so much blood?

The shouting in the main cave had almost stopped, probably because most of the Free were outside in the rain by now. Flickers of light reflecting from the roof showed that more people were coming to investigate.

A woman's body lay facedown in the center of the shambles. It was naked and smeared with gore, but it bore no obvious wounds. How was that possible? Ursula and the men were all talking at once, not a word intelligible to Alice. Some of those lumps were not rock. A leg. An arm. A couple of the men cried out at the same moment, pointing at a small boulder, coated with blood. Its eyes were open.

Revulsion! Nausea! Suddenly every shadow held a monster, every rock was a tooth. Alice half fell, half jumped from her perch and went stumbling back to the fire, moving as fast as she dared and banging her shins and elbows in the process. She threw a heap of sticks on the blaze to try and make it brighter, then hunkered down beside it, shivering. Two victims, one torn to pieces, one not visibly harmed. That made no sense at all! The sort of claws Jumbo had described could never rip a woman's clothes off without tearing her skin to ribbons as well. Where had the jugular gone?

Where had it come from?

The crowd in the main cave was silent now or else had fled out into the night. She heard voices nearby, and recognized Edward's, issuing commands. She was shaking from shock and nausea. Even the smoke from the fire seemed tainted with the reek of blood. She could make no sense of the talk, and no one was going to be speaking English for a while. She considered going in search of Jumbo, but she could not be sure he was still in the cave. With Edward's snub still rankling, he might have taken the dragons and ridden off in a huff. No, Jumbo was too much a gentleman to do that, but she had better wait here until Edward had straightened out the emergency. Her vacation was turning out to be more stressful than she had expected.

A moment later, light advanced out of the passageway. Ursula appeared with her torch, followed by Edward himself carrying the woman's body in his arms. Other men came after. As he lowered his burden to one of the heaps of bedding, Alice snatched up a blanket and went to cover her. She was only a girl.

Edward straightened, wiping bloody hands on his robe, which was already well smeared. "Thanks."

"She's alive?" Of course. He would not have brought a corpse.

"Eleal Singer. She was starting to come around. I've put her to sleep. See if you can clean her up, will you?" He turned to his followers and began giving more orders. He was paler than before, but calm, completely in command. Though they were all older men, they did not argue or hesitate. Most went out by the way Alice had entered, others returned to the scene of the accident—of the *murder?*

Ursula came to help, dragging a water skin. Alice chose a tattered cloth that might be somebody's bedding and ripped a strip from it. Together they began washing away the bloodstains. Eleal muttered and stirred as they wiped her face but did not awaken. There was little they could do about her long hair, which was caked and matted. Her skin bore only a few scrapes from contact with the rock, and there was a reddening welt around her waist that Alice could not explain. When Ursula started work on Eleal's hands, she moaned and tried to pull them loose. The tips of her fingers were swollen, some of the nails broken. Her toes were the same. Alice exchanged shocked glances with Ursula and thrust away the impossible suspicions that kept boiling up in her mind.

"How are you doing?" Edward asked.

He was standing with his back to the proceedings. This absurd display of modesty almost provoked Alice to sniggers, but she fought against them. That way lay full-blown hysterics.

Ursula pulled the blanket over the patient again. "You can look. She has serious bruising around her middle. There's something wrong with her fingers and toes."

Edward knelt down and considered Eleal's draped form. "A couple of broken ribs, too." He touched the blanket over her waist for a moment. Then he lifted one of her hands and gritted his teeth. "Swine!" He covered the girl's hand with both of his and healed the finger wounds, even the broken nails. He moved on to do the other hand, both feet.

Ursula was watching intently, but she looked more angry than impressed.

"What happened?" Alice demanded. "Can either of you explain? Does this sort of thing go on all the time?"

Ursula shook her head. "It was aimed at him, definitely. Ken'th?"

"Probably," Edward said. "Stand back and I'll—"

Pebbles rattled. The young fair-haired disciple came hurrying in. His face had a sickly pallor and there was blood on his knees and hands. He held a long strip of blood-soaked leather. From the way he offered it to Edward, it was heavy.

The two spoke for a moment. The disciple pulled a face, but nodded. He dropped his burden—it fell with a metallic clunk—and headed back out the way he had come. Someone was going to have to organize a burial for that other victim, and probably he had just been given the horrible job.

A rising murmur of voices indicated that the disciples were coaxing the crowds into the cave again.

Edward turned back to Eleal. Ursula caught Alice's arm and led her out of the way, over to the fire. Her fury was obvious now. She nudged the mysterious parcel with her foot.

"That's what did the bruising. A money belt."

Alice's brain resisted the implications. "How? And how can you know that?"

"The buckle's ripped right through the leather."

"Yes, but—" *No, don't think about it.* "Where did the jugular come from? Where did it—"

"It's sorcery," Ursula growled, "very horrible sorcery. You think I'd have gone after a real jugular with nothing but a burning stick? If there had been a jugular in the cave, it would have attacked somebody hours ago."

"But where did it go?"

The answer to that was a disbelieving glare. "Dosh has found another body, a priest. Someone bashed him on the head with a rock and took his gown."

"I don't understand!"

"Oh, work it out, girl!" Ursula shouted. "All cats are gray in the dark. All robes, too. If you wanted to get by the guards . . . We knew Eleal Singer had some sort of spell on her. We knew it made her come looking for the Liberator. We knew there was a compulsion, we just didn't know what else it did. Even I could see traces of it on her. I couldn't see one on you or Jumbo, but that didn't—"

"Jumbo! Shouldn't one of us go and find Jumbo and—"

Ursula threw up her hands and turned away. "Oh, go right ahead! Go and find him. I can suggest a good place to look. Are you completely stupid? Must I carve words in stone for you? Go to Jumbo by all means. He was a good friend of mine, Mrs. Pearson. A good friend for almost a hundred years. He deserved better than that horrible, *shameful* death. It's one more reason to settle accounts with Zath. Go to Jumbo. Tell him we're sorry. Tell him he's forgiven. There's no hurry. He isn't going anywhere now."

ᔐᕐ 47 ᔐᕐ

ELEAL FLOATED BACK UP TO CONSCIOUSNESS, AWARE FIRST OF A REVOLTING taste in her mouth. She tried to spit out whatever it was. A strong arm reached under her shoulders and raised her; someone held a gourd of water to her lips. Water dribbled down her neck, between her breasts. Coldness, darkness, and her eyelids seemed to be crusted with mud. She forced them open, shivered convulsively. Faint light, coldness again, and awareness that she wasn't wearing anything. She was on a very lumpy, prickly bed . . . someone holding her upright.

"Relax, relax!" said a voice. A man's voice.

She clutched at the blanket and pulled it up to cover her nudity. She turned her head and found herself looking into a concerned pair of very blue eyes.

"You're all right," D'ward said. "You're not hurt. You'll be quite well in a moment. We're trying to help you. Wash your mouth out again."

She discovered more aches and scrapes. Her elbows and ankles, especially. Her teeth felt as if someone had worked them over with a mallet.

D'ward holding her up. Her head against his bony shoulder. D'ward wiping her face with a wet, pink cloth. Had she been injured, somehow?

"What?" she said, and her tongue felt wrong in her mouth. "What happened?" She tried to focus, but his face was too close, a blur.

"You had a brush with very nasty sorcery, but you're all right now."

He lowered her. She still held the blanket under her chin. He was kneeling beside her.

"Relax! You're still not thinking straight. Take a little longer."

Why did her teeth hurt so? Vague, confused pictures whirled in her mind: D'ward in his priest's gown with the hood over his head, walking along a passage below her . . . a man with a mustache . . . take money to D'ward . . . *Woeful maiden, handsome lad, Met on lonely way* . . .

She peered up at him. He smiled at her, and she could make out the smile. How had she come to be lying in bed with no clothes on and D'ward beside her? She smiled back. If that was about to happen, then she would as soon it was D'ward as any. . . . What was wrong with her teeth?

"Starting to feel better?"

"Yes. What—what happened?"

"You saw a man in a robe and thought it was me."

She closed her eyes. That did sound right, but where? And what had she been doing? She opened her eyes again and tried to nod.

D'ward blinked at her a few times. "You're all right, Eleal. It's all gone now. The curse is gone."

Then the missing pieces dropped into place. She stiffened in horror. "D'ward! I came to find you! I jumped—"

"Never mind. It's over."

"Just going to surprise you . . . *I started to sing*—"

He seized her shoulders and squeezed them hard. "It's all right, I say. It wasn't me! It's all right."

"I didn't *want* to sing . . . didn't *mean* to sing—" Her voice was shrill. She felt tears, panic, and terror. Her limbs thrashed and trembled.

He steadied her, strong hands on her shoulders. "It is all *right,* Eleal! It's all over!" He made soothing noises, whispering. She calmed abruptly. The whirling terrors settled like leaves after a gust of wind has passed.

He said, "Oh, Eleal, Eleal, darling! You saved my life and—"

"What?"

"Yes! There was another curse, see? A man after me. So you saved my life again, and this time it was my turn to wash and nurse you. . . .Well, it was my helpers—not me. I mean, I didn't even peek . . ."

That struck her as funny. She laughed. "You think I would mind if you peeked?"

"Perhaps not as much as some," he agreed awkwardly.

"You think I didn't peek at you when I had the chance?"

"Er . . . That was a long time ago. The main thing is that the curse is gone."

She closed her eyes and saw the man with the mustache.

"He kissed me!"

"I expect that's his preferred technique."

"He sent me to find you, kill you?"

"Don't worry about it."

She shivered and lay still, thinking hard. "I was coming to tell you that I believe in you, not in the imposters."

"Good. Truly that makes me very happy."

"I came to give you my money."

"You don't have to."

"Some of it was his. He gave me money!" Memories were coming back. The room, the crystal figurine.

"I'll certainly take his money, if you like. And put it to a good use."

"And let me stay with you? Keep me safe, in case he tries to—punish me for failing?" She opened her eyes and watched to see what he would say.

He looked worried. "You don't have to stay, Eleal. You have two good legs now. You can go and chase that acting career you wanted."

She wanted to stay. Very much she wanted to stay, and things that worked on most men would not work on D'ward. Not quickly, anyway.

"But most of those plays—they're lies! They're about the evil sorcerers who pretend to be gods. Those plays are bad, D'ward, aren't they?"

He rubbed a wrist across his brow and looked even more worried. "If you take them seriously they are."

"Then what's to become of me!" A sob escaped her.

"Join us if you want. Glad to have you. I need someone to help with the preaching."

"Preaching? Me? You don't have to mock me." She writhed under the blanket.

"I'm not mocking you at all. You heard me last night at Joobiskby—I'll bet you could repeat almost everything I said and bring the house down with it."

She had been doing better with her eyes closed, so she closed them again. "He kissed me! I still feel his mustache on my lips. I dream of him. I'll never forget how he kissed me." She squeezed out a tear.

D'ward chuckled, very close to her ear. "You haven't changed a bit, you minx!" he whispered. "You've just learned a few more tricks. I'll see if someone can find some clothes for you."

His lips touched hers for a moment. She grabbed with both arms but he was gone already.

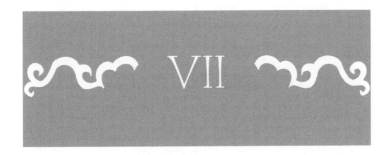

And now we have sent down unto thee evident signs, and none will disbelieve them but the evildoers.

THE KORAN, II:99

ᘒ 48 ᘓ

O N THE THIRD DAY OF HIS QUEST, WITH RAIN STILL SHEETING DOWN AS hard as ever, Julian Smedley trudged into Losby. He found the church there in disarray—which was hardly surprising, for all Randorvale was in disarray. A third of the hamlet was stricken; a dozen people had died already. Old Kinulusim Spicemerchant wheezed and sweated on his sickbed. His equally aged wife was up and about already, but still weaker than wartime beer, while young Purlopat'r Woodcutter, the baby-faced giant, had fled to the hills with his wife and children. Julian summoned a few of the faithful to Seven Stones and held a brief service to cheer them up. Then he went on his way. Having no mana, he could do no healings.

He had gathered more discouraging news: Rumors were flying that this inexplicable pestilence was the work of the Church of the Undivided. He was not too surprised. People always found scapegoats for disasters—Christians burning Nero's Rome, Jews causing the Black Death by poisoning wells. Whether or not the orthodox clergy had originated the slander, the Pentatheon would certainly use it to good effect; the Service's efforts to humanize the religion of the Vales were utterly doomed now. They might have survived the Liberator himself, but in trying to stop him, the Service had brought in the Spanish flu and was going to die of it.

On the fourth day, Julian came to Thurgeothby, a homely little ranching village at the mouth of Soutpass. The rain had ended, leaving behind a bone-chilling wind. Randorwall towered above him in the crisp sunshine, white and almost painfully beautiful against a pale winter sky. He was not looking forward to the long climb and even less to the vale beyond it, for Lappinland was not a happy place. Beyond Lappinvale lay Mapvale, and then he would be into country new to him.

In Thurgeothby he could have dropped in on the local preacher and would certainly have done so had he wanted lodgings for the night, but the day was young yet. Instead, he went to see Urbiloa Baker, who was agent Twenty-nine in the political arm of the Service and should be able to advise him on current affairs in Lappinland. She was a tall, angular widow of middle years, white haired and customarily well dusted with flour. Both residents and transients frequented her shop, and she had a gift for extracting significant information from idle chatter. She greeted him blankly, as if she had never set eyes on him before, so they went through the cloak-and-dagger rigmarole of exchanging passwords.

Then she took him through to her kitchen, hot and smelling deliciously of baking bread, sitting him at a table with some hot, soft rolls and a pitcher of buttermilk.

The news she broke to him while he ate was general knowledge that he could have gained from almost anyone in Thurgeothby. The flu was raging there as it was everywhere in Randorvale, with the deaths, as usual, especially high among young adults, the mainstay of the population. The pestilence was at least as lethal here as it had been back Home: healthy one day, bedridden the next, often dead in three. Children and old folk were mostly recovering, although slowly. The Church of the Undivided was being blamed—nonsensically, for its members succumbed like everyone else. Many had fled, some been driven out. Houses had been burned.

As if that were not bad enough, Soutpass was closed. Lappinvale was a Thargian colony, ruled by an iron-fisted military governor, and he had sealed off the pass to keep out the infection. Travelers from the south were being turned back. That was typical Thargian despotism and it wouldn't work—information traveled the Vales only by word of mouth, so the flu would arrive at the same time as the news. In retaliation, the Randorian government had forbidden entry to anyone coming the other way, but the king had not sent enough soldiers to enforce his decree and the permanent garrison was too incapacitated by flu to do anything. So a few traders were still trickling into Randorvale.

Julian leaned his elbows on the dough-stained table and gazed bitterly at the twinkling grate under the oven while he pondered his alternatives. There did not seem to be any. He knew of no other pass to Lappinvale; if there was one, the Thargians would certainly have blocked it. He could backtrack almost all the way to Olympus and then try the Narshvale road, but there he would be into the highest ranges of the Vales. Even if he could get through to Narshvale in this weather, there were no roads at all from Narshvale to Lappinvale or even Mapvale. Only dragons could cross that country. To reach Jurgvale, he would have to go round by Sussvale and Fionvale, which would take far too long and was probably impossible at this time of year anyway. He was apparently doomed to wait here in Thurgeothby until the Thargian garrison lifted its useless quarantine.

Of course the Liberator's crusade might eventually come to him, but if Exeter did make it this far, it would mean he had survived Zath's efforts to murder him. Then Alice would need no rescuing by Julian Smedley. His situation tasted nastily like failure.

He sighed and accepted it. Only fools struggled against the inevitable. Within the next couple of days, the Thargians would certainly learn that the pestilence had outflanked their swords.

He looked up at Urbiloa, meaning to ask her if he might lodge with her until then. The calculated suspicion in her shrewd eyes stopped the words in his throat. Urbiloa wore no earring. Political ran its own stable of agents, separate from the church. They all had their own agendas, their own motives for spying, although most were rewarded with gold as well, so they could be blackmailed if necessary. Some of them were not even aware that the Service and the church were related.

For all Julian knew, the Thurgeothby baker was a devoted follower of Eltiana, mother goddess of Randorvale.

He reached for his purse. "Well done, Twenty-nine. Good report. I must be on my way."

She did not try to stop him leaving. She sent no pursuit after him.

He headed east, along the mountain front, and found shelter at the lonely home of Tidapo Rancher. Tidapo was a hearty, brawny man, full of joviality and self-reliance, always glad to offer hospitality to a visiting apostle. His wife was the Undivided supporter, but he tolerated her whims, probably from a total lack of interest in anything as impractical as theology. He greeted Saint Kaptaan cheerfully and made him welcome. At dinner he apologized for the way the children were coughing, but no one in the household seemed to have heard of the plague sweeping the vale, or at least no one took it seriously.

Two mornings later, Julian had had his fill of both the rancher's trivial chatter about livestock and his wife's religious fervor. The children and the hired men were all abed with flu by then. The sun was still shining and it was time to try the pass again. Julian thanked his hosts, blessed their house, and retraced his steps to Thurgeothby.

As he had hoped, southbound travelers reported that the blockade had been lifted. They said that half of Lappinvale was down with the sickness already, which was certainly an exaggeration but bad news anyway. The Liberator had left Niolvale, last reported at Roaring Cave, on Lospass, several days ago.

That night Julian camped with a band of traders, who charged him extortionately for the privilege of bedding down at their fire. They were very worried by the damage that the sickness would do to business. Like him, they were bound for Jurgvale, so their knowledge of the Liberator came only from hearsay. They did not think he would do business any good, either.

Julian descended into Lappinvale the next day. There he began to have trouble with the language and was repeatedly forced to exercise his limping Joalian. Even that was of less use than he had hoped, because the Thargian overlords discouraged its use—Thargian itself being a throat-burning screech that he could not even attempt. He found the natives sullen but with good reason, for Thargians were hard taskmasters, and they had ruled the land for more than a century.

Two more hard, cold days brought him to Mapvale. Smallest of all the vales, it was famous only for its blossoms, which were not in evidence at the start of winter. Historically, Mapland had always been too trivial to interest the great powers, so it had rarely endured conquest—invading armies just walked across it and up the other side. Of course, on the way through they conscripted boys as soldiers and girls as harlots, but everyone expected that. Those were predictable perils in a primitive land.

The natives wrung a subsistence economy from the export of fruits and nuts. Although very poor, they seemed happier than the Lappinians—smiling, chanting greetings in an incomprehensible dialect that must be close to Niolian, for it had a singsong lilt to it. They struggled to understand his Joalian and to reply in kind. He did not think this friendly reception was all due to his stranger's charisma; they were a genuinely friendly people. He asked what they knew about the Liberator but could not follow their answers. Much pointing to the north and sign-talk of walking suggested that Exeter's crusade was still in progress.

Julian supposed that was good news.

Hamlets were few. There were no decent roads at all. He spent the day trudging along lanes that wound like snakes through trees and across fields of leafless shrubs. The ruts were frozen hard under his feet, so that he was in constant danger of twisting an ankle. Hour by hour the snowy ranges marched with him on either hand. When he met anyone or saw a man at work—usually gathering firewood—he would ask for Thamberpass and always the finger pointed east. Onward he would go again. The air smelled of snow. The weather was turning colder.

His mood was turning blacker. Regardless of what the Mapians were trying to tell him, if Exeter was still alive and his crusade still proceeding, Julian should have run into it by now, for he was much closer to Shuujooby than he was to Olympus. Admittedly, the Liberator's pace would be dictated by the slowest of his followers, but Julian had lost two days to the Thargians' quarantine. The absence of any indication that the prophet was approaching was a very bad sign. It strongly implied that he had died at the hand of either Jumbo or Alice, whichever was the poisoned pawn.

Julian supposed that was bad news.

The familiar tremor of virtuality awoke him from his gloomy reverie. He stopped and peered around at the darkening trees, trunks and branches iron black in twilight. He realized that his legs and feet ached and his belly was growling. It was past time to find shelter.

A node might contain a temple or monastery, either of which would likely offer some minimal hospitality to wayfarers. If the price was an obeisance to some idol or other, he would not be unwilling to pay it at a pinch. A resident numen, if any, would probably detect Julian as a stranger, but then Julian might do quite well out of the encounter. Being a god was a lonely business, all visitors welcome. While natives were fair game for anything, strangers were protected by the club rules.

He could not be certain which way the center of the node lay, but a faint scent of wood smoke hung in the air. Turning to windward, he set off through the trees, ducking under branches, pushing aside twigs. The virtuality grew stronger. A few minutes later he emerged in a wide clearing and abandoned hopes of a temple. There was nothing there but a desolate patch of moorland in the winter dusk: a few acres of withered weeds and an ice-bound pond. Then he noted animal dung and a tiny hovel at the forest's edge, which must be the source of the smoke. He headed straight for it, confident that his charisma would be irresistible on a node.

His approach was challenged by a flock of white, shrieking things. They looked and sounded much like geese, although they had teeth and fur. He shooed them away with his umbrella.

By then a woman stood in the door of the hut, watching him. She was small and stooped, dressed in rags. Her sparse white hair hung limp and her eyes did not meet his. Old, certainly harmless . . . and yet she made him think of the nursery tales of his youth: Hansel and Gretel, the gingerbread house. The sinister implications were not reduced by the acrid clouds pouring out around her, for this witch's cottage had no chimney, only a smoke hole.

He tried his Joalian. "Greetings. I am Julian Teacher. I seek shelter. I will gladly pay."

She stepped aside. He took one last deep breath of fresh air and stooped through into the shed.

She shared the one-room hovel with a boy and her livestock—the goose things and a rack-boned ungulate. The floor was filth. A fireplace of stones, a shelf with a few bundles of edibles, a heap of twigs for fuel, a water skin and a couple of gourds, bedding made of two piles of frondy leaves plus scraps of uncured hide . . . nothing more.

The billowing smoke stung Julian's throat and eyes, although the tiny fire barely gave light, let alone heat. Nonetheless, he sank gratefully to the ground, leaned back against his bedroll, and crossed his aching legs. Soon he was coughing his lungs out, but he was off his feet and that was all that mattered.

The woman tipped water into a small gourd and handed it to him; he drank it, assuming it was a symbol of hospitality. It tasted bad but went down well, soothing his throat. Her hands were gnarled. Indeed, her whole body was twisted. He wondered if she was eighty, as she looked, or just a badly used forty.

She knew no Joalian and he no Mapian. He established by signs that her name was something like Onkenvier *Orliel*, although he had no idea what an *orliel* did. When he pointed inquiringly at the boy, she said, "Thok," and thereafter no one spoke at all. The boy's age was a mystery too. He would have matched an English twelve-year-old in size, but if that was fuzz and not dirt on his lip, he was both older and seriously malnourished. He did not speak. Perhaps he could not. What sort of a name was Thok anyway? A nickname? It was neuter. In Joalian, a *thaki* was a cub.

The silence dragged on, broken only by stray crackles from the fire. The woman sat and stared at it with rheumy eyes. Thok sat and stared at nothing. Julian sat and shivered. He considered unrolling his blanket and wrapping up in it, but the effort seemed too enormous to attempt. The smoke had already given him a headache. Was there a husband somewhere or more children? No, because there were only two beds. How could such a life even be worth living? Earth had poverty to match this, he supposed, but he had never met it. Exeter might have done so, in his African days. The Liberator could do nothing about the plight of these people. They could have no interest in religious reformation. One of Zath's reapers might seem like a welcome release to them.

Onkenvier produced a knife made from a piece of a rib and stabbed at something in the fire. She pulled out a charred tuber, which she proceeded to hack into three pieces. Then she skewered the largest fragment, blew on it to cool it, and offered it to Julian. His stomach heaved. He shook his head, pointed to the water and made a sign for drinking. Onkenvier said something to Thok; Thok poured another drink for the visitor.

He started to cough and almost choked on it, spilling water into his beard. Again he refused the tuber. He could not imagine eating anything, the way he felt. He had walked too far, obviously. It was not only his legs and feet that ached. Everything ached. He ached all over.

Thok and Onkenvier began chewing on the smaller fragments of the tuber, eating even the charred crust. Julian wished he could call over a waiter and order a couple of steaks for them—although meat would probably make them as ill as the sight of their normal diet was making him feel. Still, he was immensely grateful just to be here. He fumbled in his purse and found a coin. He held it out to the woman.

She stared at it as if she did not know what money was, then turned a puzzled gaze on him, meeting his eyes for the first time.

"For you," he said. "Take it."

She did, peering at it wonderingly.

Thok was looking at Julian. His face bore no expression at all, so it was impossible to judge what thoughts were writhing inside that undernourished mind, but Julian realized he had made a serious error. Sleeping men had no charisma. He might wake up with a bone knife through his heart.

The prospect was strangely unworrying. He made a huge effort and rolled his bundle away, so he could lie down and lay his head on it. He did not need it as a cover, certainly. Despite his shivering, he was pouring sweat as if he were in a Turkish bath.

49

By NEXT MORNING, HE WAS ALMOST TOO WEAK TO STAND. HE HAD TO lean on Thok's shoulder when he went out to the pit, and thereafter he just lay on the smelly heap of bedding and waited to die.

Onkenvier would not let him die. She stripped off his clothes, wrapped him in his blanket, piled ancient furs over him to keep him warm. From time to time she bathed his face and rubbed foul-smelling grease on his chest. She forced him to sip a thin soup while Thok held his head up. When he needed to relieve himself, Thok held a gourd for him.

He slid into delirium. "Fools!" he told them. "You are fools. Let him die and you can bury him and keep all the money. It isn't much to him, but it's more than you have ever seen in your lives." They did not understand, so they continued to nurse him.

In his lucid moments he wept at his incredible weakness. He could hardly find the strength to cough, although the pain in his chest was unbearable and every breath rattled like a cart on cobbles. He did not want to die lost among strangers in a strange world. He would never tell Euphemia how sorry he was. She would never know what had happened to him; he would never know what had happened to her. To have lived through the Great War, to have adventured to another planet, then to die like a rat in a sewer . . . it wasn't right. It wasn't fair.

Night came again. He faded in and out of consciousness, but always when he stirred, Onkenvier was there. Did she never sleep? Breathing was an impossible effort. He was drowning in mucus. Eventually she seemed to realize that, for she roused the boy so that together they could pull Julian up to a sitting position. They propped him there somehow, and then he could breathe. Just. He wandered away into delirium that was worse than the pain. He was a kipper in a smokehouse, being eaten alive by earwigs.

Morning at last . . . He was aware of sunlight streaming in at him when the door opened, which it did a few times. Onkenvier was still fussing around him with her broth, but he was too weak to swallow it. He was dying—dying nastily, messily, irrelevantly, as everything must die. King or worm, it always came to this. He had been granted more time than those poor sods at Ypres or the Somme. A lot of them had died more disgustingly even than this, but at least they'd had the consolation that they were dying for King and Country. The universe would roll on without Julian Smedley and never notice the loss. He would leave no fame, no children, no great works. Laugh all you want at this fevered, suffering relic, but your turn will come. . . .

"*Tyika* Kaptaan!"

Julian prized his sticky eyelids open. There was nothing there but a blur. How stupid of Dommi to wander into such a nightmare! How stupid of himself not to hallucinate someone more interesting.

"*Tyika!*" Someone was shouting. Someone was trying to rub the skin off his hand. "Hold on, *tyika*! He is coming, *tyika*! The Liberator is coming. We have sent word for him to hurry."

Julian tried to explain that it was too late, but he couldn't make the words. It didn't matter. He didn't care. He wanted it to end. Come to think of it, a chap couldn't possibly accept a favor from a man he'd accused to his face of being a murderer, so it was just as well that prophet chappie wasn't there, couldn't help, wouldn't arrive in time. . . . He had probably died already anyway. See you when I get there, old man.

When the release finally came, it was almost sexual in its intensity. The end of all the harsh, labored breathing, the pain and striving, the pounding fever, the desperate effort—the sudden peace, the wonderful, wonderful peace . . . the unbearable joy.

There was a cool hand on his forehead. There were a devil of a lot of people making a damnable lot of noise outside somewhere, and the door was open again, although the sun wasn't shining on his face anymore. He opened his eyes.

He licked his lips. He swallowed. He forced himself to meet that familiar smile. "Thank you."

The blue eyes sparkled strangely. "My pleasure entirely," Exeter said. "You are a thousand times welcome."

50

"IT WAS MOST FORTUITOUSLY, WAS IT NOT," SAID DOMMI, "THAT I WAS given assignment on the advance team to this campsite and were thus identifying you?" He was methodically going through Julian's bundle, squatting on his heels to keep his fastidious self from coming in contact with that floor.

Julian pulled his blanket tighter around him, shivering now not because he had a fever, but because he did not have one to keep him warm. He was still adjusting to the idea of being alive. He was also trying to reconcile that miracle with the deaths he had witnessed at Shuujooby, for if Captain Julian Smedley (retd.) was now living on the avails of martyrdom, then he was as guilty as Exeter and a hypocrite as well. He wasn't going to tell Dommi all that, though.

"I trust that *Tyika* Kisster would have come to the aid of any invalid, not just a personal friend?"

"Oh yes, *tyika*! Many hundreds every day are succored in this wise. But I have never seen the Liberator ride any rabbit quite so hard." He laughed. "These appear to be the best of a sad assembly, *tyika*." He held up a smock and breeches.

When had anyone ever heard Dommi laugh before? His flaming hair had grown perceptibly longer since leaving Olympus, and he had sprouted an impressive layer of copper beard. Now he proceeded to hand the disparaged garments to his former employer and head for the door.

"You didn't mention where the hot tub is."

Dommi paused in the doorway and then laughed again, a fraction too late to be convincing. "Hot tub? I barely have recollection of what this is."

Mm? Times they were a-changing! "Then before you go, tell me of *Entyika* Alis and *Tyika* Djumbo."

"The *entyika* is well and keeps very busy with meritorious service. I regret to be informant that the unfortunate Djumbo has departed his recentest incarnation."

"He's dead?"

"Indeed so." Dommi's face had twisted itself into an expression of such heartrending solemnity that it looked ready to shed a few freckles for the departed. "His soul has moved to the next rung of the ladder, as the Liberator has instructed us, and because the madness into which he had fallen was a repercussion of invidious sorcery, no blame must be attached to his memory and we may be confident that his progress upward will continue. Now, if you will excuse, I have many important duties, Kaptaan."

The doorway was then empty.

Musing upon Dommi's strange transformation, Julian reached for the water skin. There was no sign of either Thok or Onkenvier, and the door had mysteriously been ripped from its worn old leather hinges. He was unbearably sticky and scratchy, so he proceeded to clean up as well as he could, although the clearing was now crowded with people. No one came to applaud his striptease. Everyone must be fully occupied. He could hear mallets thudding on tent pegs, axes cracking on trees, carts rumbling, and people singing hymns.

He dressed, combed his hair and beard, and stepped out into the brightness of a winter afternoon. The extent of the activity astonished him. He could see lines of tents, with more going up, makeshift paddocks holding at least a dozen rabbits and a few moas, five or six parked wagons, and the beginning of a camp kitchen—fires and spits and tables. His stomach growled wistfully. Hundreds of people were bustling around, all seemingly performing duties with eagerness and good cheer, even if they were doing nothing more than singing hymns. This was the county fair or the circus come to town, and the British Army could have organized matters no better. Exeter's crusade was prospering, far removed now from the turmoil of Shuujooby.

Details could wait. Julian's first duty was to find Onkenvier and give her money, all the money he had. He peered around carefully, but he could not see her. Perhaps she and Thok had fled into the forest when this unexpected invasion overthrew their world. The crisp winter air, which two days ago had been crystalline and silent, now rang with hundreds of voices. The carpet of low weeds and shrubs had been trampled flat and patterned with innumerable long shadows by the waning sun. If not terrified, she would be at least bewildered.

Another wagon rolled into camp, drawn by two rabbits. People ran to help the occupants disembark, lifting some of them out on litters, then carrying or escorting them over to the hymn singers by the pond, where Exeter in his gray robe stood ready for them. In moments the healing began, with shouts of jubilation and surges of mana that made the node tremble. The Spanish flu had met its match.

The largest group appeared to be made up of initiates; they were being harangued by an adolescent girl. On the far side of the pond, converts were being baptized. Unless Julian's eyes deceived him, one of the officials in charge was Dommi Houseboy with a shield on his back. Well, well, well! Piccadilly Circus.

The Onkenvier business would have to wait. If she failed to appear before the Free departed, Julian would just leave his purse in her cottage. Meanwhile, he was painfully aware that he was not as fit as a Stradivarius and had not eaten in at least two days. He headed for the commissary, where people were already lining up to be fed.

He had to stop for a long line of newcomers, bent under their bundles, being led by a shield-bearer to a campsite. Then he narrowly escaped being run down by a gang towing newly felled tree trunks in from the woods. He detoured around a construction site where young men were exuberantly wielding picks, hammers, and shovels, slamming posts into the ground like nails, hurling dirt with the enthusiasm of dogs going after rabbits. Their excessive energy was clearly inspired by the presence of young women, who were officially weaving withes into makeshift screens, but also commenting back and forth about muscles and stamina and related matters. It seemed like a jolly way to build latrines.

Within fifty yards he saw a dozen styles of clothing and overheard a whole Babel of dialects. The nasal Randorian accents he could identify exactly, but the others displayed varying tones of Niolian singsong, Thargian growl, or the terse staccato of Joal, as if every one of the twenty-seven Vales was represented here already.

"Captain?" caroled a voice. "Oh, Captain Sme*dl*ey! I say! Hell*o-o-o*!" The hand waving the lacy handkerchief belonged to Hannah Pinkney. She stopped waving it and metronomed her sunshade instead, until she saw that Julian had changed direction.

Hannah Pinkney! Muddled, twittery Hannah Pinkney? How the devil had she found her way to this battleground? There was no mistaking her, though, swathed in a spectacular robe, an Eiffel Tower–shaped sweep of white fur, plus a straw hat with pink bows. The effect was neither Valian nor European, but something disconcertingly in between—Ascot Week in Thargia or the Randorian Embassy at St. Moritz.

Then Julian thought, *Oh my ears and whiskers!* because the man at her side was Pinky himself—Pinky the gray eminence, the manipulator, sly Pinky, smooth Pinky, Pinky as greasy as a ha'pennyworth of cold chips, Pinky all dapper in a fur-trimmed leather greatcoat, unbuttoned to display the leather jerkin and heavy wool knickerbockers beneath, the knee-high boots, Pinky clutching a official-looking notebook, Pinky smiling a greeting without showing more than his eyelids.

"Captain Smedley! My word! Good to see you, Captain."

Julian shook Hannah's hand while he discarded all the nasty remarks lining up in his gullet: *Not good to see you!* or *By Jove, I never knew a man switch sides faster!* or even *How long do you think you can hide here before Exeter finds you?*

He said, "Pinky, old son! What brings you here?" Possible answers would be: *Pure funk!* or *Crass opportunism, old man!* or *If you can't beat 'em, join 'em.* Yet who was he to accuse Pinky of changing sides? He'd switched sides himself, and now apparently he'd switched back again, because he'd accepted a miracle cure from First Murderer himself. He was as guilty as anyone.

Pinky said, "Logistics, actually." He waved the notebook as if he were bidding on a picture at Christie's.

Julian said, "Oh my word! What sort of logistics?"

"Mm, the usual stuff. You know, Captain. You'd probably have set it up bet-ter than I did, you with your military experience. We can't afford to have the Liberator wasting time shuffling around on the roads any more, can we? Can't afford to have him waste mana doing cures in jolly ditches, either." Pinky sighed to indicate the labor involved. "We move him from one node to the next as fast as possible. That means rabbits, sometimes relays of rabbits. It means having one camp set up before we tear the last one down, and then moving it ahead to be set up for next day. It means getting all the sick to the right place at the right time. It means transportation for the halt and the lame, so they don't slow us down too much. It keeps us busy." Pinky beamed modestly, displaying his eyelids again.

Pinky, in short, was all ready to take over the Free and run them as he had run Olympus. The Pinkneys of this world—or any other world, for that matter—gravitated naturally to the bridge. Did Exeter have any say in this? Did he even know who was doing what in his name anymore, or was he so intoxicated on mana that he had lost touch with his own revolution?

Why should the prospect worry Julian Smedley? He had wanted to nip the entire Liberator fandangle in the bud, but his narrow escape from death had changed his spots. Now he wasn't sure what he wanted, except that he felt an unreasoned resentment at the thought of slippery Pinky Pinkney taking over the whole shebang.

"Us? Who's us?"

"There are quite a few of us helping out," Pinky agreed. "The Chases are here and the Coreys."

Goodness! That sounded like a lot of wedded bliss all of a sudden. "Have you seen any sign of Mrs. McKay?"

"She was at Olympus when we left."

"Don't forget the Newtons, darling," Hannah said without a blush.

Damn! The last person Julian wanted to meet now was Ursula.

"Ah, the Newtons!" Pinky said blandly. He opened his book and found a page. "Yes, the Newtons are currently with advance party two. They ought to be in Lappinvale by now, getting everything shipshape for tomorrow. Dawn departure: We shall move the Liberator over the pass in one day. That is the plan. Have to wait a couple of days for the supporting cast to catch up, of course. He will have plenty to keep him occupied in Lappinvale."

It was a good job Julian's stomach was already empty. "I take it you now support Exeter as the Liberator?"

"Oh, he's doing splendidly, splendidly! The mana's just pouring in. The flu was a godsend, of course."

"Now, now, darling!" Hannah murmured. "You know the Liberator doesn't like you saying that."

Pinky chuckled. "Well, it's an ill wind that blows nobody good, what?"

Some winds were iller than others. "Well, it's such fun to see you," Julian said. "But I mustn't keep you from your important duties. If you need a fourth for bridge anytime, just shout. Cheerio!"

He stalked off in search of food.

Hypocrite! He had been projecting his own sense of guilt onto Pinky. Healing influenza was a morally acceptable source of mana, but Exeter had begun by martyring his own bodyguard, and that was definitely not on. The martyrdom mana had been diluted by the influx of influenza mana. So what? Julian Smedley had accepted his life back, knowing where the miracle had come from. Actually, he'd had no choice at the time, but he wasn't planning to cut his throat now, so he was just as guilty as if he had agreed in advance. When the root is evil, the plant is evil. Wear gloves, Lady Macbeth, and no one will notice the bloodstains.

He went by a makeshift log table where three husky butchers were hacking a carcase into pieces. Small wonder the Liberator's cause was popular if he was giving *meat* to all who asked for it! At the next, two men and two women were chopping vegetables. One of the women was vaguely familiar—quite good-looking in a horsey sort of way. . . . As if his stare had alerted her, she looked up and their eyes met. It was Alice Prescott.

They met halfway and embraced like long-lost lovers. A trio of passing youths whooped in approval.

Then they stood back to inspect each other, holding hands, both a little breathless and flushed and abashed at having made such un-English scene in public. She was weather-beaten and faintly bedraggled, indistinguishable from any young woman of the Vales. At school, Julian had been rather awed by Exeter's cousin—older, mature, worldly. Two years ago, he had kissed her, but only once and then only to distract her attention from something else. Perhaps he should consider making a habit of it.

She laughed. "I like your beard better than Edward's, I think. And your hand? It's growing back! That's wonderful!"

"You haven't changed a bit!"

"Crikey, it's only been two years! How are you?"

"I'm splendid, thanks to Edward. And you?" He looked down at the work-ravaged fingers he was holding. "Scullery maid? Is that the best job he can find for you?"

She cocked her head and looked at him inquiringly. "It's not unworthy! I can't speak the language, so my qualifications are limited. I look after babies sometimes, help load and unload the wagons. Don't worry about me, Julian! I'm having the time of my life."

Was she? Her eyes were steady; he couldn't tell if she was lying.

"That's good. But I'm starving!"

"So am I! Let's eat and talk." She urged him in the direction of the queue. Side by side, they walked over the frosty scrub. "You went back to Olympus?"

"It's in pretty bad disarray, I'm afraid."

"Pinky told us," Alice said offhandedly.

"Pinky! How does your cousin feel about that lot being here?"

Again she gave him an appraising look. "He welcomes anyone. Why shouldn't he?"

"Because Pinky will try to take over the whole show, if I know Pinky."

Alice looked away. "I don't think anyone is going to take anything away from Edward now, Julian."

"Good. How is he?"

They joined the end of the line, edged forward as it moved. They were speaking English, so no one could eavesdrop, yet she took a moment to answer, and then she spoke softly.

"Changed, even since I came. At times he's just Edward, but not often. I'm sure he sleeps no more than two hours a night. Most of the time he's the Liberator, whatever that is. I don't mean he's acting a part. He *is* the part."

"Too much mana?"

"Overdose? What are the symptoms?"

"I have no idea. I didn't get a decent look at him." Julian's stomach rumbled loudly, having sighted the food.

Alice said, "He is different. You'll see. And of course he's collecting lots of mana from all this healing. Funny, at first it didn't work too well. He spent more than he earned, was how Ursula put it. Now . . . It doesn't take much mana to heal influenza, apparently. A lot less than blindness, say. And the audience . . . is different, somehow."

"More supportive?" Julian looked over the clearing and the crowds. "I can believe that. Watching a blind man being given his sight is impressive, true, but most of us aren't blind and never expect to be so. Pestilence is different; it can strike down anyone." He suppressed a shiver. "They're scared, all of them!"

"I expect that's it."

"The Pentatheon can cure flu too."

"They can," she agreed. "But Zath can't! You don't go to Zath for a healing. And what temple can hold a crowd like this?"

Yes, the flu had been a godsend, but Alice was not going to admit it. And it must have brought money as well as mana. There was more to this assembly than just good organization: tents, transportation, abundant food, the equipment to process it. Most of the Free were much better dressed than the rabble Julian had seen in Niolvale.

"He's certainly doing very well. The boodle must be rolling in too."

"Oh, yes!" Alice would rather discuss money than mana. "It began with a windfall from Eleal Singer, of all people. But now the rich are flocking to him. The flu brought them as nothing else could have done. Mana and money and followers."

Julian asked the question that had been hovering unsaid between them. "You think he's going to make it?"

Her face was unreadable. "He certainly has a better chance now than he did a couple of—a fortnight ago. Ursula says it's still impossible, though. Zath's been at the game too long. Edward still can't hope to win without help from the Five, she says."

And what would the price of that help be? They had reached the front of the line and were about to be served. Julian was saved from having to comment on that.

The food helped, but after he had eaten, he realized how weak his brief illness had left him. Tomorrow he would have to start walking again, for he had no doubts that he wanted to stay with the Free now, if only to watch what happened as this juggernaut rolled onward through the Vales. He did not think he would be granted a mount or a place in a wagon—not with Pinky organizing matters.

The numbers were staggering. People continued to limp in long after the sun had set, although he could not tell whether they were newcomers or stragglers from the day's march. Nothing like this crusade had ever been recorded in Valian history before, and he wondered what the Pentatheon was making of it. Trying to put himself in Zath's position, he could think of no way in which the blighter could fight this mass assault except by throwing the full Thargian army against it when it arrived on his doorstep. He was certainly powerful enough to control the weather to some extent, but the cost in mana would be frightful. If he sent reapers to nip at the edges of the crowd, he would merely create more martyrs for the Liberator, who would be so much closer to the sacrifices that he would glean more benefit from them. Exeter had found an unbeatable strategy. The big question now was how long he could hold his army together—the influenza epidemic would not last forever, and winter was coming. Like a plague of locusts, this horde must keep moving or starve. If he miscalculated, he would create a famine.

After a long search, Julian found Onkenvier, huddled down in a vast crowd of singers. She was chanting along with them, although he did not think she was making words. She looked at him blankly, not seeming to know who he was, and she stared uncomprehendingly at the purse he thrust upon her. He left it with her, sure that somebody would relieve her of it fairly soon. She remained as he had found her, in a mindless, chanting trance.

He went off to speak with Exeter. He must give proper thanks; he must try and apologize for the angry words he had said, for now he shared in the blood guilt. But getting close to the Liberator was far from easy. Even when the camp was settling down for the night under the frosty stars, he did not stop working. He preached, he answered questions, and he healed the wagonloads of sick that were still arriving.

Julian cut no corners; he joined the throng and sat with many others, all wrapped up in blankets, all spellbound, listening to a sermon. It was an astonishing performance. The words were simple, the ideas simplistic, and yet the authority in them was utterly compelling. Even a stranger could barely resist the charisma now.

"There is only one god. God is Undivided. Yet there is a spark of godliness in all of us. Have you not seen it in others? Have you not felt it in yourselves—sometimes? Not often. It rarely shows, but it is there. We strive and sometimes we succeed. We are all evil at times; none of us is evil always. And when we die, as we all must die, do you think that spark of godliness is lost? Of course not! Our bodies die, but the god-stuff in us does not die.

"So where does it go, that spark? The sorcerers promise you a place up there in the heavens, twinkling away every night. Did you ever think to ask: *Doing what?* Just watching the world snoozing far below you? Have you never wondered if perhaps you might eventually get *bored*? Doing nothing, just watching? The first week it would be nice, yes. To be free of the fear of death, to be free of pain and sickness and suffering—wonderful! But for how long could you be satisfied with that? A month? A year? A century? A thousand years? A million? I tell you that what the evildoers offer you is illusion. I tell you that their paradise of unchanging perfection would soon become a hell, and their eternity would be a torment of boredom! Fortunately the truth is otherwise."

He began to outline his doctrine of successive rebirths, and Julian found himself intrigued, despite his utter disbelief. Exeter's idea of reincarnation was not the bound-to-the-wheel sort of reincarnation from which the only escape was to a nihilist Nirvana. It was a cheerful, progressive, ladder-to-God reincarnation, a collect-your-Boy-Scout-badges-and-get-promoted reincarnation. It did not deny the world, for the world was where the medals were won. It promised that all souls could merge with the godhead in the fullness of time—apotheosis, not annihilation—and it came from no earthly creed that Julian knew. He wondered where Exeter had found it.

Who knows? said the sceptic in him, it may be right. Who ever comes back to report? It was as appealing a blueprint as any, and that would be exactly why his old friend had chosen it as the keystone of the new faith. To overcome Zath he needed followers, to gain followers he needed a faith, and all faiths needed to explain about the party after the game.

It would be wonderful to believe stuff like that, said the cynical Julian— believe wholeheartedly and permanently. In Flanders he had seen sheer terror create some steadfast, if temporary, believers, even himself. Unfortunately, God had not designed the world quite so neatly as people like Edward Exeter thought He should. At that point Julian was shocked to realize that he was now crediting Exeter with believing what he was preaching.

When the sermon was over, the disciples organized a reception line for those who felt they had a special need to meet the Liberator. He spoke a few words to each—quietly, confidentially . . . soothing, blessing, comforting, encouraging. Then the supplicant moved on, walking a little taller, and Exeter spoke to the next.

While waiting his turn, Julian studied that tall, gaunt figure in the leaping glow of the fires. From many yards back he thought he could see a difference, as Alice had said. Exeter had changed, even in a brief two weeks. Confidence, yes. Authority, without question. Certainty, certainly. But there was more, somehow, and Julian could not put a finger on what it was.

Too much mana? Was Exeter becoming a god, or at least thinking of himself as a god, just as the others did? Could occult power corrupt as inevitably as temporal power did? So soon?

Whatever had happened, this was not the Exeter he had expected to meet, and as his turn came nearer, his determination wavered. He began to feel more and more as he had in Buckingham Palace, waiting for King George to pin a medal on him. There was no need to give thanks to this person. His thanks were so insignificant that to mention them would be to waste the Liberator's time. The bitter accusations of a fortnight ago now seemed not merely irreverent but totally irrelevant, just as Pinky's petty manipulations were irrelevant. Exeter did not need anyone's apologies. Exeter had been right all along, and the sacrifice his followers had made had been as justified as the similar sacrifices so many had made on the Western Front. He had seen through the smoke to the flame, which Julian had not. Desperate evils may require desperate remedies.

Almost, he turned and fled. But in the end he stayed, and a last step put him in front of the Liberator. Tongue-tied and dismayed, he stared into those piercing sapphire eyes—and was unable to remember even why he had come.

The spell snapped like an icicle. It was only the old familiar Edward Exeter who laughed and took his hand. "Now you're a thousand and one times welcome, old man! Come. Let's talk." He gestured to the closest fire.

"But . . ." There were hundreds still waiting to meet him.

"They won't disappear. Time for a tea break."

Thus Julian found himself sitting at a fire with the Liberator, served a hot, spicy beverage by worshipful disciples, while a few hundred envious worshippers watched like tigers peering through bars.

"I never doubted you would return."

"Actually I came to check up on Alice. Since I'm here, I'd like to stay and do my bit."

Smile. "Very glad to have you."

"Look, old man, I'm frightfully sorry about—"

"Stow it!" Exeter said sharply. Then he grinned sheepishly. "If I can't let bygones be bygones, then I'm in the wrong trade."

"You're doing very well in it."

"Got a few lucky breaks. How bad are things in Olympus?" He seemed totally relaxed, fresh, ready to cruise along all night.

His humor was a twinkling armor, deflecting all effort to pry. Only once did Julian manage to nudge the conversation close to Exeter himself.

"Your blueprint for the afterlife intrigues me. It isn't any form of Buddhism I've met. Is it Hindu? Where'd you find it?"

Just for a moment, Exeter seemed startled. "Find it? I don't really know. It just sort of came to me one day when I was preaching. Felt like something they'd like to know . . ." Then his eyes focused on Julian again and suddenly flickered amusement, as if he had a very shrewd idea of what his old chum was thinking. "It's all this mana, you know. I take dictation directly from God now."

He didn't *seem* to be serious.

When the brief audience was over, the prophet returned to the reception line to greet the next devotee. Julian walked away into the darkness, humming cheerfully. He paused once to look back at a scene made bleary by wood smoke—the Liberator foretold, receiving the adulation of his admirers by night. There were a dozen people grouped in the warm gold glow of the fires against the dark. It could have been a picture from an illustrated Bible, or even a study in chiaroscuro by some would-be Caravaggio, but the light did not shine any more brightly on Exeter than on the rest. Despite Alice's misgivings, he had not really changed. Exeter was playing a role and playing it magnificently, but he was still the same old Exeter underneath.

A little later, when he had found a cramped corner of a crowded tent in which to curl up, Julian Smedley discovered that he now had two normal hands.

VIII

He leaves his own country and goes to another,
But he brings the five evils with him.

ADI GRANTH: PRABHĀTĪ M.V.

51

GIVE PINKY HIS DUE—IF IT WAS HIS DUE—THE ORGANIZATION WAS IMpressive. Pilgrims were already starting to move out when Julian awakened at first light. He had promised to wait for Alice, and by the time she and the other commissariat staff had struck camp and loaded up their wagons, Onkenvier's clearing was almost deserted again, a wasteland of gray mud dotted with smoking ash piles and abandoned latrine fences. Snow was falling gently but with persistence, as if determined to hide the mess the Free had left behind them. The Liberator himself was still there, healing some last patients straggling in, while a fleet of moa taxi chariots was being assembled to carry him and his handlers to the first staging point.

Alice explained that she normally walked with the pilgrims, helping the old or the very young, but that morning she was scheduled to ride with other kitchen workers in a rabbit cart, and she insisted on Julian's joining her. He suspected that she was not being completely truthful, but accepted gratefully, feeling very much a scrimshander because there were thousands of other people who had been just as sick as he. He promised himself that he would pull his weight tomorrow.

The express could not travel very fast through the multitude packing the Fainpass trail, but it did arrive at the next campsite soon after the vanguard. When Captain Smedley offered to assist, he was armed with a knife and aimed at a mountain of several tons of a tuber much like a potato. It was one of the most joyful moments of his life: He had been assigned a job that needed two hands and he could do it.

The node Exeter had specified was marked by a single standing stone in the center of bleak winter pasture a couple of miles from a small village. Soon the Free were settling on it like flies on a cow pat. There was no snow in Lappinvale; the sun shone at times. Seated on an upturned bucket with his back to the wind, Julian peeled spuds into another bucket to his heart's content. He had companions—two women jabbering away in Lappinian, a very deaf old man, and three disgruntled girls who thought they deserved much better. He was quite happy to ignore them and just peel spuds.

Then a shadow fell across his bucket and a voice spoke his name. He looked up in fury. She was swaddled in moth-eaten furs like a shapeless teddy bear, her hair blowing untidily across her face. She wouldn't care how she looked, though; she never had. And she was actually smiling at him as if he should be pleased to see her!

Never in his life before had he wanted to hit a woman, but he did now—very much. "Go away!" he shouted. "Get out of my sight!"

She backed a step. "What's wrong?"

He rose to his feet, trembling with fury. "The word is rape, Mrs. Newton. You raped me!" None of the onlookers would understand English, but he would not have cared if they did.

"Oh, that."

"Yes, that!"

She looked at him uncertainly. "That's a rather extreme way of describing what happened. I suppose I used mana on you. I didn't mean to, Julian."

"Didn't *mean* to?" He took a step forward, and she retreated again. He was glad to see that she was starting to look alarmed. His anger had surprised her.

"No," she said. "You know how . . . Perhaps you don't. You never had much mana, did you? When you have mana and you want something, it's very difficult not to cause it to happen. The power leaks out. You couldn't stop your hand healing, could you? I wanted you to come to my tent. You did. I wanted you to—"

"I did not want you!"

She frowned as if he had said something a gentleman should not. "I suppose I should have been more careful. I'm sorry, Captain Smedley, truly I am."

But she didn't care. She would have been much more sorry if she had knocked over his teacup. Now he was waving his knife at her, and the onlookers were becoming alarmed. The deaf old codger had struggled to his feet. Julian was so furious he could not find words.

"When I saw what was happening," she said patiently, "I should have stopped, I suppose. Or asked you, perhaps. I didn't think you'd mind. Men usually don't." She smiled knowingly.

"You make a habit of it? Is that the only way you can get a man?"

"Oh, your hand!" Ursula cried, changing the subject. "It's better!"

Julian threw down the knife and made a fist. "A present from an old friend. I should hate to put it to work by knocking your teeth down your throat, Mrs. Newton, but if you don't get away from me now and stay away from me in future, then the Liberator is going to have more healing to do. Now go to hell and stay there!" He was bluffing, of course. She could bring him weeping to his knees with a whiff of mana.

She didn't, but she obviously thought he was making an awful fuss. "I am sorry, truly I am. I just didn't think you'd mind." With a shrug, she turned and walked away.

Shivering with frustrated rage, Julian resumed his seat and began hacking madly at the tubers.

ᏋᏋ 52 ᏋᏋ

Light snow was falling as the Free crossed Fainpass, but the weather was fine in Lappinvale. Alice had heard predictions that the Thargians there were sure to cause trouble. They would try to block a mass invasion heading for their homeland, and they certainly did not want their Lappinian serfs taking the opportunity to escape over the border.

The doubters had forgotten that the pandemic still raged in Lappinland. Governor Kratch himself brought his wife and children to be healed by the Liberator. Gratitude was not a prized virtue among Thargians, but they always put expediency ahead of principle, and their garrison was outnumbered a hundred to one. The Free marched on unopposed, gathering recruits as they went. These refugees were free to desert as soon as they reached Randorvale, of course, but surprisingly few of them did.

Alice was enjoying herself enormously. London seemed far away now, but she had never truly been a Londoner. Tents she associated with childhood safaris, Uncle Cam and Aunt Rona in Kenya. The climate and the scenery were different, but roughing it did not bother her. Her Norfolk depression forgotten, she helped with the cooking, tended babies, cared for the sick waiting for Edward to arrive, and generally did work that felt more useful than any she had done before in her life. Now that she knew how much fun crusades were, she could understand why the Middle Ages had put on so many of them.

Even so, having Julian Smedley around was an improvement. She needed an interpreter to help her learn some basic Joalian. During her first few days with the Free, she had been forced to rely on Ursula, Dommi, and Edward himself, and they were all too busy with other duties to spend much time with her. Various Olympians began turning up and enlisting after that, but they were quickly put to work as well. Julian was not fluent in Joalian and usually enlisted a native as tutor, translating back and forth and learning along with her. It ate up the hours on the daylong treks and the sometimes monotonous toil, for he pitched in with the lowly work of the commissariat, leaving religious affairs to others.

Captain Smedley qualified as an old friend. Alice had more in common with him than anyone else in this world except Edward, and she rarely saw Edward. Julian had flicked in and out of her life for years, her cousin's closest chum, a different person every time she met him: bean sprout boy, then spotty, unsure adolescent, debonair youth, shell-shocked hero. And now? Now a lean, competent young man, not quite handsome but certainly attractive, old beyond his years. If he still had daylight nightmares, he hid them behind a cheery façade. He never discussed his own affairs, but he was too personable not to have at least one sweetheart somewhere. Recalling the bedroom roulette that Mrs. McKay had described that long-ago evening in the dining room of the Bull, Alice concluded that Julian Smedley would be regarded as a prime target but might not be ruthless enough to play such games well.

From Lappinvale by Soutpass into Randorvale—and still the sun shone. Randorland might be tricky, Julian warned, because it was home ground for the Lady, the Church was being persecuted there, and Doc Mainwaring still lay in jail. But the prophecy was encouraging, verse 318: "From Randor the mighty shall seek out the Liberator, sleeping in the woods and ditches, crying: aid us, have mercy upon us, and they will shower gold upon him."

The first thing that happened in Randorvale, though, was that Ursula and Dommi disappeared.

"They'll be back," Edward promised. "Dommi's appointed himself apostle to the Carrots. Ursula's going to report to whatever's left of the Service."

The following morning, King Gudjapate summoned the Liberator to an audience and the Liberator declined the invitation.

Two days later, the king tried again, delivering an emaciated but otherwise unharmed Doc Mainwaring as a peace offering. Edward still refused, although he kept Doc.

On the Free's fourth night in the vale, when they were camping close to the western end and thus not very far from Olympus, several hundred copper-haired Olympians poured into camp and greeted the Liberator with hysterical adulation. With them came Ursula and some familiar faces: Betsy and Bill Pepper, Iris Barnes, Prof Rawlinson, and others.

Julian learned of the evangelists' return as he was wrapping himself up in a fur robe beside a campfire. There were still not enough tents, and he could not see why a seasoned campaigner like himself should be given preference. He was quite healthy now, just a little weak, and Flanders had been much worse than this. A man knelt down at his side and grinned at him like a starving crocodile. He sat up quickly.

"Dommi! You're back? How's Ayetha?"

"Indeed she is most excellently in good health, Brother Kaptaan. And I am very proudest father of very loud son."

Julian, formerly *Tyika* Kaptaan, thumped him on the back and shook his hand. "Congratulations, Brother Dommi! And what is his name?" He could guess the answer. The Vales were going to be swarming with D'wards from now on.

"By gracious permission he is named after our esteemed Liberator."

"And was *Entyika*— Was she there?"

Dommi grinned even wider and nodded. "I have brought missive for you."

Julian snatched it from his hand and ripped it open. He forgot to say thank you, and he did not see Dommi depart.

my dearest darling captain hook,

it was very clever of you to guess were i had gone. i am staying hear with one of tims ants not a man. i would have staid in olimpus if i new you were coming back so soon. and i am sorry to miss you. i miss you very much. i am sorry we quareled but all lovers quarel sometimes. all your promises made me cry and i wont hold you to them because i think you will repent at leshur but if you do realy mean them then i am yours always on any world. body and soul and espeshly body.

*your ever loving
wendy*

That letter very nearly cost the Free one of their number, but in the end he decided to stay aboard. The crusade would not last very much longer, whereas his future with Euphemia could be stretched out for centuries. A few days more would be very little by comparison, however long they might seem.

The following morning, the royal family and most of the court drove into the camp in a caravan of fine carriages. Edward greeted them politely, cured every last runny nose, and did not insist that they sleep in ditches. He accepted their gold and gave it to Dosh to buy more food and more pack beasts.

Prophecy was a two-edged weapon, and next stop was Thovale. By now everyone knew that verse 404 of the *Testament* held some ominous words about D'ward and hunger in Thovale. The encounter was unavoidable—a man of destiny could not pick and choose.

"Should make an early start in the morning," Julian said. "Beat the rush."

Alice could see only a sheer wall of mountain, fit to challenge a fly. "Certainly. How is the pass rated?" She knew now that Joalian had a dozen words that might be applied to a mountain pass, depending on its difficulty. Difficulty was a matter of judgment, though. If it couldn't stop a mountain goat, then it ranked as easy.

"Figpass is a *jaltheraan*."

"I'm not familiar with that one. What does it mean?"

"Bloody-awful-even-in-summer."

"Will an hour before dawn be early enough?"

The Figpass trail began rising at once, climbing steeply through scrubby trees, and it soon opened out to reveal vast hills of an impossibly green green under a pure white sky. The Free were a gray rope dropped by a giant, scrolled over the mountain face and ultimately vanishing into clouds thousands of feet above. And that was only the vanguard. There were many, many more behind.

Alice leaned into the slope, trying to keep up a steady plod. In an hour or two she would stand up there and look down to see the masses following. "It seems so unreal! I keep trying to think of earthly equivalents and I can't find a single one. Visigoths . . . the Children of Israel . . . Xerxes crossing the Hellespont—none of them quite fits."

Julian puffed, his breath already white in the cold. "Peter the Hermit?"

"Don't even think that!"

"Right-oh, I won't. It is real. It is also very transient. All of us will remember these days for the rest of our lives. A century from now one or two of those children may still be alive, bragging that they marched with D'ward, following the Liberator into Thargvale."

These days were also the most important of Alice Pearson's life. If she lived to be a hundred, like those hypothetical children, everything else would be anticlimax. The Vales were only a small part of the world, and only a tiny fraction of their population was actually involved, but surely this was a moment in history. Who would refuse a grandstand seat at the Hegira, the parting of the Red Sea, or Caesar crossing the Rubicon? She tried not to include the People's Crusade or the Crucifixion in that list. Whatever was going to happen at Tharg, she would never again see anything to match this. She assumed she would eventually go Home. She had already overstayed the four-week limit she had set with Miss Pimm, but it was certainly not time to leave yet.

No one, even Edward, knew how many followers he had now. The organization alone was a miracle, growing of itself to keep pace with the mushrooming numbers. Having learned over the past five years how incompetent armies were, Alice would not have believed that a large group of people could cooperate so well. The credit was all Edward's, for he had chosen a superlative team of disciples and inspired them with fanatical loyalty. There were no personal feuds or squabbles over precedence among the shield-bearers.

Their strength as a team sprang from their differences. No one understood human weaknesses better than Dosh, the reformed criminal and libertine. Dommi had scaled up his experience at running households to run the commissariat. Ursula Newton was an irresistible force, a human tidal wave to overcome all resistance, while Eleal's preaching could wring tears from a field of rocks. Of Edward's two age-group brothers from the old Nagian days, Tielan was a shrewd trader and Doggan was dogged and untiring in humdrum tasks that drove others crazy. Piol Poet was official archivist, keeping Eleal's sermons theologically orthodox. Pinky Pinkney moved people as the wind moves snow-flakes, usually without their knowing it. Bid'lip had been a soldier, Kilpian a drover, Hasfral a midwife, Gastik a farmer, Imminol a herbalist, and Tittrag a mason.

The Liberator himself could outperform any one of them at anything, but he could not be in a dozen places at once. Whatever he needed done, he had a disciple to do. There were twenty shield-bearers in all, and Edward remarked to Alice in one of his wry asides that he could not imagine how Jesus ever got by with only twelve.

In the last two weeks, she had seen very little of Edward. When he offered apologies, she refused them. "You are working; I am on vacation. I can't speak the language, so I can't help much. If you want to talk, then send for me and I'll come gladly. Otherwise, do what you must do and don't give me a thought. One thing I am not is bored."

He did send for her a few times, always late in the day, when others were ready to relax. He seemed to need no rest, but his helpers did, or perhaps he chose the hour merely from habit. She was amused to notice that the two of them were never completely alone, so no tongues would wag, and yet she doubted that the danger of scandal had consciously occurred to him. His instincts were perfect.

At those sessions he would always inquire if she was happy, and she would always assure him that she was. She let him lead the conversation, and thus they talked of England, of the war, of poetry, of their childhoods. Only once did he mention what might happen when the Free arrived in Tharg, and then almost offhandedly.

"They can only be a cheering section," he said, "but of course it is their cheers that make it possible. There is just one event on the bill—the heavyweight championship of the Vales, between the reigning champion, Zath *(boo! hiss!)* in the black corner and the Liberator *(hip! hip!)* in the gray. We've all read the result in the *Testament,* so it should be a very dull. . . . What's wrong?"

"Nothing. I just tend to forget that Zath is a real person, not just an allegory."

"Oh, he's real all right." Edward's eyes narrowed, and for a moment he stared out bleakly at the night. "But what I'm planning is not murder, it's execution. You know which victims' names head the indictment."

Then he shrugged and changed the subject. If he had any doubts about the outcome, he could hide them even from her. But he must know that the battle was not always to the righteous and that most popular uprisings ended in disaster: Wat Tyler, Jan Hus, Peter the Hermit. The People's Crusade had taken thirty thousand people to slavery or slaughter.

Sometimes he was the Edward she had known. He had shown this same courage and quiet determination when the Blighters were trying to kill him. Sometimes she sensed more, a fearsome coiled power waiting to be unleashed, a calculated hatred for an evil foe—unless that was only her imagination seeing what it wanted to see. Yet, sitting demurely across the fire from him, she would watch the play of light on the angular planes of his face and wonder what her cousin had become.

Once, and only once, he let his inner feelings show. He fell silent for a while, staring at her. She waited, pretending to watch the flames, and finally he said wistfully, "Dear Alice! What would have happened if the war hadn't come? Happened to us? If there had been no *Filoby Testament*? Do you ever wonder?"

"I can't imagine." She studied the pictures in the embers, which was just as practical an occupation as indulging in useless might-have-beens.

Softly, he said, "I was very much in love with you, you know. I still am, but now . . . well, things are different now. Let's not complicate matters by talking about that. Would you ever have taken me seriously?"

"I always took you seriously, Edward, dear. Very seriously. I was very frightened of hurting you. I was sure you would find another girl soon enough, probably lots of girls. I was the only one you'd ever known."

"One's enough. I don't think I'd have found another. I don't think I'd have given up—not even when I learned about D'Arcy."

She met his eyes then, and the question in them. "I was in love, too. Crazily in love."

"And if the war hadn't come?"

"I would have continued to be a fool, I suppose. His wife's still alive."

"Were you really a fool? Do you think that now?"

"Yes." She felt disloyal to the memory of a man who had given her so much happiness, but she owed loyalty to Edward also. "He wouldn't risk losing his career and her money."

"Jolly watery sort of love!"

"Yes. I suppose I'd have come to my senses eventually. Why I didn't become pregnant, I can't imagine—that would have done it! Too late, of course. I should be grateful that the war did come."

He pouted. "Don't think that! And Terry?"

"Rebound, only rebound." Terry had been even younger than Edward, with the same black hair and blue eyes—an odd coincidence. "A wonderful man, and yet in the end that would have been worse. We were madly in love, both of us, but we'd nothing else in common. It wouldn't have lasted. We'd have lived unhappily ever after."

After a moment, he said, "Thank you."

For what? Sauce for the gander? "What about Ysian? Didn't you love her?"

He shook his head in sad amusement, as if unable to credit her disbelief. "No. I told you. Love between native and stranger is unthinkable. It doesn't matter which world you choose, one must age while the other doesn't. I could have loved her. I didn't *let* myself fall in love with Ysian."

"Then what of Miss Eleal, who follows you around all day with those big, big mooncalf eyes?"

His eyebrows arched. A corner of his mouth quirked. "Alice, darling, you're not, um, just a little bit—"

"Me? Of course not. As far as I'm concerned, she's perfectly welcome to her classic profile and her overabundant mammary tissue and her life as one vast dramatized tragic *tableau vivant*. I just wish she'd keep it a little farther away from me, that's all."

"Her own father bewitched her," Edward said. "Can you imagine that—his own daughter? I took the spell off."

"With another kiss?"

He laughed aloud. "Don't blow steam at me, Mrs. Pearson! Yes, if you must know. I didn't enthrall her, though."

"She managed that all by herself?"

"Yes, she did! She was hurt and vulnerable; she picked the first man she could find to fill that terrible gulf in her soul. And the answer is still the same—love between stranger and native is unthinkable."

Alice was still winding herself up to apologize when he shrugged and said, "I just hope she's strong enough not to turn suicidal when—when she discovers I can't respond."

"Or when—what?"

"Let's talk of happier things," he said. "Do you remember . . ."

How many men could resist a piece like Eleal? Life would be much simpler if more of them were like Edward.

Figpass was bad going up and worse coming down. Alice stopped in the shelter of a rock to take a break, while wet-flannel mist drifted by and the column of Free trudged past without a break. Julian was looking very weary, but his sense of humor was still operational.

"Thovale?" he said. "It's very small and very strategic, because it connects to several other vales. The Thargians have always known the gods meant it to belong to them; they have never quite convinced the Thovians of that self-evident truth. Thovians are wild hill men. They make the Scots or the Afghans look like bunny rabbits.

"Thargia has tried to annex the vale several times. The clansmen came down from the hills by night and cut throats. The Thargians couldn't do much to retaliate, because they prefer to fight in straight lines and the terrain here won't allow that. Their armies had to cut their way through every time, both going and coming, which cramped their foreign policy *vis-à-vis* everyone else. So they came to a gentlemen's agreement. Thovale is officially independent, but it won't hinder Thargia marching through and won't support its enemies. Now the Thargians are free to bully everyone except the Thovians and the Thovians can carry on feuding among themselves. Everybody's happy, doing what they enjoy most."

She laughed. "You are a cynic!"

"I learned that on Earth," he said grimly.

Even as the Free poured down into Thovale in their thousands, a sudden blizzard closed the pass. Snow fell in shiploads, day after day after day, trapping the pilgrims within their camp.

Very few of the wagons had arrived in time. Fuel ran out first, but that hardly mattered. People had crammed into every available tent and the tents were buried in snow, so although their interiors were dark, damp, and stank horribly, they were not really cold. Walkways between them became trenches through the drifts. The food ran low. Rations were cut and finally stopped altogether, with the last reserves being issued only to children and nursing mothers—for there were even nursing mothers on this crusade.

Edward came around regularly, visiting every tent at least once a day. Shield-bearers came more frequently, especially those who were good preachers: Eleal, Pinky, Dommi. Influenza came, and was dispatched by the Liberator. Boredom came also. Hymn singing palled. Doctrinal arguments palled. Alice was very glad she did not understand enough of the language to have to listen to all that. Tempers grew shorter as the hunger bit harder.

Gradually fear began to seep into the Free. The *Filoby Testament* said that the

Liberator would take death to Death, but it did not mention his followers. Perhaps they would all die first? Alice worried about that, having heard of the fruits of martyrdom from Julian, and she was certainly not alone. A word from Edward or even a shield-bearer cheered everyone up again, but the doubts returned.

It was night on the second day without food. Tempers were brittle. Somewhere in the pitch-black tent, two men were arguing, ignoring the rising grumbles of their neighbors. Alice was cramped from sitting with her knees up, but it was not her turn to stretch out yet. The shapeless furry lump she was leaning against was Julian, leaning against her. She was fairly certain that there was no one else in the tent who understood English.

"Julian?"

"Mm?"

"He's been imitating Jesus."

"Mm." Meaning, *yes*.

"How far do you suppose he's willing to go?"

"Driving out the money changers? Last Supper?"

"You know what I mean. Being crucified."

He sighed. "I wouldn't put it past him if he thought that was what was needed. Fortunately, I don't think it's relevant. I asked Prof and he agrees. There's no way that the Liberator's death would in itself destroy Zath. Edward's in terrible danger, of course. The odds are still long against him, so he may well die. If he does, I'm sure it won't be by his own wish."

The argument in the corner sounded as if it was about to come to blows. The protesters were growing louder too.

"He might pull down the temple, like Samson?" Alice asked.

"No, that won't work. It's got to be a straight, heads-down contest of mana. The stronger wins, the weaker loses. If Edward isn't powerful enough to win that, then he would gain nothing by pulling down the temple. Zath would just trap-door himself out of there. Edward would have used up far more mana than he would."

She thought of the other two men she had lost in her life and wondered if she was about to lose a third. Not a lover like them, of course, but a very dear foster brother. Just that. It was enough. Of course, if Edward survived his ordeal and then renewed his suit . . . She shied away from such thoughts.

"You still believe he needs help from the Pentatheon?"

"Zath has been collecting mana for a hundred years or so."

"But Edward has done far, far better than anyone expected, hasn't he?"

"Thanks to the Spanish flu, he has. I know we mustn't say that, but it's true." Julian chuckled, and Alice felt it through her backbone. "Fallow always claimed it taught us leadership, but no old Fallovian has ever led anything on this scale before. He's done far, far better than the Service ever dreamed possible. I think the only one who foresaw this was Zath himself. I hope the bastard's been worrying about this for thirty years."

"How do you think the Pentatheon feels?"

"Pretty bucked, if we're right in thinking they don't like Zath."

"But the more powerful Edward is, the greater the risk they take if they help him, surely? They'll just create another Zath to threaten them, and they must know Edward doesn't approve of them either." His own success might doom him.

"I don't know." Julian squirmed into a new position. "Nobody knows. It's a waste of time theorizing." He wasn't contradicting her. He couldn't, because he had said much the same things himself in the past. "I will say this: Prof and I went over the *Testament,* and this is almost the end. This is verse four-oh-four, hunger in Thovale. There's only one prophecy left. Edward's fulfilled all the rest—all those that mention the Liberator, all those that mention D'ward, all those that seem to be relevant but don't name him at all. The only one left to go is verse one thousand one: 'In wrath the Liberator shall descend into Thargland. The gods shall flee before him; they shall bow their heads before him, they will spread their hands before his feet.' "

"That's certainly encouraging, but you're forgetting three eighty-six. It's not finished yet."

"Well, of course."

Everyone knew verse 386:

Hear all peoples, and rejoice all lands, for the slayer of Death comes, the Liberator, the son of Kameron Kisster. In the seven hundredth Festival, he shall come forth in the land of Suss. Naked and crying he shall come into the world and Eleal shall wash him. She shall clothe him and nurse him and comfort him. Be merry and give thanks; welcome this mercy and proclaim thine deliverance, for he will bring death to Death.

The arguing men had been forced into silence by their neighbors. People were whispering and coughing, and a child wailed in another tent somewhere. Snow smothered all other sounds.

Thinking over what Julian had said, Alice realized that there was another verse in the *Testament* that had not been completed yet, one that mentioned someone called the Betrayer. Who was he?

53

DOSH HAD SET OFF OVER FIGPASS WITH FIFTEEN HELPERS AND TEN WAGONS. Five men and six tusk oxen froze to death on the way, but four days later he led the survivors into Thovale, arriving two hours after dawn, just as a warm wind mockingly turned the snow to rain. A crowd of men and women ran out to meet the train, shrieking and cheering, slithering and stumbling through drifts already shrinking. The famine was over.

Dosh was dead on his feet, soaked and frozen and exhausted, aching in every bone. If he were in a fit state to find anything amusing, he would be finding that welcome amusing, for the rescuers were being greeted like the long-lost son in that parable D'ward told. Tielan and Doggan were the first to locate Dosh himself amid the bedraggled band of rescuers. They embraced him as if they were planning to rape him. Doggan kissed him. Tielan screamed that he loved him. Oh, how times changed! The last time the three of them had been in Thargdom together, those two would not have been seen within arm's length of Dosh Houseboy. That was what the Liberator had wrought. That was what virtue was all about, and it felt good. He could not deny that it felt good.

More people flocked around him to pummel, hug, and congratulate. He was too weary. He shook them off, turned away . . . and came face-to-face with the one man he really wanted to see.

"Well done!" D'ward said harshly. "You delivered the goods again. You saved the day!" He clasped Dosh's shoulder briefly, a squeeze hardly detectable through its covering of wet fur.

Dosh stared up at him in dismay. "Master? What's wrong? What have I done?"

"Nothing! I mean everything. We've got a famine on our hands, and you've saved us. You're the best, Dosh! I can always count on you."

The Liberator bared his teeth in a death's-head grin, thumped Dosh's shoulder again, and trudged away to greet the others. His eyes had not said what his voice had. Something was wrong.

Dosh found a tent and fell into the bottomless sleep of total exhaustion. By the time he awoke, it was the following morning and the Free were already on the move, under a roof of cloud that seemed to rest on the treetops. A steady drizzle still fell; slush had become a soup of mud, black and pungent and knee-deep.

Most of the tents had been struck; all the livestock had gone. The remaining wagons were being hauled away by teams of men.

Stiff as an oak rafter, he limped off in search of food and news. The rumors were thicker on the ground than the mud. The Thargian army was holding Mestpass. The Thargian army had been devastated by the sickness. No, it had been devastated a fortnight ago but was now recovered. The ephors had sent word that the Free were welcome to enter Thargia, or must not enter Thargia. The ephors had demanded D'ward be handed over to them. D'ward had demanded Zath. The ephors were dead and Tharg was burning. All guesswork, obviously.

The poles were genuine, though. Men had been tearing down a forest, cutting poles. D'ward had decreed that every able-bodied pilgrim should henceforth bear a pole topped with the circle of the Undivided. He had demonstrated by cutting a sapling, trimming off all the branches except one at the top, curling that one around, and tying it with a length of creeper. The camp was full of them. They were being issued to everyone departing.

"What the blazes are those for?" Dosh demanded of the Fionian woman who heaped his platter with boiled vegetables. The meat he had brought had not stayed around long enough for him to share.

"Symbols of the One, dear." Fionians called everybody "dear."

Dosh considered the matter as he headed off to find a seat. The Free had never needed such emblems before; D'ward spurned even the earrings that the old Church of the Undivided had issued to its followers. So what was he really thinking?

Thargia maintained the only real standing army in the Vales, commonly estimated at no less than ten thousand men. That number might be doubled or tripled in an emergency, but what had the pestilence done to Thargland's fighting strength? Moas would not accept substitute riders, so the cavalry had certainly been weakened. It was not impossible that the Free would outnumber whatever forces the ephors sent against them, although numbers alone were misleading. A trained Thargian soldier could eliminate half a dozen peasants without spitting on his hands. When every peasant bore a quarterstaff, the odds were a little better. Moas had very fragile legs.

So D'ward was anticipating trouble. What of morale? Would even Thargians fight for the hated god of death? Furthermore, the Liberator had gone from strength to strength for the last three fortnights, from nothing to leader of a mighty host. This was the hand of the One, of course. Even the pagans must be wondering which side their phony gods supported.

If he were one of the ephors, Dosh concluded, he would let Zath and the Liberator settle their own quarrel first. Then he would decide whether to let the Free go or round them up and send them to the mines.

He was still very shaky, but his duty lay with D'ward and Dosh did not want to be left out of the excitement. Having checked on the condition of his helpers—

because that was what D'ward would have done—he acquired one of the circle poles and set off in pursuit.

Mestpass was classed as easy, but no pass was truly easy in winter. Much of the trail ran through a broad, flat valley, made difficult now only by mud, but in some places it narrowed to a canyon. Normally placid Mestwater had become a boiling torrent, glutted with melted snow. Half the bridges had gone and must be replaced before the Free could cross. Consequently, they had not progressed very far, and Dosh caught up with the main body before midnight. The next morning he was ready to resume his duties.

By midday, he was walking over the green hills of Thargslope. Snowy peaks dwindled away to west and south, for Thargvale was so wide that its far side was hidden beyond the horizon. The sun shone in a sapphire-pale sky as if spring would jump out of the ground at any moment. Yet this was midwinter! Thargvale was blessed with a much finer climate than its inhabitants deserved.

"The old place hasn't changed much, has it?" D'ward said cheerfully.

"No, master." Dosh eyed the Liberator's smile and decided that there was nothing wrong with it. He must have been imagining that odd greeting two days ago. He had been very tired, after all. "I don't suppose the people have changed much either."

"Well, you never know. It does look as if they're up to their old tricks, though, hiding the silverware."

"Master?"

"No welcoming committee, no livestock in sight. You think perhaps they don't trust us?"

"We're being watched," growled Bid'lip Soldier from D'ward's other side. "I'd swear I saw something on that hill a moment ago. And the back of my neck's itching."

"Fleas," D'ward said. "Fleas in bronze armor. You can see the sun flashing off them every few minutes. Watch over there."

Four years ago, Dosh had traveled across Thargvale with D'ward—and with Tielan, Doggan, Prat'han, and all the others. Then it had been springtime, with the trees shining in a million shades of green and gold and purple and blue. Then he had been young and crazy. Now most of the woods were bare, although here and there he could see patches of evergreens—also everblues and everpinks, for all Thargian vegetation was colorful. A few patches of snow still lingered in the hollows. Mestwater swirled along the valley floor, deep and dark, spread beyond its banks. It was burdened with floating logs that had been cut in the summer and were now on their way to market.

By marching into Thargvale, the Free were blatantly provoking a fanatically xenophobic warrior state. This was the second time in four years that D'ward Liberator had led such an invasion. The air seemed to crackle with danger.

The countryside was much as Dosh remembered it: prosperous, well-tended farms in the lowlands, stone walls trailing like pencil lines over the fertile, rolling hills. The big houses of the nobles were more noticeable with the trees bare.

Silos, haystacks, windmills. As D'ward said, no visible people or animals. Since Jurgvale, his progress had been marked by groups of the sick and their attendants, waiting for healing: people on foot or in wagons or even in tents, camped out until he should arrive. Here, there was no one. Had the pestilence avoided Thargvale, or were the people forbidden to seek the aid of the heretic?

No one in sight except the Free themselves, a wide column that stretched back out of sight, many thousands, carrying thousands of circles . . . or quarterstaffs, if that was what they were. With them came their wagons and pack beasts, oxen and llamas, and even a few moas and rabbits that had appeared after the snow melted. It must be the greatest movement of people in the history of the Vales.

Where was D'ward taking them? That morning he had placed himself at the front and given orders that the inevitable stragglers be herded up as much as possible. He was setting a very gentle pace. He had detailed no advance party and had refused Bid'lip's request to send out scouts. Obviously he anticipated trouble, but he would have to be insane not to anticipate trouble in Thargvale. A little while ago, he had passed the word for Dosh and Bid'lip, but so far he had said nothing of substance.

Then he did. "How's the money?"

"All gone, master."

He nodded. "Thought it would be. Well, Bid'lip? You're our expert on strategy. How does our situation look?"

The big Niolian scrunched up his luxuriant black eyebrows. He had been known to remark that he had the sort of face that looked best when he put his helmet on backward, but he was not in a joking mood today. "Shaky." He pointed to the river. "Mestwater's in spate. Somewhere up ahead it must join Thargwater. There'll be other tributaries, I expect, and likely all of them in flood too. The Thargians can cut down the bridges, if the rivers haven't done it for them. Is Tharg on the south bank or the north?"

"North. But you're right about the tributaries."

When D'ward said no more, Dosh spelled out his own worries.

"No supplicants, no fresh recruits, so no source of funds. Buying food in Thargland won't be as easy as it's been in other vales. There's no villages here, only those big estates. They trade with one another or send their produce directly to the city. Dommi's moaning about supplies, master."

Still the Liberator continued to stroll along in silence, wielding his pole like a staff. His face was giving nothing away. He seemed to be enjoying the walk and the sunshine.

"But we have the One True God to rely on?" Dosh snapped.

His impudence earned him a reproving frown. "He doesn't expect to do all the work, Brother Dosh. Good intentions are not enough by themselves." Then D'ward smiled to take the bite out of his words. "Yes, I know it looks bad. I'm not unaware of that. Here's what I want you to do. See that little hill? The one with the trees and the house on top? We're going to camp there. Bid'lip, I want you to post guards around the house to keep people out. I'm going to use that as my headquarters. I think it'll be empty. It was half a ruin when I last saw it. Don't let anyone except shield-bearers in . . . and anyone else I send for, of course."

The soldier nodded. "Yes, sir."

"And post guards around the perimeter. I don't expect an attack, but they may try a feint or two, just to see what our reaction is."

"And what is it?"

"We can defend ourselves, if we must. Try to avoid violence."

The big man rolled his eyes as if to imply that he would not attack Thargia with a force comprised of civilians and two armed Nagians.

"I'll want you at the house," D'ward continued, "so appoint deputies. Tell them to let any sick people into camp, of course, as usual—any genuine supplicants. They're to escort those to me in the usual way. But if messengers come or emissaries, they're to make them wait and send to the house for Dosh. All right?"

"Yes, sir."

"Good. Then go and get started."

D'ward sent him on his way with a smile. Dosh waited for his orders. And waited. The Liberator continued to walk in silence. He was frowning now, though.

Eventually Dosh couldn't stand it any longer. "How many days from here to Tharg?"

"I don't know. Four, maybe?"

Dosh almost gasped aloud. That was a shock! Until now, the Liberator had always known exactly where he was going. Sometimes the weather or the crowds had delayed him unexpectedly, but always he had known the route he was going to follow. He had scouted it out in advance. Now he did not know.

D'ward glanced behind him, as if making sure that there was no one close enough to overhear. "Dosh?"

"Master?"

"We've been friends a long time."

"The only real friend I've ever had."

D'ward winced. "Surely not?"

"It's true."

"I wish it wasn't."

"Well it is! Everyone I've ever been close to just wanted carnal pleasure of me, one way or another. You're the only person I ever knew who liked me as a person. I have friends among the Free, now, of course. But they wouldn't be my friends if I wasn't the new man you made me."

D'ward's face twisted as if he was in pain. "Well, you've certainly been a good friend to me, these last few fortnights. I don't think I'd have managed what I have without your help. I want you to know that, Dosh. I wasn't nearly as sure as I pretended I was that you'd manage to reform. You've succeeded beyond anything I ever dreamed of. You've been wonderful."

"It was you, master. D'ward, I mean. Or it was God. You brought me to God, and every night I thank God for sending me to you."

D'ward groaned. "Well, I need your help again. I need you to do something for me."

"Anything. Anything at all."

"Oh, Dosh, Dosh! It isn't going to be that easy. It may cost you your life, or worse."

How could he doubt? "Just tell me, master! I swear I will do it, exactly as you tell me. I know I failed you in Roaring Cave, letting those intruders—"

"You did *not* fail me! Those two both had magic to help them. Don't blame yourself for that. But I said then that I gave you all the tough ones. There isn't another soul in all the Free that I could trust to do this."

Dosh laughed aloud. He felt almost as excited as he'd ever felt in all his years of perversion and debauchery. "Tell me! Tell me!"

D'ward put an arm around his shoulders. "I'm not clear on the details yet. But if I give you an order tonight or perhaps tomorrow . . . We'll need a signal. Suggest one."

" 'Good old days'?"

The Liberator's brief smile acknowledged the humor. "Yes, that'll do. So if I mention the good old days, that means I want you to do whatever I ask then, however wrong or crazy it may sound. Or it may seem absolutely trivial, but it will be deathly important. Whatever it is, will you do it with no argument?"

"Yes, master. Of course."

"Thank you. That's all I can tell you now."

"I promise."

The Liberator gave Dosh's shoulder another squeeze and then took his arm away. He had left a burden there, though. What orders could possibly be so terrible that Dosh would be tempted to refuse them?

ᔧ 54 ᔧ

"I KNOW YOU ARE HUNGRY!" ELEAL CRIED. "SO AM I. SO, I AM SURE, IS the Liberator, for he will not eat when you cannot. Remember how he spoke to us in Thovale, saying that those who hunger and thirst after righteousness shall be filled?"

She must hurry up and finish now, for it was almost dark and she was supposed to be up at the house. Pity! Her speech was going very well. She was enjoying it, and she thought her listeners were enjoying it too. They were certainly attentive. The little clearing was so packed with people that she could barely see the campfire. The woods all around were packed also, and yet when she paused for breath the night was still. Barely a cough, only the ticktock of woodcutters in the distance. Earlier she had caught snatches of other shield-bearers preaching elsewhere on the hill, but not anymore. Hurry.

"But he has also warned us that mortification of the flesh can be carried too far. And so that message I gave you, that you will feast tonight!" She paused while a sigh of wonder swept the wood like a breath of wind. Did they think the Liberator might have changed his mind since she began her talk? "Be patient, therefore, brothers and sisters! It will be a sign unto you! Tonight Trumb will eclipse."

They all knew that. The great moon hung over the jagged teeth of Thargwall like a green plate, glistening in the winter night. Before dawn it would certainly fill out to a circle and then fade to black.

"No matter the misguided pagans worship that disk as one of their false gods, for the Liberator has taught us that it is only a blessing from the One, to brighten darkness. Is not the circle His symbol? It is a sign of God, not of the so-called Man. You know how the pagans tremble when that light is eclipsed, believing that Zath will send reapers to steal away souls. Well, Zath's days are numbered. It is written that the Liberator will slay him, and he has come to Thargvale to do that."

Another sibilant murmur.

"We are greatly blessed to have traveled with him, all of us. Friends and family behind at home will revere us all our days because we are here and they are not. Harken to what the Liberator said to us at sunset! He said that before Trumb eclipses again, *Zath will be dead and there will be no more reapers!*"

Louder, longer, came the reaction. Naturally—the shield-bearers themselves had cheered when they heard that news. Trumb's eclipses often came nine days apart, sometimes only four, rarely more than a fortnight. She raised her voice over the rumble.

"And therefore tonight, when the green moon darkens, we feast! We are the Free, and we shall celebrate tonight the certain death of Zath! So promises the Liberator, in the name of the One True God. He bids us remember this night all our days and all our years, so that evermore, when midwinter comes and the sun turns, we shall feast and make merry in remembrance and thanksgiving. This be his command to us. Let us pray."

She kept the prayer brief, made the circle sign, and stepped down from the stump. Her head was pounding with reaction as if she had just come offstage after playing some great role. Which was apt, she supposed. What greater part could there ever be than this? Voices were rising excitedly all around. She looked for her shield before remembering that it was still slung on her back. Willing hands passed her staff and her pack. The crowd parted to let her through. She saw eyes glinting with tears in the moonlight, she felt hands reach out to touch her gently as she passed. She did not enjoy that for it reminded her of how men had fondled her flesh in the Cherry Blossom House. Here they were doing it for other reasons, of course, but she still did not like it. She was only D'ward's mouthpiece, unworthy of such adulation. She hurried off, up the hill.

Since she had joined the Free, she had never known D'ward take over a building. It was yet another sign that things were changing. The absence of any new recruits today, the fact that they were now in Thargvale, which had always been their objective, D'ward's unique promise of a feast . . . events were hastening toward their climax, and one tiny part of it was Eleal Singer.

Singer? She did not sing now, except when everyone else did. She really ought to change her name. Eleal Preacher? She considered asking Piol's advice and chuckled as she imagined his reaction, telling her not to get swelled-headed. Eleal Actor? She performed before great audiences now, greater than any Grandfather Trong had ever imagined, but she wasn't really acting. Plays were fiction, mostly sinful nonsense about evil people who claimed to be gods, but every word she spoke now was true. She only repeated what she had heard D'ward say, or what Piol and Dommi had written, which again was only what D'ward had said in public or in private instruction.

Puffing and leaning on her staff, she emerged from the wood at the entrance to the house. It was a spooky place, two storeys high, long abandoned. The windows were empty eyes, the door a vacant mouth. Once there had been gardens around it, but they had run to weeds, dead winter straw crackling under her feet. Stark, unsightly trees raised branches against the sky in frozen agony.

Two young men sat on the steps, chatting. They jumped up when they saw a shield-bearer and made the circle. She, having both hands full, raised her staff in salute instead. She paused to catch her breath. "Blessings of the Undivided! Am I the last?"

They exchanged worried glances. One said, "Don't know, Mother. There's another door."

Mother? Now that was amusing! She was younger than they were. Mother Eleal? Eleal Mother? "Well, D'ward says that the last shall be first." Making a mental note to ask him or Piol what that meant, she went on up the steps.

She found the others gathered in a large, high-ceilinged room. A fire crackled cheerfully in a fireplace at one end, but most of the light came from Trumb's great disk, blazing in through three huge windows. Cobwebs festooned the gaps between jagged edges of glass, and the mullions cast hard shadows on the floor. The floor, she noted, had probably been a fine expanse of mosaic at one time, but it was so littered with a mulch of dead leaves that little of it was visible. Someone had thought to sweep a clear space in front of the hearth, or the first spark would have sent the whole place up. The air was musty and earth scented.

She made a hasty count and decided she was not the last. In the absence of furniture, the shield-bearers were sitting in twos and threes on their own bedrolls, not clustered at the fire but grouped around the walls. Seeing Piol's shiny scalp alongside Hasfral Midwife's silver mop, she went to join them, dropping her pack and sitting on it before she dealt with shield and pole. She released a sigh of content.

"I heard you speak," Hasfral said, leaning around Piol. "Some of it. You were marvelous! I do enjoy your sermons!" She patted Eleal's knee and smiled her motherly smile.

Eleal mumbled thanks. She would have been ecstatic to receive such praise had she been *acting*. For preaching, it seemed inappropriate. All she did was quote the Liberator. With a little practice, anyone could do the same. Besides, talent was a gift from God, D'ward said, more an obligation than anything to get swelled-headed about.

"Where's D'ward?"

"Out there," said Piol, "with Kilpian and Dommi. And don't ask us what they're doing, because we don't know."

"Not so," Hasfral corrected. "We know what they're doing. We just can't decide why."

The windows looked out on a courtyard enclosed by two wings of the house and a high wall. Like the gardens outside, it had degenerated to a wilderness of trees and shrubs run riot. In summer it would be a dense jungle of greenery. In winter it was a brown tangle of death and decay. What might have been a lawn had become a small hayfield. Three men were moving around there—dragging away thornbushes and brushwood, apparently.

"They can't be planning a bonfire. It'd burn the house down."

"They're clearing a space," Hasfral said. "I think we're going to have a ball. May I have the first dance, Piol?"

He coughed his dry little laugh. "If you promise not to tramp on my bunions. Personally, I hope we have the feast first."

"Has D'ward ever promised a feast before?" Eleal asked. She could eat a mammoth, medium rare with lashings of mapleberry sauce.

The others said, "No," in unison.

"Must have been a lovely garden once," Hasfral said wistfully. "That's a lantern tree and a giant spindle nut. Those small ones are sesames; beautiful in spring, they are."

Footsteps scrunched outside. A small man marched in, his blond halo identifying him instantly as Dosh Envoy.

"Twenty!" said Tielan, from somewhere near the fire. "Now we can start."

"Twenty-three," Dosh retorted. Two others followed him in. "Alis and Kaptaan, and you mustn't forget D'ward himself."

While Tielan protested that he hadn't, the newcomers found places. The men outside must have concluded their work, for they were approaching.

Eleal had almost never seen all the shield-bearers gathered together like this, with nobody else. Well, almost nobody else. Alis and Kaptaan didn't count— they were special. They were not shield-bearers or friends. They did not preach or undertake specific responsibilities. They just were. The Liberator knew what he was doing. Laws were for evildoers, he said. The righteous were guided by principles.

Kilpian and Dommi stepped over the low sills and stamped across the room to their bundles. D'ward followed, looked around, counting. He remained standing.

"Blessings!" he said. "Are you hungry?"

"Yes!" said almost everyone.

He sighed. "So am I! We'll have to wait awhile yet, I'm afraid." He strolled over to the fireplace and turned his back on it. "A few of you may be worrying that I'm about to produce a sacramental supper. I'm not. That is not what we're here for. We have no bread and no wine, anyway."

He began to move again, sauntering along the big room. "You wonder what's going to happen. The One will provide. Bid'lip? Any signs of trouble?"

The soldier's deep growl came from the darkest corner. "No, sir. But they're out there. Lots of 'em. You can smell moa on the wind."

"I'd rather smell a moa than its rider! Colleagues . . ." D'ward turned and started wandering back, peering at faces. "Yes, I am proud to call you colleagues. You have all realized, I'm sure, that we have arrived at an ending. I marvel that the Thargians let us come even this far. I will not tempt them further, for there are thousands of people out there who would make good mine workers."

He continued to wander, speaking now to one group, now to another, but audible to all. "Yes, this is an ending. All those good folk we brought with us have played their part. Like wedding guests who lead the bride and groom to the chamber, they must now depart in peace, their portion done."

And would the Liberator also depart? Vanish in a blink as he had come into the world, the Free dispersed, scattered, perhaps persecuted. What then of Eleal Singer? She could not go back to the Cherry Blossom House. There was little call for a preacher of heresy. Although her leg no longer barred her from the stage, her eyes had been opened and she knew how evil most of the plays were, filthy pagan legends; she would certainly never dream of entering Tion's Festival. As for marriage, a woman's normal lot . . . no matter what husband she found, she would compare him with D'ward every time she looked at him. She must pray, and the One would provide.

Even if He didn't, D'ward would never forsake her.

He was still talking. "An ending but also a beginning. I was told of this house by a friend who lives not far off. He said that its owner and his sons were taken by reapers, many years ago, and the old place had remained deserted ever since, as no one knew who owned it. It was a noble place once and it will be noble— Aha!"

Footsteps crunched on dry leaves outside the door and then halted. Eleal could not see who was there, but D'ward could, and he smiled a welcome. "Kuchumber Boatman, isn't it? You came for Dosh, I assume."

Dosh was already on his feet, heading for the exit. D'ward watched them go until there was no more sound, and then began to pace again.

"That means we have visitors, so the house must wait till later. Let us plan the feast. How much food is left?"

Dommi said, "None, master!" and a few others muttered agreement.

"None at all?" D'ward stopped in the center of the room. "No food! There is no food, but the Liberator promised us a feast, so now he will call on the One, who will shower miracle wheat from the heavens like hail?" His voice was soft and bantering, yet it had a razor edge. "Oh, my friends, have I not told you that you were given brains to think for yourselves? You would die of thirst underwater. The Lord has already provided what you need, if you will but look. Did I not just tell you that we have reached an ending? Dommi, how many wagons would be needed just to haul the infirm and small children?"

"Four, perhaps five—"

"So save five oxen and— Ah, now you see?" The Liberator smiled as the old house rang with laughter.

ᔕᖇ 55 ᖇᔕ

JULIAN WHISPERED A QUICK EXPLANATION TO ALICE. SHE CHUCKLED. THE shield-bearers began planning the feast, joking about the best ways to cook llamas, rabbits, and tusk oxen. They would be edible but tough as rope, likely. D'ward listened with tolerant amusement.

What a performance! Could have used more like him in the trenches to buck up the lads and lead them into battle with their heads high. But this wasn't really funny, dammit! The Liberator must meet Zath alone, man to man—that was the sword above the throne. That had always been the plan, David and Goliath. Exeter had specifically not staged a travesty of the Last Supper, but he was sending the Free home, and he'd dropped bags of hints that he was pulling out.

Alice tapped Julian's shoulder. "He said *all* the rabbits?"

"Yes. Why? What's wrong?"

She frowned. "Nothing."

Yes there was. What?

A quick look the other way showed that Pinky was wearing his sleepy-eyed thoughtful look as he watched the byplay. He, too, had noticed something awry.

"Tell me," Julian whispered.

Alice shrugged. "If they slaughter the excess oxen and *all* the rabbits, then how is he going to Tharg?"

"Good question." Julian mentally kicked himself for not seeing that. It would take days on foot, and Thargians did not tolerate strangers wandering around their vale. They would especially resent the man who had laid a historic humiliation on them only four years ago. Zath would lay his own traps. Of course Exeter had enough mana now to defend himself from mundane attack—or even teleport himself across country from node to node if he chose—but either would be a foolish waste of power. He might have hidden one rabbit away somewhere for his own use.

Alice had been expecting to go to Tharg with him.

And so had Julian Smedley. Damn! He didn't want to be sent home with the children. Exeter knew what he was doing, certainly—clearing ground in the courtyard, sending Dosh off on a secret errand. How and where did he expect to meet Zath? Was he even going to Tharg at all?

Now he was raising a hand for silence. Ye gods, but he was a cool one! Only his tendency to pace around showed the strain he must be feeling, and that might be due to the virtuality of this node. It was localized, but very intense.

"We are about to have visitors." Exeter walked over to the central window and sat on the sill, so that the light was behind him, leaning against a mullion and stretching out his legs, cool as the proverbial cucumber. The great room fell silent. A bat-owl warbled its ghostly call out in the trees. Farther off, some of the Free had begun a singsong. Footsteps approaching. . .

Dosh entered first and stepped aside. Three men followed, coming to a halt just inside the doorway, looking around for the leader.

None of the three was dressed for riding moas. The chappie in the center was a massive figure in full armor, boots and crested helmet making him tower over the others. His clean-shaven chin showed he was a Thargian, had there been any doubt. His scabbard hung conspicuously empty at his side. Wee Dosh had done extremely well to persuade him to disarm. From a Thargian point of view that would be a very poor start to negotiations. The other two wore civilian garb: fur hats, long fur robes. The one on the right sported a trim, gray-streaked beard, the one on the left a heavy black mustache. Now there was a surprise! Julian glanced at Alice, but she was still studying the visitors and probably did not know the significance of that facial hair.

If they were waiting for introductions or words of welcome, they were evidently going to be disappointed. No one spoke a word. Then the soldier picked out the man in the window as the likely head boy and marched forward, his heavy boots scuffing up dust clouds from the litter of humus. When he was in the center of the room and just into the moonlight, he stamped to a halt. His greaves flashed streaks of Trumb's green fire.

"I am Kwargurk Battlemaster, ephor of Thargia." His accent was as thick as road tar, but— Good Lord! An ephor *in person*? And speaking Joalian, too!

"I am the Liberator." Exeter showed no awareness that he was being granted an unprecedented honor.

Kwargurk grunted contemptuously. He waved a hand to indicate his companions. "Petaldian Ambassador from Joalia and Tanuel Ambassador from Niolia." Neither moved.

"I am the Liberator," Exeter repeated. He crossed his legs. He was in the presence of one third of the Thargian government and representatives of the other two great powers. Julian suppressed a strong desire to whistle a cheery tune.

The ephor growled deep in his throat. "Let us speak in private."

"No. These are my friends. I hide nothing from them."

"Friends? How many cohorts can you field?"

"None. I am armed with the word of the One True God."

The ephor glanced around the desolate, unfurnished chamber and then down at the young man lolling on the windowsill. His voice was a sneer. "He does not pay you well."

Exeter's voice was higher pitched and quieter, but it was steady and plainly audible. "He pays better than you can imagine, Ephor Kwargurk, but you did not come here to trade insults. State your business."

"You and your rabble have violated our borders. Your persons are forfeit. The penalty is death or slavery."

"I know that."

"Why? What is the reason behind this insanity?"

"Our business is God's business. It does not concern you, Ephor. You came to offer terms. State them."

"Not offer, heretic—dictate! Hear, then. You who call yourself the Liberator will proceed to Tharg with all deliberate haste, taking no more than ten companions, and will present yourself there to the authorities, who upon examination may decide to put you on trial. The rest of your followers have two days in which to leave Thargvale or endure the consequences."

Julian heard Pinky utter a faint hiss of surprise or relief. Make that both. By letting the Free leave unscathed, the irascible Thargians were breaking all their own rules. If Exeter had not been tipped off in advance, he was a fantastic guesser. Obviously this was how he planned to journey to his rendezvous with Death—as a guest of the Thargians. Would he accept the offer of ten companions or insist on going alone?

Julian whispered a hasty explanation to Alice: "He's done it! He can go on to Tharg and everyone else is free to depart!" He squeezed her hand and she returned his grin. Triumph!

Exeter uncrossed his legs and rested his forearms on his knees. "What are Joalia and Niolia doing in this?"

The ambassadors exchanged glances. Tanuel cleared his throat loudly, or perhaps he was just blowing his mustache out of the way. "You have deluded many citizens of Nioldom and even some of Niolia itself into following your mirage. I made representations on their behalf to the noble ephors and their excellencies agreed to treat the matter with the outstanding leniency that Ephor Kwargurk has just described. You have many persons from Joalia here also. Honorable Petaldian Ambassador will confirm, if you wish, that his government's views are concurrent with mine. We have assembled a stock of foodstuffs to provision the refugees' return journey—at no small cost, I may add. You should know that the Thargian government's concessions are historically—"

"I think we understand. Thargia would love to load up its slave pens, but it doesn't want to antagonize all the Vales at the same time. The chance to take so many hostages must be mouthwateringly tempting, though. A more weighty consideration would be that the omens and auguries are especially ambiguous just now?" Edward stood up, revealing that he was as tall as the ephor. His next words cracked out like pistol shots. *"Your terms are rejected. Leave this camp."*

Alice understood the tone, and her nails stabbed hard into Julian's hand. Pinky gasped. Others among the shield-bearers were reacting similarly. Petaldian Ambassador uttered undiplomatic obscenities. A six-foot pillar of bronze viewed from the side in partial moonlight should not be able to express astonishment without speaking, but somehow Ephor Kwargurk managed it.

Tanuel Ambassador hurried forward, his voice emerging as a trembling bleat. "Young man, you will have the blood of innocent thousands upon your head! Ever since your destination became obvious, I have worked night and day to persuade the Thargian—"

"Your motives are honorable. The One will not be unmindful of them, nor of Petaldian Ambassador's. But we will be guided by our God and heed not the butchers who reign in Tharg, worshipping evil. The blessings of the Undivided go with you all."

"You really are insane," Kwargurk growled. "My colleagues and I did not believe that so many would follow a maniac." Turning slowly, he surveyed the hall. "Will none of you break free from the madman and seek to avert bloody catastrophe?"

No one spoke. Not that Julian was not tempted . . .

"Truly," Exeter remarked, "this concern for the welfare of others is a welcome innovation among Thargians. There is hope for you yet, when I have ripped out the foulness that contaminates your city. Go, ephor. Go back to Tharg and tell your murdering Zath that his hour has come."

For a moment the giant seemed to balance on his toes, poised to seize the insolent preacher and snap his neck. Possibly he tried to, although no tremor of mana disturbed the virtuality of the node. Then all three envoys turned and stalked away. The two diplomats were doubtless downcast at their failure. It was hard to believe that the Thargian was feeling anything short of homicidal mania. All three vanished out the door, crackling dead leaves into the distance.

As Dosh was about to follow and see them off, Exeter called him over. For a moment the two conferred, then Dosh departed also.

Julian was returning Alice's wide-eyed stare. "He had it all! They gave him everything he could have asked for, and he turned it down flat. This is insane! He's bloody bonkers."

"It's a rum go," Pinky muttered.

"Never thought I'd agree with a Thargian. He *is* crazy, as the man said. He must be."

Alice chewed her lip. "He knows what he's doing, I'm sure."

"I'm not," Julian growled. He turned to regard Pinky. If anyone had a mind devious enough to understand this, then he did. "You make head or tail of it?"

Pinky lowered his eyelids dreamily. "Indeed we must suppose a complex gambit, mustn't we, mm? A ploy being made on several levels, I suspect. Wouldn't you agree with that? Different message being passed to different listeners, as it were . . ."

Alice said, "Sh!"

Exeter had moved to the center of the hall. He had just declared war on

Nextdoor's equivalent of the Prussian Empire and now he was talking of trivialities as if nothing at all had happened.

". . . was telling you of this fine house, fallen on hard times. We must now consecrate it to greater service than it knew before. Let us make this building the first temple of the Undivided, to give witness to the Truth, to minister to the suffering and unfortunate. A temple must have a high priest or priestess, some holy person well fitted. Who among you is most worthy?"

He stopped and looked around. No one spoke. Julian wanted to scream, Who cared about a bloody temple? He glared at Pinky, but Pinky was frowning at this latest Liberator outrage. The Church of the Undivided had staunchly refused to establish permanent chapels in the belief that they would attract persecution like wasps to a picnic.

Exeter sighed. "No nominations from the floor? Oh, my friends, do you not see yet? Is it not obvious? Only two of us here are mentioned in the *Filoby Testament*. She knows what it is to be penniless and wretched. She knows what it is to be crippled. I have even heard tell of those who mutter that she should not hold up her head among *honorable* people. Shame, shame! It is those proud popinjays who should hang their heads in her presence. Eleal Highpriestess, come forward."

At the far end of the hall, Eleal clambered to her feet, apparently being pushed by her companions. She walked forward slowly, shoulders hunched, her arms tight around her breasts. Superb actress that she was, she could not possibly be faking that shock and reluctance. Exeter embraced her.

"Now, priestess," he said, releasing her, "we need a Circle. There is a nail in the wall above the fireplace, and you have a shield that would sanctify this hall without any further words from us. May it ever remind us of the Warband who fell so bravely as the first martyrs of our church. . . . They will not be the last. I shall consecrate it and this temple in the name of the Undivided and all of you shall watch and listen and remember, for soon you will carry the word to all the Vales and to lands beyond."

Horsefeathers! Either the blighter had come completely unhinged or he was killing time until something happened or . . . or . . . or Julian Smedley was a monkey's uncle. *Why had Exeter spurned the ephor's offer of safe conduct for the Free?* Pinky knew, or suspected, if he could ever be persuaded to get to the point.

But Pinky was glaring at the ceremony now being organized before the fireplace. Again Exeter was going his own way with his own schismatic sect—the Church of the Liberator, probably. . . . And Eleal as high priestess! Not a stranger, even. A girl in her teens, a native, and an actress! A former harlot! No wonder Pinky was seething. It was surprising the man hadn't turned in his shield already. Of course, he must assume that he would be able to overrule a mere—

No! If Exeter cut loose and left the Church of the Liberator to fend for itself, then certainly Pinky would expect to run it as he had run the Service, the rat behind the wainscot. But that program depended on the believers surviving tomorrow's apocalypse. The Thargians would come at dawn in fire and slaughter. The old, the infirm, the children, would be put to the sword and the able-bodied marched off to the mines in their thousands.

The awful truth reared up like a monster in a nightmare: Exeter had brought all those innocents here to die for him, just as the Warband had died. That was why he had refused the Thargian terms. More martyrdom, more human sacrifice! Wholesale massacre—wholesale mana! He was going to try and beat Zath at his own game.

⁊ⱳⱳ 56 ⱳⱳ⁊

Dosh TROTTED DOWN THE STEPS AND SET OFF AFTER THE THARGIANS, crunching leaves under his boots. The night was calm but turning cold, and Trumb's disk was almost a perfect circle, so the eclipse would start soon. He could find his way along the path by moonlight. If it had gone by the time he returned, the fires twinkling among the trees would guide him. Snatches of hymns mingled with popular folk songs told how the Free were celebrating the Liberator's triumphant promises. They were showing their faith.

Shamefully, Dosh's faith had not been as strong as it should be. He knew Thargians and how jealously they guarded their borders. He had been very relieved when he heard them promise to let the Free depart unmolested but also very astonished, which he should not have been. He should have trusted more in D'ward and the power of the Undivided.

Catching a glimpse of the envoys in front of him, he slowed down. D'ward had told him to speak to them when they had left the woods and not before. He could hear the mutter of their conversation, the clink of the ephor's armor.

When D'ward rejected their terms, Dosh had been as surprised as everyone else. He should have had more faith. Just why the Liberator had chosen to proceed in the way he had was still a mystery, but he always knew what he was doing. Trust in the One! It would be the Thargians who would be surprised when they heard the message Dosh brought. They would curse, undoubtedly, but they would certainly accept, and it would be fun seeing their faces.

The real mystery was why D'ward had made so much of this mission. He had used the code words that meant Dosh was to obey without question, but it had not been necessary. Dosh would have been overjoyed to undertake this task without that. He could not imagine what problem D'ward had foreseen. Perhaps he had expected something else to happen, or had been considering several plans, and the worst had not happened. Why, then, had he used the code words "Good old days"?

"Dosh, darling?" A figure stepped out of the trees before him, from deep shadow to bright moonlight.

He yelped in horror and reeled back. His heel caught against a root and he fell, landing on his seat with an impact that knocked all the breath out of him. He gaped up at the apparition.

She was stark naked. She was hardly more than a child. She was also very pregnant, her breasts and belly distended. Her golden ringlets hung below her shoulders.

He turned his head away and closed his eyes. "Sister! You must not display yourself like that! It is unseemly. It is contrary to decency."

In midwinter, too! She must be having some sort of brainstorm. He'd heard that imminent motherhood could have strange effects on women. He was not sure if this sort of madness was commonly one of them, but madness was the only possible explanation. She was in need of help. He scrambled to his feet.

She laughed, a laugh like a tinkle of silver. "You always liked me like this before, lover."

Dosh reached out and clutched a tree for support. The roughness of its bark under his hand reassured him that he was awake and not dreaming. The voices of the Thargian embassy had faded into the distance. He stole a quick glance out of the corner of his eye and she was still there. In fact she was closer.

"Go away! Go back to your husband at once!"

"Husband?" She laughed again, nearer than ever. "Don't you remember me, Dosh? After all the happy times we had together?"

He stole another glance—at her face, only her face. It was a very lovely face, soft and fair and smooth. She was much too close. He looked away.

"I have never seen you before in my life!" he squealed.

"Well not like this," she admitted. "This is last year's model. Lovely, isn't she? Or she was. One of the guardsmen did the damage, I think."

Dosh's knees trembled with the shudder of terror and horror that ran through him. Oh, God preserve me!

She laughed again, and somewhere in the deep crypts of his mind, down in the foulness where the nightmares lurk, there was something unbearably familiar about that laugh. "Memories starting to come back, are they?" she teased. "It's easier to wipe them clean than bring them back, but we'll see what we can do. Aren't you going to kiss me?"

Nausea burned in his throat and cramped his gut. He pressed his face against the prickly tree bark. "Go away! In the name of the One True God, I bid you begone!" He began to pray, but silently, so she would not hear how frightened he was. God would hear. God would help him.

After a moment, she said sweetly, "I'm still here, Dosh. Are you sure you don't want to kiss me?"

Never! Never, never again! That sort of sin was all behind him now. He had a job to do, a very important job. D'ward was depending on him. He spun around the tree, bypassing the girl, and sprinted away along the path, stumbling and staggering, trying to fend off the trailing branches but missing some of them, which stung him across the face.

"Goodness, what a hurry!" she trilled, right at his back. "It isn't very good for this body to run like this, Dosh. Suppose it drops its brat right on the path here? And you won't get away from me like this, you know. What a surprise the ephor will have when we turn up together! Will he take your message as seriously as he should, do you suppose?"

Dosh stopped dead. The girl cannoned right into him and wrapped her arms around him, laughing gleefully. He struggled to free himself, and of course she was far stronger than she looked. She weighed as much as he did, and her mountainous belly seemed to get in his way more than in hers. The two of them staggered to and fro, banging into branches and saplings. He cursed between clenched teeth, he tramped on her bare toes, and she just trilled her ghastly mocking laugh. At last he managed to free an arm. He punched her in the face as hard as he could, hurting his knuckles.

She released him and fell back a step. Again she was in full moonlight.

"Darling, does this mean you don't love me any more?" Her smile displayed a missing tooth and blood coursing down her chin from a gashed lip. Her swollen bosom heaved as she panted. "Or are you just remembering how I enjoy rough play? Hit me again. Kick me!"

He was trembling so hard now that he could barely speak. "You are not a god! You are a foul, evil sorcerer—like that pair of mummies that call themselves Visek!"

"This is true," she said, looking down at the dark stream flowing over her breast and splashing onto her protruding belly. "It was naughty of D'ward to tell you, but it is true. That needn't come between us, lover. We can still do all the things we used to do."

"You bewitched me!" His voice broke. Tears of frustration blurred his sight. Memories were starting to writhe in his mind like worms in rotten meat. Naked girls, naked boys . . . Worse, the faces were starting to come back, and the sounds of laughter and screaming and gasping and pleading. "You cast spells upon me. . . ."

She stepped forward. He retreated until he ran into a tree and could go no farther. She was so close that her nipples touched his coat and he could smell her sweat.

"Sometimes I did," she said huskily. "But you didn't really need them. You were the most inventive playmate I have ever had, Dosh. So tough, so versatile, so resilient. You're too old to be Tion now, of course, but we could still have fun together. Even if all we do is just watch the others—"

"Go away!" He closed his eyes. His fists hurt, he was clenching them so hard. "I will have nothing more to do with you ever again!"

"You will if I want you to!" she said sharply. "I can take you away from here before D'ward knows a thing about it. Well, if last year's model doesn't interest you, how about this year's?" A man's voice added, "These ones wear better."

The change of pitch warned Dosh what had happened. Reluctantly he looked.

Now Tion was a boy—slim, narrow shouldered, dark haired, and startlingly handsome. Naked, of course. He pursed his lips invitingly.

"Go away!" Dosh screamed. He was powerless against such sorcery, and yet D'ward was relying on him. If he failed to deliver the message, thousands would die and all the Liberator's plans be ruined.

The incarnation shook his head pityingly. "You are being terribly foolish, Dosh. You want to go and tell the ephor that the Liberator was only pretending and really does accept his terms. But you haven't seen what that message is going to do to *you*, Dosh. D'ward is being very nasty and unfair to poor Dosh. Can't you work it out?"

"What if he is? I don't care! I'd do anything for him because he is my friend, a true friend, not a blood-sucking lecherous monster like you, Tion Sorcerer!"

The boy pouted. "I never treated you any worse than D'ward is treating you now. For your sake, you really shouldn't deliver that message, love."

Dosh clung to the thought that Tion the Youth was evil incarnate. Whatever he wanted was wrong, wrong! To escape by force was impossible, so deception was the only alternative.

"What message should I deliver then?"

"Let's see. You could tell them that D'ward says Thargians are cowards. You could tell them he's calling Ephor Kwargurk a turd in a tin tankard." The boy chuckled and then his eyes narrowed. "Don't try to fool me, love. You never could before, and you're terribly confused at the moment. D'ward is just another sorcerer, like me. That invisible god he's invented doesn't exist. D'ward doesn't even believe in him himself."

"That's not true! You're lying. You're on Zath's side! You want D'ward to die!"

The kid sighed, fluttering his long lashes. "No, love, no! You're wrong again. I am on D'ward's side, believe me! I always was. I had him in my power years ago and I let him go. Didn't you know that? I set you to spy on him, but just out of curiosity. I never tried to stop him, did I?"

Dosh moaned, unable to speak. His mind was whirling like a moth as it tried to find some way out of this. His efforts to pray were being choked off by all those ghastly memories bubbling up in his mind. D'ward had told him many times that the Youth was crazy. He'd said so to Visek, and they hadn't denied it.

"So you see," Tion said, "I really do want to see that horrible Zath dead, and this is the only way to do it. D'ward himself still isn't strong enough. He has to do one of two things. Either he lets the Thargians kill the Free, or he gets help from me and the others—all of us, the Five he has been slandering so nastily. I'd gladly help him, truly I would, but I won't dare to, because I know that the others won't. It would take all of us, all Five together and all our flunkies as well. And that won't ever happen, because none of us trusts the others enough. Somebody would be sure to break faith and help Zath, and then Zath will win."

He reached up a hand to stroke Dosh's cheek. Dosh jerked his head away and banged it on a branch hard enough to make stars fly in front of his eyes.

The boy tweaked Dosh's beard playfully. "You can guess what Zath will do then! It's called the Great Game, lover. The secret is to always choose the winning side, and D'ward isn't the winning side."

"You're lying!"

"No, Dosh, dear, I'm not. So I'm not going to let you deliver that message. We're going to let the Thargians think he meant what he said the first time. The silly boy changed his mind, but they're not going to hear that. You won't understand, but this way D'ward may just have a chance without our help. Zath will outsmart himself, and that will be a very elegant solution."

Dosh tried to lunge past. The kid caught him with one hand and held him like a steel bracket, so his feet shot out from under him and he thought his arm had been jerked from its socket. Tion supported the weight without even tensing his slender muscles. Dosh regained his footing and swung a punch at the beautiful face. He howled as his fist cracked into something as hard as a stone wall. Tion apparently felt nothing at all.

"Oh you do want to play rough games?" He glanced up at the sky and frowned. The light was fading fast as a stain of black spread over Trumb's great disk. Stars were returning.

"Well!" the sorcerer muttered. "Now that's interesting!"

Dosh squirmed, trying to pry the slender fingers loose and failing utterly. Tion ignored him, apparently staring at the eclipse.

"Very interesting! That changes things." The sorcerer chuckled. "All right, Dosh. You go and deliver your message. Stop the massacre if you can."

With that he vanished, fading away even faster than the green moon.

57

T HE CEREMONY WAS OVER. ALICE HAD UNDERSTOOD NOT A WORD OF IT, but the actions had been plain enough. Eleal, that silver-tongued ingenue, had now been installed as bishop of Thargvale or perhaps archbishop of the Vales. She had recovered from her shock and was already warming to her new role, accepting congratulations from the shield-bearers with matronly grace. Edward had certainly made some very odd decisions tonight. Pinky's face was a picture. Ursula's would rank as a whole art gallery. Even Julian had gone into a black sulk about something. With the fire shrunk to a few red embers, some subtle difference in the overgrown garden beyond the windows hinted that the eclipse had begun.

Edward must have given orders to start the feast, because people were leaving.

He was standing by the door, speaking to each shield-bearer in turn, but his tone sounded cheerful enough, more like personal instructions than final farewells. He would not dispose of Cousin Alice quite so easily. She wanted to know what he was planning to do next, and she was not leaving until she found out, so there! She stood up and eased her stiffened limbs.

She peered up crossly at Julian's scowl. "What's the matter? Don't you think Eleal will make a good pope?"

He shrugged, not caring about that. "I wish I knew why he rejected the Thargian offer. And the way he did it! Dammit, Alice, an ephor is like a king or a president, one third of an absolute tyrant."

"I think I know why. I'll tell you if you promise not to repeat it."

Julian said, "Right-oh!" too quickly. He obviously thought he did know the answer and she didn't.

She looked around. Edward wouldn't hear her. He was saying good-bye to Eleal at the door, but she was the last.

"It's the old problem of church and state. . . .This is isn't easy to put into words. I'm not sure Edward could, even. I think he was acting on instinct—"

"Instinct! *Instinct?* He's likely to get us all killed or enslaved with his bloody instinct."

"In a sense that almost doesn't matter." She wondered if she could ever explain to a man who couldn't see it already. Julian was a downright, earthy Anglo-Saxon. Edward was a realist too, but he also had a Celtic streak in him, an artistic undercurrent that defied logic. "The point is that this is the climax of everything he's worked for, yes? So even details are very important. What we saw tonight may become legend for thousands or millions of people. This was his night, his apotheosis almost, and he would not be seen currying favor from the Thargians."

"If you think that, then you're as mad as he is! This is Thargia, woman!"

It must be her turn to shrug, so she did. "I just don't think Edward saw that man as Ephor Kwargurk. I think he saw Pontius Pilate."

Julian's mouth opened. Then closed.

"He was irrelevant," she explained, "like Pilate. Sometimes military force just doesn't matter. Generals and armies are forced to dance to other tunes and serve purposes they cannot comprehend."

Julian was a former soldier. "That is the most ridiculous—" His eyes shifted to look over her shoulder.

She turned. Edward was approaching, but he wasn't looking at them, he was staring out the windows. He spoke as if one of them had said something.

"It's too late to ask questions."

Julian said, "But—"

"No. There's only faith left now." Edward glanced briefly at him and held out a hand, but his attention went back to the garden.

Julian ignored the hand. "Just tell me why—"

"No. Good-bye, Julian. Thank you." Edward put his arm around Alice as if to lead her away.

"Thank me for what? I haven't done a thing, and——"

"You will." Edward steered Alice over to the wall. "If you stand back here in the shadows you should be safe. Don't draw attention to yourself."

She put her hand over his. It was icy. His face was rigid.

"Edward! What's . . ." She grabbed his shoulders as he tried to leave. "What are you going to do now? Tell me!"

"You must have faith, too." He flashed her a grotesque smile and left her there, heading for the windows. His sort might die of fright, but it would be on its feet, doing its duty.

The ghastly green moonlight was fading fast. She folded her arms tightly around her and watched as he stepped over the sill. He strode through the weeds and brambles, hastening to the patch he had cleared earlier.

She had thought Julian was leaving, but he changed his mind and came and stood beside her. Neither spoke, but her hand found his to hold. She was grateful for the company.

Dimmer and dimmer grew the light. The night seemed to close in, growing colder as well as darker. Edward was standing with his arms folded, waiting, barely visible through the branches. Waiting for what? Clocks in the Vales were primitive contraptions. With no uniformly accepted standard time, how did one set up an appointment? *Meet me when Trumb eclipses* would do very well. Waiting for whom?

It could not be Zath. He would not have let her stay if he expected Zath. He did anticipate trouble or danger. No one had ever said that his campaign would be anything other than dangerous, but she had been thinking that the threat was still a few days off. The sudden urgency had caught her unaware. It could not possibly be Zath, the main event. It must be vital, or Edward would not have been so tense. She said a small prayer. *Lord, two men I loved have been taken from me. Be with him and keep him safe.*

Another man stood in the clearing, facing Edward and about ten feet from him. He was slim, dark haired. . . . He had no clothes on.

Julian sucked in air through his teeth. "Tion! It must be!"

Alice edged closer to his side. Cold and tension were making her shiver. That boy out there would freeze to death unless he was using mana to keep himself warm, or unless he wasn't really there at all, just some sort of moving picture.

The Liberator and the Youth might be exchanging words, but if so they were too soft to hear. Then another figure . . . This man was larger, husky even, decently clothed and black bearded. That must be Karzon, the Man. Two more people appeared almost simultaneously. They were only vague shapes, but they could have been a girl in a blue robe and a mature woman in a red. That was what the mythology of the Vales would dictate.

"It won't work!" Julian whispered.

"Sh!"

"No Visek, see! The Five can never all cooperate . . . been squabbling for centuries . . . won't trust each other, let alone a . . ." His voice trailed away.

What was being said out there in that unworldly meeting? Alice would give

her front teeth to be allowed to eavesdrop. And where was the fifth, Visek? The
Free had a legend that the Liberator had met with the Parent in Niol. As far as
Alice knew, Edward himself had never described such a meeting. The story was
attributed to Dosh—the gospel according to St. Dosh.

The light had almost gone when the node shimmered again and the gap in
the circle was closed by two more figures. Their arrival showed only because
they were wearing white or something close to it. Starlight glimmered on silver
hair. Seven people—the Liberator and the Pentatheon.

"There!" she whispered. "He's got all of them!"

Julian snorted. "He'd be crazy to trust them. And why in hell should they
trust him?"

"You think he's asking for their help? He wants to borrow their mana?"

"What else? But all he has to offer them in exchange is Zath removal, and
they have to gamble that he'll pay them back afterward. They'll stick with the
devil they know."

Alice did not reply. She had no idea, really, but she was confident that Edward
had worked it out a long time ago, before he even started his crusade. He had
gambled his life to arrive at this one point, so he would not let the Pentatheon
cheat him out of everything he had won. Yet they must know he had his back
against the wall. Events were rushing to a climax and if he needed their help, he
needed it now or never. That was not a good bargaining position.

Have faith!

The darkness was total. This, above all, was the time when the reapers pursued
their grisly work, when Zath might be distracted by the inflowing surges of
mana. Was that another reason to choose the eclipse as the time of meeting?
Starlight showed only as a gleam on rimy branches and on the walls around the
courtyard. Whatever was happening, whatever was being negotiated, the scene
was invisible and inaudible. She wanted to run out there and shout, "You can
trust him!"

For Edward *was* trustworthy. An Englishman's word was his bond. That creed
had been drummed into him all his life, and no one believed it more strongly
than he did. If he borrowed mana on a promise of returning it later, then he
would do exactly that, even if it killed him. He would repay every penny of it.
Yet how could those age-old pseudogods ever believe that? He had set out to
prove himself to them, but why should they believe? Far more likely, they would
judge him to be what they were themselves—sly, devious players of the Great
Game. The whole point of that game was to lie and cheat. It would be no fun
at all if a promise could not be broken at will.

"This is crazy!" Julian muttered at her side. "They'll cross their hearts, but
when the chips are down, they'll pull the plug on him and leave him holding
the bag." Metaphors were never his strong suit.

"Wait!" she said.

They had no choice but to wait. Even the fire had disappeared. They stood
in darkness, broken only by faint outlines of windows. She could not have found
the door had she wanted to. Oh, what a wonderland this Alice had found! She

did not belong here in the dark and cold, on another world, meddling in tumultuous events; she never had. She should return to her own place soon, as soon as possible, if indeed it was still possible at all, for the Service had collapsed. The old Church of the Undivided had been overthrown and Edward obviously intended his new church, whatever it would be called, to be a populist movement with little place for world-jumping elitist strangers. Go Home. She tried to frame a prayer in her mind, for the act of putting her fears and wants into words often clarified her thinking. First, let the good triumph here on Nextdoor. Let Edward survive, his purpose achieved. Go Home, yes—she did not belong here. Go Home with Edward . . . yes again, wonderful! If he still wanted her. His name was still on a murder warrant, but the trail was cold, and perhaps Miss Pimm could solve the matter anyway. Norfolk? The cottage? It would be spring there now. London was gorgeous in spring, and this first spring after the war it should blossom beyond imagining. But neither prospect thrilled her. Africa did; return to Nyagatha. The war was over; it should be possible. No warrant would find them there. Heat and starkly brilliant sunshine and the scenes of their childhood. That was really Home. *Thy will be done, but if I had my dibs, Lord, it would be that.*

The light had begun to return. The trees came first, then the roofs and the general shape of the courtyard. Soon she made out the ghostly glimmer of Visek's robes, the pallor of Tion's bare flesh. The circle was still there, still presumably negotiating—the Liberator and the six who made up the Five.

Tion sank gracefully to his knees. Mana rippled. Then more. Julian gasped. The node writhed with surges of power, wilder and wilder until reality itself seemed to twist and the house undulated. Karzon went down, then the Maiden, the Lady . . . and finally, slowly, the two who were together Visek. A silent thunderstorm of mana rolled through the courtyard, dim flickers of sepulchral color playing over the kneeling Pentatheon and the one triumphant figure looming over them.

"My god!"

Edward Exeter stood in the clearing and the paramount sorcerers of the Vales knelt before him, fulfilling the prophecy: *They shall bow their heads before him, they will spread their hands before his feet.* Then, suddenly, everything vanished again into darkness, blacker even than before.

Alice and Julian had their arms around each other, although she could not recall who had started it. "He's done it! They have agreed to help!"

"Shush! And don't be so bloody sure! I wouldn't trust any one of that lot as far as I could throw a battleship."

The scene changed almost too fast to register, the Five gone and Edward trudging back to the windows. Alice ran forward to meet him as he stepped over the sill. She hugged him. He drooped in her arms like a man exhausted. There was no doubt now—he was shaking. Relief, of course!

"You did it!"

He sighed, leaning his head on her shoulder. "Think so," he mumbled.

"Oh, Edward!" There was nothing else to say. Just hug him, hold him.

He endured her embrace without returning it. She discovered she wanted to tell him to get a good night's sleep, so he wasn't the only one suffering from reaction. She had not realized how taut her nerves were. She clung as he made a halfhearted effort to break away.

"Things to do, Alice."

"But the worst is over, isn't it?"

He made a sound that was half a laugh and half a sob. "The worst hasn't even started."

She looked at him in alarm and did not like what she saw. His forehead was beaded with sweat like dew.

"What more? What happens now?" she demanded.

He shook his head. "Have faith, remember?" Then he did laugh, a bitter, hollow laugh. "What does it matter? Even if Zath wins, he can't stop what I've started. The Five can't. They've pushed their own theology so long that they have no idea how flexible faith can be. Even if I die tomorrow, some people will go on believing I brought death to Death in some mystical way. *I am the resurrection,* or something. They'll find a faith to fit."

"Stop that! You're going to fight and win."

He pulled free and straightened up to his full six feet. "Even if I do, what do you suppose they'll make of it all? What will the Church of the Liberator be like a hundred years from now? Religions don't spring up fully armed. They sprout, they grow, they change. They split off heretical sects and persecute them until the best creed wins." His voice was dangerously shrill. "As soon as the Caesars stopped torturing Christians, Christians tortured Christians. What would Jesus of Nazareth have thought of the Inquisition? What would Saint Paul have said to a Borgia Pope? Will the Free do that now? Or have I convinced them enough? Do they believe my lies about the Undivided? Have I convinced anyone? Who really believes in that hodgepodge god of mine?"

"I do."

"No, you don't!"

"Yes, I do! Details don't matter. The principle does. I believe a god sent you to them."

He studied her for a moment, as if trying to decide how serious she was. Then he forced a smile. "Wish I did, but thanks anyway." He kissed her.

Well! If that was the best kiss he could manage at his age, she ought to be ashamed of herself. She pulled him back to her and showed him what a real kiss was. Eventually he put his arms around her and cooperated clumsily.

Afterward he just said, "Oh!" For a monosyllable it seemed to convey an awful lot of meaning.

"You need lessons." She was breathless herself.

"Would you give me lessons?"

"Gladly, oh gladly!"

He glanced around the big, empty room. Julian had gone. Another man stood in the doorway, leaning limply against the jamb as if he had just run over Figpass. It was only Dosh, with his blond hair awry and some lurid welts across his face—

how long had he been there? Why did little Dosh look so sinister, so ominous, waiting there?

Edward shuddered and broke free from her embrace. "Too late. Time to go."

"Not just yet!"

He took a step or two and stopped. He looked back unwillingly and bared his teeth in a snarl. "I have to go, Alice. Got a job to do. I promised. God knows I don't want it but I asked for it and I can't evade it now."

"What job? Promised what? Promised whom?"

"Pray for me," he whispered.

Then he turned and hurried over to join Dosh. The two of them went out together.

ℰℛℛ 58 ℛℳℛ

THERE WAS PRICKLY GRASS IN HIS FACE, AN EARTHY SMELL IN HIS NOSTRILS. The back of his head thumped a sickening beat, keeping time with his heart. He was cold.

"I don't think you should lie there like that, love," said a man's voice. "It isn't good for you, and it's likely to get a great deal worse very shortly."

Dosh groaned. If he spoke he would throw up, or die. Dying would be better. He opened his eyes a crack and made out a bare knee close by. He closed them and tried not to groan again.

"I suppose I can waste a little more mana on you, just for old times' sake," Tion said. "There, how's that?"

Cool fingers touched his scalp. The pain and nausea disappeared. Dosh felt infinite relief and then shame at having accepted a favor from the sorcerer. "Go away."

"Oh, I shall! But I do think you ought to make yourself scarce, too, lover. They're going to tear you into small pieces if they catch you."

Dosh raised his head. He could hear a strange, low roaring noise in the distance. Like a waterfall. He did not know what it was. Come to think of it, he didn't know what he was doing here or how he had come here or even where here was.

Keeping his face averted from the sorcerer, he scrambled to his feet. Trumb blazed green in the sky again, drowning out the stars, shedding its unholy light on the peaks of . . . er, Thargwall. Yes, this was Thargvale. He was in a meadow, just below the wood where the Free were camping. He turned around to look for the two lonely bristlenut trees, and they were right beside him. This was the rendezvous he'd set up with . . .

He spun around. "D'ward? Where's D'ward?"

Tion was on his feet also, wearing the same appearance as before, the dark-haired boy of ethereal beauty. He shrugged. "Almost at the river. But I think you ought to worry more about those irate peasants, lover."

Reluctantly, suspecting a trap, Dosh glanced again toward the woods. It was shedding a tide of stars, a dark flood full of twinkling lights, flowing down the hill. The roar was growing louder. The dark mass was . . . people with torches.

"The Thargians! They took D'ward?"

"Well, of course. They cracked you on the head. You're of no value to them. You are to me, of course, lover, but not to them. They broke your skull with a sword hilt. Didn't want to get the blade dirty."

"But it was a parlay!" He had delivered the Liberator's message. He had promised that the Liberator would come in person to confirm the agreement, as D'ward had told him to. They had agreed on these two trees as a landmark. . . .

"Dosh, Dosh! You know Thargians!"

"They took him! They're taking him to Tharg?"

Tion rolled his eyes. "I can't heal stupidity, lover."

"They can't kidnap the Liberator! He'll perform a miracle. He'll escape!"

"No he won't. He promised not to."

"Promised who?"

"Me—and my associates."

Filthy lies! Who would ever believe Tion?

"The river?" Dosh looked at Mestwater, a brilliant silver highway looping through the valley. It was in flood, deadly—but it would lead to Thargwater and then the city. "They've got boats?"

"Even ephors can't walk on water, Dosh, dear."

Treachery! If the Thargians had boats ready, then the perfidy had not been a sudden impulse. The swine had planned it. Rescue? Rescue! There might be time for the Free to overtake them before they reached the water with D'ward and were swept away to safety.

He had taken two steps when Tion's hand closed on his shoulder and effortlessly stopped him in his tracks. "Think, Dosh, think! Somebody saw you. They're coming already. But I really don't think they want your help now, darling."

"But—"

"Think! You haven't forgotten verse two twenty, have you? 'In Nosokslope they shall come to D'ward in their hundreds, even the Betrayer'? Where did you enlist, Dosh?"

Dosh screamed. "I was only doing what D'ward told me to!"

"But they don't know that, do they, dearest?" Tion chuckled. "You were seen leading D'ward out of the camp. Now the Thargians have got him. What would you think? If you want to die horribly, then I suggest you stand pat, and your wish will be granted very soon. If you want to live, then your best course is to get down to the river before the last boat leaves and before D'ward's friends can catch you."

The lights were much closer. The roar was louder, and distinguishable now as the sound of mob fury. Being a loner, Dosh had always hated mobs. Panic! He turned and sprinted downhill, running as hard as he had ever run in his life, leaping and stumbling over the rough pasture. When he came to a stone wall, he hurdled it recklessly and kept on going. His shadow raced ahead of him. The river was a hatefully long way away.

Tion loped along easily at his side. "I did warn you that you shouldn't deliver the message, didn't I, dear? I told you it wouldn't do you any good."

Dosh tripped, regained his balance, and went on. He thought he could feel a stitch starting in his side. He had no breath to argue with the evildoer.

"I did tell you D'ward was being nasty to you, didn't I?"

And so had D'ward. D'ward had warned Dosh that the mission might kill him. He had known.

Dosh ran. He had always hated mobs. They would never give him a chance to explain. He thought of Tielan and Doggan, of Bid'lip. . . . They wouldn't stop to listen to reason or explanations. It wasn't fair. But he'd always done best when he expected the worst. D'ward knew the truth. If he could get to D'ward, he would be all right.

It wasn't D'ward's fault, it was Tion's. If Tion had left him lying unconscious in the field, then the Free would have found him like that and known he hadn't helped the Thargians. He would have been a *betrayed,* not the *Betrayer.* He ran. D'ward had known the physical danger. He had foreseen the probability of Thargian violence. He couldn't have expected Tion's meddling.

The river was closer. Dosh looked around, and the pursuit was closer also. There were hundreds of them, spread out now. Some of them would be younger and faster than he. The leaders carried no torches, and they were gaining on him rapidly. It would only take one stripling to bring him down and let the others catch up.

"A little more to the left," Tion said quietly, "over by those sheds." That was the last Dosh heard of him. At some moment after that, the sorcerer disappeared. Soon, though, Dosh made out the Thargians, two or three score of them, dragging boats across the grass to the river. The boats had been beached for the winter, pulled up high, away from floods. As he ran, he watched one after another being launched and swept away in the swirling torrent. He could not see D'ward, but he would have been loaded into the first. Tree trunks and ice floes and ice-cold water: Without a boat, the river was death.

Reeling and gasping, he arrived at the bank just as the last boat was loading. The men were armored and armed. A couple of them drew their swords. Somewhere he found breath enough to scream, "They'll kill me!" in Lemodian, which was close to Thargian. Men laughed, but someone shouted an order. The soldiers sheathed their blades and vaulted over the side as the dory began to move. Dosh splashed through water so cold that it burned his legs. He grabbed hold of the gunwale and tumbled over it headfirst.

Howls of fury and frustration from the shore faded swiftly into the distance as the little craft was seized by the current and swept away on its long trek to Tharg.

ℰ℩ℭ 59 ℘℩ℭ

WHATEVER EDWARD WAS DOING, ALICE KNEW SHE COULD BE NO HELP, only hindrance, but she wished she knew what it was, where he was. She strongly suspected he had set off for Tharg already, with only Dosh to keep him company. That would explain Dosh's mysterious errands—filching a couple of rabbits and concealing them somewhere.

Lugging her bedroll along on her shoulder, she went in search of the feast. She investigated two or three campfires, hoping to find Julian, Ursula, or anyone she knew who could speak English. In a community of thousands, that was not very easy. Eventually her hunger drove her to join a group of—she thought— Lappinians. They jabbered at her cheerfully, laughed at her halting efforts to reply in Joalian, and presented her with a slab of roasted meat on a scrap of bloody hide as a plate.

It was disgusting and absolutely delicious. She ate all the meat, handed the skin on for someone else to use, and licked her fingers. A woman offered her a rib to chew on, but she declined with thanks. She had a strong desire just to lay out her blanket and go to sleep. Her eyelids weighed tons.

On the other hand, her nerves were still jangled and jumpy. She heaved her bundle up on her shoulder again and renewed her search. She had not reached the next campsite when the shouting began. It spread like ripples on a pond. Soon the whole camp was in an uproar, people racing around howling and waving torches that threatened to set the entire hill on fire. Unable to understand a word of what was going on, she just stood her ground, a rock in a whirlpool, and watched the faces streaming by. Were the Thargians attacking already? Should she flee with the mob or go to the house for a last stand?

Then a woman with carroty red hair going past in a shrieking crowd . . . Alice grabbed her arm.

"You speak English?"

The woman glared at her, then at her vanishing companions.

"Yes, *entyika*. I must go."

"Just tell me what's happening!"

She did, then she ran.

In some sort of herd reflex, Alice found herself racing down the hill with thousands of others. The night was a madhouse. People were falling and being trampled, screaming, yelling. Others were pushed by the mob into the freezing river. A few crazier souls went as far as the Thargian army camp, four miles away, and were repulsed with heavy casualties. It was useless, of course. The mob rampaged along the flooded meadowland for hours, but their Liberator had long gone.

As the sky began to brighten toward a chilly dawn, Alice trudged wearily back into the grove. The fires had gone out, the landscape looked as if a plague of Brobdingnagian locusts had slept in it. Not many people had. Now they were returning, as she was, broken and bewildered. Exhausted children clung to their parents and wept. Lost children howled in terror for theirs. Adults prowled the ruins in search of scraps left over from the feast.

Someone was trying to restore order, though. Tracking down the shouts, she found a shield-bearer, but it was Kilpian Drover, who knew no English. She could just make out enough of his words to understand that he was trying to collect all the Niolians.

Farther up the hill, Ursula Newton was bellowing for Joalians, Lemodians, and Nagians. There was nothing wrong with her voice, but her eyes were red-rimmed pits, her hair a briar patch, and she obviously had not slept. She paused, leaning on her pole and staring blearily at Alice.

"You heard what happened?"

"I heard. Can any boat survive in that torrent?" That was the first danger—that the fates had made a mockery of human ambitions once again and the Liberator was floating facedown in some weedy backwater, his mission forever incomplete. (But mana should have taken care of that danger, shouldn't it?)

Ursula pulled a face that declined comment. Then she seemed to change her mind. "It's possible. That river's flowing forty miles an hour or I'm a Dutchman. He could have reached Tharg hours ago."

"So what are you doing?"

Another pout. "I'm carrying out the last orders he gave me. I'm to lead the exodus to Joalia. Can't leave the kiddies here for the Thargians."

Alice looked over the group Ursula had collected so far and concluded that she might be several hundred short, although who knew how many Joalians had come to join the crusade? "Will they let you go?"

"Can't know till we try. Excuse me." She started shouting at a group of men, gesturing vigorously with her pole. They nodded reluctantly and moved off, separating and starting to shout in their turn. "Bid'lip and Gastik are taking the Niolians. Don't know who else is doing what the hell else." She thumped the end of her pole at a helpless rock a few times. "Shite, what a mess! I hope those ambassadors come through with the rations they promised."

"And that the Thargians cooperate too. Who's staying here?"

"Don't know. I imagine Eleal Highpriestess will be wanting to put her temple in order. Don't know if the Thargians will allow that either, of course."

Alice rubbed her eyes and thought about it. "That will probably depend on what happens when Edward gets to Tharg, won't it? Once he's killed Zath, he won't have to tolerate backtalk from the ephors."

Ursula responded with long bellows of, "Joalians! Here, Joalians!" like a bull elk summoning his harem. She resumed the conversation in her normal voice, eying Alice pensively. "You really think he's still alive?"

"I'll believe it until I know he's dead."

Mrs. Newton pursed her lips skeptically. She was a hardheaded, practical woman, not given to wishful thinking. Julian detested her for some reason he would not discuss, but she would do as good a job as anyone could in shepherding a few thousand pilgrims back to their homes.

She said scornfully, "With the mana he had, the Thargians should never have been able to ambush him, you know. And certainly not overpower him. Doesn't that suggest that it was Zath's doing?"

"Why abduct him? Why not just kill him and leave his body for the Free to find?"

"I don't know." Ursula sighed. "Because Zath wants a public execution in Tharg, perhaps. It'll take a few days for them to get back with the news."

Ah! "Someone did go?"

She nodded absently. "I heard Doggan, Tielan, and Julian. Possibly Dommi. They may have had a few others with them, I don't know. They found a boat farther upstream. Shouted to someone as they went by."

Alice's knees trembled with weariness. If she didn't sit down soon she would fall down. She compromised by leaning against a tree.

"That doesn't sound like enough people to stage a rescue, and I don't imagine Edward needs rescuing anyway. I mean, if he overcomes Zath and gets all his mana—that is what's going to happen, isn't it?"

Ursula was peering around as if to spy out ill-intentioned Joalians hiding in the bushes. "I don't think rescue was uppermost in their minds. They wanted to catch that scummy, yellow-haired Tinkerfolk pervert and knot his guts round his throat."

"What? You mean Dosh?"

"Dosh! Dosh the Betrayer! He turned Exeter over to the Thargians—didn't you know that? Well he did! And if I ever get my hands on him, he'll rue the day he was born, I'll tell you. Where are you going? You want to go Home? There's a portal over in Thovale we know the key for."

Alice shook her head. "Not until I find out what happened. Are you quite sure Dosh . . ." The look in Ursula's eye was answer enough. But it still seemed incredible. "Edward valued Dosh very highly. He put him in charge of the money, remember."

"Christ trusted his to Judas!"

"Hell! So he did." Alice felt very, very weary. "Think I'll go up to the temple and help the bishop with the housework. If I don't ever see you again . . ."

They made a subdued farewell. Leaving Ursula Newton to her bull moose impressions, Alice dragged herself up the hill on aching feet.

60

THE SOLDIERS HAD APPARENTLY BEEN LAUNCHING THE BOAT STERN FIRST, because Dosh found himself in a pointed end, which he assumed was the bow. He huddled down on the thwart and hoped to be forgotten and overlooked—not an unreasonable ambition, for the helmsman would be fully occupied in trying to steer by moonlight and the four oarsmen must face the rear. His first thought was to pull off his wet boots and massage some life back into his toes, but he discovered he needed both hands just to hold on. Even then, the boat rocked and pitched so violently that he was hard put to stay on his seat. Besides, there was bilge slopping around already, so he might as well keep his boots on. Then something hit the side with a shuddering crash and the sergeant screeched something in Thargian.

Dosh realized it was intended for him. He also realized that the other four were not rowing, they were frantically fending off logs, ice, and other debris, using the oars as poles. Both ends of the boat were pointed; he was at the stern. A shower of spray half blinded him. The thwart tried to buck him overboard.

"Speak slowly!" he said and repeated it in Lemodian, which he had learned in bed from Anguan, four years ago.

One of the sweating troopers knew enough Lemodian to swear in it vividly. He concluded his invective with, "You want us to sink?"

Dosh turned his attention to the river. It was a ghastly heaving soup pot of black water, surging in glistening waves, frothing and juggling tree trunks, many of which were bigger than the boat, some still furnished with branches and roots. Uphill one minute, downhill the next. They wanted a lookout? No. When a trooper kicked a wooden bucket at him, he realized they wanted him to bail. He should have known not to expect charity from Thargians.

He reached for the bucket and promptly tipped headlong into the bilge and a melee of struggling men. Spluttering and cursing he sat up, edged back out of the crew's way, and began to bail.

He bailed until his arms were ready to fall out of their sockets, until the night became a nightmare of bailing. The ancient cockleshell sprang more leaks with every impact. Bilge surged back and forth, drenching him. One moment he was half afloat, the next he thudded down on the boards again, and then another wave would throw him over backward against the thwart.

Mestwater flowed into Saltorwater which flowed into Mid'lwater which flowed into Thargwater, spreading out to a great width, drowning fields and forests. The current seemed just as fast, if a little smoother. Collisions became less frequent—fortunately so, because the little craft was steadily settling lower in the water. The troopers began using their oars more for rowing and less for fending, struggling to keep the waterlogged boat in the main channel, away from the half-submerged trees and fences that marked its normal banks.

Dosh's cramped muscles moved more and more slowly. The bilge grew deeper, tipping the boat as it surged. Eventually one of the Thargians snatched the bucket away from him and started throwing water overboard at three times the rate Dosh had been managing. He hauled himself up on the thwart out of the way and curled into a knot to try and get warm.

The first light of morning was brightening the sky now, but a mist was rising from the river. A bridge came hurtling out of the fog. The sergeant screamed orders. Oars creaked in the oarlocks. The boat wallowed sideways, straightened, and hurtled between two piers on a long spout of water. The underside of the bridge shot over their heads with inches to spare, and they plunged down into foam. For minutes it seemed they must founder. Dosh clung to the gunwale to avoid being washed overboard. Then the man with the bucket gained on the flood and the boat was still floating. Another man took over the bailing.

Soaked and shivering, Dosh peered out at the ghostly fog and wondered about escape. The troopers were shouting and pointing, identifying landmarks. Obviously they were very close to Tharg itself now, but they were also very close to sinking. If they decided to lighten the boat, Dosh knew what they would throw overboard first. The water was running very close to the top of a levee, well above the countryside beyond. Vague shapes of trees and buildings loomed out of the murk and then vanished again.

The troopers were as exhausted as he was. The sergeant's yells grew louder and more urgent. The two men still rowing strained to obey and the helmsman leaned on a third oar, but their efforts had no effect. The irresistible river swept them straight for a levee—steep, muddy, and partially undercut, so that great trees had canted outward and overhung the water or floated in it like booms, still anchored by a few roots. The boat struck just upstream, stabbing into the mud, tipping perilously. The current spun the stern around into a tangle of branches and twigs, slapping and cracking over them. The Thargians threw themselves flat. As the boat began to pick up speed again, Dosh saw a thick trunk across his path and stood up.

The impact winded him, doubling him over. He scrabbled with frozen fingers as someone's head knocked his feet from under him. Then he was sprawled over the log and the boat had gone. His perch trembled ominously; black water raced past underneath him. He managed to get a leg up and lay there, nauseated and shivering, but safe from the Thargians.

★   ★   ★

The tree creaked and shuddered as more roots pulled free. He worked his way in along the trunk to the bank and clambered up to a footpath. The river raced by below him, and all the rest of the world was washed away to shadows by white mist. Deathly cold had seeped into his bones and his whole body was shaking. He must keep moving or freeze. He removed his boots to get the water out of them, then found his fingers were too stiff to retie the laces properly. Letting the boots flap, he began to jog. By the time he realized that he was heading toward Tharg, he had gone too far to think of turning back.

Besides, he probably had more chance of finding some food and shelter in the city than in the country. And there was D'ward. Unless his boat had sunk, he was probably in Tharg now, perhaps already confronting Zath. When the prophecy was fulfilled, he might have a moment for Dosh.

D'ward was his only hope. The Free assumed he had betrayed the Liberator. Why in the world would he ever do such a thing—for money? That was infinitely unfair, because it had been a Joalian's offer of thirty silver stars to betray the Liberator that had led Dosh to him in the first place. He hadn't taken that money, so why would he have changed his mind after all that D'ward had done for him? He must find D'ward to clear his name.

Tired, cold, starving, he staggered on as well as he could, muttering prayers through chattering teeth. As the day brightened, the fog grew thicker not thinner. Nothing was clear or solid anymore. His repentance had brought him no better luck than his former sins.

He met no one on the path; he seemed to inhabit a ghost world all his own. All the friends he had cherished would be against him now; he was a traitor to the Free and a heretic to the Thargians. The track became a road, then a street. His story was repeating itself. Four years ago he had come to Tharg with the Liberator. Then the ephors had been planning to execute poor old Golbfish, thinking he was the Liberator, and D'ward had wanted to take his place on the anvil. The Man himself had stepped in to stop him throwing his life away. Golbfish had died anyway, fulfilling the prophecy: *Shame! Shame! To the Man goeth D'ward, saying, Slay me! The hammer falls and blood profanes the holy altar. Warriors, where is thine honor? Perceive thy shame.*

Now D'ward was again coming to Tharg. . . . Had he planned this? He might have done. He had warned Dosh of the dangers of those orders, so he must have had an idea of what was going to happen. Would Karzon interfere again? But D'ward wasn't asking to be slain this time, was he? Or was he?

Which visit had been prophesied?

Ugly, ugly city! Narrow streets, houses like fortresses with barred windows and armored doors. The fog didn't really help, it just laid a wet dreariness over everything. Cheerless, gloomy place! Very few women to be seen, just smooth-faced, grim-faced Thargian men. Every one of them bore a sword, for only slaves went unarmed. They all wore the same brief tunics they wore in summer, scorning to cover their legs. Drab, brown colors. Drab, brown city. Fog.

Where to go? Dosh slunk from doorway to doorway, careful not to antagonize those strutting warriors, not even by meeting their eyes. He knew no one in Tharg. He did know where the Tinkerfolks' hole was, but anyone there would likely be some of old Birfair's band, and they would cut out poor Dosh's liver before he could speak a word. He doubted he could make it that far in any case. If he did not eat soon, he would faint. If he fainted, he would be thrown in the river or slapped into a chain gang.

"I see you made it." Tion was dressed like a Thargian youth, but only just, because his buttercup tunic was indecently skimpy and practically unlaced, while his soft leather half boots barely covered his ankles. The rapier at his belt, in contrast, reached almost to the cobbles. The too-beautiful face wore an authentic-seeming Thargian sneer.

Dosh leaned against a doorpost and shivered. The street rocked, wet clothing clung lankly to his skin. "Where is D'ward?"

"He's presently standing trial for blasphemy against the beloved gods."

"And what's going to happen next?"

"Well, he's not being very cooperative. I'll bet he'll be acquitted if you'll give me ten million to one." Tion simpered.

"And then?"

Mist swirled along the alley. The Youth moved closer, but grew no more solid. He draped an elbow against the wall and smiled down at Dosh. "You know the Thargians. A court can impose capital punishment for public farting if it wants to. They'll smash his brains out in the temple, right in front of Zath's statue."

"You, boy!" A burly Thargian had stopped in front of Tion.

Tion raised his classic eyebrows. "Warrior? How may I serve you?" He did not move from his languid posture against the wall.

"Fasten that tunic! It's indecent to expose yourself like that!"

"Oh, dear!" Tion sighed. "That is the whole idea. Do go home and disembowel yourself, Warrior."

The Thargian saluted smartly. "At once, Warrior!" He turned and hurried back the way he had come.

Tion shrugged. "Now, Dosh, darling, where were we?"

"D'ward came here to kill Zath!"

"So he did. And Zath is definitely going to die. He doesn't know it yet, but he is. Probably. He has become a serious nuisance. The problem is that D'ward is going to die too."

"No!"

"I'm afraid so, Dosh. It's a shame, don't you think? He's such a *nice* boy! But he's much too dangerous for the Pentatheon to let him live. He's too good at the Game! Why, in only four fortnights, he's managed to outmaneuver Zath himself, the greatest player of us all. Who knows what he might try next? D'ward must die, dearest!"

"No!"

The sorcerer displayed a hint of interest. "No? I promised ever so faithfully that I would not try to rescue him. I should hate to break my word on that, Dosh!"

Dosh shuddered. To trust Tion was insanity. He was total evil. He did not know what truth or fair-dealing were. "Can you rescue him?"

"Probably not. It would be very tricky. But if I were to try . . . What would it be worth to you, Dosh dear?"

"Anything! What do you want—my soul? My body?"

"Probably both," Tion admitted. "And your life too?"

"Yes!"

"My goodness! Love is a beautiful thing." The sorcerer held out a slender hand.

Dosh took it in his own, which Tion raised to his lips.

"Well, we'll see what we can do. It certainly won't be easy. I only say I'll try, not that it'll work. Now why don't you run on up to the temple and find a good spot to watch the proceedings? Close to the altar at Zath's end would be best. Very close. The crowds are starting to move already, so you'll have to hurry."

"You're coming?" Dosh demanded suspiciously.

"Not just yet. It would not be wise for me to come too close yet. But I do hope to see you there, love." A pained expression . . . "Trust me, Dosh! I haven't told you a lie yet. Not recently, anyway. Off with you now!"

History repeating . . . Isn't this the same trench of a street he came along four years ago? Then, too, he was following D'ward. The crowds were thicker then, but there are crowds now—a crackle of excitement in the air, people heading for the temple . . . Do they know of the Liberator, or does any public execution bring out the vultures? There is the Convent of Ursula, with the festoon of blue net over the door, unchanged. So much else has changed in four years. Here D'ward had brought Ysian. *Oh, Ysian, little firecat, it was your death that roused him!*

Crowd's growing thicker, almost no women. Yes, jostle me, see if I care. Draw your swords, it hardly matters now. All this swirling fog, is it real or is poor Dosh faint? People recoiling off him in disgust because his clothes are wet. The great square, with men hurrying across it like scurrying bugs. The huge pillars of the temple, tops almost hidden in the fog, giant granite cage, ugliest building in the world.

Cold, oh so cold. Poor Dosh. Is there any warmth left in the world? Has there ever been warmth since he left Amorgush's bed? Climbing the steps. Passing between two great plinths. The temple floor packed already, a-buzz with whispers . . . Karzon . . .

Zath . . .

The Man, taller than a tree, green-stained copper. The mighty bearded face with its hooked nose—a fair likeness—the hammer clutched against the brawny chest in two hands, the draperies of his wrap exquisitely rendered by the great

K'simbr Sculptor, trailing from the belt to the ground to support the weight, one foot forward, one shin bare. A noble work.

Turn, damn it, turn! Look at the other end of the great rectangle. The matching colossus in blackened silver, swathed in a cowled robe, one hand holding a marble skull . . . stooped, head bent, looking down on the altar. Splendid evil.

Shivering, teeth chattering, must go to that end, must meet Tion. Drums starting, crowd reacting, announcement coming. People don't like wet bodies against them, edge aside, let me through, not enough room to draw swords, ignore the looks, the oaths, the jabbing elbows. Getting closer.

The altar is an anvil, set on the plinth, a black altar, or is it all old blood? Coming to the edge of the steps, crowd jam-packed, unwilling to be pressed up onto the steps, closer to that awesome, dread god. Go on, look! Look up at the face of Death.

No, no!

Don't look again. Men coming out, priests coming out, coming around the base of the silver statue, soldiers. D'ward, bound, limp, bloody. What have they done to him? Roll of drums. Silence, hushed, pregnant. White fog, black fog. Is it only the crowd swaying or the temple? Proclamation.

"In the name of the ephors and people of Thargland, in the name of the Man, the heretic D'ward convicted of blasphemy and condemned to die on the anvil. To the glory of Zath, the Last Victor, so be it."

Rumble. Whispers. *Where is Tion? Can't see Tion. They have D'ward on the anvil.* The masked executioner with the hammer. Coming forward. *Where is Tion?! He tricked me.* D'ward prone on the great anvil. *Is he even conscious? They've beaten him. Can't fight Zath if he isn't conscious. So tiny below that titan. Evil, evil.* Black fog swirls. White fog swirls. Executioner coming forward. *Up, D'ward! Arise. Rise up like a giant, a giant of fog. Grapple with him. Choke him.* White fog, black fog. *Don't lie there waiting for the hammer! Rise as the Liberator, great as the One God. Tower over the temple, D'ward. Awe the crowds, D'ward. Seize the monster Zath. Crush him. Strangle him.* Feel the ground sway. Hear the people cry. *Help him, God. You are mightier, greater. Stand tall, D'ward. Fulfill the prophecy. Reveal the Liberator. Come, brothers, save him from the anvil. Leave him not there as the hammer falls. Cry out. Cry out. Let Karzon come striding over the multitude. Let Visek appear white as fog bright as sun through cloud. . . . They come. They come. See Eltiana red as blood, see blue Astina and her sword of justice. Shake the pillars. Heed the cries of the people, God. Zath trembles. He's failing. It's not enough. . . . Where is Tion? Where is the Youth? He needs you, Tion. Come now, Tion. Save him, Tion. Don't let him die, Tion. If you want me I am yours, Tion. Anything anything . . . Help him, Tion! Save him. . . .*

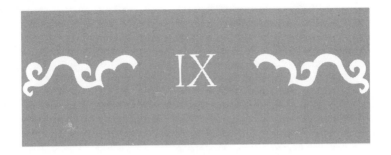

We can see why throughout nature the same general end is gained by an almost inÆnite diversity of means, for every peculiarity when once acquired is long inherited, and structures already modiÆed in many different ways have to be adapted for the same general purposes.

CHARLES DARWIN, THE ORIGIN OF SPECIES

61

TINY FLAMES FLICKERED IN THE DRY GRASS, STROKED THE SHREDS OF BARK, grew taller and braver, and reached up for the twigs. Alice blew. The bark began to burn hotter, brighter. She laid a thicker twig across the logs, then another. The fire uttered a crackle like a baby's first cry, and she sat back on her heels to admire her handiwork. There was something very satisfying in building a fire this way, much more satisfying than putting a sixpence in a gas meter. It came with the world. She began building a castle of thin branches. That should keep it going until she returned. Beyond the high and narrow windows, clouds blushed red in a winter sunset.

She stood up to survey her day's work. This chamber was now the refectory, by decree of Eleal Highpriestess, and for the time being would also serve as chapter house. It was a mess, but this morning it had been a disaster. The floor lacked so many of its tiles that not all Alice's hours of sweeping and scrubbing had made it look clean. Half the plaster had fallen off the rough stone walls; what was left resembled mange. The men had brought in four benches and a couple of tables they had found upstairs, badly worm eaten but apparently safe enough to use. Well, it wasn't the Savoy, but it beat camping in the woods. She hoped the chimney was not plugged with birds' nests.

Now for the little ritual she had promised herself. She walked out the door and along the corridor. Here the filth had been swept to the sides, leaving a narrow path in the center, but tomorrow or the next day it would be cleaned out properly. She passed the chapel, hearing a murmur of voices from Eleal and a translator as Br'krirg and some of his people received instruction. Someone— almost certainly Tittrag Mason—was chopping wood in the courtyard beyond, clearing out the firetrap. If the monotonous thumping did not bother Eleal, then it should not bother Alice. She peered morosely at the blisters on her palms. They were taking a long time to turn into calluses.

Arriving at the main door, which was only an archway with nothing to open or close, she was met by the cool evening breeze. The red-tinged clouds to the west were a sailor's warning if she had ever seen one, not that Nextdoor had any sailors to speak of. She did what she had come to do—walked out and stared down the long, overgrown driveway. It was deserted, as she had expected.

"You too?" Pinky Pinkney stood on the steps, resting one foot on a bulky roped bundle of sticks, calmly smoking a cigar. Where the blazes had he acquired that? Trust Pinky! There was an ax at his feet, though, and she could not deny that he had been pulling his weight these last few days, working as hard as any native.

He smiled smugly and blew a stream of smoke. "Watched roads never, um, get traveled. That isn't a very melodious proverb, is it? I really cannot imagine a road ever *boiling*, though, can you? Not that one, at any rate."

"This is the first time I've dared look. Three days at the very least, we were told, so I swore I would not start looking until the end of the third day." Alice felt unreasonably irritated at having been caught doing so, and even more annoyed at herself for making excuses.

"But four was described as much more likely, was it not? And six or seven quite possible. Considering the floods. And even that assumes that they did not stay more than an hour or two in Tharg. But where are my manners?" He took his boot off the bundle. "Do sit down, my dear Mrs. Pearson!"

She declined, being quite certain that the sticks would be an intolerably uncomfortable seat. Pinky replaced his foot on it and leaned an elbow on his knee to help support the cigar.

"I am reasonably confident that they will have decided to remain in Tharg. For a day or two. I should allow no less than two. So we may anticipate hearing the news, whatever it may be, from our local friends. Br'krirg has promised to inform us right away if he hears anything. Anything at all. Right away."

"I shan't mind, so long as they don't remain in Tharg permanently, six feet under."

He drew smoke, closing his eyes in rapture. "This is a concern, of course. A real concern. The hazards of the river journey disturb me more than the civil authorities do. Much more. But the other is a factor, definitely. Not under, by the way. Thargians cremate their dead. Almost all vales do."

That information was hardly comforting. "I must get back to work. I was lighting a fire."

He chuckled. "May I offer you some firewood, then? Very reasonable! My rates are competitive."

"I shall have to requisition funds from the temple bursar. Do we have one?"

"I am prepared to serve, if asked. When we have some funds. Ahem! I understand that you plan to return Home, Mrs. Pearson? Ultimately."

She felt her defenses rise like a drawbridge. "Well, that depends on what the news is when it comes." If Edward was now safe from Zath's murderous attentions and if he chose to settle down on Nextdoor and if that kiss had meant anything more than a farewell . . . "Possibly."

"Of course," Pinky said blandly, as if he were not capable of interpreting implications, which he certainly was. "That is understood. There is a portal in Thovale, only a day or so from here, which connects to a provisioned portal in the New Forest. The Goldsmiths were planning to use it. When they went Home on leave, you understand. The Peppers inspected it and confirmed that it is still in operational condition."

"What exactly is a provisioned portal?"

"One not actively tended by Head Office but with clothes and money to hand. Not one where you will drop in unexpectedly on a funeral. Or Divine Service, what? General consternation. Let us give thanks for this sign unto us! You are expected to restore whatever you take, mm? At your convenience. I should be happy to instruct you in the key. And guide you there of course."

"That is most kind of you, Mr. Pinkney." She would not have expected it of Pinky, somehow. She had underestimated him. Or overestimated him, if his interest was in watching her dance around in the nude. "My fire will be pining for attention, so I— *Someone's coming!*"

A rider had just turned the corner at the far end of the driveway. A rabbit, not a moa, so not military. Only one, but a rabbit was not a herd animal and chose its own pace. There might be others following.

"Bless my soul!" Pinky stood up straight. "Not one of ours, surely? Where could they have acquired a rabbit? They had no money. Cannot be one of ours."

The rabbit was halfway to the temple now, and a second had come into view behind it.

"Red hair!" Alice shouted. "It's Dommi!" She leaped down the steps and raced to meet him.

ᘒᕊ 62 ᘎᕗ

Halfway up the drive, Julian's rabbit saw the people ahead and tried to bolt off the road. Julian reined it in and just sat there, not sure if he was too weary to fight with the stupid beast any longer or too cowardly to help Dommi break the news. Soon a boy he did not recognize came trotting down the road, gangly and bare legged. He said something in Thargian, smiling and obviously offering to take charge of the rabbit. Utterly disinclined to argue, Julian exchanged places with him, and the boy rode the brute off to be confined somewhere. That chore complete, Julian had no choice but to totter up the driveway and join the wake. Lordy, but he was stiff! Also filthy, hungry, exhausted, and in dire need of a pint of bitter.

Alice was coming to meet him.

He saw that she knew.

When they met he hugged her. She accepted the hug, ear to ear.

"He did what he set out to do." He was surprised at the harshness of his own voice. "I don't think he would have . . . I mean, even if he had known what the result would be, he would have accepted . . . He would not have done things differently."

"He did know." She pulled back and looked at him. Only her pallor and a sparkle in her eyes betrayed her. "I'm sure he did. There is no doubt about Zath?"

"Well, there was no corpse. Not in public, anyhow. But the statue fell. I mean, that's pretty definitive, isn't it? There were many reports of former reapers confessing. I believe it, Alice: Edward killed him somehow. I'm convinced."

She was pale as a corpse herself, but her chin was steady. "And no doubt about Edward?"

He shook his head. "None at all."

She nodded and took his hand. "You must be all in! Come on up to the temple and we'll find you something to eat."

They began to walk. Her fingers were icy. He knew that she had not had much luck with men lately: her secret lover, her husband, even her former guardian the Reverend Roland—and now her cousin . . . foster brother. She must be used to bereavement, and she was certainly bearing up admirably. Wonderful pluck! Why wasn't she asking questions? Dommi could not have told her everything in those few minutes.

He found the silence unbearable. "Who are all those people?"

She smiled witlessly at a passing tree. "Believers! When the Free left, the army followed. As soon as they had gone, the locals began coming to investigate. The white-haired one's Br'krirg Something, a big landowner. He's been wonderful—sending men over to help with the clearing, providing food and tools and things. And Eleal's been giving him lessons in the new faith. We're short of Thargian speakers, but she can pretty much make herself understood, and he found some people who understood Joalian. They translate, sentence by sentence."

The Thargians would be the men with bare legs and the two women with shawls over their heads. That left Dommi and four of the Free, distinguishable even at that distance by clothing that was an obvious rag bag of castoffs. The group divided, the Thargians taking their leave with much bowing and curtseying, disappearing around a corner of the house. The others headed for the doorway.

Alice continued to chatter. "We've been terribly busy ever since you left! The place is almost habitable now apart from the beetles and I had no idea that Nextdoorian beetles had eight legs. The Thargian army did let the Free go and the ambassadors did come across with the food they promised, or at least they were doing so the first day. We haven't heard since, but we assume they're all safely on their way home now. And the few of us left here have been working our fingers to the bone getting the place Bristol fashion and Eleal makes a slamming good highpriestess. Even Pinky addresses her as 'Your Holiness'! Dommi says you cremated him?"

"That's the law there. I don't think he would have minded, do you? We arrived just after it happened. There was a frightful shemozzle, people fleeing in thousands, so it took us a while to fight our way through to the temple. . . . You want to hear all this?"

"Tell me everything."

They began to climb the steps. The others had disappeared inside.

"It was rather like a very local earthquake. Zath's statue collapsed, Karzon's turned on its plinth, some of the pillars shifted. The Convent of Ursula next door sustained some damage, and a couple of the minor shrines were badly hit. The rest of the city was not affected at all. In other words, it was pretty much confined to the node. Edward was right in front of the idol."

"In front of Zath?"

"In front of Zath. That's where they do all their executions. That idol was sixty feet high, Alice! The inside of it was masonry, covered with silver plating, and it collapsed like a heap of rubbish. Why there weren't a lot more deaths, I can't imagine. Apparently it rocked a few times, and the priests and people had enough time to run."

Her grip tightened on his hand. "And why couldn't Edward run?"

"He'd been laid out on the altar—"

"Bound?"

This was the part that did not bear thinking about, Exeter just lying there while it happened. "When we found him, his hands were tied, but his legs weren't. The witnesses agree he was conscious—although the buggers had roughed him up a fair bit, I'm afraid. So why didn't he run? Or at least roll off the anvil? I don't know. I can only assume he was too busy dealing with Zath somehow."

"Go on!" she said dully.

"Well. You know how they do it. The executioner uses the hammer of Karzon to crack the victim's skull. But he didn't hit Edward! When he raised his hammer, the temple began to shake. Zath's idol collapsed in a storm of dust and rubble. No one else was hit. Everyone else fled in terror, of course. Even more amazing, nobody was trampled in the panic. There were a few injuries, I heard, but no deaths."

"You found him?"

"We found him quite easily, lying beside the remains of the altar. He looked very peaceful." Julian concentrated on memories of the face, suppressing thoughts of the rest. "He couldn't have felt a thing. A big block crushed him; he must have died instantly." A marble skull the size of a potting shed—no wonder the damned statue had been unstable. "We just took him. The priests were too dazed to object. . . . I think everyone who was near the altar got blasted by mana—they were gibbering and babbling, not making much sense."

He paused to peer into the big chamber he remembered. It was swept and clean, furnished with some plank benches. The shield above the fireplace was the only decoration. The courtyard outside had been stripped of much of its jungle and now two rabbits were grazing on the rest. "By Jove, you've been busy here!"

"It was Pinky and Tittrag's doing. We call this the chapel. Eleal has designs for stained glass in the windows. It'll look very . . . Well, come along. The chapter house is this way."

A bloodcurdling scream echoed through the empty house.

Julian's nerves were at breaking point. He jumped. "What in hell was that?"

"I think," Alice said drily, "that Eleal Highpriestess has just been told."

An hour or so later . . .

Fire crackled irascibly in the fireplace, two candles twinkled on one of the tables, but most of the light still came from the windows. There were half a dozen or so people standing inside the doorway, all talking at once in a jabber of Joalian, Randorian, and English. Julian did not want to attend this inquest. He wanted to go away and lie down—sleep, yes, but mostly just stare at the ceiling for a fortnight and let his jangled thoughts settle. Alice seemed to want him, so he must stay.

"You are a most welcome sight, Brother Kaptaan."

He turned and looked blankly at the girl who had spoken. Recognition came as a sudden shock: a taller, older Eleal Singer. She had lowered her voice to a contralto and tied up her hair in a bun on top of her head. It suited her; she had pretty ears. Her robe was faded, patched, and threadbare as if discarded by some convent after generations of use, the staff she wielded like a jeweled crozier was only a pole and a loop of twig, and yet she portrayed real dignity. Her eyes were rimmed with scarlet, but she was in control of herself. Embarrassed by his failure to identify her at once, Julian bowed low.

"Thank you, Your Holiness."

She nodded graciously. "We seem to be assembled. Let us begin." She walked to the head of one of the tables—where the only chair in the room happened to be located—and thumped her staff on the floor for silence.

Dommi was recounting the boat ride in staccato Joalian. Alice said, "Where did you get the rabbits?" just as Prof Rawlinson exclaimed, "Captain Smedley!"

"Almighty God!"

Everyone jumped, turned, fell silent, bowed heads.

"We give thanks for the safe return of these, our brothers Dommi and Kaptaan and for the glorious news they bring us. Let us see Your purpose through our grief and may our joy at the destruction of the evil Zath be tempered by recognition of Your hand in all things. Guide our debate, we pray You, and lead us in the path of Your truth and justice. Amen."

"Amen," chorused the congregation. They shuffled to the benches along the sides of the table. Julian caught Alice's eye, and for a moment a twinkle of laughter shone amid the grief. This stripling bishop knew what she wanted! Eleal took the chair and called the meeting to order.

So it had come to this. Only nine of them left, out of thousands! Julian was seated between Alice and the intimidating bulk of Tittrag Mason, who completely hid Prof Rawlinson at the end. Opposite sat the saturnine Kilpian Drover, Pinky Pinkney, Piol Poet, and Dommi—whose freckles were barely visible through his windburn. The church itself was down to six, since Prof, Alice, and Julian himself were not officially disciples, not shield-bearers. Yet there were both natives and strangers gathered here, sitting as equals—that was one of Exeter's legacies. How long would it last? How long before Pinky had the Church of the Liberator knocked into shape? Charisma would soon bring back his bearers and silverware and freshly ironed sheets.

At the moment, the Church of the Liberator did not have two coppers to rub together. All religions began in poverty.

"We wish to hear the whole story," Eleal proclaimed. "But first, tell us of Brothers Tielan and Doggan who went with you?"

Julian did not want to talk at all, not to anyone, not for a long time, so he silently tossed the query to Dommi, who might even enjoy being raconteur.

"They stayed behind, Your Holiness, hoping to find the trail of the accursed Dosh Betrayer. They promise to return very shortly, having both received directives from the Liberator—as I did myself, and must attend to."

"We are glad to hear that they did not come to grief. Would you begin at the beginning now, please, Brother?"

Dommi spoke Joalian, with an occasional repeat in Randorian. When he wasn't strangling English, he was notably articulate, was Dommi. At his side, old Piol Poet scribbled frantically on scraps of paper, his nose almost on the table and his wispy hair in danger of catching fire from the candles. Pinky had his eyes closed; Kilpian Drover wore his usual morose expression, which didn't mean anything. Eleal was engrossed, but remembering to keep her chin up. Whatever Prof Rawlinson was doing was concealed by Tittrag's Himalayan mass. Alice . . .

Julian stole a few sideways glances at Alice. She was chewing her lower lip as she struggled to follow the story. He suspected she would decide to go Home now, for götterdämmerung had taken all the fun out of Olympus. In fact he would not be surprised if the station was abandoned completely. He really ought to take her off somewhere and tell her the whole story in English. He was just too tired. He was oppressed by guilt and sorrow. Why, why, why had he not guessed sooner what Exeter was up to? It was obvious now, but if no one else could work it out, then he wasn't going to tell them, not even her.

Dommi had run into trouble, hemming and hawing.

Julian stirred himself with a mental pitchfork. "I'll tell this bit. We loaded the Liberator's body onto a sheet of silver plate from the Zathian junk heap and carried him out of the temple. We stopped to rest outside, at the edge of the big square. A crowd gathered, and Dommi began preaching to them. He was absolutely wonderful! He told them of the death of Zath and the prophecy fulfilled and how the Liberator had laid down his life for it. He had them all weeping. He had me weeping, dammit! And I think he stumbled onto . . . No, I think he was inspired! He said, 'D'ward Liberator sacrificed his life to show us the way to the One True God, for now he assuredly has reached the top of the ladder and is united with the Undivided. By following his teachings we shall also climb until we are united with Him. He brought death to Death—not in the sense that our bodies shall not die but in the sense that death is no longer to be feared. We, too, shall become the Liberator. We, too, shall become God.' I think that should be the creed of our Church, Your Holiness."

Who had ever guessed that Dommi was so fluent in Thargian, or that he could be so convincing? Dommi was a miracle, and Exeter had seen that years ago. Julian had not. Eleal was another, of course. She was still inexperienced and impetuous, but she would soon grow out of that. Pinky would take her in hand.

Piol was busily writing down the new official creed, aided by Dommi and Eleal. Exeter would probably have hated it. He had never claimed to be Buddha or Jesus, but all sects must attribute perfection to their founders. Even Mohammed, although he had remained human, was a unique human.

Hesitantly, Dommi took up the story again, telling how the crowd had built a funeral pyre right there in the plaza. His voice broke and the room fell silent. The candles burned brighter in the deepening darkness.

Prof Rawlinson was eternally impervious to atmosphere. "And where did you find the rabbits?"

"Some of our new Thargian supporters provided them," Julian said. "They showered us with hospitality. Doggan and Tielan are still with them. You may expect a flood of pilgrims to arrive within days, Holiness."

Eleal nodded. Her eyes were brimming, but she recalled herself to her role. "We give thanks for this wonderful story."

Prof cleared his throat. "Three days ago?" he muttered in English. "It should be about time, shouldn't it?"

Alice gasped and looked at Julian.

He peered around Tittrag. "Time for what?" he snapped. "What are you implying?"

Rawlinson pursed his lips and blinked as if he had mislaid a pair of very powerful spectacles. "Come, come, Captain! We all know the model on whom Exeter based his actions. The saga is not yet complete."

Julian ought to be angry, but he was too numb to feel anything more than disgust. "If you're expecting a resurrection, Rawlinson, then you will be disappointed. Exeter isn't going to appear as Christ appeared to the Apostles, showing his stigmata. Exeter was smashed to pulp. We watched his body burn away to ashes. Don't be obscene." He leaned his head on his hands.

"You are overlooking the logic of the confrontation, Captain." Prof had assumed his lecturing mode. "Zath is dead, we agree. So Exeter killed him. So Exeter was the survivor and acquired all the mana. With that kind of power, it would be fairly simple to fake one's death, I am sure."

The Valians were looking puzzled, all except Dommi, who understood English. "I am assuring you, Brother Prof, that the person we found was most assuredly the *tyika,* and he was most assuredly dead. His face was not damaged. He had a birthmark on his leg, often which I have been observing when he was bathing."

"I remember it from school days," Julian said. "And I noticed it too."

The infuriating drawl would not be hushed. "Mana could simulate that. It would be easy enough to alter the appearance of some other corpse—"

"There were no other bodies."

Prof laughed. "Precisely! A most fortunate miracle? Or does it sound like the hand of our friend, taking charge of events when he had overcome the opposition and was free to exercise his powers as he wished?"

Sudden fury blazed up in Julian. He slammed a fist down on the table with a crack that made everyone jump—his right fist, which the Liberator had given him. "No!" he roared. "It sounds like plain, damned, good luck! I tell you that Edward Exeter was not a shyster! He would never stoop to that sort of deception. However powerful he became, he would not have been immortal, so to stage a resurrection would have been the cheapest sort of trickery. *He would not have done that!* Don't you see? Don't any of you see? He knew he was leading his Warband to their deaths in Niolvale, and he did so *because even then he knew that he would have to die himself!*"

Alice whispered, "Oh, no!"

"Oh, yes! Those were the only terms on which he would ever have sacrificed his friends. He wouldn't just send them over the top without him. He avenged his parents and all Zath's other victims, but he knew the necessary price and paid it. Zath died and so did he!"

Prof was shaken but not convinced. "Simultaneously? How is that possible? Where did the mana go?"

Julian wanted to scream.

"For heaven's sake, man—*Exeter didn't have any mana!* Haven't you worked it out yet? We all wondered how he could ever convince the Pentatheon to support him, to give him enough mana to win the battle. We all knew that the stronger he became, the less likely that they would ever trust him."

Pinky's eyes were open wide, for once. "And how did he persuade them to trust him?"

"He didn't!" Julian shouted, leaping up. He was horribly afraid he was about to start weeping as he had wept in Tharg, as he had wept when he was shell-shocked. Shell shock felt just like this. He yelled louder. "He summoned the Five here, to that courtyard. Alice and I saw them, right out there. But he didn't ask for their help. He didn't ask them to trust him. *He* trusted *them!* He didn't beg mana from them. *He gave them his!* All of it. That was why the Thargians were able to arrest him and drag him off to a fake trial and beat him and take him to be executed. He had no mana left! Zath had never thought of that gambit. Nobody had. But Edward planned it right from the beginning, as the only so-lution to the problem. Remember the prophecy that the dead would rouse him? He saw the war in Flanders. If millions of ordinary men could lay down their lives to defeat an evil cause, then he would do no less, and he could avenge his parents and the friends who had died. . . ."

He took a deep breath and forced himself down on the bench again, shivering like the guv'nor when his malaria took him. "Zath must have been horribly puzzled when his mortal foe was delivered to him bound and helpless. He must have suspected a trap. And while he was engrossed in watching Exeter die, the Five took the chance that Exeter had given them, and the extra mana he had given them, and *they* killed Zath!"

He stopped, choking. Alice put a hand on his arm.

"You imply that they cooperated?" Pinky asked dubiously. "The Five?"

"They had to! Edward had left them no choice, because the winners would share out Zath's mana, so none of them could afford to be left out. They took the only opportunity they would ever get to deal with Zath. The opportunity Exeter gave them as a gift, no strings attached."

After a moment, Prof said doubtfully, "I suppose that is possible. But . . . You'd have thought one of them would have had the common decency to save the Liberator's life."

"That bunch? Oh, no! They don't know what gratitude is. And they certainly did not want Exeter running loose again. He could play their game better than any of them. He would have gathered more mana next year and then pulled them all into line, at the very least. They got rid of the two men they feared at one stroke. I bet they're all celebrating like a bunch of drunken sailors."

But they would never again make the mistake of permitting human sacrifice. That was one good thing.

"Julian is correct," Alice whispered. "There was another prophecy, you see. A gypsy told him he must choose three times: honor or friendship, honor or duty, and finally honor or his life. He chose honor every time. He knew he must die."

This time the silence was longer. At last Pinky said, "I do believe we should speak in Joalian. Holiness, brothers, we were just discussing the evil sorcerers, and how much they may have come to the Liberator's assistance. We conclude that they did not, of course."

"They are doubtless rejoicing in their wickedness," Eleal agreed majestically. "But the good shall triumph, as the One wills."

"Yes, it will," Julian said hoarsely. Tears ran cold on his cheeks; he felt nauseated, ashamed of his outburst, ashamed that he could not conceal his grief as the others could. "And they don't know the power of an idea. What D'ward has left us is a church built on a true historical event, whereas the pagans' beliefs are merely legend and deceit. We must build in his memory." There would be persecutions and martyrdoms, and the church would feed and grow on them. . . .

"I believe—" Piol Poet said. From somewhere he produced a wad of papers and began to thumb through them. "I believe I have some . . . Ah! Yes, these were words the Master spoke regarding a church." Holding a sheet dangerously close to the candle and his nose even closer, he read, "In Jurgvale on Thighday, the Master said:

" 'Is not a church a living thing? It is conceived in union, when a father drops a seed in a ready womb. It comes forth in pain and blood, and they smile who hear its first cries. Is not a church like a child, for it grows and changes and makes errors and learns? Is not a church like a young person, zealous and vigorous to improve the world, but apt to blunder into violence? Is not a church like a mother, who should love her children but not smother them? Is not a church like a father who should defend and discipline his family without hurt to them or others? Is not a church like anyone of us, who may grow in wisdom and compassion or sink into lazy and meaningless old age? Wherefore judge faiths as you judge persons. If they are greedy for gold, spurn them. If they lie, deny them. If they threaten, defy them. If they slay or harm or persecute, seek other counsel, for a false guide is worse than ignorance. And if they repent, forgive them.' "

Julian could recognize Exeter's sentiments, but the actual words were Piol Poet's. The evangelists were ornamenting already.

Eleal was beaming at the old man. "Assuredly, that was his hope. He entrusted me to guide his followers here in Thargvale, and he instructed Ursula Teacher to found a temple in Joalvale."

"And he directed me to do so in Niolvale," Dommi said quietly. "I have been remiss, but I shall leave at dawn."

"And you, Kaptaan?" the high priestess inquired.

Julian shook his head. How shameful his repeated lack of faith seemed now! He had never truly trusted Exeter—he who had known him since boyhood. Oh, how he wished now that he could call back those angry words he had spoken after the death of the Warband at Shuujooby! "I am no shield-bearer, Holiness. In fact, I have never even been formally baptized into the Church. I ask now for that honor, although I do not feel worthy of it."

She gave him her best reverend-mother smile. "Indeed your request will be granted! Is there one among us you would especially ask to perform this sacrament?"

Julian looked hopefully at Dommi.

Dommi beamed wider than ever. "I shall be most honored, Brother Kaptaan!"

Eleal nodded approvingly. "In his last words to me, the Master said that he hoped you would go into Randorvale and found a church, Kaptaan, because he thought you would be a very great apostle. We have one shield with no bearer. He said that if the previous bearer did not return to claim it, then it was to be yours. It is the most cherished shield of all, for it belonged to the holy Prat'han, first among the Warband."

For a moment Julian just stared at her. Then he babbled, "I should like nothing better than to take the Church of the Liberator into Randorvale. I shall be honored." Yes, he would take on Eltiana and her gang and stuff Edward Exeter down their throats. And one day he would burn her filthy brothel temple and dance on the ashes. If it took him a thousand years.

"Previous bearer?" growled Pinky. "You mean Dosh Betrayer, of course? Was that his shield? I just hope he had the grace to hang himself, like the original Judas."

Unfair! It was possible, of course, that Dosh had taken silver from the Thargians to betray Exeter, but Julian was fairly certain that he had only been following orders. In order to deceive Zath, Exeter had been forced to deceive everyone else as well. It would be better not to say anything to damage the burgeoning legend. The calumny would not matter unless Dosh himself showed up, and he must know that he would be torn to pieces if he did. Better to have poor Dosh remembered as a traitor than to admit that the Liberator had set up his own martyrdom. Julian decided he must tell no one about that, not even Alice.

Nor even Euphemia. But on his way to Randorvale, he would stop in at Olympus and assure her that he had meant all the promises he had made in his letter. And he would hold her to hers. No one had suggested that the Liberator's clergy were required to be celibate.

ᏐᏒ 63 ᏖᏋ

W HEN THE USUAL WAVES OF NAUSEA AND DESPAIR HAD FADED AND HER muscles stopped trying to knot her up like a string bag, Alice gingerly raised her head to survey the clearing. It was very small, tightly encircled by dense trees and shrubbery. There was blue sky above her and dew below. The fresh air on her skin was a little too fresh for comfort, but this was an April morning in England. She could probably have guessed that from the smells alone. By the time she had struggled to her knees, she had spied violets, primroses, and cowslips. The branches were dipped in the first green fuzz of spring, and a cuckoo hooted its demented refrain not far off.

Muttering, "Too true!" she staggered to her feet.

The hut was so small and overgrown that she might have overlooked it had she not been told of its existence. The key, they had said, was in the squirrel hole in the third tree to the left. The Service had never outgrown a juvenile obsession with cloaks and daggers.

Half an hour later, she was trudging north in clothes that were at least a generation out of date, but the buttoned boots fitted tolerably well and she had several gold sovereigns in the pocket of her coat. A lorry driver gave her a lift into Southampton and was much too polite to inquire why a lady should be tramping the New Forest dressed for a masquerade ball. Such things had never happened before the war.

She took the train to Waterloo and crossed London by bus, breaking her journey to visit Thomas Cook and Son and inquire about passage to East Africa. At Liverpool Street, she caught the 4:15 for Norwich with seconds to spare. The travel information would wait; she divided her time between a selection of newspapers and just staring out the window. England had not changed in two months, not as much as she had. Spanish flu was raging again, although in a less deadly form. It had almost killed the American president.

On another world, it had killed Zath.

By evening, she was sitting in a rattling, wheezing taxicab, bound for her cottage. The driver himself belonged in a museum. He looked too old to know much about trains, let alone motorcars, and when he tried to make conversation, his lack of teeth combined with his scrambled Norfolk accent to defeat her completely. Worse than Thargian. She gathered only that this was the first sunshine in weeks, and it had been the worst April since Noah.

The shops were all shut, but she could eat sardines tonight and face the real world tomorrow. London had seemed even more of a madhouse than she remembered it. Not London. And not Norfolk. If she shut herself up in her hermitage with her memories, she would be talking to the gulls inside a week. No, it must be Africa. What she would do there she could not imagine, but she'd find something. She would look when she arrived.

One thing she would not look for was romance. Three men in less than three years! She was Lucretia Borgia. She was Typhoid Mary. One heart can only break so often before it forgets how to heal. She would let no more men enter her life, not ever again.

Methuselah stopped at the end of her muddy little drive, perhaps not trusting his chariot to extricate itself if he went in. She overtipped him, and he sprayed her as he gushed his thanks, touching his cap. His rattletrap ground its gears and roared away, one wheel wobbling precariously.

She trudged up the driveway, unburdened by luggage but still feeling the aftereffects of her cramps. Miss Pimm had promised no intruders—and there were the tire marks from Miss Pimm's motorcar, still showing in the mud outside the door. The garden . . . oh, dear, the garden! Tomorrow the garden. Home was where your heart was? Not in her case, because she had left her heart in Thargvale. But the little place was a welcome sight. After all those weeks of sleeping in tents, it would feel like the Ritz. It did seem quite homely, with the smoke drifting from the chimney. . . .

A broken heart could still leap into its owner's throat. Alice did not need to be an Embu or Meru tracker to know that those tread marks were recent, or that an untended fire did not burn for two months.

Three empty paint tins lay by the doorstep. There was a muddy footprint on the step itself. *Panic!* No, steady . . . Think this out. . . . There's nowhere to run to anyway. Concentrate! Miss Pimm herself? Getting it ready for its owner's return? Nobody except Miss Pimm knew of this place, but even Miss Pimm could not have known she was coming, not today, not to have a fire ready. It was a man's footprint.

Faint strains of music . . . That was why he hadn't heard the taxi. He was playing one of her records, Galli-Curci singing "Un bel di vedremo." Even as she listened, the soprano dwindled to a mournful baritone and then soared triumphantly again as he wound up the gramophone.

Paralyzed, Alice could only stare at the door. D'Arcy, the horrible mistake and the prison camp fantasy? Or Terry? But Terry's ship had gone down in the Channel, not off some desert island. Edward? Julian and Dommi had vouched for the body and watched it burn. . . .

Magic? Mana? He had given all his mana away to the Five. Prof Rawlinson had said: *It should be easy enough to alter the appearance of some other corpse. . . .*

He had said: *You'd have thought that one of them would have had the common decency . . .*

Alice threw open the door.